CODE OF HONOR

THE BUREAU BOOK FIVE

MICHAEL NEWTON

WOLFPACK
PUBLISHING
— EST 2013 —

Copyright © 2018 by Michael Newton
All rights reserved.

Published in the United States by Wolfpack Publishing

Wolfpack Publishing
6032 Wheat Penny Avenue
Las Vegas, NV 89122

wolfpackpublishing.com

Paperback ISBN: 978-1-64119-385-6
Ebook ISBN: 978-1-64119-384-9

Library of Congress Number: 2018956106

To the memory of Hank Messick (1922-99)

DRAMATIS PERSONÆ

- *Aloysius Gantt*: agent of the Federal Bureau of Investigation.
- *Colby Gantt:* his son, agent of the wartime OSS and postwar CIA.
- *Devon Gantt*: his son, agent of the FBI.
- *Declan O'Hara*: agent of the FBI.
- *Nolan O'Hara*: his son, an FBI agent.
- *Fiona O'Hara*: daughter of Declan and Abigail, an attorney.
- *Gregory Jordan* (né Gregorio Giordano): legal counsel for the Giordano crime family.
- *David Jordan*: his son, born 1924, an attorney.
- *Isaac Sawyer*: agent of the Federal Bureau of Narcotics.
- *Payton Sawyer*: his son, joins NYPD 1950.
- *Keisha Sawyer*: his daughter, born 1933.
- *Frederick Douglass Sawyer:* his youngest son, born 1938.
- *Leonid Babin*: Soviet intelligence officer, once deported from the United States.

AUTHOR'S NOTE

The Bureau is a work of fiction, but real-life public figures, institutions and events often appear within its pages. Where that occurs, personal conversations and actions are the author's invention, except where drawn directly from reliable nonfiction sources. Timelines of historical events, likewise, may be rearranged, compressed or extended as required for dramatic effect. Anachronistic terms now often deemed offensive—"Negro," "colored," "queer" and the like—are used within these pages as they were applied during the years portrayed. Obsolete geographical names are used as they were normally applied during the years of 1947 to 1955.

CODE OF HONOR

PROLOGUE

HAVANA, CUBA: MARCH 20, 1947

IF LUCKY LUCIANO had been capable of insight, he might've blamed himself. But as it was, he knew it must be someone else's fault.

Maybe the freelance journalist, that Henry Wallace guy, no plausible relation to America's current Vice President of the same name. On January 31 he'd rolled into the Jockey Club in Mariano, the sedate casino whose executives—Dr. Indalecio Pertierra, a Cuban congressman, and his brother Dr. Julio Pertierra—served respectively as president and director of racing for the Oriental Park racetrack. Both were friends of Lucky's and his partners in the Jockey Club, with Meyer Lansky and associate Charles Simms.

Wallace started betting heavy on roulette and didn't like the way it went for him, so he'd beefed it to the manager, Carlos "The Goat" Miranda. At a nod from Luciano, Carlos called a couple of his bruisers and they tossed Wallace onto the street. He'd spotted Lucky on his bum rush to the sidewalk, and from there he ran straight to the *Havana Post,* an English-language daily that was glad to run the scoop, which made it into half a dozen papers on the mainland.

Still, it could've been all right til February 9, when four loud-mouthed *Yanquis* dropped by the club and started betting on—that's right—roulette. One of them hit a number, claimed it should've paid $432, but what the croupier delivered was $342. Call it a counting error, easily resolved, but the four of them were making so much noise, Lucky and Meyer sitting there together, taking it all in, that Lucky gave The Goat another nod and out they went.

So what? How could he know one of the four was Perrine Palmer Jr., the Republican mayor of Miami, accompanied by an FBI agent and two flacks from the local press?

That time, the story showed up in the tourist section of *Tiempo en Cuba*, a weekly that started echoes Stateside. Bright and early the next morning, FBI headquarters issued a report on Lucky being in Havana, promising a full investigation of the circumstances.

Even then, he might have ridden out the storm, except for Harry Anslinger. In Washington, that bald son-of-a-bitch went running to the State Department first, howling for Lucky's deportation, but the State couldn't swing it with President Ramón Grau's so-called Authentic Cuban Revolutionary Party. Next, Anslinger pulled an ace out of his sleeve on February 21, announcing that Havana would receive no more legitimate narcotics from America as long as Lucky stayed on Cuban soil.

Two days later, Lucky was dining at a café in Havana's Vedado district, a short stroll from the Hotel Nacional, when two cops entered with hands on their pistols and placed him under arrest. Benito Herrera, chief of Cuba's secret police, told reporters he'd ordered the arrest in fear, that Luciano "might cause public disorder." When the scribblers got to Lucky, he'd said, "If I'm going to have trouble on this side, I'll go back to Italy. I just want to be nice and quiet. I don't want to be kicked around like this for no reason."

But it wasn't that simple, in fact.

While Lucky sat in Tiscornia detention camp, President Grau signed his deportation order on February 27, prompting Lucky's lawyers to file a writ of *habeas corpus*, demanding the government show cause for deportation. Havana's Fifth Criminal Court accepted the petition on March 1, but Lucky failed to appear for his hearing three days later and was slapped with a contempt charge. Lucky fought that charge with complaints to the Bar Association and Cuba's Supreme Criminal Court of Justice until March 10, when Minister of the Interior Alfredo Pequeño canceled the hearing, declaring that Lucky would be shipped to Genoa by way of the Canary Islands, aboard the Turkish freighter SS *Bakir*. To top it off, the *Bakir*'s skipper said he couldn't guarantee his passenger would make it back to Italy.

So here he was taking his chances, not sure whether he'd wind up in Italy or get tossed overboard, somewhere at sea. He'd left Congressman Pertierra facing charges of accepting $50,000 to let Lucky and Meyer run the Jockey Club's roulette and poker tables, plus $600 to replace fourteen no-show Cuban dealers with American ex-convicts.

And screw him, anyway.

The *Bakir* looked more like a garbage scow than a cargo steamer, and once on board, it smelled of piss and vomit. Lucky hadn't even made it to his tiny cabin when he saw the first rat blinking at him from a greasy corner of the passageway.

A fuckin' month of this, he thought and started drawing up a mental list of men he wanted dead.

CHAPTER 1

ALOYSIUS GANTT SAW how the world was turning, and while none of it was unexpected, the reality of global *Realpolitik* was still depressing.

Back in January 1942, eleven months before Pearl Harbor, FDR had used his State of the Union address to outline what he called the goal of "Four Freedoms": freedom of speech and worship, freedom from want and from fear. Now, five years later with fascism crushed—at least for now —none of those airy dreams seemed any closer to reality.

Freedom from fear, especially, was out the window with the dawn of a Cold War against the Reds.

Take Eastern Europe and the Near East for example. Moscow had ended World War II, expecting free passage of ships between the Black Sea and the Mediterranean through the Turkish Straits, but İsmet İnönü, president of Turkey since 1938, refused. That sprang from tension with the Soviets in Eastern Anatolia and threatened violence

5

after the Brits pulled out of Turkey. But Harry Truman had stepped in with a show of force, sending the battleship USS *Missouri*, and left Stalin fuming.

But Joe didn't have "The Bomb"—at least, not yet.

Then there was Greece, where the National Liberation Front (EAM), run by the Greek Communist Party (KKE), had purged Axis invaders in 1944. The Brits showed up to meddle as they often did, unseating the victorious EAM, propelling right-wing forces into a reign of "White Terror" against Reds, leading to all-out civil war, then declared in February that they could "no longer guarantee security" of Greece or Turkey and were bailing out. President Truman looked at Greece and saw a Russian pincers movement toward the Med and Middle Eastern oil, appearing before Congress on March 12 to announce the creation of the "Truman Doctrine," its goals simply stated, if you could trust them.

"I believe," he'd stated, "it must be the policy of the United States to support free peoples who are resisting attempted subjugation by armed minorities or by outside pressures. I believe that we must assist free peoples to work out their own destinies in their own way. I believe that our help should be primarily through economic and financial aid, which is essential to economic stability and orderly political processes."

Concise, and maybe even laudable, but who believed that Truman *really* meant to leave struggling nations free from "outside pressures"? Who thought "free peoples" would be free, in fact, to plan the future "their own way"? And how far could a flood of economic aid proceed without the shadow of armed force arising from the West, as it was bound to do from Moscow?

Talking to his son Colby, Gantt knew that America's

Central Intelligence Group planned to use every trick in the books—and some new ones, besides—to swing the world America's way, by fair means or foul.

And how else had it ever been?

Another brooding fear involved a creeping paranoia over Reds at home. Nine days after his speech to Congress, Truman had signed Executive Order 9835, creating a Federal Employee Loyalty Program to weed out any Commies from the U.S. government. A side effect of that, the White House clearly hoped, would be the cessation of flack from Republicans who'd already started branding the Democrats in power as "soft on communism."

Just look at Yalta and Potsdam. Hadn't FDR and Truman handed Stalin most of Eastern Europe, grinning for the cameras while they did it? Wasn't China locked in civil war right now, at risk of going Red?

Truman's executive order created 150 Loyalty Review Boards, scanning lists of three-plus million federal employees, sniffing out any "derogatory references" on file. From there, it came down to the Bureau, mounting full-fledged field investigations of each suspect, trying to find out if he or she was Red, "pink," or "lavender"—a homosexual, presumably vulnerable to Soviet blackmail. Whatever was decided, curt dismissal by a loyalty review board came with no right to appeal.

In theory, "disloyalty" fell into five major categories: sabotage or espionage; treason or sedition; intentional, unauthorized disclosure of classified information; membership in any group deemed totalitarian, fascist, communist or subversive; and advocating the overthrow of the U.S. government. Tom Clark helped out in April, with the creation of an Attorney General's List of Subversive Organizations, an expansion of the 1941 "Biddle List" that increased the original list of thirteen groups to forty-one, most of them branded "fronts." From what Gantt saw, it didn't seem to matter if a group had been disbanded years ago, with no remnants surviving to the present day. What mattered was the list itself, a roster that seemed to grow longer by the day.

And while the said list was meant to help federal loyalty boards screen government employees, a blind man could've seen that it would filter down from Washington like water seeping into sand. In no time, Clark's list was employed by state and local governments, by the Treasury's Bureau of Internal Revenue ruling on tax exemptions, and the State's Bureau of Passport Control. From there, it filtered down to the civilian workplace, used by hoteliers, restaurateurs, theater managers and damned near anybody else you could imagine to winnow their staffs down to the local waitress, janitor, and street sweeper.

The roster's application hinged on where a suspect lived, of course, and which "subversive" group he or she might've joined, donated money two, or simply dropped in to observe from idle curiosity. Take Georgia. While the Klan was listed as subversive, redneck politicians courted the Grand Dragon at his birthday parties and Atlanta cops, like John "Itchy Trigger Finger" Nash with thirteen dead blacks on his record, routinely earned promotion.

Some world, Gant thought. *Some freedom.*

But however busy Edgar Hoover was with new assignments, he still had time to coddle Number Two. In February he'd created a new job for Clyde Tolson, naming him the Bureau's first Assistant Director, allegedly saddled with "duties in budget and administration." So far, in practice, that meant dining out with Speed, swanning around nightclubs, and making "field office inspections" with an emphasis on racetracks and resorts.

After nineteen years and counting, Tolson had made no move to use the Bureau as a stepping stone to something better, as he'd indicated on his application, and Gantt had found no way to bring him down.

Maybe this year, Gantt thought. *We all have shady secrets, right?*

And kept his fingers crossed that none of *his* would be exposed.

———

FEDERAL BUREAU of Narcotics Manhattan Field Office, *June 30, 1947*

THE FILES and memos on Ike Sawyers desk assured him that he'd have no shortage of assignments during the eight years until Civil Service forced him to retire at sixty-two. He could've quit with an annuity in 1953, at sixty, but preferred to hang in where he was and go for the full pension he had earned.

On top of which, drug traffickers on both sides of the law kept coming up with new twists to intrigue and vex him.

Just this year, cocaine smuggling had started to increase, conducted by mules—often adventurous young women—from all over Latin America: including Argentinians, Bolivians, Brazilians, Chileans, Cubans, Mexicans and Peruvians. Most of them carried an ounce or two at a time, from leaves grown in the Andes and refined in crude jungle labs or some willing farmer's barn. It hadn't reached the epidemic stage—not yet—but Ike could see it coming if the trade wasn't shut down.

As far as epidemics were concerned, to Sawyer that

meant traffic in amphetamines, most of it legal, doubling last year's annual sales of Benzedrine and Dexedrine by Smith, Kline & French to a total of $5.7 million this year. Regulation was bound to occur sooner or later, but in the meantime, fumbling efforts continued at home and abroad without much to show for it.

Stateside, the National Research Council's Division of Medical Sciences had earnestly debated narcotics problems since 1929, then transferred that function—whatever it was —to the Public Health Service Division of Chemotherapy ten years later, going dormant after Pearl Harbor, now reconstituted as the Committee on Drug Addiction and Narcotics. Study was precisely that, complete with doping monkeys at the University of Michigan, but anyone with half a brain already knew how morphine, heroin and other drugs affected people—namely breeding addicts—but proposals for real-world solutions had been few and far between.

On the legal front, the Tokyo Trials were proceeding after a fashion, though some fifty of the tribunal's original defendants had already been cut loose. Emperor Hirohito and his Imperial Family had already been absolved, President Truman and Douglas MacArthur bargained for royal approval of changes they'd planned for occupied Japan.

Of the twenty-eight defendants held for trial, two— Admiral Osami Nagano and ex-Minister of Foreign Affairs Yōsuke Matsuoka—had already died from natural causes at Tokyo's Sugamo Prison. Yoshisuke Aikawa, founder of Nissan Industries, was freed when his conglomerate disbanded prior to trial. Ex-Surgeon General Shirō Ishii also got a pass on charges of human experimentation since leaders of Fort Detrick, Maryland's biological warfare project, deemed his data "absolutely invaluable" and "obtained fairly cheaply." General MacArthur weighed in with advice that "additional data, possibly some statements from Ishii, probably could be obtained by informing the Japanese involved that information would be retained in intelligence channels and will not be employed as 'War Crimes' evidence."

So, Ike supposed, the thousands of Chinese, Koreans, Mongolians, Soviets, and other Allied POWs who suffered vivisection, frostbite and weapons testing, infection with venereal diseases or rape and forced pregnancy hadn't suffered and died in vain. It all came down to the good of America.

One strange Tokyo defendant, author and scholar Shūmei Ōkawa, was found unfit for trial after he put on a floor show for the tribunal, dressing in pajamas, shouting, "This is act one of the comedy," and slapping General Tōjō's bald head with a cry of "*Inder! Kommen Sie!*"—translated from German to English as "Come, Indian!" A U.S. Army psychiatrist confirmed that Ōkawa was nuts, whereupon presiding judge Sir William Webb dismissed his charges.

That still left a handful of defendants charged with wholesale drug trafficking, aside from their other war crimes, but Sawyer couldn't guess what would become of them.

On the dismal domestic front, echoes of last year's Moore's Ford lynching continued in Georgia, where redneck brothers James and Tom Verner attacked Negro victim Lamar Howard at work in Monroe's municipal icehouse, beating him while they shouted questions about his testimony to a 1946 federal grand jury, white manager Will Perry watching while they beat Howard for a quarter-hour. Charged with intimidating a federal witness, the brothers raised $20,000 bail from a friendly local planter and were freed at trial by a white jury.

In February, South Carolina claimed the year's only lynching victim so far. Pickens County Sheriff J. G. Hood charged Negro Willie Earle with stabbing a white taxi driver, whereupon a mob, mostly of cabbies, "overwhelmed" jailers and took Earle to a country road near Greenville, beating and slashing him before a point-blank fusillade finished him off. Twenty-eight defendants confessed, but Judge J. Robert Martin vowed that he would "not allow racial issues to be injected in this case." The defense attorneys didn't bother with evidence, blaming the trial on "northern interference" and calling Willie Earle a "mad dog" deserving his fate. White spectators found that hilarious, and jurors acquitted the whole mob in May. When Earle's mother tried to collect a $2,000 state benefit for relatives of lynching victims, officials rejected her claim on grounds that the mass acquittal proved no lynching occurred.

Tom Clark added the Klan to his list of subversive organizations in April, but that made no difference in Dixie, where Dr. Green called his order "America's social conscience" and railed against the "Commie Jews" in Washington.

One tiny speck of hope for optimists appeared in April when CORE—the Congress of Racial Equality—announced a "journey of reconciliation" to challenge state segregation on interstate buses in Dixie. Sixteen CORE members were naïve enough to think the Supreme Court's 1946 ruling in *Morgan v. Virginia* meant something in the South when they followed black Quaker Bayard Rustin aboard their chartered bus, but southern cops and courts soon disabused them of that foolish notion. As Judge Henry Whitfield elegantly stated it after they were arrested in North

Carolina, "It's about time you Jews from New York learned that you can't come down here bringing your niggers with you to upset the customs of the South. Just to teach you a lesson, I gave your black boys thirty days, and I give you ninety."

Maybe that was on Harry Truman's mind when he addressed a June gathering of the NAACP on the steps of the Lincoln Memorial, broadcasting his comments nationwide via radio. "It is my deep conviction," he'd declared, "that we have reached a turning point in our country's efforts to guarantee freedom and equality to all our citizens. Recent events in the United States and abroad have made us realize that it is more important today than ever before to ensure that all Americans enjoy these rights. When I say all Americans, I mean *all* Americans."

Ike had nearly choked on that, remembering Truman's record; briefly a Klansman in 1922, while seeking local office in Missouri and a long outspoken bigot whose conversations and writings proved it. Twice, after dining at the White House under FDR, he'd described liveried waiters as "an army of coons" and the occasion as a "nigger picnic day." Three decades earlier while courting his fiancée, HST had written, "I think one man is just as good as another so long as he's honest and decent and not a nigger or a Chinaman. Uncle Wills says that the Lord made a white man from dust, a nigger from mud, and then threw up what was left and it came down a Chinaman. He does hate Chinese and Japs. So do I. It is race prejudice I guess. But I am strongly of the opinion that negroes ought to be in Africa, yellow men in Asia, and white men in Europe and America."

Now Sawyer and his people were supposed to think that everything had changed?

Believe it when I see it, Ike thought. *And not one damned minute sooner.*

———

FBI HEADQUARTERS: July 1, 1947

DECLAN O'HARA FINISHED READING a small story on page ten of the *Washington Post,* then laid the paper aside. After nearly five years, three separate indictments, and ungodly court costs, the Great Sedition Trial had finally lurched to a close yesterday, when D.C.'s Circuit Court of Appeals affirmed dismissal of all charges. Six of the final thirty defendants were still imprisoned for state sedition convictions or violations of the Foreign Agents Registration Act, but unlike those caught up in Moscow's show trials, none would face a firing squad. The only dead, in fact, were elderly defendant Elmer Garner and Judge Edward Eicher, both killed by heart attacks in 1944.

What a waste of time it all had been.

Declan preferred to think about his son Nolan, busy training for his own place in the FBI, and daughter Fiona, accepted at Columbia Law School, specializing in criminal law and procedure, nose pressed firmly to the grindstone now, seeking a Juris Doctor degree and hoping to have it by May 1950. With her brains and ambition, Fiona could've found a lucrative place on the corporate side, but she'd somehow developed a passion for justice that made her crave a place as a defense attorney, staking out a legal foxhole in the murky realm of civil liberties.

What would that mean in postwar, paranoid America? Declan didn't like to think about that, but at least he knew

Fiona had picked a top-flight school to get her prepared. She had regaled her parents and anyone else who'd listen, touting her praise for Columbia Law. Founded in 1858, successor to King's College, it had turned out legal luminaries including John Jay, first Chief Justice of the U.S. Supreme Court, and Alexander Hamilton, first Secretary of the Treasury and co-author of *The Federalist Papers*. Other alumni included two U.S. Presidents—both Roosevelts—plus two more Chief Justices, one Associate Justice, one Solicitor General, twenty-eight members of Congress, nine U.S. Cabinet members, and eighteen governors of states or territories.

It was a stellar cast all right, but where would Fiona fit in?

In a country pledged to purge Reds and homosexuals, where thirty-four states still practiced some form of Jim Crow and police used third-degree tactics as they saw fit, would a young female lawyer with ideals simply be swept away?

————

Little Italy, Manhattan: August 14, 1947

THESE DAYS, whenever Greg Jordan passed by a mirror, he could see a grandfather regarding him with skepticism from the looking glass. On Sunday, his daughter Gemma had delivered Luccia Bianca Ricca at Mount Sinai Hospital on Madison Avenue, officially making Greg a *nonno* and leaving him open to gibes from his brothers.

Officially, the baby had been premature, conceived on Gemma's January wedding night, but no one in groom Paulo

Ricca's family or Gemma's honestly believed it. She'd been pregnant at the altar, and Luccia's birth weight—seven pounds two ounces—ruled out any honest speculation that she was a preemie.

So, Grandpa, it was and would always be, though Greg was having trouble getting used to it. And he could say the same about the rest of his life, tethered to the Syndicate.

In January, triggermen Cockeye Dunn, Squint Sheridan and Danny Gentile shot the waterfront hiring boss Andy Hintz six times, but he lived for three weeks, naming them all in a dying declaration that sent them to trial on a capital charge. Three days before Hintz passed, pathetic Al Capone preceded him in Florida, finally taken out by a cerebral hemorrhage from his tertiary syphilis.

Frank Costello remained a running joke in headlines, fighting on in court to reclaim the $27,200 he'd dropped in a taxi, back in June of 1944. The wrangling endlessly delighted Gotham editors, even if Frank couldn't make out the humor in it.

In other courts, the Boccia murder case continued to unravel between February and June. First, the D.A. dropped Michele Miranda's indictment, followed by dismissal of the murder counts against Pete DeFeo, Cosmo Frasca, and Blah-Blah Smurra. The only charge that stuck, against Frasca and Smurra, was dodging the draft.

In New Orleans, after seven years of stalling, Immigration agents finally deported *capo crimine* Sam Carollo in April. Before he left, Carollo joined his capos at the Black Diamond nightclub, naming ambitious underboss Carlos Marcello as his successor. While Carollo packed his bags in New Orleans, Charley Luciano reached Palermo and was jailed on arrival, held for a month before a regional commission freed him with a warning to keep his nose clean.

Closer to home, in June, Gurrah Shapiro joined partner Lepke Buchalter in the Great Beyond when a heart attack killed him at Sing Sing. He'd died believing that Dutch Schultz was right when he'd suggested killing Tom Dewey in 1935. Meanwhile, Albert Anastasia followed Joe Adonis from Brooklyn to Jersey, buying a house near Joe's in Fort Lee. They now met frequently at Duke's Bar & Grill in Cliffside, with Willie Moretti and Genovese confederate Anthony "Tony Bender" Strollo.

But the year's big news from gangland was the scandal swirling around Chicago's imprisoned Hollywood extortion defendants. Attorney General Clark had helped them once in 1945, with transfers from Atlanta's lockup to Leavenworth, but he wasn't done yet. Only days ago, Clark had finagled early parole for the whole gang, each with six and a half years remaining on their ten-year sentences. As Jordan heard the story, Missouri lawyer John Dillon reached out to Dallas fixer Maury Hughes, who'd, in turn, cajoled old buddy Clark. Aside from pushing the parole, Clark also had outstanding fraud charges against the gang dismissed in Gotham.

Granted, Paul Ricca and Louis Campagna still owed $600,000 in back taxes and penalties, but under pressure from Clark, the Treasury cut that back to $126,000—none of it paid by the two Outfit honchos. Instead, they contacted Joe Bulger, "supreme president" of the *Unione Siciliana*, who told his 25,000 members, "The boys need some money." G-men counted forty-two separate deliveries to *Unione* head-quarters, the bagmen simply saying, "This is for Paul" or "This is for Louis." Another $500,000 came from some-where, doled out among members of the U.S. Parole Commission before they freed the Outfit's leaders. Afterward, none of the commissioners would challenge any tales of bribery.

Paul Ricca's take on the Attorney General: "That man must want something; money, favors, a seat in the Supreme Court. Find out what he wants and get it for him."

And from where Greg Jordan sat, that had the ring of prophecy.

———

COLUMBIA UNIVERSITY, Upper Manhattan: September 9, 1947

REGISTRATION AT COLUMBIA had fallen into place more easily than Dave Jordan expected, part of his tuition handled by the G.I. Bill, the rest and various other expenses covered by two part-time jobs he'd picked up at the law school's library and bussing tables at Bernie Glassman's restaurant on West 112th Street, facing the Cathedral of St. John the Divine across Amsterdam Avenue.

The fall term had begun just after Labor Day, with Dave enrolled in the general studies program. Columbia offered no specific pre-professional majors, though advisors helped students prepare themselves for professional graduate schools, including required applications. For now, Dave had declared a major in history, concentrating on the discipline of American politics that included constitutional law with studies of elections, national and local governments. He shared a room at John Jay Hall with freshman chemistry major Zack Aaronson and got his daily exercise walking to classes on campus or two blocks south from his digs to Glassman's.

Dave knew his leg was getting better, and he sometimes

left his cane stashed in his room, but he was still self-conscious about limping on his daily rounds while clearing tables and shelving items at the law library. Most days, he had a budget breakfast at the campus cafeteria, skipped lunch, and either came back to the cafeteria for dinner or wolfed down the biggest meal Glassman allowed employees on their breaks. Between his jobs and classes, Dave supposed he'd manage reading and assigned papers.

Tonight was one of his library nights, which fell on Mondays, Tuesdays and Thursdays. Fridays and Saturdays were reserved for Glassman when they had a heavy trade and waiters shared a fraction of their tips with kitchen help. Jordan preferred the library, with its quiet, and law students whom he hoped to follow if he made it through to join the class of '54.

His sister Gemma should've been a sophomore by now, chasing her dream and working toward Columbia's graduate school in journalism—first in the nation, founded by Joseph Pulitzer in 1892—but she'd found love instead, and just last month had made David an uncle. Complications with daughter Lucia's birth had left Gemma incapable of having any other children, and Dave wondered at odd moments how Paulo Ricca, his new brother-in-law, felt about losing *his* dream of a big, traditional, *famiglia italiana*.

Jordan hadn't seen the baby yet, but he would have to squeeze that in somehow, and fairly soon. So far, his two meetings with Paulo had occurred at Sunday dinners with Dave's parents, all small talk and Gemma's belly growing visibly between the monthly sessions. These days, Jordan found his ties to family as strained as his connection to the church he had been raised in from infancy.

Not that his father was a regular at mass—likely afraid he might burst into flames upon crossing the church threshold—but Uncles Primo and Carlo still turned up with their wives most Sundays, from what David understood, although their wayward sons were typically no-shows. Dave guessed his reasons for avoiding church were different from those of cousins Fausto, Dominic and Angelo, but what the hell? They all had sins that wouldn't bear confession, even with a guarantee of confidentiality, and even if Dave's weren't the Mob-related kind, he still had bloody hands.

Killing in service to his country, sure...but did that make it any different to the Big Man floating on a cloud somewhere?

David had gotten reacquainted with the so-called Holy Bible at Camp Edwards, urged to read it in his spare time by an Irish chaplain who had plainly never seen a battlefield. Jordan had mostly found it boring, then gave up entirely while he labored through the wit and wisdom of Isaiah. In those scriptures, he had learned that God, Jehovah, Yahweh —call Him what you will—had known "the end from the beginning," seeing every petty sin and gross atrocity that would occur on Earth until its final days. Worse yet, the same Heavenly Father bragged, "I form the light, and create darkness; I make peace, and create evil; I, the Lord, do all these things."

What kind of life was that for humankind? If God existed, was He a sadistic psychopath playing a long, sick game on offspring He'd created in His own image?

David could pass on praying to a god like that, and hopefully get on with steering his own life through the maze, unknown to nearly all the planet's 2.3 billion inhabitants. Except for those he'd slaughtered with his own hands, fascist bastards.

Maybe, if there was a Hell, he'd seem them there someday.

FBI Training Academy, Quantico, Virginia: September 16, 1947

Nolan O'Hara felt like he was back in the Marine Corps, even training at their base that sprawled across four counties, but this wasn't boot camp and he found it all considerably easier after the war. Drill sergeants didn't curse him up and down for every move he made, and he was spending time in classes totally divorced from combat exercises—some echoing subjects from his studies at GW Law, three nights a week—but he'd found that the firing range suited him best.

As long as he remembered that the war was now behind him and he couldn't simply shoot suspected enemies on sight.

Gunwise, he'd started with the Bureau-issued Colt Official Police revolver, chambered for .38 special rounds and having a four-inch barrel. It was lighter than the Colt .45 O'Hara had used in the Corps and held two rounds fewer when loaded for bear, but it felt good in his hand. Before he fired it on the range, Nolan had to learn the Bureau-approved mode of drawing, brushing back his suit jacket to reach the open holster on his hip, pulling and practicing the weapon's double-action trigger squeeze. Once a new agent mastered that, he passed on to the pistol course with only five rounds loaded at a time, although the weapon's cylinder held six.

The FBI's practical pistol course involved fifty shots overall, simulating real-life crisis conditions as closely as possible. Ten shots were fired from hip level, seven feet from a target that bore John Dillinger's face. A would-be agent failed unless he managed ten rounds within twenty-five seconds. The rest of the course, also timed, took five and three-quarters minutes: five shots lying prone at sixty yards; five shots at fifty yards while seated; ten rounds from behind a barricade at the same range, five with each hand; then running to the twenty-five-yard line and going through another fifteen rounds from the same positions held at fifty yards. K-value scores—the "K" standing for "kill," hits in a lethal portion of each target—were totaled for all targets afterward, then multiplied by .4 to produce a trainee's score. No one scored perfectly after they'd fumbled with loose rounds reloading, but Nolan was satisfied with his performance.

A separate pistol course taught shooting from the hip, using the basic course's ranges and postures, but firing twelve shots singly, twelve shots fired two in succession, six shots in groups of three, six shots singly, four shots in groups of two, then ten shots in groups of five, for a total of fifty rounds.

Next up came the rifle course, using the Bureau's choice, a Remington Model 81 Woodsmaster pioneered in 1936, feeding .300 Savage cartridges from box magazines of five, ten or fifteen rounds. The Remington weighed in at eight pounds, compared to 9.2 for the M1917 Enfield he'd first carried to war, 9.5 for the M1 Garand, and 5.2 for the M1 carbine that saw him through Okinawa. It was semiautomatic, firing 150-grain bullets at 2,600 feet per second, with a top range around 300 yards.

The Bureau's rifle course was more abbreviated that O'Hara's training in the Corps, requiring only twenty shots in all. Shooters started 200 yards from their targets, firing five rounds prone and five while seated. At 100 yards, they fired five prone and five while kneeling. The 200-yard course was slow-fire, while shots from 100 yards were timed, allowing trainees one minute to fire all ten, including a magazine reload.

From the rifles, future G-men proceeded to shotguns, specifically the pump-action Ithaca 37 with a twenty-inch barrel, holding five twelve-gauge rounds in its tubular magazine. Shooters inserted cartridges through a loading port underneath the receiver, from which they were also ejected once fired. The dual-action port made the Ithaca equally convenient for right- and left-hand shooters, laying down deadly fire as rapidly as one could work the weapon's slide action.

The Bureau's shotgun course used moving "bobber" targets to simulate a ducking, dodging enemy. The shells loaded were double-aught buckshot, with nine lead pellets in a single round, the pellets spreading from the weapon's muzzle at about one inch per yard. "Effective" range was said to be 100 yards, but if you did the math, that meant a spread exceeding eight feet, when your average man stood five foot six and had a torso fourteen inches wide. Firing one cartridge from 100 yards you might, just *might* inflict one wound—or two, if you were lucky—ranging from a graze to an unlikely kill shot to the head or heart.

On the shotgun course, accordingly, trainees fired five shots from the hip at bobber targets from a range of fifteen feet, the targets placed four feet apart. Another five rounds from the shoulder, directed against numbered targets standing ten, fifteen, twenty, thirty, and forty yards away, two seconds to fire each round after the Rangemaster called a target's number.

Finally, successful trainees moved on to the submachine-gun course, firing Thompson M1A1 weapons, modified from the original his father might have carried in the

1930s to accommodate the needs of World War II. Specifically, the stylish pistol grip below the early Tommy's barrel was supplanted by a horizontal foregrip, and its cocking bolt was mounted on the right-hand side of the receiver rather than on top. Beyond that, the receivers had been altered to accept only "stick" magazines, bearing twenty or thirty rounds apiece, eliminating larger and more awkward drums. Additionally, barrels were not ribbed, muzzles lacked the Cutts compensator, and the new model had fixed rear sights without triangular guard wings. Beyond all that, it was the same old Thompson, weighing ten pounds empty, firing 700 .45-caliber rounds per minute, with an effective range of 164 yards.

The Bureau's submachine-gun course consisted of forty shots fired from half-loaded twenty-round magazines: five semiautomatic rounds and five in short bursts from the hip at fifteen yards; then ten shots on semiauto and ten in short bursts from the shoulder at twenty-five yards from the targets, and finally ten shots fired on semiauto from the shoulder, at a range of fifty yards. Each hit scored two and one-half points, with the first thirty rounds timed at twenty-five seconds, reloading included.

Aside from marksmanship, each trainee was thoroughly drilled on safety standards; cleaning and oiling all firearms, and releasing tension on each weapon's firing mechanism, hammer, and recoil springs before he returned it to the gun vault. That was simple, after Nolan's service with the Corps, and he would have no problem keeping up with monthly practice sessions at the firing range. He was equally at ease with boxing, grappling, control holds, disarming techniques and handcuffing, though he'd have to pull his punches, unlike anything he'd picked up in the Corps when any adversary was supposed to be dead meat. Academic courses in criminal law overlapped his GW studies, while others included interviewing and interrogation methods, forensics and crime scene investigation, ethics and preparation of acceptable Bureau reports.

Somewhere in the midst of all that, Nolan also had to find time for his role as a husband and father. Keely had delivered daughter Erin ten days earlier, sharing her brother's birth month but two weeks apart. Together, they'd agreed that two kids were enough, and when Keely felt up to it again, they would be using condoms until Nolan had the time to schedule a vasectomy at GW's hospital, taking full advantage of his student discount and the G.I. Bill.

Ryan, already looking forward to his fourth birthday—but not so much to kindergarten, coming up next fall—hadn't decided how he felt about his baby sister yet, but what could you expect?

Nolan was simply glad he'd made it home after the Corps, much less to sire a second child and steal whatever time he could away from school and Bureau training, spending it with Keely and the kids. He didn't know where they'd end up, once he was clear of the Academy and law school, but his parents had survived Chicago in the "Dirty Thirties," hadn't they? So how bad could it be?

Impulsively, he felt like knocking wood and had to settle for his Thompson's walnut stock, hoping nobody saw him, thinking him a superstitious fool.

————

THE LUBYANKA BUILDING: *October 6, 1947*

LEONID BABIN'S son was now nineteen months old and

cutting teeth—although, as Dr. Lazar Serbsky had informed him, baby teeth do not cut through the gums. Rather, hormones released within an infant's body prompt some fleshy cells to die and separate while teeth emerge. Another year or so might be required for Stefan to be weaned from suckling at his mother's breast, assuming Babin chose to wait that long.

But could he wait? Should he?

Employment of a wet nurse was one possibility, but that meant Babin would be forced to deal with three surplus adults, instead of just two. He had already earmarked Dr. Serbsky for a fatal accident, come winter—icy Russian roads could be so treacherous—and he would also have to deal with Darya Sokolva when it was time. Stefan would not be brought up in the care of his birth mother, something Darya had not bargained for in any case, although she still seemed to believe she had a payday coming, with her dossier purged of all sins.

And she was partly right, of course. When it was time, both Darya and her police file would vanish simultaneously and forever, not for her to lead a happy, independent life somewhere abroad, but simply to stop living altogether.

No one must survive who could betray Babin and under-mine his plan.

The couple who would raise and educate Stefan in the United States was already in place. On paper they were Mark and Isabella Barnes, Canadians who'd emigrated from Toronto back in 1939, now living in New Jersey, where Mark owned a radio repair shop as a source of legal income and a cover for his interest in all things electronic. Isabella was what most Americans referred to as a "homemaker," and both of them were naturalized citizens. A convenient lame leg had exempted Mark from military service during World

War II, although he'd set a local record selling war bonds in Burlington County and had done his bit for the Civil Defense Corps, repairing public utilities. Both were impeccable, above reproach, and anxious to adopt a child if one became selectively available.

It was the child they lived for now while keeping cautious track of movements at Fort Dix, lately a U.S. Army basic training center and home of the 9th Infantry Division. On weekends, they might go to Philadelphia, with its naval shipyard, or to the Jersey shore, snapping casual photos of naval and Coast Guard maneuvers. The odd jaunt into New York City put them near Fort Hamilton, home of the 5th Coast Artillery Regiment with its 120-mm guns and the archaic U.S. Army's Chaplain School.

While Mark and Isabella waited for the perfect son, Stefan Babin—still unnamed on his birth certificate—would be conditioned at a special training school in Balashikha, overlooking the Pekhorka River east of Moscow. There, he would learn both Russian and English, drilled to treat the latter as his first language for conversation, while he studied basic facts of U.S. history, geography, and politics. Above all else, he'd be impressed with duty to the State and to the Party, things that he could not discuss with anyone except his teachers—and, in time, with his adoptive parents.

The mechanics of delivering a Russian child into America were flexible, requiring great finesse by specialists who could place Stefan in New Jersey and arrange the paperwork for his adoption at age five or six as "Stephen Barnes." From there, his further training and eventual deployment as an agent of the FBI relied on Mark and Isabella, both of whom had loved ones in the USSR whose well-being, and indeed survival would depend on how well the two sleepers did their job.

What could go wrong? At least a million things, Babin realized. The smugglers who transported him from Moscow to Durrës, Albania, might run afoul of law enforcement or of bandits who outnumbered them. Stefan's ship might be lost at any point between Durrës and Moncton, in New Brunswick, from which point he'd be transported into Maine. The border crossing could be perilous, although a simple drive from Canada into the States was relatively safe, and Stefan's faux uncle would have the finest travel documents the MVD's technicians could produce. From Bangor, it should be a long but not-too-grueling drive to Trenton, where a special agency created to perform just one adoption prior to dissolution would accommodate the childless Barnes couple and make their lives complete.

Only a car crash could derail the plan, as Stefan's "uncle" shuttled him along the Eastern Seaboard to his newfound home. From that point on, all Babin had to fret about was a laundry list of potentially fatal childhood diseases, abduction by some psychopathic stranger who could ruin everything, then Stefan's orderly progression through the grades of public school, matriculation at a suitable college, and eventual acceptance to the FBI Academy at Quantico. Other concerns: diversion and corruption of his son by daily life in the United States, or some betrayal on the part of Mark and Isabella Barnes that would ensure their execution by whatever heinous means Babin was able to devise.

A simple plan? Hardly. But it was doable.

And while he waited, Babin had to stay secure in Moscow while his native country and the agency he served transformed from day to day. Viktor Abakumov still led the MVD, but there were changes in the wind. On the last day of May, Moscow's "Committee of Information"—a newly created foreign intelligence agency within the MVD's First Chief Directorate, led by Lieutenant Pyotr Fedotov—decreed an "upgrading coordination of different intelligence services and concentrating their efforts on major directions," whatever in hell that meant.

Only yesterday, Stalin had created a new Information Bureau of the Communist and Workers' Parties, "Cominform" for short, to coordinate Communist parties under Soviet control in Albania, Bulgaria, Czechoslovakia, France, Germany, Hungary, Italy, Poland, Romania and Yugoslavia. Ideally, Cominform would script and direct Party activities throughout Europe, but Babin had his doubts, especially in Yugoslavia, where Prime Minister Josip Broz, commonly called "Tito," had revealed a stubborn independent streak while firing randomly on U.S. planes that entered his airspace.

What would become of Babin's grand design if one side or the other set off World War Three, with A-bombs bursting over Moscow and environs? Would it even matter to him, then?

Of course, it would. Babin had pledged his life to bringing down the FBI *himself,* with the assistance of his bastard son, and nothing else would satisfy him, even if his ashes lay in an irradiated grave.

———

FBI FIELD OFFICE, Los Angeles: November 30, 1947

HOLLYWOOD WAS GOING crazy over Red influence on the movies, and since Devon Gantt received his marching orders from Chief Hoover, filtered through Los Angeles SAC

Leland Stafford, he had to at least pretend he thought the "menace" was legit.

And who was he to say it wasn't, after all?

Bill Wilkinson, before he fled L.A. last year, had published a column in *The Hollywood Reporter* titled "A Vote for Joe Stalin," naming eleven Hollywood screenwriters as Reds. In March, Chief Hoover warned the House Committee on Un-American Activities (nicknamed "HUAC" with the vowels reverse) that communists had launched "a furtive attack on Hollywood" as early as 1935. Another loud voice was that of something called American Business Consultants Inc., founded this very year and run by a group of ex-G-men who denied any "affiliation whatsoever with any government agency," while their published broadsides came straight from Bureau and HUAC files.

J. Parnell Thomas brought HUAC to Hollywood in May, grilling a list of witnesses mostly named in Wilkerson's columns. October found the panel back in Washington, for public hearings that quickly became a paranoid sideshow. Dick Nixon, a HUAC member since February, was in the thick of the action, attacking film stars Katherine Hepburn, Charlie Chaplin and Edward G. Robinson. Screen Actors Guild President Ronald Reagan—alias Bureau informer "T-10"—basked in the limelight, hoping to feather his own nest by smearing union rivals. Walt Disney helped out with warnings of a "serious threat," branding some of his ex-employees as Reds. Sterling Hayden, home from service with the OSS, swallowed his admiration for Red wartime partisans to denounce fellow actors and wound up hating himself as a coward. Actor Adolphe Menjou proudly declared, "I am a witch hunter if the witches are Communists. I am a Red-baiter. I would like to see them all back in Russia."

Eric Johnston, dual president of the Association of Motion Picture Producers and the Motion Picture Association of America, assured Chairman Thomas he would never "employ any proven or admitted Communist because they are just a disruptive force, and I don't want them around."

Others, to Devon's surprise, had resisted HUAC by pleading the Fifth Amendment or reading defiant statements. Director John Huston joined Humphrey Bogart, Lauren Bacall, and Danny Kaye to found a Committee for the First Amendment, but it soon fell apart, Bogey raging at Kay, "You fuckers sold me out!" As the dust settled, HUAC set its sights on eleven defiant witnesses, soon reduced to the "Hollywood Ten," as émigré playwright Bertolt Brecht crumbled and answered committee questions. On November 17, Reagan's SAG voted to make its leaders swear an anti-communist pledge. One week later, HUAC cited the Hollywood Ten for contempt of Congress, followed one day after by the creation of an official industry blacklist, drawn up by studio chiefs at a Manhattan sit-down.

The Ten—reduced to nine when director Edward Dmytryk recanted—faced fines of $1,000 each and six to twelve months in jail, but that wasn't the end of it. As Devon knew, the Bureau was already stalking their legal defender, lawyer Bartley Crum, building a file on him, reading his mail, tapping his phones, and generally doing anything Chief Hoover could devise to ruin him.

When Devon wasn't tied up shadowing some actor on the set or monitoring wiretaps, he was busy playing Daddy to his newborn son Wyman—an October baby, hale and hearty—or doing small favors for Camille around their place. Gantt loved his wife and son, of course, especially the boy, but still wasn't convinced that he'd been meant to raise a child. Camille claimed Wyman was the spitting image of him, but Gantt couldn't see it, personally, knowing damned well that *he* wasn't bald or toothless and he didn't cry all frigging night.

And when he wasn't hunting Reds or changing shitty diapers; Devon studied crimes he'd never be allowed to solve.

One was the case of Bugsy Siegel, blasted with an M1 carbine on June 20, while he killed time with Al Smiley at the mansion in Beverly Hills that he normally shared with Virginia Hill. She missed the fireworks, since she'd flown out to Chicago twelve days earlier, a specially chartered flight, and on from there to Paris, where she heard about her lover's death while at a yacht party. The rumor was that she'd been told to leave, either by Siegel or an old friend in Chicago who could read the writing on the wall.

Siegel was still recovering from the original Flamingo flop in Vegas, shutting down his dream in January, with the gaming tables $275,000 in the red. Casinos *never* lost money, as his New York backers knew from personal experience, so what in hell was going on?

The joint reopened on March 1, renamed the Fabulous Flamingo, with would-be reporter Hank Greenspun playing cheerleader, and it seemed to turn around. By May, Bugsy was some $300,000 in the black—but then he had to close again, to finish off lagging construction. By then, even Meyer Lansky had wearied of pleading his childhood friend's case to the Mob.

Thus came the Friday night when someone fired nine rounds through Siegel's living room window, turning the Bug's handsome face into hamburger and shattering a white marble statue of Bacchus that stood atop Siegel's grand piano. Miss Hill skipped the funeral, busy with the first of several suicide attempts in Europe. Only Ben's brother and a rabbi turned out for the burial at Hollywood Forever Cemetery.

Mickey Cohen took the killing hard, barging into the Hotel Roosevelt on Hollywood Boulevard, firing two Colt .45s and shouting for the slayers to meet him outside in ten minutes. No one responded, and Mickey fled before squad cars arrived, launching a turf war against *mafioso* Jack Dragna. On June 21, mobsters Dave Berman, Moe Sedway and Gus Greenbaum took over the Flamingo, lowered its admission standards to accommodate all comers, and the place was making dough in no time.

And while LAPD got nowhere with Siegel's murder, a madman was prowling their city, butchering women. On January 15, a woman and her child found the mutilated, bisected corpse of twenty-three-year-old would-be actress Elizabeth Short in the Leimert Park neighborhood. Reporters claimed she was a British war bride, citing shoddy dental work, until a check of Bureau fingerprint files identified Short as a Massachusetts girl, arrested once for underage drinking with soldiers. Next, headlines dubbed her the "Black Dahlia," conflating her fondness for black clothing with Alan Ladd's mystery film *The Blue Dahlia,* released in June of 1946. Detectives eyeballed hundreds of purported suspects, logging dozens of false confessions from nutjobs, but made no arrests.

On January 21, someone claiming to be Short's assassin phoned editor Jim Richardson of the *Los Angeles Herald Examiner*, congratulating him on coverage of the crime and telling him to "expect some souvenirs of Beth Short in the mail." The package—swabbed with gasoline to erase finger-prints—arrived three days later, including a cut-and-paste letter with Short's birth certificate, business cards, photos, a handwritten list of names, and an address book embossed with the name of local nightclub and theater owner Mark Hansen. Hansen pled ignorance, while a girlfriend of Short's claimed he'd hated the Dahlia for rejecting his sexual overtures.

While cops went through the people named in Hansen's address book, a typewritten letter reached the *Herald Examiner*. It read: "Here it is. Turning in Wed., Jan. 29, 10 am. Had my fun at police. Black Dahlia Avenger." Cops staked out the address cited for the surrender, but nobody showed. Another cut-and-pasted letter to Richardson followed, declaring: "Have changed my mind. You would not give me a square deal. The Dahlia killing was justified."

And the rest was silence, more or less—until February 10, when someone beat Mrs. Jeanne French to death and dumped her nude body on Grand View Boulevard. Scrawled on the corpse in red lipstick was "Fuck you P.D." and "TEX," maybe then killer's signature. Again, the police got nowhere, but the press was way ahead of them, linking the Short and French slayings to the murders of February victim Evelyn Winters, Laura Trelstadt in May, and Rosenda Mondragon in July. By then, headlines had dropped the "Black Dahlia Avenger" angle and labeled their resident psycho "The Werewolf."

How many more women would die before somebody caught or killed the slayer? Would they *ever* bag him? Were the crimes even committed by a single individual?

Too many mysteries and none counted as violations of a federal law. Officially, unless some copper asked for fingerprint records, the Bureau didn't give a damn. That pissed Gantt off, but there was nothing he could do about it, and a stack of unrelated files kept growing on his desk while Wyman and Camille awaited him at home.

Some "Angeltown," this was. Some "Big Orange," ripe

and juicy for the picking. Some "City of Flowers and Sunshine"—as long as you had the Kleig lights and big bucks.

None of it coming my way, Devon thought and went to fetch a mug of subpar java from the office urn.

———

FOGGY BOTTOM, E Street Northwest, Washington: December 31, 1947

THE WORLD WAS CATCHING fire again, "Cold War" be damned, and Colby Gantt was anxious to be part of it. Unfortunately, he was blocked, at least for now, by paperwork at headquarters, accommodating major changes in the intelligence world, and by demands from his wife Eileen at home.

Too much falling upon his shoulders all at once.

In March, Eileen bore a son whom they'd named Hardy, after someone on her mother's side who'd died before Gantt married her. Colby accepted that, had no objection to a decent, rugged-sounding name, but he was still waiting for those paternal instincts everybody talked about to visit him.

On May 1, President Truman named Rear Admiral Roscoe Hillenkoetter as the CIG's third director, but that wouldn't last long. Twelve weeks and two days later, Truman signed the National Security Act of 1947, a major restructuring of the U.S. government drafted by CIG chief counsel Lawrence Houston that created a National Security Council, merged the Departments of the Army and Navy into a new Department of Defense with its own cabinet secretary, and liberated the Army Air Forces into a separate U.S. Air Force. It also created a new Central Intelligence Agency, still led by

Hillenkoetter, replacing the old CIG after eighteen months of service.

The law's provisions took effect on September 18, one day after the Senate confirmed James Forrestal as America's first Secretary of Defense. While OSS veteran William Peers fleshed out a CIA training program, the Agency—minus cipher clerk Eileen Gantt, on maternity leave—undertook its four broad duties: advising the NSC on matters related to national security; making recommendations to the NSC regarding coordination of intelligence activities between government departments; correlating and evaluating intelligence while providing for its appropriate dissemination; and finally, performing "such other functions as the NSC will from time to time direct."

The CIA was clearly meant to collect and assess foreign intelligence, but guidelines for operations inside the U.S. remained vague, and headquarters was already taking advantage of that, collaborating with the navy on "Project Chatter," a search for drugs useful during interrogations and for "the recruitment of agents." Dr. Charles Savage was in charge at the Naval Medical Research Institute in Bethesda, Maryland, proceeding with laboratory tests of both synthetic and natural drugs on animals, as well as human subjects.

Colby supposed that project had potential, but the real action right now was going on in war-torn Europe. In Germany, for instance, the CIA was taking over ex-Major General Reinhard Gehlen's spy ring, formerly tasked with feeding information to the *Wehrmacht* from the Eastern Front. A born survivor, Gehlen had cozied up to the U.S. Army's Military Intelligence Corps after V-E Day, debriefing escapees from the Soviet Bloc. Now he was the Agency's pet Nazi, operating from a villa once owned by Martin Bormann in Pullach, a Munich suburb, and bossing "Operation Rusty" to collect intel from nations under Russian sway. The U.S. public wouldn't like it if they knew of Gehlen switching sides and thus evading the Nuremberg trials, but who was going to tell them?

Across Europe, winners and losers from the war were grappling with their homegrown communists, often admired these days as leaders of the resistance against fascism. In vanquished Italy, Prime Minister Alcide De Gasperi wanted his piece of the Marshall Plan, Washington's $13 billion European Recovery Program, but he couldn't score until his Christian Democrats suppressed the Italian Communist Party and its parent group, the Italian Socialist Party. The Mafia and local bandits like Salvatore Giuliano were helping out with that, turning their guns on leftist rallies, killing dozens at a whack.

France was a mess since Charles De Gaulle had briefly retired from politics in January 1946, leaving governance to a *Tripartisme* regime including the Christian Democratic Popular Republican Movement, the socialist French Section of the Workers' International, and the French Communist Party. That was too much leftist crap for Washington to swallow, so the Agency had been recruiting more gangsters —*Le Milieu* in Paris and Marseilles, the *Unione Corse* out of Corsica—to crush strikes and make "radicals" disappear. When De Gaulle bounced back in April 1947 with a new party, dubbed Rally of the French People, mobsters became his strong-arm crew, rewarded with a free hand in heroin smuggling by friendly agents of the National Gendarmerie, Customs, and the CIA's French counterpart, the External Documentation and Counter-Espionage Service. And if Agency men skimmed their piece of the take when French smack reached New York, who'd be any the wiser?

Greece was another hotspot, with civil war raging since March 1946, between the lawful government's Hellenic Army and the Democratic Army of Greece, the military arm of the Greek Communist Party. America was backing Prime Minister Konstantinos Tsaldaris, while the USSR, Albania, Bulgaria and Yugoslavia piled on to help the Reds, shifting from guerrilla action to conventional warfare by September 1947. It was anybody's game, so far, unless advisors from the Agency and money from the Marshall Plan could swing the balance.

Poland, where the last World War officially began, presented CIA operatives with another kind of problem in the form of WIN—short for *Wolność i Niezawisłość*, or Freedom and Independence. Ostensibly an underground anti-communist group, resisting Soviet domination of the new Polish People's Republic, WIN had been feeding intel to the Gehlen Org hand over fist, but now a whiff of rot strongly suggested that WIN had been founded and led from day one by the Soviet Ministry for State Security, its reams of information worse than useless.

Czechoslovakia's Third Republic, established in April 1945, was another problematic three-way operation, totally leftist, comprised of the Czechoslovak Social Democratic Party (ČSSD), the Czech National Social Party (ČSNS), and the Communist Party of Czechoslovakia (KSČ). After V-E Day, President Edvard Beneš had expelled 2.9 million ethnic Germans, stripping them of their citizenship and all property with Allied approval, and cozied up to the USSR. The parliamentary election of May 1946 was a split decision, with the KSČ winning ninety-three seats, the ČSNS claiming fifty-five, and forty-six left over for the ČSSD. In July 1947 the Czechoslovak government welcomed Marshall Plan aid, but then Stalin summoned KSČ leader Klement

Gottwald for a chat in Moscow, whereupon Gottwald reversed his decision, claiming that a reactionary coup was imminent, requiring immediate action to prevent it. What form that action might take was still up in the air, but Agency analysts smelled a Red *coup d'état* in the making.

Meanwhile, Romania, ruled by Nazi henchman Ion Antonescu during World War II, now labored to pay Moscow $300 million in reparations while "SovRoms"—tax-exempt Soviet-Romanian companies purportedly formed to generate revenue for postwar reconstruction—cheerfully looted the enfeebled government of King Michael I. In November 1947, King Michael visited London for the wedding of his cousins, Princess Elizabeth and Prince Philip of Greece and Denmark, then returned to find that Romanian Reds had been busy during his absence. Only yesterday, while prepping for a New Year's party at Peleş Castle in Sinaia, Michael was summoned home to Bucharest by Prime Minister Petru Groza, one of Stalin's lapdogs, and compelled to abdicate at gunpoint.

Devon Gantt could almost hear the *clang* of Churchill's "Iron Curtain" falling in Europe, but the CIA was gearing up to fight it, authorized by the National Security Council on December 17 to perform covert action abroad.

Gantt planned to grab himself a piece of that, as soon as possible, and if he missed out on the rumored joys of early fatherhood...well, that was life, when he was tasked to save a world at risk.

CHAPTER 2

NOLAN O'HARA FELT like a true April fool, uprooting his family the same way that his father had in 1933 with the short-notice move from D.C. to Chicago. At least the kids weren't in school yet or leaving their best friends behind, and Florida was almost always warm, unlike Chi-Town—but what a very different world it was.

Some days he wondered whether they were still in the United States, but there were other Deep South states, he realized, that could be worse.

And that was Bureau life when Edgar Hoover had a transient whim.

Miami's SAC was Austin Hunnicutt, a twelve-year Bureau veteran sent here in 1942, after a short sting as Agent in Charge of Birmingham's field office. He was a rangy, thirty-something fellow, with an accent harking back to his Georgia roots, who'd killed a bank robber while still a six-month rookie in Milwaukee and moved on from there to

41

climb the Bureau ladder. Presently, he had 150 agents under his direct command, covering nine counties in the Sunshine State's southern sector, with resident agencies in Daytona Beach, Fort Lauderdale, Jacksonville, Lakeland, Orlando, St. Augustine, St. Petersburg, Sarasota, Tampa, and West Palm Beach. Proximity to Cuba, only ninety miles offshore, also made Hunnicutt the Bureau's primary liaison with Havana.

The biggest shock to Nolan, stranger than the year-round warmth and the seasonal hurricane threat, was Jim Crow, legally enshrined after the Civil War when a northern newspaper dubbed Florida "the smallest tadpole in the dirty pool of secession." Segregation of races began at birth and went on to the grave, with a maze of laws that could sound humorous if you weren't one of the people despised as second-class citizens.

Take interracial romance, for example. Florida law prescribed a year in prison and/or a $500 fine for "any black man and white woman, or any white man and/or Negro woman, who are not married to each other, who habitually live in and occupy in the nighttime the same room." If marriage sounded like a loophole, just forget about it; other laws forbade courtship between a white person and any person "of Negro descent to the fourth generation inclusive," while interracial marriage was "forever prohibited." All public facilities were likewise subject to Jim Crow, including "separate but equal" schools and juvenile detention centers, which required cell blocks separated by at least one-quarter mile, so that "white boys and Negro boys shall not, in any manner, be associated or worked together."

White police and courts enforced those laws, or if they proved inadequate, the state fell back on vigilante outfits like the Ku Klux Klan—whose ranks included many lawmen, ranging from command positions to patrolmen on the beat, often attending Klan rallies in uniform—or *ad hoc* lynch mobs that had slaughtered one out of every 1,250 Florida Negroes between Reconstruction and 1930. Convictions for those homicides were nonexistent, even on the rare occasions when arrests were made. In fact, black residents of Florida were twice as likely to be lynched as those in Georgia, seven times as likely as North Carolina's Negroes.

Keely had understood the "White" and "Colored" signs all right, while frowning disapproval and their kids were still too young for explanations, thankfully. Around the all-white Bureau office, no one seemed put off by the discriminating rules, and Agent Hunnicutt set an example for the rest by dropping racial slurs into his daily conversations—as had some of Nolan's teachers at the FBI Academy and even Chief Hoover himself from time to time.

The focus of white rage in Florida was Harry Tyson Moore, age forty-three, state secretary of the NAACP during the 1930s, founder of his own Progressive Voters League four years ago. Moore made a habit of investigating lynchings, registering Negro votes, filing anti-segregation lawsuits, raising hell in Tallahassee to get Ku Klux sheriffs fired, suspended, or at least ordered to do their jobs impartially. Aside from getting more Negroes on voter rolls, his biggest win so far was Florida's Minimum Foundations Project, granting more money to county schools in hope that Uncle Sam would leave Jim Crow alone.

In short, he was a royal pain in the ass.

If racial terrorism wasn't bad enough, the Sunshine State was also a paradise for mobsters, both homegrown and visiting from out of state. The late Scarface Capone had started it, back in the Twenties, and a flock of them had followed, notably Meyer Lansky and his cohorts planting illegal casinos up and down the state's Gold Coast while branching out to Cuba.

Otherwise, the Mafia—which Bureau headquarters still didn't recognize and maybe never would—was based in Tampa, the seat of Hillsborough County on the Gulf Coast. A Sicilian-born thug named Ignacio Antinori had started the Florida "family" during Prohibition, waging ceaseless war with local gangster Charlie "Dean of the Underworld" Wall, until someone blasted Antinori with a shotgun in October 1940. Son of a former Tampa mayor, Wall was still around these days but fading in the stretch, while another Sicilian, Santo Trafficante Sr., rose from being Antinori's underboss to rule the roost. Santo had strong ties to New York, sending son Santo Jr. off to learn the business from Tommy Lucchese, then shipping him to Cuba in '46, to help manage one of Lansky's Havana casinos. Meanwhile, Santo Sr. posed as an innocent cigar manufacturer, hiding behind frontmen Salvatore Italiano, an Antinori cousin, and glad-handing James "Head of the Elks" Lumia.

Florida's motto was "In God We Trust," first stamped on U.S. two-cent pieces back in 1864, and that told Nolan all he had to know about the Sunshine State, a place where money talked and bullshit often landed in the seat of power, if money came with it. Now, he'd have to buckle down and do his job the best he could, until the time came for him to move again.

———

FBI FIELD OFFICE, Los Angeles: July 5, 1948

L.A.'S "WEREWOLF KILLER" as still on the prowl, slashing

survivor Viola Norton on St. Valentine's Day, rebounding two days later to slaughter realtor Gladys Kern in one of the empty houses she showed to potential buyers. Between those crimes, police received a rambling hand-printed letter on Biltmore Hotel stationery, claiming the killer or his accomplice wanted to "help" detectives, but no one stepped up to surrender.

Devon Gantt wished he could be a part of that pursuit somehow, but there were still no federal laws involved for him to hang his hat on. He could say the same about the Red Light Bandit case, although LAPD had seemingly been able to solve that one on its own.

The guy they'd settled on was Caryl Chessman, twenty-seven, who had changed his given name from "Carol" in a bid to sound less feminine. As a child, he had survived encephalitis, asthma, and his mom's paralysis after a car wreck, stealing food to help his family during the Depression, moving on from there to auto theft, armed robbery and prison. One month after his latest parole, in January 1948, he had returned to his old tricks, adding a twist where he robbed couples parked on lover's lanes. He'd mounted a red spotlight on his car, to make victims believe he was a cop, then raped the girls while threatening their boyfriends' lives. Arrested after four attacks, he'd been arrested and indicted under California's "Little Lindbergh Law" on eighteen counts of robbery, rape and kidnapping, the latter crime involving his removal of one girl from her date's car to his, parked twenty feet away. Chessman claimed police had tortured him into confessing—not a stretch of the imagination with LAPD—and after choosing to defend himself at trial in May, he was convicted on seventeen counts. The twist: under state law, harming a "kidnap" victim, which included forcing oral sex, would send him to the gas chamber.

Gantt felt no sympathy for Chessman, but he knew the verdict laid grounds for appeals that could drag on through higher courts for years, giving the two-bit punk the publicity he craved. Celebrities had already lined up to plead his case, including poet Robert Frost, former First Lady Eleanor Roosevelt and Christian evangelist Billy Graham.

Whatever, Gantt mused to himself. *It takes all kinds.*

HUAC's foray to Hollywood last year had failed to turn up any Red subversives, but the movie industry was nonetheless transformed. Fallout from the hearings and resultant blacklist prompted Floyd Odlum to quit the business, selling RKO Pictures to aircraft builder Howard Hughes in May, around the same time the Supreme Court made its ruling in the case of *United States v. Paramount Pictures,* citing antitrust laws to ban studios from owning their own theaters. That seven-to-one decision with Justice Jackson abstaining, spelled doom for the "Big Five" studio system, raising rates the studios charged theaters while clearing the way for independent productions and "art house" theaters, weakening the Hays Production Code with an influx of films made outside the censors' jurisdiction. Hughes settled that case, then fired half of RKO's employees and closed the studio for six months while he probed the politics of those remaining on his payroll.

In court, the Hollywood Ten stood convicted of contempt of Congress, drawing one-year sentences, but their case was on appeal, with an amicus curiae brief signed by 204 sympathetic movie professionals. Outside the industry, L.A.'s city government had seen the writing on the wall, firing seventeen employees who'd refused to sign loyalty pledges.

Speaking of movies, Johnny Rosselli had barely hit the street after his early parole before he'd returned to Hollywood, teaming with Bryan Foy at the "B" pictures unit of Warner Brothers to try his hand at producing. Ironically, three of the films he'd worked on since his 1947 release had gang-busting themes, including *T-Men, He Walked by Night,* and *Canon City*, the latter featuring a prison break.

When not playing producer, Rosselli flexed his muscles by prodding Columbia Pictures president Harry Cohn into hiring starlet Marilyn Monroe, née Norma Jeane Mortenson. Monroe had spent her share of time on Cohn's casting couch, but he'd still dismissed her as a "second string no talent with tits" until Rosselli stepped in, with the weight of Chicago's Tony Accardo behind him. Next thing you know, with no credits to her name except a silent walk-on in *Dangerous Years* and one line of dialogue in *Scudda Hoo! Scudda Hay!*, Monroe landed a six-month Columbia contract starring with Adele Jergens as mother-daughter burlesque girls in *Ladies of the Chorus*, then having her photo briefly used in Gene Autry's *Riders of the Whistling Pines*. Her contract tanked when Marilyn pronounced herself "madly in love" with crooner Frank Sinatra, whom Cohn detested while shunning an offer to spend the weekend aboard Cohn's yacht.

Another L.A. mobster, Mickey Cohen, divided his time between battling *mafioso* Jack Dragna and aiding the new state of Israel—or maybe the latter pursuit was just a con job. Gantt knew this much; Cohen had staged a bash at Slapsy Maxie's Wilshire Boulevard comedy club, ostensibly to raise cash for Israel's Irgun guerrilla army, coaxing a roomful of bigwigs to open their wallets. Mickey had kicked things off with a $25,000 pledge, ending the night with some $120,000 from bookies, Jewish gangsters, movie stars, and Burbank's chief of police. Supposedly, the money went for guns, loaded aboard the USS *Altalena* and shipped off to Israel in June. Alas, eleven days after she sailed, the *Altalena* sank off Tel Aviv, shelled by Israeli Defense Force gunships. Nobody knew if there were actually any arms aboard, or if Cohen had kept the cash himself.

In politics, Dick Nixon was busy cashing in on his HUAC stardom, cross-filing for reelection to Congress in both party primaries, unopposed as a Republican and grabbing 53 percent of Democratic votes as well. No pundit alive was betting against a November landslide, particularly after Nixon teamed with South Dakota's Karl Mundt to write a bill requiring all CPUSA members to register with the U.S. Attorney General. It died in the Senate, in June, but so what? In red-baiting, it's heated words that count.

The Las Vegas Strip, meanwhile, was growing by leaps and bounds since Bugsy Siegel's murder. From bloody red ink, the Fabulous Flamingo had turned a $4 million profit this year, suckers dropping money en route to its showroom, lured by the likes of Dean Martin and Jerry Lewis, Sammy Davis Jr., Lena Horne, Sophie Tucker, Spike Jones and Danny Thomas. Horne and Davis, as Negroes, were banned from booking rooms at the Flamingo during their appearances, shunted to cheap motels in West Side's ghetto while they raked in heaps of moolah for the Mob.

Indeed, the Fabulous Flamingo proved so profitable that Nevada politicians wanted more than just their share of the casino's skim. When the Thunderbird Hotel opened for business—featuring Indian artwork, a Navajo-themed restaurant and the Strip's only bowling alley—its owner of record was Lieutenant Governor Clifford Jones. Rivers of cash were flowing *somewhere*, but until a federal indictment was returned, or til Director Hoover pulled his head out of the sand, the Bureau would be sitting on its hands.

San Francisco D.A. Edmund Brown might call America "the most lawless country in the world" while venting to reporters, but the Bureau couldn't just charge in and solve that problem for him, much less in L.A., where Sheriff Gene Biscailuz and LAPD Chief Clemence Horrall were wallowing in graft, focused on Reds and Mexicans as the root of all evil.

That left Gantt and his fellow G-men chasing bank robbers and fugitives who crossed state lines, and L.A. had its share of both to keep the local Bureau occupied. Devon had yet to make his first headline arrest and hoped he wouldn't have to wait much longer for his moment in the spotlight—if it ever came at all.

———

WEST 112TH STREET, *Manhattan: August 30, 1948*

DAVE JORDAN FINISHED CLEARING off another table while he eyed the television set mounted in Glassman's dining room, a little something extra for the paying customers. Station WJZ-TV, owned by the Columbia Broadcasting System, had begun broadcasting three weeks earlier as Manhattan's sixth TV station and the second to premier so far this summer. The rest had gone on-air while he was busy over-seas or working overtime to get his life back at Camp Edwards, where the entertainment had been limited to radio.

The big hit for CBS was *The Ed Sullivan Show,* but that aired on Sunday nights, leaving Mondays to a kids' puppet show called *The Adventures of Lucky Pup,* followed by local programming of news and sports. The big news for the past month had been New York International Airport, already nicknamed Idlewild after a land developer's earlier tag for a failed golf resort on nearby Jamaica Bay, Queens.

Less than captivated by the puppets, David concentrated on his work and getting through another shift, although his mind strayed of its own accord to family and school. He wasn't spending any more time with his parents or with Gemma and her husband than when he'd come back from Massachusetts, but that didn't trouble him. His mother worried too much, while his father always seemed preoccupied with business, which meant shady deals. Gemma and Paulo were so wrapped up in the only child they'd ever have that it was hard to get a word in edgewise with them about anything except Lucia walking for the first time, uttering her first word—"Dada," if it wasn't just some kind of stammer—and whatever else she'd done of late that was the cutest thing recorded throughout human history.

As far as Cousins Dominic and Angelo, they spent most of their free time—which was damned near *all* the time, apparently—running the streets with hoodlum friends, drinking and getting laid, stealing whatever caught their eye, or skirmishing with Puerto Ricans and Negroes. Someone was likely to get hurt there, even killed, but David didn't see it as his job to save their lives or souls.

As someone in the Bible he'd abandoned might have asked, was he his cousins' keeper? And his answer: not a chance.

At university, his classes were proceeding well, his grades all As and Bs as they had been in high school. He enjoyed studying history, delving into the motives that had driven great or evil men—and sometimes women, too—to change the world. Dave also liked his job at the law library and had already made one friend among the students who spent so much time among the stacks.

Her name—yes, *her*—was Fiona O'Hara, a pretty redhead one year older than Jordan but further advanced in her studies since she'd been exempt from the war. He'd checked her out a little, on the sly, and learned she hailed from D.C., that her grade point average was kissing-close to 4.0, and that she'd been a star on Columbia's female swim team as an undergrad. A time or two, he'd pictured her in one of those two-piece bikini swimsuits that were getting popular right now, named by its French designer for an atoll in the Marshall Islands where America had shipped the native population out to detonate bigger and better A-bombs since the war.

When he thought of Fiona swimming, it was usually at the beach, not in a pool—someplace like Rockaway, Fort Tilden, even Coney Island—but Dave knew he'd never see her there. The beach wasn't for him, swim trunks revealing all his scars while he tried hobbling across the sand without taking a spill.

To hell with it.

The "hot" thing at Columbia this term was a new School of the Arts, just opened for a range of courses that included theater, writing, and film. Beyond that, most of what he picked up from the news was murder, war, and politics. In India, some nut had killed the nation's final hope for peace, Mahatma Gandhi, and ensured religious war between Hindus and Muslims. Stateside, in March, the Supreme Court had prohibited religious education in all tax-supported schools, provoking howls of outrage from churches craving government handouts. And after three decades of terrorism against British occupation forces, Zionists had formed a State of Israel back in May, one day before the armies of four Arab nations charged across its borders and began to get their asses kicked by Jewish troops.

Sometimes, it made Dave wonder what he'd nearly lost a leg defending, most particularly when he read about the rising cost of living in America. Inflation stood at close to 8 percent, with the average family earning $2,950 per year and new houses averaging $7,700. New cars averaged $1,250, but if you wanted to drive one, a gallon of gas cost more than a whole loaf of bread. Movie tickets had jumped to sixty cents since the antitrust lawsuit in Hollywood, and if you had spare cash to burn, the new Polaroid Land Camera with self-developing film could be yours for a mere $89.75.

Dave was already looking forward to the end of school, passing the New York bar exam—and then, what? He still didn't have a clue, beyond knowing the last thing that he wanted was to join his father in the Giordano business, alternating between shady deals and standing up in court with criminals.

Why had his old man gone that way after his own war with the Germans three decades ago? Had it been easier than striking out alone or slaving as an underpaid associate at some Manhattan firm? David had never asked and didn't plan to now.

Some things, he fervently believed, were better left unsaid.

————

Berlin: September 9, 1948

Leonid Babin hated being 1,800 miles from home right

now, but he'd had no choice in the matter. Viktor Abaku-mov, the Minister for State Security, had ordered him to visit Germany, and here he was amidst chaos, wishing he could be back in Moscow, overseeing the preparation of his son for the fulfillment of their destiny.

According to reports, the boy was doing well at two years old, not large enough to handle weapons yet, but taking to a regimen of exercise and early education custom-tailored to develop him in mind and body. Dr. Lazar Serbsky was no longer Babin's problem, such a shame about that accident he'd had, approaching Gorky one night last December. Who could have imagined that a tanker truck would change lanes unexpectedly and crush the doctor's GAZ-M20 like a tin can, afterward exploding to incinerate both drivers? Tragic.

Nor was that the end of tragedy in Babin's secret life. It had not pleased him to dispose of Darya Sokolva, the mother of his bastard son and tool of sweet revenge, but Babin had gone through with it, regardless. What was a brief personal pain compared to destiny's demand?

As luck would have it, a madman was stalking Moscow Oblast, five young women slain and mutilated, heads and hands removed in some demented ritual. Officially, such crimes did not occur in Russia, being limited to decadent Western nations enslaved by evil capitalists, but Babin had learned of a misfit Militsiya private imprisoned for rape and slashing the faces of two *prostituki* on nights with full moons. His acts had not rated a death sentence, and it had been child's play to spring him from prison, borrowed for "special testing" by the MGB's chemical warfare program. Instead, the young man was restrained and handed victims from the streets of Moscow until it was time to carry out the task for which he had been liberated.

Poor Darya. She'd been so beautiful in life.

At least her soul could rest, if such a thing existed in this godless world, knowing her slayer had himself been shot by Babin personally, planted in the freshly-poured foundation of a new building in Moscow, never to be seen again.

And now, Berlin.

The trouble had begun in March, three months before Tito's rebellious Yugoslavia was expelled from the Cominform. Angered by economic advances in the American, British and French sectors of Berlin, Stalin had blocked the Western Allies' railway, road, and canal access to their respective quadrants of the former German capital, then offered to stop the blockade in exchange for the withdrawal of newly issued Deutsche marks from West Berlin. Instead, the Western Allies organized a military airlift of supplies beginning on June 26, while Soviet fighter planes began intermittent harassment, one Yakovlev Yak-3 colliding with a British European Airways Vickers Viking near Gatow airfield, claiming fifteen lives.

The whole world watched a crisis in the making, fearing the outbreak of World War Three. At the outset, West Berliners had five weeks' worth of food and six weeks' worth of coal. The U.S. had 98,000 soldiers in West Germany, but only 31,000 combat troops, versus 1.5 million Red Army soldiers surrounding Berlin. Even with that disparity, residents of Berlin required some 1,534 tons of foodstuffs daily, plus 3,475 tons of coal, diesel and petroleum fuels. Call it 5,000 tons per day on average, for nourishment and heat alone.

The Allied position seemed untenable, but as the Kremlin soon learned, it was not. Hundreds of daily flights from Frankfurt, Hamburg and Hanover delivered the goods to Berlin's Templehof Airport in "Operation Vittles." The siege was relieved but not lifted. Stalin seethed, ordering incessant radio broadcasts warning Berliners that Allied forces would soon cut and run, placing all of Berlin back in Soviet hands. Noncommunist civic officials elected in 1946 faced daily police harassment when they went to work at City Hall in the Soviet sector. In the sky above Berlin, U.S. Air Force pilots claimed 733 incidents of Russian provocation including air-to-air gunfire and rocketing, coupled with flak from ground fire.

None of it stopped the airlift, and today, Babin stood near the Brandenburg Gate, adjacent to the ruined Reichstag in the British sector of Berlin, watching a mob of some 500,000 anti-communist citizens. They, in turn, watched Ernst Reuter, the mayor of West Berlin, broadcasting an appeal to the so-called Free World.

"You peoples of the world," he cried, "you people of America, of England, of France, look on this city, and recognize that this city, this people, must not be abandoned —*cannot* be abandoned!"

At that, the crowd surged forward, eager hands ripping down a Soviet flag from the Brandenburg Gate. Russian police responded with scattered gunfire, wounding several rioters, before a British deputy provost intervened, forcing the officers back with a swagger stick, his pistol still pointedly holstered.

Babin turned away, wondering if winter would defeat the protests as it had destroyed Hitler's *Wehrmacht* in the midst of Operation Barbarossa. Either way, his function was to write and submit a report of his findings to Minister Abakumov, then get back to Moscow as soon as it could be arranged.

The good news from this unwelcome diversion: Berlin's crisis might drag on for months yet, helpfully distracting Abakumov and Lavrentiy Beria from Babin's private moves behind the scenes. He didn't care how many Germans starved or otherwise met death during the siege if their mass sacrifice concealed his own.

That simply proved that destiny, indeed, was on his side.

————

MARSEILLES, France: October 15, 1948

IT WAS good to get away from home, away from fatherhood if only for a little while, and get back in the thick of things. Colby Gantt sat opposite a lieutenant of the Gendarmerie Nationale in that worthy's office, watching his host chain-smoke unfiltered Gauloises cigarettes. Beside him sat the *sous la tête*—underboss—of a prominent family within the *Unione Corse*.

"You understand, *Messieurs*, that the collaboration you propose must be beneficial to all parties, *oui?*"

"Of course," Gantt answered for himself and for the Corsican, who had a strong aversion to direct contact with lawmen.

"Services exchanged for payment as it were, *n'est-ce pas?*" said the lieutenant, lighting up another smoke.

"We all know the procedure," Gantt replied. "We're simply here to set the terms."

"And there is still the *Service de Documentation Extérieure et de Contre-Espionnage* to be considered, eh?"

"They're already on board," Gantt answered back. "We're here to deal with you."

"Of course. As long as everything is...how do you say it? Simpatico?"

"That's one word."

"So, the terms, as I've been led to understand by my *Capitaine* who shall remain nameless, include continuing disruption and suppression of the *Parti communiste français* and safe passage of certain cargo shipped by your associates, shall we say, to which my agency agrees for the sum of one million *nouveaux francs* per month."

Gantt did the math in his head, reaching a monthly total of $8,417—chump change when you considered the results. Suppression of the French Communist Party in itself was worth much more to Washington, while shared profits from heroin imported to the States would nicely pad the CIA's "black" budget for covert operations.

"That's agreeable," he said.

"And this month's payment...?"

"Is right here." Gantt opened his attache case, removing a cigar box neatly stuffed with 200 banknotes in 5,000-franc denominations. "Smoke them in good health," he said and smiled as the lieutenant took the package off his hands.

That had been quick and clean, as well as reasonably cheap, facilitated by President Truman's April signature formalizing the Marshall Plan. Elsewhere, Gantt thought, as he prepared to leave the spartan office, matters thus far had been neither as neat or economical.

Czechoslovakia had undergone a Red *coup d'état* in late February, its twelve noncommunist ministers resigning en masse, while Foreign Minister Jan Masaryk was found dead on March 10, in the courtyard of Prague's Czernin Palace, wearing only his pajamas. That case smacked of assassination, but detectives from Public Security professed themselves unable to find any evidence of foul play. President Beneš refused to sign the new Communist Constitution in May and resigned on June 7, succeeded by Red loyalist Antonín Zápotocký. The KSČ established a Workers' Militia, banned non-Communists from television broadcasts, and occupied all non-Communist ministries.

The only bright spot on that scene came courtesy of the Gehlen Org, presently tapping the Agency's budget for $1.5 million yearly. The win was "Operation Bohemia," a Czech-run operation, penetrating their Military Intelligence and thereby revealing a spy ring run by Yugoslavia's secret police, or State Security Administration, reporting from several cities in western Europe.

Colby's next stop would be Italy, where parliamentary elections in April worried the Truman White House and Henry Luce at *Time* magazine. The weekly had already warned that leftist victories at the Italian ballot box would lead to "the brink of catastrophe," and the Agency meant to prevent it. As it turned out, in fact, De Gasperi's Christian Democrats won the day on behalf of a Roman Catholic, conservative and capitalist Italy, drubbing a leftist coalition of the Popular Democratic Front, Italian Socialist Party, and Italian Communist Party.

Colby knew for a fact that CIA paymasters had laid out $1 million to ensure that victory, while elves in the covert workshop ginned up forged letters, discrediting Communist Party leaders. *Time* backed that effort without saying where the cash came from and put Prime Minister De Gasperi on its cover after the election. The Mafia, as usual, had played its part, assassinating socialist trade union leader Placido Rizzotto in Corleone, then hiring a physician, Dr. Michele Navarra to slay 11-year-old witness Giuseppe Letizia with a lethal injection.

Colby had hands to shake in Rome and in Palermo, but Romania, alas, was closed to him, at least for now. Two days ahead of Italy's election, the land of Dracula and Ion Antonescu proclaimed itself the Socialist Republic of

Romania, nationalizing private companies and moving toward collectivized farms. Secret police, operating as the Department of State Security, suppressed dissent wherever it was found, purging "enemies of the state," but resistance had coalesced in the Carpathians, with anti-communist guerrilla bands enlisting several thousand fighters.

Back home, where gathering intelligence had turned into a new growth industry, the U.S. Air Force Office of Special Investigations opened for business on August 1. Not to be outdone, the CIA created its own Office of Policy Coordination exactly one month later, geared up to pursue covert action under Frank Wisner, former OSS chief in southeastern Europe during 1944-45.

In Greece, the civil war dragged on, with the Democratic Amy of Greece (DSE) fielding 26,000 soldiers, controlling 70 percent of the Peloponnese. Even so, the Hellenic Army, reinforced by Brits and American troops under General James Van Fleet, had the Reds outnumbered with more than a quarter-million soldiers. In these haggard, brutal days, both sides had taken to rounding up children: the DSE kidnapped some 30,000, shipping them off to Eastern Bloc nations "at the request of popular organizations and parents," while anti-communist forces removed 25,000 more from their DSE parents, stashing them in "reform camps" and "child towns" devised by Frederica of Hanover, the German-born Queen Consort of Greece. Triumph in the cradle of democracy could still go either way.

More jarring news—if not entirely unexpected—came in early September, with the formal establishment of the Democratic People's Republic of Korea above the 38th parallel. Its premier was Kim Il-sung, né Kim Sŏng-ju, a rolly-polly thirty-six-year-old who'd founded a Down-with-Imperialism Union in 1926, joined the Communist Party of China five years later, and in 1935 took his present name, meaning "Kim become the sun." The Soviets had trained him with other Korean guerrillas at a camp near Khabarovsk, winding up with a puppet whom they had "created from zero" in the words of one Agency mole inside the Ministry of Internal Affairs. The USSR had recognized Kim's government on October 12 and withdrew its soldiers, leaving Ambassador Terentii Shtykov in Pyongyang to pull the puppet's strings.

South of the 38th parallel, UN observers watched an unwieldy three-month election install Syngman Rhee—as corrupt a would-be tyrant as Colby had ever seen—as president of a new Republic of Korea. Rhee hated Kim and communism; Kim returned the favor, and then some. You could almost hear the fuse sizzling.

Well, Colby thought, *I can't be everywhere at once.* But he was hoping for a shot at more than one exotic battleground as the Cold War went on. His service with the OSS had given him a taste for high adventure, besides which, the joys of hearth and home unfortunately paled.

———

New York Cancer Hospital, Manhattan: November 3, 1948

"It breaks my heart to see 'im that way," Carlo Giordano said. "I mean, for Christ's sake! What's even the point in hangin' on?"

"I know," Greg Jordan told his older brother, knowing there was nothing he could say to ease the pain they shared.

Primo, their firstborn sibling, was dying in the hospital behind them, nicknamed "The Bastille" by locals for its large, broad towers built in 1884 and for the high attrition rate amongst its patients. Truth be told, Primo smoked himself to death and there was no recovering from that, despite doses of radiation and the latest chemotherapy involving nitrogen mustard and folic acid, only tried and tested in the past five years. He'd done it to himself, but placing blame supplied no palliative for grief.

The hospital, modeled after a chateau from the Loire Valley in France, took up a full block of Central Park West between West 105th and 106th Streets on Manhattan's Upper West Side. Patients confined to its circular wards— built to eliminate corners for breeding of germs—seldom enjoyed a view of Central Park itself except on entering or, for the very fortunate, a carriage ride around the park, weather permitting. Most, like Primo, came to die here and departed in a hearse.

"Sometimes I wish he'd just get on with it, you know?" said Carlo. "Kick the fuckin' bucket, already."

"Carlo—"

"I know it's blasphemy, okay? But Jesus Christ, where's all the mercy Father Santovito always blathered on about in church?"

Greg knew exactly what his brother meant and couldn't argue with it, but once they had cleared the antiseptic-smelling hospital, his mind was moving on to other members of his family.

David seemed to be doing well in all his classes at Columbia, eschewing any aid that tainted Giordano money could provide. He came to Sunday dinner once a month on average, held up his end of the small talk conversations that were getting old, enjoying sister Gemma's daughter on the rare occasions when they met.

That was a pisser for you if there ever was one. On delivering Lucia fifteen months ago, Gemma had suffered major hemorrhaging. The only way to save her life had been an emergency hysterectomy, precluding any further children unless Paulo Ricca managed to accept the idea of adopting someone else's kid. Greg personally didn't mind having only a single grandchild, but he knew that Angelina grieved the loss, perhaps more than their daughter did.

Carlo was the leader of the Giordano family these days, had been since Primo finally broke down and saw a doctor who diagnosed stage four lung cancer, metastasized through his body to invade his liver, bones and brain. Carlo had the street smarts and required ferocity to keep the money flowing from a multitude of rackets, coping with the other *Cosa Nostra* families, but he'd never be the gangland statesman and civic philanthropist that their eldest brother had been in his prime.

And hard times might be coming round again for the *italiani* in America, despite war's end and removal of their stigma as potential enemy aliens. Back in January, speaking to Bishop Thomas Molloy's Cathedral Club of Brooklyn, Attorney General Clark said, "Those who do not believe in the ideology of the United States shall not be allowed to stay in the United States." To prove his point, in March, Justice decreed that left-leaning Italians couldn't immigrate or even visit the U.S.

Another headache for Greg Jordan was the hoopla over Governor Tom Dewey's campaign for the White House, prompting leaders of the Syndicate to wonder what he'd have in store for them as president. Most newspapers seemed to believe he was a shoo-in, the *Chicago Daily Tribune* prepping headlines for Election Day that read "DEWEY DEFEATS TRUMAN." Bad luck for publisher Robert McCormick: Truman scored a surprise upset, beating Dewey by some 2.2 million votes and carrying twenty-nine states.

Across the country, *mafiosi* heaved a great sigh of relief when the results were tabulated on November 3. In Michigan, Bill Tocco and Joe Zerilli bought a controlling share of Hazel Park Raceway, built as an auto racetrack now earmarked for horses. Kansas City's Binaggio family made the difference in Forrest Smith's election as Missouri's next governor, spending an estimated $200,000 on his race in St. Louis alone. In Milwaukee, *Don* Giuseppe Vallone lost face when *la Commissione* made his family subordinate to Chicago. Ray Partiarca ruled New England from his base in Providence, Rhode Island, while John Sicandra kept his grip on northeastern Pennsylvania. Frank Amato had Philadelphia under his thumb, drawing strength from his Brooklyn roots and marriage to the only daughter of rising New York *mafioso* Paul Castellano. Stefano Badami ran Elizabeth, New Jersey, while Willie Moretti shared Newark with Longy Zwillman, rubbing out rivals Charles Yarnowsky and John DiBiaso during the summer of 1948.

Out west, the *Cosa Nostra* had its share of problems. Brothers Jack and Tom Dragna were still battling Mickey Cohen for control of Los Angeles and might be for years to come. Anthony Lima and underboss Michael Abati ran San Francisco's rackets, briefly sidetracked by indictment for murdering Chicago transplant Nick DeJohn in May 1947, but D.A. Pat Brown dismissed those charges mid-trial, after "losing confidence" in key witness Anita de Venza, a police informer and brothel habitué associated with Frisco "Queen of Vice" Inez Burns. In San Jose, forty-eight miles farther south, *Don* Onofrio Sciortino shunned publicity while he grew ever richer from gambling, counterfeiting, shylocking, prostitution and extortion.

Sometimes, it all felt like a house of cards to Jordan, or a mansion built on shifting sand. His function now, as he approached age fifty-two, was to protect his family as best he could, and to respect son David's wish to stand outside the Syndicate milieu, maintaining a safe distance from his father, uncles and cousins.

What greater hope could any true American cherish for these days, than for his children to be better than himself?

————

FBI Headquarters: November 17, 1948

DECLAN O'HARA KEPT WAITING for Edgar Hoover to explode over his epic disappointment on Election Day. It hadn't happened so far, but he knew the Chief too well to think his rage would simply fade away.

Not that Speed was stable at the best of times, these days. In April, after United Automobile Workers president Walter Reuther narrowly survived a shotgun blast through the kitchen window of his home in Detroit, UAW attorneys asked Attorney General Clark to launch an investigation. Clark spoke to Hoover and came back shamefaced, telling them, "Fellows, Edgar says no. He says he's not going to send the FBI in every time some nigger woman gets raped."

What did *that* mean? The lawyers, being sane, couldn't make any sense of that and neither could O'Hara.

Then again, what could he make of the Bureau's obsession—meaning Hoover's—for recruiting lapsed Reds as informers, paying them thousands of dollars and looking the other way when they double-dipped from other sponsors? And why were the most prominent among them

Catholics who'd strayed, then flipped back from the CPUSA to the Mother Church? Was it a passion to "believe" some kind of psychiatric syndrome?

One of them, Elizabeth Bentley, was a confessed Russian spy or had been from 1938 to '45. Before that, she had joined a fascist student's group in Italy and bedded its leader, proclaiming communist literature "as dry as dust," before she came back to the States and stated her migration to the left. She'd volunteered to serve the FBI, naming 150 fellow spies, including thirty-seven federal employees—some also fingered by the chatterbox Whittaker Chambers. Granted, she had nothing to corroborate the tales she sold, but once she was code-named "Gregory," supported by 250 G-men working in shifts, she'd made a killing from the Bureau, from HUAC, and from whoever else cared to hear her sing. Her loose lips cost the NBC network $10,000 to settle a September libel suit from government economist William Remington, but Bishop Fulton Sheen had put her on the public speaking circuit, quenching her endless thirst for booze at $300 per lecture.

Another one was Louis Francis Budenz, an Indiana labor organizer and allegedly ran his own spy ring for Moscow until he repented in 1946, declaring, "With deep joy, I wish to announce that by God's grace I have returned fully to the faith of my fathers, to the Catholic Church." Lately, he'd wriggled into the Alger Hiss case, telling HUAC that the CPUSA "regarded him always" as a member acting "under Communist discipline." On the stand, with cash in pocket, he also corroborated accusations made against others by Whittaker Chambers.

But Reds aside, the Chief's crushing November disappointment was Tom Dewey's fault, of course—or maybe Harry Truman's. Hoover had despised Dewey as long as

Declan could remember, back to the mid-Thirties, when the mama's boy from Michigan had scored gang-busting headlines as Manhattan's special prosecutor, then as district attorney. When Dewey ran for president, however, they struck a deal, worked out by Chief of Bureau Crime Records Lou Nichols and Dewey's top aides. The bargain: once Dewey occupied the White House—something most pundits agreed was a sure thing—he'd name Hoover as Attorney General, with Clyde Tolson as his chief assistant, while Nichols became Director of the FBI. Next time a vacancy came up on the Supreme Court, Hoover would ascend once more, ultimately slated to become Chief Justice.

All the pieces were in place, with G-men in the field searching for every speck of dirt on Truman to advance his rival's cause. HUAC Chairman Parnell Thomas set up special hearings on the case of former Yalta delegate and secretary of the UN conference Alger Hiss, hoping to smear incumbent Truman by association, and American newspapers gobbled it up. By September, when Truman launched a whistle-stop tour across America, 65 percent of all daily papers were backing Dewey and he led Truman in every poll. Truman's defeat seemed even more likely when former FDR Vice President Henry Wallace left the fold to run on behalf of a new, left-leaning Progressive Party, and southern racists defected en masse over Truman's civil rights concessions, creating their own States' Rights Democratic Party, better known as "Dixiecrats."

Those rifts seemed fatal to the mainstream Democratic Party til Election Day when Truman rebounded to amaze the country and the world at large. Dewey went back to Albany, wiping the egg off his face and trying to decide if he should run again in 1952, while Hoover's dreams of glory vanished in a puff of smoke. He'd never be Attorney General now, much less Chief Justice of the nation's highest court, and there was nothing he could do about it except sulk.

Aside from Dewey, Hoover blamed Lou Nichols, grousing to whoever would listen, "I wouldn't be in this mess if it weren't for Nichols. He pushed me out on a limb that got sawed off."

On November 5, Truman had returned to Washington for a triumphant motorcade down Pennsylvania Avenue, from Union Station to the White House, Vice President-elect Alben Barkley seated next to him in an open limousine. It felt like a rehearsal for next January's inauguration, but Chief Hoover couldn't face the celebration. He stayed home from work that day—and for the next eleven days as well, in an unprecedented lapse. When he finally came back on November 17, the Associated Press told a presumably worried populace, "J. Edgar Hoover returned to active duty at FBI headquarters today, fully recovered from a bout of pneumonia."

Bullshit, O'Hara thought. Speed's absence was the action of a spoiled, dyspeptic child. The only question now in Declan's mind, was who might take the brunt of Hoover's pique. Would it be Harry Truman, Nichols, lesser agents under his control, or all of the above?

O'Hara reckoned he would keep his head down for the next few months and wait for the Chief's brooding rage to dissipate a bit so that he wasn't caught in the fallout. In fact, it might turn out to be a long four years ahead.

————

FEDERAL BUREAU of Narcotics Manhattan Field Office: December 13, 1948

IKE SAWYER HAD a world of worry on his mind, and no solutions seemed to present themselves.

First up was family, specifically his eldest living son, Payton. On the surface, there appeared to be no problem with him: he'd made first-rate grades at Benjamin Franklin High School, while starring as point guard on the basketball team, graduating in June 1947 with an athletic scholarship to Monroe College in the Bronx. Their men's basketball team, the Monroe Mustangs, was in Division I, meaning the scholarship paid full tuition, fees, books, housing and meals, renewable yearly if Payton kept his grades high enough to please the National Junior College Athletic Association.

No problem there, with Payton's record. It should've set Ike's mind at ease.

The problem was his son's major and Payton's chosen life path. He was studying up for a two-year degree in criminal justice, setting his sights on the NYPD—the same department that had dealt with near-continuous investigation of corruption from the 1890s onward, not to mention allegations of brutality against minorities and anybody else who fell into their clutches, some cases observed by Payton personally on the streets of Harlem.

What in hell was Payton thinking? *Was* he even thinking? Ike had tried to talk him out of it, but that proved useless. Who could talk sense to a young man, going on nineteen, who thought he knew it all?

At least the younger kids weren't giving Ike too many headaches, yet. Keisha, fifteen, enrolled at Benjamin Franklin in September, and Frederick was still five years behind his sister, putting in his time at Patrick Henry Elementary. The street held no allure for either of them, which was great, and both of them had brains to spare, Fred was likely to become an athlete in his older brother's mold when he hit high school, though he favored football.

So, two out of three, and there was no way Ike or wife Talitha could restrain their eldest now. Payton would have to make his own mistakes and live with them, if he survived that long behind a badge.

And who knew, maybe he'd wash out of the Police Academy.

Meanwhile, Ike kept chasing drug smugglers, pushers on the street, and turning any addicts he could motivate into his private snitches, looking for his next big bust.

For whatever it was worth, United Nations headquarters, located in Geneva, Switzerland, was trying to be helpful. Recently, its thinkers had drawn up a new rule with a long-winded title: Protocol Bringing under International Control Drugs Outside of the Scope of the 1931 Convention for Limiting the Manufacture and Regulating the Distribution of Narcotic Drugs. The first go-round tried to place controls on drugs derived from natural raw materials—natural alkaloids, like morphine or cocaine, and their semi-synthetic derivatives, like heroin—but manufacturers kept running ahead of the law. Thus, the 1948 Protocol targeted all drugs liable to similar abuse, addiction, and harmful effects, including all those to be found or whipped up in the future.

An impossible dream? Hell, yes. But any nation signing on to the new Protocol was "obligated" to inform the UN's Secretary General of any new drugs discovered or invented down the road, whereupon the existing Commission on Narcotic Drugs would place said substances under "provisional control."

That all sounded like hot air to Ike, whose interest outside the States was focused on the Tokyo War Crimes

Tribunal. The defense rested its case in September 1947, after which the judges spent another fifteen months deciding guilt or innocence, poring over testimony from 419 witnesses, affidavits from 779 more, plus 4,336 exhibits. Reading the final judgment had consumed eight days and finished yesterday, with verdicts listed in the *New York Times.*

Of the twenty-eight defendants who stood trial, seven were sentenced to hang, sixteen drew life prison terms, one was sentenced to twenty years and another to seven. Ike's primary interest was in those who'd organized the drug trade in Manchuria. Of those, nooses waited for General Seishirō Itagaki, Lieutenant General Akira Mutō, and General Hideki Tōjō—who had tried and failed to kill himself in 1945 and was nursed back to health so he could hang. The panel dealt life sentences to Field Marshal Shun-roku Hata, ex-Finance Minister Okinori Kaya, Admiral Takazumi Oka, General Kenryō Satō, and General Yoshijirō Umezu. Two former foreign ministers, General Yoshijirō Umezu and Mamoru Shigemitsu pulled sentences of twenty years and seven years, respectively.

With justice, like the rest of life, you had to take the bitter with the sweet.

Speaking of bitter, Ike had lost some sleep this year over the rifts that threatened to destroy the Democratic Party. He'd preferred Wallace to Truman, even knowing the Progressive Party had already doomed itself by February, five months prior to its Philadelphia convention, by welcoming outspoken Reds into its ranks. Wallace's running mate, Senator Glen Taylor from Idaho had gone to jail in Birmingham for failure to observe the Jim Crow signs. Ike's real worry, however, was the Dixiecrat walkout from the Democratic National Convention, also held in Philly, followed two days later by a "States' Rights" convention in

Birmingham that looked and sounded more like a Klan rally. Amidst flapping Confederate flags, graced by the presence of bigots including Gerald L. K. Smith and Jess Stoner —expelled from Dr. Sam Green's Klan for advocating mass murder of Jews—the delegates had nominated South Carolina Governor Strom Thurmond for president with Mississippi Governor Fielding Wright as his running mate.

Nine days after the Dixiecrats got organized, President Truman had called a joint session of Congress, announcing Executive Orders 9980 and 9981, which fully integrated the armed forces and the rest of the federal government's workforce. A move was also underway to ban the poll tax southern states employed to keep most colored voters from the ballot box, but racist senators had killed that with a five-day filibuster winding up on August 5. It was a weak rejoinder from the West in October, when California's Supreme Court voided a law from 1880, banning interracial marriages.

The Dixiecrats worried Sawyer, not because he thought they had a chance of winning— they'd only carried four states on November 2—but because they had legitimized hatred and sparked new violence against Negroes below the Mason-Dixon Line. By 1948, Dr. Green's Klan occupied all 159 Georgia counties, with chapters in six other states, and Green himself had been named aide-de-camp to gubernatorial candidate Herman Talmadge, telling Klansmen that if elected, Talmadge had promised the Klan "a free hand in any racial rioting." Green's rivals included William Morris's Federated Knights in Alabama and Alton Pate's Original Southern Klans in Georgia. In June, the Federated Knights raided Camp Fletcher, a Girl Scouts' retreat outside Bessemer, threatening two white counselors.

For pure gall though, Ike had to give the prize to Dr.

Green. On the night before Election Day, Green staged a monster rally of Atlanta's premier chapter, praising Patrolman John "Itchy-Trigger-Finger" Nash for slaying his thirteenth black victim, purportedly in self-defense. After auctioning off fifty .45-caliber cartridges, Green suggested that the bidders donate their bullets to Nash, and the Klansmen happily complied. Nash, nearly blushing, said, "I'm much obliged, but I hope I don't have to kill all the niggers in the South without getting some help from my brothers."

To that, one knight replied, "Don't worry. You'll get plenty of help!"

As in Lyons, the seat of Toombs County, where a gang of twenty robed and hooded white men shot and killed "uppity" Negro Robert Mallard in front of his family, on November 20. Police initially jailed widow Amy Mallard for her husband's murder, then embarrassed by a storm of public ridicule, charged white triggermen, Roderick Clifton and William Howell instead. Predictably, an all-white jury acquitted Howell, then the D.A. dismissed Clifton's charge.

Meanwhile, Georgia was caught up in what headlines called the "three-governors" wrangle, its leadership in limbo. Eugene Talmadge—a rabid racist and Herman's father—was elected in November 1946, but died in December, eleven days prior to the inauguration. State legislators chose Herman to replace him, but rival Melvin Thompson took the case to Georgia's Supreme Court, which ruled against Talmadge in March. Meanwhile, incumbent Ellis Arnall stayed in office, refusing to step down until a legitimate successor was elected. Time dragged on, including Talmadge's grinning appearance at Dr. Green's birthday party, while Klansmen marched in Herman's favor, burning crosses and littering the porches of Negro homes with miniature caskets bearing the initials "KKK." A special primary election in September 1948 chose Talmadge as the Democratic Party's nominee, and one of the few blacks who'd voted that day, Isaiah Nixon, was murdered hours later at his home in Montgomery County, abutting bloody Toombs.

November's election had cinched it for Talmadge, and while Robert Mallard hadn't tried to vote, he'd still been assassinated seventeen days later. Sheriff R. E. Gray escorted a Klan parade through Lyons in October, grudgingly admitted that Mallard's slayers had worn "some white stuff," but panned any suggestion of a politicized murder, calling the victim "a bad Negro." Governor-elect Talmadge turned the investigation over to the Klan-infested Georgia Bureau of Investigation, followed swiftly by Lieutenant W. E. McDuffie telling reporters the KKK had been "falsely accused" of killing Mallard. Sam Green released an affidavit to that effect, signed by helpful Sheriff Gray. NAACP attorney Thurgood Marshall called for an FBI investigation but none was forthcoming.

Bad times, Ike thought, *and likely more ahead.* Desegregating federal employment was a forward step, all right, but when Negroes were being killed for voting—or for no reason at all—it didn't mean fuck all.

And Payton, spending two more years in school to join the ranks of NYPD, promised more trouble in store. Ike knew that barely one percent of New York City's officers were Negroes, hampered daily by discrimination on the job. The first black cop appointed, Samuel Battle, hadn't joined the force until 1911, facing two full years of stony silence from his white colleagues, taking fifteen years to make sergeant and nine more to make lieutenant. Could Payton beat that record? Could he even stay alive?

MICHAEL NEWTON

"Out of my hands," Ike muttered to himself and wondered why that made him feel so small.

———

Tenleytown, Northwest Washington, D.C.: December 31, 1948

ALOYSIUS GANTT PASSED an uneasy New Year's Eve, worried that he had stepped into a pile of shit, and it was all the goddamned Commies' fault—or maybe Edgar Hoover's when he thought about it, working on his second glass of Jameson's.

The trouble dated back to August 3, when fat-assed Whittaker Chambers presented himself to HUAC, called by Chairman Thomas at the Bureau's urging, to smear Harry Truman and put rival Tom Dewey over the top. As usual, Chambers denounced Alger Hiss, branding him a member of "an underground organization of the United States Communist Party" founded by agriculturalist Harold Ware in the 1930s. As Chambers told it, "the purpose of this group at that time was not primarily espionage. Its original purpose was the Communist infiltration of the American government. But espionage was certainly one of its eventual objectives." G-men had already questioned Hiss twice, before he left the government to lead the Carnegie Endowment for International Peace, recording his flat denials.

Harold Ware, conveniently dead since 1935, couldn't defend himself, but Hiss could and did on August 5. He denied ever joining the CPUSA or personally meeting Chambers, speaking so ardently that committee member Dick Nixon described his testimony as "insolent," "condescending," and "insulting in the extreme." Unwilling to

74

accept denials, Nixon sought to forge ahead and reap free publicity in the process. His wedge: when shown a photograph of Chambers, Hiss admitted that his face "might look familiar," perhaps belonging to one "George Crosley" who'd posed as a freelance writer in the Thirties, subletting an apartment from Hiss and taking a free used car off his hands. Chambers publicly denied using the "Crosley" pseudonym but confessed to Hiss's lawyer that it "could have been" one of his many pen names.

Hiss asked Nixon to arrange a face-to-face with Chambers, and HUAC had obliged on August 17. That day, under oath, Chambers denied ever posing as Crosley "to my knowledge" or subletting Hiss's apartment, though he admitted occupying the flat with his wife and child. When Hiss asked Chambers to explain the contradiction, Chambers replied, "Very easily, Alger. I was a Communist and you were a Communist."

Hiss couldn't sue for statements made to Congress, so he'd challenged Chambers to repeat his claims elsewhere and Chambers complied, calling Hiss a Red on *Meet the Press*. Hiss slapped him with a libel suit, and that was when the whole thing went to Hell.

Thus far, both Hiss and Chambers had denied spying for Russia, but when faced with litigation, Chambers changed the tune he'd sung since 1945, accusing Hiss of espionage. Justice investigated once more in October, announcing it found no basis for charges of spying. In November to support that altered claim, Chambers produced four retyped State Department documents, plus four scribbled notes allegedly in Hiss's handwriting, summarizing contents of various State teletypes, all from 1937 and '38. Chambers claimed Priscilla Hiss had retyped the original documents since Alger couldn't cope with their typewriter. Next, Chambers led HUAC members to a pumpkin patch on his Maryland farm, extracting five rolls of 35mm film from a hollowed-out gourd. When developed, the photos depicted more State Department and U.S. Navy documents, ranging from additional teletypes to instructions for painting fire extinguishers aboard warships.

Proof positive of spying? A New York grand jury thought so, indicting Hiss on two counts of perjury for his HUAC testimony, skipping the espionage since the statute of limitations had long since expired. By then, the race was on to find Hiss's missing typewriter, and what a race it was.

On December 4, Hiss told G-men that he and Priscilla had owned a typewriter, "possibly an Underwood," from 1936 to "sometime after 1938." Priscilla's father, Thomas Fansler had provided it, and while Hiss never used it, his wife had. Priscilla for her part, couldn't recall the typewriter's make or what became of it, but agents and chief defense investigator Horace Schmahl kept digging. Mr. Fansler was deceased, but his surviving partner, Harry Martin, recalled buying a new Woodstock typewriter from salesman Thomas Grady in 1928. Fansler kept it when he retired, saying he planned to let his daughter have it, but no further records existed, no company documents were typed on the machine. Bureau analyst Robert Feehan *did* announce that three letters sent to Priscilla's sister were typed on the same machine as forty-two of the State Department documents.

Next, G-men located Thomas Grady, who amazingly recalled the sale two decades earlier, insisting that it must have happened sometime between June 1927 and December 3 that year, when he'd retired. In Chicago, the Woodstock's manufacturers had no relevant sales records, but they supplied a roster of serial numbers for their machines, ranging from #160000 to #176999 for 1927. Now, if they could only find the actual machine itself...

That hadn't happened yet, but the FBI's lab rats banged away on their stockpile of typewriters used for document comparisons, reporting yesterday that the Chambers documents "mostly closely" matched a typeface used by Woodstock during 1929, when Woodstock serial numbers ranged from #204000 to #239999. If they'd continued with that typeface during 1930, serial numbers might range as high as #275999. Finally, the lab decreed, "proper consideration should be given to obtaining specimens from machines having serial numbers lower than 204000."

Two things were crystal-clear: someone would have to find the Hiss typewriter, then match it to the stolen documents.

How that task fell to Gantt, he wasn't sure, except that Chief Hoover had summoned him that morning, telling him in no uncertain terms that he *must* find the missing Woodstock and be damned sure that it matched. Hoover was in a rotten mood, his shot at the Supreme Court gone for good, and no demurrals would suffice.

At first, Gantt almost felt relieved. He'd been assigned the case of Judith Coplon, a Brooklyn native who'd joined the Justice Department's Economic Warfare Section in Manhattan at age twenty-two, in 1943. A background check pegged her as a former member of the Young Communist League who'd published pro-Soviet writings in the *Barnard Bulletin*, her college weekly, but Moscow was a U.S. ally then so no one seemed to care—until October of that year, when code-breakers cracked an NKVD document referring to a "Judy Coplon" who "works in the U.S. Justice Department."

By then, Coplon had transferred from Gotham to D.C., as a political analyst in the section of Justice that registered foreign agents. That same month, January 1945, G-men learned of Coplon's meeting with Vladimir Pravdin, the NKVD station chief in Manhattan. Messages from Pravdin to Russia soon followed, announcing Coplon's recruitment as a spy, code-named "Sima," working with "local compatriots" from the CPUSA, anxious to serve directly for the Comintern. Her first delivery had been a Bureau document detailing senior OSS agent Duncan Lee's intent to resign, prompting handler Anatoly Gorsky to wire Moscow that Coplon "treats very seriously and honestly our task and considers our work the main thing in her life." In late October 1945, Coplon told Pravdin that the FBI had been eavesdropping on conversations between Manhattan Project physicist Robert Oppenheimer and college friend Haakon Chevalier since May 1943, probing for security leaks.

Three years elapsed with no action from Coplon's bosses or the FBI. In October 1948 she'd been transferred to the Bureau's Internal Security Section, reviewing files on Russian agents and CPUSA members in search of federal violations.

How could agents wrap her up? Wiretaps, of course.

Still, it took a while—until December 1948 to be exact—before Chief Hoover thought Justice could bring Coplon to book in court. His hope was to catch her red-handed, making a pass to the Reds, and Gantt had been working on that when the Woodstock conundrum fell into his lap. Now, he'd been saved from doing a difficult job, landing one that seemed damned near impossible.

But could he pull it off?

Why not? Gantt had done stranger things before, and as he'd told son Devon once upon a time, when you were in the FBI you went along to get along.

Beginning bright and early New Year's Day.

CHAPTER 3

LEONID BABIN MADE a show of window shopping on the block between East 15th and East 16th Streets, hoping he would be inconspicuous to his marks on the west side of Third Avenue. The twenty-something brunette woman held no interest for him, but her male companion—shorter than average, mid-thirties, with a fleshy face beneath his gray fedora—was the one Babin had traveled some 5,000 miles to meet.

So far no luck, but Babin meant to pull it off today.

It was his first time back in New York City for nearly three decades, since he'd been deported in December 1919 with 248 other alien radicals aboard the USS *Buford,* nicknamed in headlines as the "Soviet Ark." His fellow passengers included anarchists Alexander Berkman and Emma Goldman, both dead now: Berkman a suicide in France, Goldman slain by a stroke in Canada at seventy. The man who'd booked their package, Edgar Hoover of the FBI, had

79

watched the ship from dockside with a grim smile on his face.

Babin scarcely remembered his shipboard companions now—though Hoover occupied his mind each day—nor could he claim that much of Gotham looked familiar to him after so much time had passed. The city New Yorkers called their "Big Apple" had managed to survive the Roaring Twenties and the Great Depression, weathered an epic hurricane and a deadly blizzard, hailed a Harlem ghetto "renaissance" and watched two race riots against police brutality, plus all the other tremors and upheavals that befell Earth's largest city in the present century. Its population had topped 5.6 million in 1920, the year of the Wall Street bombing aimed at robber baron J. P. Morgan. Three years later, ludicrously, residents had rioted for nine straight days against men who donned straw hats prior to September 15, thereby defying idiotic fashion. Monuments to capitalist swine had been erected—the Pierpont Morgan Library in 1923, the Frick Collection art museum in 1935, sandwiching the Wall Street crash that should have proved great private wealth was modern society's cancer.

By 1925 the city's population topped 7.7 million, and many were clearly dissatisfied with their lot, while skyscrapers rose around them: the Chrysler building, Earth's tallest at 1,046 feet in 1930, surpassed eleven months later by the Empire State Building's 1,454 feet. Below, at street level, 35,000 marched on International Unemployment Day in 1935, battling with police. Two years later, while 4,740 strikes occurred nationwide, 1.8 million Gotham department store workers staged a ten-day sit-down spanning Easter week.

And beneath it all ran a crackling current of Socialist discontent that gladdened Babin's heart. When the RCA

Building opened in May 1933, furor erupted over a mural by Mexican artist Diego Rivera called "Man at the Crossroads," depicting Moscow May Day scenes and a portrait of Vladimir Lenin, obscured in the initial sketches. Janitors masked the painting with paper until the Rockefellers found a suitable replacement. Meanwhile, no one sensed the irony when Edsel Ford—son of Nazi sympathizer Henry —announced the creation of the Ford Foundation in 1936 to "advance human welfare," thus far without any progress. An elusive wraith dubbed "the Mad Bomber" planted his first device in 1940, addressing it to the giant capitalist firm of Consolidated Edison with a note reading: "CON ED CROOKS—THIS IS FOR YOU."

Through it all, grassroots New Yorkers managed to distract themselves with professional sports and a semian-nual "Press Week" for fashion designers, mourning their loss of the SS *Normandie* but failing to notice the American mili-tary's first collaboration with the Mafia in "Operation Underworld."

The time was ripe for spying, so Babin had been sent to New York by Minister of Security Viktor Abakumov, ordered to contact the man who now stood opposite him on the far side of Third Avenue: Valentin Gubitchev, a Russian engi-neer, MGB agent, and a member of the UN Secretariat.

There was no Russian consulate in the United States for Babin to contact, not since July of 1948 when Oksana Kasenkina, a Soviet citizen and teacher of Russian UN diplomats' children, had appealed for sanctuary to a Russ-ian-language newspaper in Manhattan. Friends conveyed her to Reed Farm, run by the White Russian Tolstoy Foun-dation in Valley Cottage, Rockland County, where she wrote to Soviet Consul-General Jacob Lomakin, saying, "I implore you, don't let me perish here. I am without willpower."

Lomakin and Vice Consul Zot Chepurnykh retrieved Kasenkina without opposition on August 7, followed two days later by a missive from Ambassador Alexander Panyushkin to the U.S. State Department, claiming the Tolstoy Foundation had kidnapped Kasenkina. In Moscow, Minister of Foreign Affairs Molotov echoed that complaint to U.S. Ambassador Walter Bedell Smith, while Gotham newspapers accused the Soviet consulate of abducting Kasenkina and New York Supreme Court Justice Samuel Dickstein issued a writ of habeas corpus for the teacher's delivery to police. Ambassador Panyushkin dismissed that, citing international law.

The question became moot on August 12, when Kasenkina leapt from a third-story window of the consulate on East 61st Street. She'd survived the fall, and when an NYPD detective questioned her six hours later, her reply "indicated a stronger desire for deliverance than for asylum," whatever that meant. As a result, Moscow closed its consulates in Manhattan and San Francisco on August 25, while expelling the U.S. consular staff from Vladivostok. Chepurnykh set sail for home the next day, while Lomakin, packing his bags, predicted a permanent severance of U.S.-USSR diplomatic relations.

There *was* a Russian embassy, of course, in Washington, D.C., where Ambassador Alexander Panyushkin spoke officially for Moscow, but that was too far off—226 miles from Manhattan—and constantly watched by the Central Intelligence Agency.

Thus Babin had been left to prowl Gotham's streets, seeking a chance encounter with Gubitchev, avoiding any trespass at the UN's offices. Perhaps today, if Gubitchev would ditch the woman who accompanied him, that goal might be achieved.

Babin thought he had found his window when the couple separated, moving off in opposite directions, but neither of them got very far. Instead, a group of obvious plainclothes policemen swarmed the pair and placed them both in handcuffs, leading each in turn to separate black sedans.

Cursing, Babin flagged down a tax and directed its driver to West 86th street, seven miles south from the scene of the double arrest to a small appliance shop in Washington Heights, on Manhattan's Upper West Side. The proprietor, sexagenarian immigrant Sasha Yushkov, was a low-ranking MGB agent who sent messages from the Big Apple to Moscow at need.

The cab arrived at Yushkov's store and Babin tipped its driver adequately, ample for a "thank-you" but nothing the cabbie would recall later. Inside the shop, a small bell rang to announce his entrance, Babin used the code phrase of the day, telling Yushkov, "I need to send a message home."

Yushkov, frail and balding, blinked at Babin from behind an antique register, replying in a heavy Slavic accent that time had not erased. "We don't do that. You should try Dostoevsky's on the next block south."

Dostoevsky? Perhaps the author of the Russian classic *Crime and Punishment,* published in 1866?

Frowning, he thanked Yushkov and left the shop, hearing that bell again, before a quartet of grim men in snap-brim hats and overcoats surrounded him. Their seeming leader told Babin, "FBI special agents. You'll be coming back to headquarters with us."

Babin put on a smile as he replied, "*Yob tvoyiu mat', sookin syn.*"

One of the agents snapped, "What's that, Pal?"

Babin smiled and lied. "I said there must be some mistake."

"You made it, Ivan," said their spokesman. "Hands behind your back."

As he was cuffed and hustled to a waiting car, Babin wondered what impact the arrest would have upon his greater plan. Stefan was still progressing well in school, and Babin was not aware of any threat to his future foster parents, Mark and Isabella Barnes. How Moscow might react to his exposure was another question altogether, but Babin could feel it slipping from his hands.

———

KATZ'S DELICATESSEN, Lower East Side, Manhattan: May 13, 1949

"THEY SAY this is the best pastrami sandwich in the city."

"I believe it," Dave Jordan replied, embarrassed to be caught with his mouth full.

The sixty-year-old deli should've looked rundown, but its brand-new façade at the corner of Houston and Ludlow Street sparkled, facing the lot where its builders first opened for business in 1888. Now, their menu was famous citywide, and well beyond Manhattan.

Some dreams *did* come true.

Their lunch together—Jordan wouldn't let himself regard it as a "date"—had been Fiona O'Hara's idea. She'd asked him yesterday in the law library, apparently on impulse. Dave added his own surprise to that shock by accepting the invitation. They were going Dutch of course, no strings attached, and while he could've driven eight miles south from campus to the deli if he'd had a car, he rode the subway and left the cane he rarely used these days back at his dorm.

Now, even halfway through his sandwich and potato salad, Jordan couldn't quite believe that he was here, seated across a window table from Fiona. They were dining amiably, making small talk about school. She loved the law and couldn't wait to pass the bar, jump into the shark pool, and start defending clients she assumed would all be innocent. Whether that would be in Gotham or back home in Washington, maybe even out west, she hadn't yet decided.

When she asked, Jordan allowed that he was doing well enough in class—no mention of his current GPA, not wanting to compete with hers in case it took a nosedive in the fall semester—but he didn't mention anything about his father's practice in New York. What would he say, especially since he'd found out Fiona's father was a longtime FBI agent?

Not that the Bureau seemed to give a damn about the Syndicate.

That doomed any idea of a relationship right there, as if his leg and lesser scars weren't bad enough.

"Oh, I almost forgot," Fiona said, dabbing her full lips with a paper napkin bearing Katz's logo. "I saw 'Salesman' Friday night."

Dave didn't have to ask *which* salesman. It could only be "Death of a Salesman," Arthur Miller's play that had opened to rave reviews in February, graced with a Pulitzer Prize for Best Drama in April, reportedly up next month for that new-fangled Antoinette Perry Award for Excellence in Broadway Theatre.

"Mmm. Did you like it?"

"*Loved* it. 'Course, I had to go alone."

Dave nodded sympathetically but wasn't touching that line with a ten-foot pole. He half imagined sitting in a darkened theater, Fiona soft and fragrant at his side, knowing that everything from time and money to his goddamned gimpy leg was stacked against him.

So he changed the subject, asking, "What about that tunnel?"

"Such a tragedy." She seemed to mean it, eyes downcast, but maybe she was only looking for the perfect French fry on her plate.

The Holland Tunnel had been moving cars between New Jersey and New York beneath the Hudson River, since David was three years old, without a hitch. That very morning, though, a truck loaded with 4,400 pounds of volatile carbon disulfide industrial solvent had gone off like a German SC50 bomb, damaging the tunnel's infrastructure and injuring sixty-odd people, mostly from smoke inhalation.

A tragedy? He guessed so, although nobody had died. It could've been much worse, he thought, imagining the tunnel rupturing and hundreds of morning commuters drowning in their crumpled cars.

Time for a lighter mood, so Jordan asked Fiona, "Do you miss the swim team, now that you're in law school?"

She blinked green eyes at him, her turn to be surprised. "You know about that?"

"Hey, you're famous."

"Oh, well hardly."

"You're too modest. I bet you could've made the team for London, if it wasn't for the war."

"Swimming in the Olympics? You've gone gaga now."

"I wish I could've seen you," Jordan blurted out, then tried to reel it back. "Swimming, I mean. You know."

"But you were off saving the world. That's more than I could ever do."

"A good thing, too." He forced a smile. "You see how that turned out for me."

She actually blushed. "I didn't mean—"

"It's fine. Forget it."

"No. I was about to say not bad, all things considered."

Right, he thought. *Considering the limp and all the scars you'll never have to see.*

Knowing it would sound lame before he spoke, Dave said, "So, maybe we're both where we need to be."

Before he made things even worse, he took another bite of his sandwich.

———

FBI Headquarters: July 15, 1949

Reds were the rage this year, and Aloysius Gantt had a new boss to help him hunt them down. D. Milton Ladd —"Mickey" to friends, if he had any—was a senator's son from North Dakota who joined the Bureau three years after Gantt, in 1920, appointed Acting SAC for New Orleans in 1924, then serving over the next eight years as SAC in St. Louis, Saint Paul, Chicago and D.C. From 1942 until this May he'd been the Assistant Director of the Domestic Intelligence Division, now holding the number-three spot behind Clyde Tolson as Assistant to the Director.

Ladd knew Reds, and he'd been dogging Judith Coplon from the first report of her shady activities. In early January she'd approached Agent William Foley—Ladd's former boss at Internal Security and head of the Foreign Agents Registration Section—asking to peruse the dossiers of certain Russian spies. By January 6, Attorney General Clark had authorized a tap on her home phone in Washington and G-men had begun to shadow her. On the fourteenth she'd gone to New York City with Foley's permission, "to visit family," and her tails stuck with her, logging her protracted, roving conversation with Valentin Gubitchev, a Soviet national employed by the United Nations Secretariat. They'd dined together, then embarked on a subway ride from which Gubitchev bolted, losing his trackers.

A background check on Gubitchev revealed that while he'd entered the States on a diplomatic passport, he'd changed jobs since then, working directly for the UN on the construction of its rising complex in Manhattan. The upshot: no diplomatic immunity from arrest or prosecution if the Bureau caught him breaking any laws.

On January 24 Clark had approved a second tap on Coplon's office telephone. That soon revealed her romantic affair with a DOJ lawyer, one Harold Shapiro. They'd spent a weekend at a Baltimore hotel, signed in as man and wife, but Bureau eavesdroppers dismissed it as a simple sleazy pastime and scratched Shapiro off their list of suspects.

On February 1 the Bureau started tapping Gubitchev's phone in New York—no mentions of Coplon—and Agent Foley blocked Judith's future access to internal security files. She'd been angry, calling it a slight on her ability, and soon approached her successor, attorney Ruth Rosson, requesting access to any such files tagged "R" for Russia. Rosson, none the wiser, had delivered fifty-odd files without question.

Coplon went back to New York on February 18, again forewarning Foley, and agents watched her second known meeting with Gubitchev, strolling about aimlessly, sometimes separating briefly, then rejoining, constantly looking over their shoulders for watchers. No files changed hands as far as they could see, but G-men on the detail granted that they didn't have the duo constantly in view.

Haley and Ladd decided it was time to set a trap.

On March 3, when Coplon told Haley she'd be traveling by train to Gotham the next day, Peyton Ford, Assistant Attorney General for the Civil Division, gave Haley a mocked-up file stamped "Strictly Confidential," describing the Soviet-based Amtorg Trading Corporation's quest to purchase atomic research equipment. Before Coplon left to catch her 1:00 p.m. train on March 4 Haley gave her the file, which he described as "quite hot and very interesting."

Coplon made her trip as planned, met up with Gubitchev, and went through the same old evasive song and dance. Around 9:30, fed-up agents jumped the gun, arresting both of them without warrants or waiting for any exchange of documents. Inside her purse, they found twenty-eight pieces of Bureau memoranda: nothing from the Amtorg file, but notes on FBI surveillance of actors: Danny Kaye, Frederic March and Edward G. Robinson; 1931 Oscar winner Helen Hayes, a devout Catholic and pro-business Republican; presidential advisor David Niles; and Manhattan Project physicist Edward Condon. The Bureau's interest in most of them began with their support for presidential candidate Henry Wallace last year and leapt to false claims of CPUSA membership.

On March 10, a federal jury in Manhattan indicted Coplon and Gubitchev with conspiring to gather and transmit classified defense information. A separate count charged Coplon alone with attempting to pass said information to Gubitchev, although no such attempt had been observed. Six days later, a second grand jury in D.C. charged Coplon with stealing government files between December

1948 and the day of her arrest, plus willfully and unlawfully removing said records from Justice HQ.

Meanwhile, the Bureau "routinely" destroyed most recordings, notes and resumés of the Coplon wiretaps sixty days after they were created. That still left ten recordings, plus various other logs and summaries, but word came down from Edgar Hoover's office demanding the destruction of all further records "in view of the immency of her trial."

No trace, no crime.

Ironically, Hoover's nemesis and now ACLU Director Larry Fly had testified before a special committee of the New York County Criminal Courts Bar Association shortly after Coplon's arrest. Fly called Governor Tom Dewey the "founding father" of legalized wiretaps in the Empire State, then fired off a letter to Nevada Senator Pat McCarran, chairman of the of the Senate Judiciary Committee, declaring that the ACLU and Americans for Democratic Action vehemently opposed tapping. No problem, since McCarran, HUAC, and most other far-right cheerleaders considered both groups to be Commie fronts.

For whatever reason, Coplon faced trial first in Washington, convened on April 25 before Judge Albert Reeves, once a commissioner for the Supreme Court of Missouri and lecturer at the Kansas City School of Law, appointed to the federal bench in 1923, elevated to chief judge in 1948. Oddly, a CIA memo that found its way to Gantt from son Colby referred to Reeves as "feeble-minded," while tagging Coplon's *pro bono* attorney, Archibald Palmer, "an inexperienced buffoon"—this, despite the fact that he'd been practicing since 1905.

Experienced or not, Palmer grilled Supervisory Special Agent Robert Lamphere in court, producing a claim that

Coplon was originally fingered by an unnamed "confidential informant." From the files on Hollywood actors and others retrieved from Coplon's handbag, Palmer correctly deduced that said "informant" must have been a string of wiretaps. Coplon explained her meetings with Gubitchev as lovers' trysts, though he was married and they'd never booked a room. As for Harold Shapiro, she admitted spending one night with him in a Baltimore hotel but claimed they never got around to having sex.

Judge Reeves helped the defense by ruling that conviction for unauthorized possession of classified documents required submission of FBI originals, a strict no-no as Hoover tried to protect the sensitive "VENONA" operation, decrypting Soviet intelligence messages in conjunction with the U.S. Army's Signal Intelligence Service. In fact, as Gantt well knew, VENONA had collected several hundred thousand messages since 1942 but had only decrypted 3,000 by 1948, when the Reds changed their methods and rendered decoding hopeless. Nonetheless, Bob Lamphere feared that "to release the basic file reports might not only endanger security and compromise informants but also bring to light many unsubstantiated allegations, which would do no one any good."

No one, that is, except Coplon's defense.

In May with the trial in full swing, Larry Fly struck again, petitioning Attorney General Clark to ensure that his New York agents, at least, respected the federal ban on wiretaps. To make his case for its abuse, Fly listed 300 known authorized wiretaps by NYPD in 1948 alone, theorizing that innumerable other taps must have occurred without legal permission. For further emphasis in August, Fly wrote to the *Washington Post*, saying that taps both nullified the law and "fertilized the breeding ground of crime itself." One day later, Attorney General McGrath announced that the Bureau's wiretaps would continue and that he planned an "anti-tycoon" conference, whatever *that* was, to discuss new means of capturing subversives. The *Post* opined that taps might help, along with thumbscrews and the rack, but noted that "every free and civilized society has forbidden its police to use such methods."

Larry Fly chipped in with an ACLU amicus curiae brief, blasting "the conduct of government attorneys and FBI representatives who, by a process of concealment and infantile denial, misled the trial court on this vital issue and in the teeth of their knowledge of the true facts." In a letter to the *New York Times,* Fly quoted Hoover's order to destroy "all administrative records in the New York office" before Coplon's trial, which Fly described as part of "a routinized scheme and practice of destroying public records." When petitions reached Congress, calling for an investigation of the Bureau, FBI Assistant Director Louis Nichols named Fly as the petitions' author. Dissatisfied with a bland response to Fly from U.S. Solicitor General Philip Perlman, Clyde Tolson fired off a memo urging that someone "tie into Fly and nail his lies once and for all."

Other problems soon became apparent with the Bureau's case. Of thirty agents tailing Coplon on the night they busted her, none saw her passing anything to Gubitchev. On top of that, although they'd followed Coplon for eight weeks, laying a final trap to reel her in, no one in all of Justice had suggested swearing out a warrant— mandatory under the law unless the agents observed a crime in progress, which they hadn't.

Nonetheless, after a nine-week trial, jurors convicted Coplon on June 30, of both counts charged against her. She immediately told the court, "I'm a victim of a horrible,

horrible frame-up." Next day, before Judge Reeves slapped her with ten years on one count, three on the second, she'd declared, "I understand that I can plea for mercy. That, I will not do, because pleading for mercy would mean an admission of guilt and I am innocent."

Gantt would've loved to sit in on that trial, but he'd been busy chasing Alger Hiss's typewriter. It helped to have a spy on the defense team, P.I. Horace Schmahl, feeding the Bureau tips on legal strategy, and he was Johnny-on-the-spot when one of Alger's lawyers, Edward McLean, found the Woodstock on April 16. Despite lacking the FBI's resources, he had traced it from Priscilla Hiss through four subsequent owners to a moving man, one Ira Lockey, who'd been paid to haul it off as scrap in 1945. Instead, he'd passed it to his daughter who'd returned it to him later, and he sold it off to the defense.

That raised a problem for the prosecution, since the Woodstock bore Model No. 230099, proving it was manufactured sometime during 1929 or '30, two to three years *after* Priscilla's father bought their typewriter in 1927. Even though it obviously couldn't be the same machine, Justice used it in court, marking it as Exhibit UUU. Bureau experts also knew the Woodstock's typeface hadn't entered use before 1930.

Edgar Hoover realized all that, of course. He'd had the Woodstock's serial number in hand by May 14, ordering his agents to "conduct all possible investigation to determine the history of this typewriter since its manufacture, including sale, resale, and repair." Three days later, Hoover warned his SACs "that the definite possibility exists this typewriter is not the one received by Priscilla Hiss from her father Thomas Fansler." Next, on May 25—six days before Hiss went to trial—Speed cabled an outrageous fiction to the field, claiming that Woodstock #230099 "has been identified by the FBI laboratory as being the machine used to type documents QG through Q69" from the Chambers collection. Curiously, on the same day, Hoover ordered the Milwaukee office to interview Thomas Grady "to obtain an explanation as to how he could sell a machine which was manufactured in 1929 to the Fansler-Martin partnership in 1927."

How indeed, when it was physically impossible?

Grady stood by his report of when he sold the Woodstock, shortly prior to his retirement in December 1927, while Harry Martin pronounced himself "positive this typewriter was not traded in on a new one at any time during the Fansler-Martin partnership."

With that chaos in mind, Bureau witnesses limited their testimony on the Woodstock, Agent John McCool declaring the machine was "operable," while Agent Ramos Feehan swore, "the same machine"—unspecified—had typed forty-two of the documents Hiss allegedly passed to Chambers.

But *which* machine? Alger's defense team didn't bother cross-examining Feehan.

They *did* grill Chambers, who freely admitted he'd committed perjury by falsifying sundry dates throughout the stories he'd told HUAC and the press. Both Alger and Priscilla Hiss denied spying, while Alger's character witnesses included former Democratic presidential candidate John Davis, Illinois Governor Adlai Stevenson II, and two Supreme Court justices, Felix Frankfurter, and Stanley Reed. Outside the courtroom, President Truman branded the trial "a red herring."

Prosecutor Thomas Murphy had no qualms about lying in his summation, telling jurors that the stolen documents "were typed on that machine. Our man said it was." Judge Samuel Kaufman tried to help Justice, repeating its unsupported claim that stolen documents were typed on Exhibit UUU. On July 7, confused jurors reported themselves deadlocked, eight-to-four for conviction, and Judge Kaufman declared a mistrial.

But that wasn't the end. Not even close.

On July 8, juror Fred Gaffney visited Murphy, claiming another panelist had noted errors common between letters Priscilla Hiss admitted typing and several Chambers documents. Specifically, the letter "r" was used instead of "i," while "f" stood in for "d" and "g." When Murphy passed that to the FBI's lab, analysts reported back that "it would be impossible for an expert to testify to the fact that because of the similar or common errors, it followed that Priscilla Hiss actually typed the questioned documents." Another strike against the prosecution, but nobody bothered sharing it with the defense.

Instead, Donald Doud, a Detroit expert on the questioned documents, floated the theory that Priscilla's father had acquired "a second Woodstock" at some point, without the knowledge of surviving business partner Harry Martin. Nothing indicated that was true, but the alternative was a forgery by tricking out a separate machine Priscilla never owned to match the Chambers documents.

And that, as Gantt knew personally, was exactly what had happened.

Now he wondered how he could avoid being discovered as the one who'd done it all.

FBI Field Office, Los Angeles: August 22, 1949

REDS REMAINED a hot topic around L.A., particularly in the small enclave of Hollywood. Democrat John Wood had replaced Parnell Thomas as HUAC's chairman in January, keeping up the heat while drawing flack for his avoidance of examining the Klan in his native Georgia. Devon Gantt found that ironic since Wood had retrieved the corpse of Ku Klux lynching victim Leo Frank in 1915 with a local judge, to guarantee a decent burial, but investigating Klansmen wouldn't fly with Herman Talmadge in the governor's office.

Meanwhile, private groups were busy expanding the Hollywood blacklist. The American Legion's so-called Americanism Division produced its own list of 128 Hollywood bigwigs immersed in a far-flung "Communist Conspiracy." One of their targets, renowned playwright Lillian Hellman, had penned scripts for eight movies since 1935, winning the New York Drama Critics' Circle Award for Best American Play, but now she found herself unemployable in California and went back to Broadway, where the lowbrow Legion had no further interest.

On the crime front, L.A.'s "werewolf" killer was still prowling, wounding survivor Violet Norton in February. slaughtering Louise Springer in June, Jean Spangler and Mimi Boombauer in August, but he—or she—still hadn't violated any federal laws.

In the Syndicate venue, crusading evangelist Billy Graham had welcomed Mickey Cohen, of all people, to the Christian fold. Their connection came through Jimmy Vaus, an LAPD eavesdropper who'd wired up Cohen's house but was caught at it, whereupon Mickey paid Vaus to flip and spy on the police. As Cohen told the story, Graham had come to his Brentwood mansion for dinner, "and before we had food he said—What do you call it? That thing they say before food? Grace? Yeah, grace." A partnership of sorts evolved from that four-hour meeting, Mickey tapping Graham for a hefty loan, or so he claimed, and airing plans for a joint vacation to a Tucson dude ranch.

Where else on Earth could shit like that go down, except in La-La Land? And Devon had a ringside seat, regretting only that he couldn't lift a finger in the Bureau's name to intervene.

———

FEDERAL BUREAU of Narcotics Manhattan Field Office: September 6, 1949

FRESH BACK FROM LABOR DAY, Ike Sawyer checked his in-box, hoping for a breakthrough on the drive against narcotics but came up with nothing new. The National Research Council's Committee on Drug Addiction was pleading for funds, but so far, eight huge pharmaceutical firms had contributed less than $19,000. Meanwhile, Smith, Kline & French alone had earned $7.3 million this year, despite patent-busting competition from meth-amphetamine-based weight loss and antidepressant products, including Abbot's Desoxyn and Wellcome's Methedrine.

On the illegal side, Lucky Luciano and Sicilian *Don* Calogero Vizzini had established a "candy factory" in Palermo, shipping their product to dealers throughout Europe and America. Police in Rome briefly jailed Luciano in July, then released him after twenty hours' questioning, with orders to stay out of Italy's capital.

Matters were even more depressing if you could believe it, on the racial front in Dixie. Authorities had logged three lynchings so far, including victims Caleb Hill Jr., "mysteriously" snatched from jail at Irwinton, Georgia, in May, beaten and shot for allegedly wounding a cop in a juke joint melee; Malcolm Wright, beaten to death by three whites in July for "hogging the road" with his mule-drawn wagon near Houston, Mississippi, en route to grocery shopping with his wife and five kids; and Hollis Riles, an affluent farmer in Decatur County, Georgia, shot by five whites in September after he told them to stop poaching fish from his pond. Sheriff A. E. White sought FBI help in the Riles case, but got no response. Two men were detained for Hill's murder, one a cousin of Sheriff George Hatcher, but nothing came of that. One of Wright's killers went to trial after the first judge —another relative—recused himself, but white jurors acquitted him and the D.A. dismissed charges against his cohorts.

In mid-July, false claims of rape from Groveland, Florida, rallied a white mob that burned Negro homes for six days until National Guardsmen arrived. A local paper, the *Mount Dora Topic,* defended the rioters, claiming, "The mobs didn't just wantonly burn Negro homes in wild vengeance for the crime. No—it was a cunning mob. The mob burned the homes of a Negro engaged in voodoo, and another who ran a Bolita game." Illegal gambling, that was, which Ike supposed made arson hunky-dory.

Five weeks later, Negro CPUSA member Paul Robeson scheduled a benefit concert for the Civil Rights Congress at Lakeland Acres, just north of Peekskill, New York. It was to be his fourth local appearance, but this time American Legionnaires and other local yahoos turned out in force, stoning concertgoers and clubbing them with baseball bats, chanting "Dirty Commies" and "Dirty Kikes." After the riot, newspapers reported that Klan headquarters in Georgia had

received 748 new membership applications from Westch-
ester County.

Fools never learn, Ike thought, then had to wonder, *What
am I, when I keep hoping for a happy ending to the same old
story, after all?*

———

T AVARES, *Florida: September 7, 1949*

NOLAN O'HARA HAD GROWN TIRED of Florida, though no one
in the Bureau gave a damn about his personal opinion.
Lately, he'd been tied up looking into a Lake County case
that that had already spawned mayhem and threatened
worse at any moment, drawing him 267 miles north from
Miami to another world where lawmen freely hobnobbed
with the Klan and any accusation against a Negro, true or
false, was prone to draw a mob of lynchers from the woods
and farms to wreak havoc.

The case at hand arose in mid-July, six months after ex-
Klansman Fuller Warren was elected governor. His Republican opponent, Bert Acker, raised the issue during 1948's
campaign, but Warren shrugged it off, recalling that during
World War Two he'd joined the navy, battling Nazis, whom
he dubbed "first cousins to Klansmen." Today's Kluckers, he
said, were "hooded hoodlums and sheeted jerks" whose
parades "made a disgusting and alarming spectacle."

But if they'd voted for him in November, that was fine.

July 16 marked the beginning of Lake County's trouble,
when teenage housewife Norma Padgett appeared on the
highway near Groveland, claiming four Negroes abducted
her while she was on a date with husband Willie—labeled a

wife-beater by her relatives—and that she'd been raped at gunpoint. Hard-nosed Sheriff Willis McCall was traveling when that occurred, but his deputies responded with alacrity. They'd focused on four suspects, two of whom had never met the other pair before, but that was no impediment to framing all of them for rape.

Two of the four, war veterans Sammy Shepherd and Walter Irvin, were well known to local officers beforehand. Sheriff McCall had scolded them for wearing their army uniforms in public and ordered them to stop, dress down, and find suitable grunt work in some white planter's orange groves. Since Shepherd's father owned his own farm, Sam refused. Another worry for McCall was Harry Moore's Progressive Voters League, which had doubled Florida's number of registered Negroes to 116,000 since 1947, threatening the sheriff's job.

The other two suspects were sixteen-year-old Charles Greenlee and an acquaintance, Ernest Thomas, who'd lured Greenlee from Gainesville with rumors of plentiful jobs around Groveland. Officers found Greenlee at the railroad depot, waiting for Thomas, and hauled him in. Thomas got wise and ran as if his life depended on it—which, in fact, it did.

The deputies who'd busted Shepherd and Irwin drove them to an isolated spot, beating them both with fists and blackjacks while demanding a confession. Failing there, they took their prisoners to where the rape supposedly occurred and tried again, but still no luck. Deputy James Yates tried to match their shoes against visible footprints, but he failed.

Next stop: the county jail, where officers stripped all three suspects, hung them by their wrists from ceiling pipes, barefoot over a floor littered with broken Coke bottles, and whipped them all with rubber hoses until Shepherd and Greenlee confessed, but even then Irvin refused. He did, however, mention having different shoes back at the Shepherd home, where he'd been staying overnight.

Voila! Deputy Yates went back and found the second pair of shoes, which proved to be a perfect match—or so he claimed. Nolan had doubts, but couldn't verify them yet.

Sheriff McCall returned next morning to a town inflamed by racist rage; with three rapists in his jail, one in the wind. Before the usual lynch mob arrived, he'd stashed Irvin, Shepherd, and Greenlee in a nearby orchard for safekeeping, prior to dropping them at Raiford Prison farther north. Having deprived the mob of its intended prey, McCall watched it roar off toward Groveland's colored neighborhood for six long days of rioting before National Guardsmen finally arrived. In the midst of chaos, Flowers Cockroft, leader of the mob, promised reporters, "Next time, we'll clean out every nigger section in Lake County."

On July 20, State Attorney Jesse Hunter had convened a grand jury—all white, of course—that rapidly indicted Greenlee, Irwin, Shepherd, and Thomas (still on the run) for capital rape. Mabel Reese, editor of the local *Mount Dora Topic*, told readers that the jury's haste "bespeaks the caliber of the county's law enforcement officers."

O'Hara couldn't argue with that sentiment, although he guessed that Reese was blind to irony.

Fugitive Ernest Thomas lasted six more days until a ragtag "posse" of 1,000 men caught up with him in swampland some 200 miles northwest of Groveland. Sheriff McCall, onsite, claimed Thomas had resisted; local Negroes said the mob had found him sleeping, propped against a tree. In either case, 400 gunshots didn't give the coroner a lot to work with, but he'd deemed the slaughter "justifiable."

Soon after that, NAACP attorney Franklin Williams interviewed the three surviving suspects at Raiford, recording their tales of torture and photographing their wounds. He called the FBI, and that was when O'Hara got involved, driving 380 miles north from Miami to the prison with another agent, Joe Sturgis for backup.

"You don't want to go up there alone," SAC Hunnicutt had cautioned. "Local whites don't like us much, these days. You'd better take a shotgun, just in case."

Nolan started out expecting trouble from the prison's warden, Leonard Chapman, but he'd proved to be the easy-going sort, at least where fellow lawmen were concerned. Nolan and Sturgis met him at his house—a mansion, really, freshly painted white by cons—and he had introduced them to the "Groveland boys," as they were called in newspaper reports. All three described their ordeal in Tavares while O'Hara took more photos of their injuries, ranging from lacerated scalps and bruised faces to lash marks swollen testicles, and gashes on their feet. Beyond that, there'd been little else for him to do but write up his report in duplicate for Agent Hunnicutt and Washington.

That document concluded that two deputies—James Yates and Leroy Campbell—had abused the inmates in their custody and urged U.S. Attorney Herbert Phillips to file charges, but a federal grand jury turned thumbs down.

On August 12 the prisoners returned from Raiford and Judge Truman Futch set the trial to start on August 29. Jesse Hunter would be prosecuting, aided by Assistant State Attorney Sam Buie. Eleven white attorneys had refused the case by then, so Futch appointed Harry Gaylord, to defend the three. Another, Alex Akerman Jr., replaced Gaylord on August 22, three days prior to argument of pretrial motions. At that hearing, he petitioned for a change of venue and more time to prep his case. Futch wouldn't grant the move but pushed the trial back slightly to begin September 2.

Nolan and Sturgis wedged themselves into a packed courtroom that Friday morning to observe the show. Judge Futch amused himself by whittling a chunk of cedar while reporters—white men only, no colored photographers allowed—snapped pictures of the grim proceedings. Franklin Williams, fearing he might be shot for questioning a white witness, left Akerman to do the heavy lifting, with southern decorum limiting the questions he could ask. He dared not question whether Norma Padgett had, in fact, been raped at all, but tried, gently, to challenge her ID of her alleged attackers. Steadfast in maintaining her original account, she'd pointed to "those niggers" who'd assaulted her, while jurors fumed and gnashed their teeth.

A savvy gamesman, Jesse Hunter didn't introduce the two confessions deputies had gained by torture at the county jail, which stymied Akerman from introducing medical reports and X-rays of his clients' injuries. Instead, Hunter relied on Norma Padgett's tearful testimony and the footprint "evidence" Deputy Yates had managed to contrive, using the second pair of Walter Irvin's shoes. Jurors wasted no time returning guilty verdicts on all three defendants. As a minor, Greenlee drew a term of life imprisonment, while Futch sentenced Shepherd and Irvin to the chair, adding, "God rest your souls." Before the crowd dispersed, Futch summoned Jesse Hunter to the bench, shook hands with him, and said, "I've never heard a better argument in all my life."

Not bad, O'Hara thought, *when you consider that the prosecutor never spent a day in law school. Good old Florida.*

The white press was ecstatic, starting off with Mabel Reese, whose headlines in *The Topic* trumpeted "Honor Will

Be Avenged" and cheered the jury with a rousing "Our Thanks, Gentlemen." The *Orlando Morning Sentinel* ran a front-page, full-color cartoon of three electric chairs with the caption "No Compromise."

Alex Akerman filed an appeal for Shepherd and Irvin on September 6. He dropped Greenlee from that appeal, fearing legal delays would age him out of adolescence and he would be sentenced to death row next time around.

Typing what he presumed would be his last report about the Groveland case, O'Hara frowned, then let it go, remembering his father's words: *To get along in the Bureau, you go along.*

At least for now.

———

FBI Headquarters: November 5, 1949

Declan O'Hara laid aside his copy of the *Washington Post,* detailing recent leadership changes at the DOJ. A heart attack had killed Supreme Court Justice Frank Murphy on July 19, and President Truman had nominated Tom Clark to replace him two weeks later, recalling to O'Hara's mind Paul Ricca's order during the parole scandal of 1947: "That man must want something: money, favors, a seat in the Supreme Court. Find out what he wants and get it for him."

Now it was in the bag, but not without a tidal wave of opposition. Critics charged Truman with "cronyism," while the *New York Times* called Clark "a personal and political friend of Truman's with no judicial experience and few demonstrated qualifications." Ex-Secretary of the Interior Harold Ickes opined, "President Truman has not 'elevated'

Tom C. Clark to the Supreme Court, he has degraded the Court." Clark had declined to testify at his own confirmation hearing, telling reporters he "didn't think that a person who had been nominated to the Supreme Court should testify, as it jeopardized his future effectiveness on the Court, and that he would invariably testify to something that would plague him."

One who did appear before the Senate Judiciary Committee was former DOJ attorney Oetje Rogge, once fired by Clark, who lambasted his ex-boss for trying to "out-Dies the Dies Committee," promoting blacklists, approving wiretaps, and promoting "a loyalty witch hunt" that spawned "a cold war against anyone who engaged in independent thinking." To Rogge, confirming Clark meant the "erection of an American type of fascism."

Maybe so, but the Senate confirmed Clark on August 18, with only eight dissenting votes, and he'd taken his seat on the court one day later, appointed for life. At Justice, Clark's successor was James McGrath, ex-Governor of Rhode Island and chairman of the Democratic National Committee since October 1947.

And if that wasn't cronyism...well, what was it?

At Bureau HQ, Chief Hoover continued his feud against Detroit's Reuther brothers. Assassins nearly killed Walter last year, and they'd tried for Victor in May, blinding him in one eye with buckshot. Waking in the hospital, Victor told his surgeon, "Take my eye, or my arm or leg, but spare my tongue. I've got a living to make." He'd survived, and despite a Senate vote urging the Bureau to investigate, Hoover did nothing.

In the Chief's defense, Declan knew he was tied up chasing Reds. One suspect, economist William Remington, held various federal jobs until professional witness Elizabeth Bentley accused him of spying for Russia. They'd been casual acquaintances during the war, before Bentley ditched the CPUSA, rediscovered Catholicism, and went on the Bureau's payroll in 1945. Two years later, G-men questioned Remington, then employed by the President's Council of Economic Advisers, leading to a Gotham grand jury appearance where he denied any wrongdoing. Next, to prove his innocence, Remington sent the FBI a list of fifty-odd supposed Reds, most of whom he'd never met aside from his estranged wife Ann and her mother, both avowed CPUSA members.

A second probe of Remington followed in early 1948, prompting suspension from his job in June. In July, while the Senate Permanent Subcommittee on Investigations questioned Bentley, the *Washington Post* branded Remington "a boob who was duped by clever Communist agents." At his loyalty review hearing, he blamed the CPUSA for dissolution of his marriage and called Bentley a liar. When Bentley repeated her charges on NBC Radio's "Meet the Press," Remington filed a $100,000 libel suit and Bentley dropped from sight, leaving NBC to settle the claim out of court for $10,000. Remington got his job back and hoped the ordeal was behind him.

Next up came Harry Bridges, an Australian-born leader of the International Longshore and Warehouse Union, naturalized as a U.S. citizen in 1945, whose success at leading strikes marked him in Edgar Hoover's mind as an obvious Red. In 1948, the DOJ—hoping to deport Bridges as they'd tried and failed to do in 1939 and '41—collected a gaggle of "witnesses" including racketeers, disbarred attorneys and convicted perjurers to take another shot at it, augmented by Hoover's standard illegal wiretaps.

In fact, Bridges had known about the taps, at one of his

hotel rooms, since 1940. He'd started playing games with G-men, typing notes, shredding them and leaving them in a trashcan for agents to find, then switched to another hotel and used binoculars to watch the scavengers piecing his bogus notes back together. Matters seemed more serious in 1949 when Bridges hired Larry Fly to defend him against the government's latest deportation bid, which sought revocation of his citizenship. Specifically, he was accused of perjury for lying at his naturalization hearing, denying that he'd ever been a CPUSA member.

Over the past four years, Hoover's minions had smeared Harry's name in newspapers and urged friendly congressmen to pass a bill specifically commanding the Attorney General to deport him, but that farce died in the Senate. Still, nothing seemed to work, and Fly was standing fast beside his client, declaring, "I think this is a civil liberties issue. Illegal means have probably been used here, and I feel very strongly on this question of individual rights and wiretapping." What a jury might decide, of course, was anybody's guess. Fly was also pursuing Judith Coplon's appeal for the ACLU on identical grounds.

Bridges aside, in July 1945 Hoover ordered his men to collect info on CPUSA members at large, documenting their "subversive" goals. A year later, he passed Attorney General Clark a 1,850-page report detailing prosecution strategy, but that was stalled until July 1948, when a federal grand jury indicted twelve CPUSA leaders for violating the Smith Act, plotting to overthrow the U.S. government. Alphabetically, the defendants included Benjamin Gates, Chairman of the CPUSA's Legislative Committee; General Secretary Eugene Dennis, aka "Francis Xavier Waldron"; John Gates, né Solomon Regenstreif, leader of the Young Communist League; Gil Green and Gus Hall, National Board members;

Furriers Union official Irving Potash; Jacob Stachel, chairman of the Party's Education, Agitation and Publications Department; Robert Thompson, Party chief for New York; native Scotsman and Central Committee member John Williamson; Henry Winston, a black Marxist civil rights activist (three strikes in one); and Carl Winter, head of the Party in Michigan.

Hoover was disappointed by that haul, hoping all fifty-five members of the CPUSA's National Committee would be charged, reminding Clark that in 1917, "the IWW was crushed and never revived, and similar action at this time would have been as effective against the Communist Party." Worse yet, Foster was dropped from the case due to poor health, but that still left eleven "kingpin Commies," as *Time* magazine labeled them, ready and ripe for conviction.

Before trial convened at the Foley Square federal courthouse on November 1, the defense launched a letter-writing campaign that swamped the White House and Judge Harold Medina with pleas to dismiss the indictments. Medina, only on the bench for eighteen months, stood fast and proceeded with jury selection, wrapped up on January 17. The defendants made their first courtroom appearance on March 7. Dennis opted to defend himself, while the rest put their trust in a legal team led by British Zionist Harry Sacher, backed by leftist lawyers George Crockett Jr., Richard Gladstein, Abraham Isserman, and Louis McCabe. The ACLU kicked in an amicus brief endorsing a motion for dismissal, which Judge Medina denied.

Lead prosecutor John McGohey hit a snag immediately, on the fact that no defendant charged had ever called for violence. His narrative maintained that as members of the CPUSA, based on the revolutionary works of Marx and Lenin, all had, in effect, conspired to overthrow the government since 1945. As proof, McGohey introduced *The Communist Manifesto*, published 100 years ago, plus various pamphlets and other writing from subsequent years. Federal witnesses included Angela Calomiris, hired by Justice to infiltrate the CPUSA in 1942 and burrow in for seven years; born-again Catholic Louis Budenz, spinning convoluted tales of "Aesopian language," in which "the fact that a man denied he was a communist might prove he was a communist since all communists had instructions to deny it"; and another FBI mole, Boston ad man Herbert Philbrick, doubling as Party publicist and Baptist youth leader.

The defense employed a three-pronged strategy: first, casting the CPUSA as a conventional party, promoting socialism by peaceful means; second, with a "labor defense" branding the trial a rigged capitalist sideshow; and finally, using the courtroom as a forum to publicize Party policies. Attorneys argued that the prosecution's choice of aged documents to prove its case was spurious, most of the "evidence" predating the Comintern's 1935 Seventh World Congress, which urged conversion to socialism through education. Judge Medina disallowed most of the documents submitted by defense attorneys, which set the tone for all that followed.

The Gotham trial quickly devolved into rancor, described in the press as a "circus-like atmosphere," requiring 400 cops on duty for security. Defense attorneys seemed to goad the court deliberately, prompting Judge Medina to declare, "I will not be intimidated!" Amidst a blizzard of motions, objections, and outbursts, Medina briefly sent five defendants to jail, Hall for shouting, "I've heard more law in a Kangaroo court," and Winston for crying out, "More than five thousand Negroes have been lynched in this country." He also cited each of the defense attorneys for contempt, warning that punishment would be delivered at trial's end. Later, during jury deliberations, one juror reportedly told other members of the panel, "We must fight communism to the death," voicing his urge to "hang those commies."

Public opinion generally echoed that sentiment. *Time* magazine ran two cover stories on the trial, one labeled "Communists: The Presence of Evil," the other branding Eugene Dennis "The Little Commissar." The *Christian Science Monitor*, although more moderate, predicted that "The outcome of the case will be watched by government and political parties around the world as to how the United States, as an outstanding exponent of democratic government, intends to share the benefits of its civil liberties and yet protect them if and when they appear to be abused by enemies from within."

Not that all voices supported the state's view, by any means. Outside the courtroom, pro-defense protesters chanted, "Adolf Hitler never died. He's sitting at Medina's side." Congress proposed a bill to ban pickets from federal courthouses but it died in the Senate. Henry Wallace blamed Harry Truman for inciting a new Red Scare, writing, "We Americans have far more to fear from those actions which are intended to suppress political freedom than from the teaching of ideas with which we are in disagreement." On October 10, a delegation from the National Non-Partisan Committee that included Paul Robeson and Oetje Rogge petitioned Justice, in vain, to quash the New York indictments.

Four days later, the defense rested and jurors deliberated for nearly eight hours before convicting all defendants. Judge Medina sentenced each in turn to ten years, plus $10,000 fines, then turned to his unfinished business with their lawyers, slapping all five with contempt sentences ranging from thirty days to six months. While their lawyers sat in jail, two awaiting potential disbarment, the defendants appealed and posted $260,000 bail in negotiable government bonds, provided by the Civil Rights Congress.

And if anybody thought that was the end of it, Declan decided, they should look a little closer at the writing on the wall.

———

L*ITTLE* I*TALY, Manhattan: November 10, 1949*

G*REG* J*ORDAN* WALKED into the kitchen of his brother's *ristorante*, finding Carlo huddled with his sons Dominic and Angelo. Carlo was stirring a large pot of aromatic marinara sauce, but from the bit of conversation that he overheard, Greg gathered that his nephews were receiving pointers on conducting family business.

Passing on to Carlo's office, he was studying the books when Carlo entered, on his own and smiling as he said, "Ya know, I think the boys might do all right once they get made."

"You *do* remember that the books are closed?" Greg asked his brother, not referring to the open ledger on the desk in front of him, but to the *Cosa Nostra*'s membership rolls, officially closed to new members for seventeen years.

"Yeah, but they gotta open up some time. An what's a *babbo* good for, if he don't talk to his *figli mashi*?"

"Sure. Okay."

"Speakin' a sons, what's up with Dave these days?"

"Just school."

"You say, 'Just school,' like it was nothin'. It's *Columbia*. He's goin' places, that one. Pass the bar like you, then who knows what?"

Who knows is right, Greg thought. And said, "He's still got two more years before he graduates, then three in law school."

"Maybe O'Dwyer will be out by then," Carlo replied.

Bill O'Dwyer had been reelected to a second term as mayor, polling 49 percent against five outspoken opponents, but that was down eight points from last time and the tough campaign left him looking haggard. He had shaken off the 1945 grand jury's claims of laxity and maladministration, but a new police corruption scandal had been making news, unearthed by D.A. Miles McDonald, and one tabloid had begun calling O'Dwyer "The Mob's Man at City Hall."

But things were tough all over, right? Sam Carollo returned to the United States from Sicily, then was deported once again. July saw Cockeye Dunn and Andy Sheridan fried at Sing Sing for killing Andy Hintz two years ago. At Valley Stream, western Long Island, shooters eliminated one of Meyer Lansky's partners, Philip "Little Farfel" Kavolick, in mid-September. One week later, Ernie Rupolo walked out of prison on parole, unfazed by speculation that he might be hit for testifying against Vito Genovese. Acting casual, he'd told acquaintances, "Hey, Vito beat the rap. I did him a big favor. They can't try him twice for the same murder." In Milwaukee, Joe Vallone retired, succeeded as *capo crimine* by Salvatore Ferrara. Mother Nature took out John Sciandra in northeast Pennsylvania, his family passed on to Russell Bufalino.

Changes, Jordan thought. *And I don't even know which way my kids are going, one day to the next.*

He didn't mind Dave breaking from the family—that

was the plan—but he was still haunted by what he'd seen and suffered overseas. As for Gemma, raising the only child she'd ever have, life had seemingly settled down.

But in the crazy world these days, who really knew?

———

IT FELT good being back out in the field, but Colby Gantt couldn't help wishing that he'd been dispatched to the Far East. Granted, any escape from Washington—from home, Eileen, and two-year-old Hardy—was a relief, and while that also brought a twinge of guilt, he wouldn't look a gift horse in the mouth.

As far as Gantt could tell, the action was wrapped up in Germany, at least for now. On April 9, twelve nations led by the U.S., Britain, and France had formed a North Atlantic Treaty Organization to protect members from Red expansion beyond Eastern Europe. Eleven days later, the Russian news agency TASS announced Moscow's willingness to lift the Berlin blockade, formally brought to an end on May 12, at one minute past midnight. On May 23, the Federal Republic of Germany was born with President Theodor Heuss, mirrored four months later by the announcement of the German Democratic Republic, led jointly by State President Wilhelm Pieck and Prime Minister Otto Grotewohl.

Would that mean the permanent division of the former Reich? It looked that way to Colby, standing quayside on the River Havel, staring off toward East Berlin. A few blocks to his west on Wilhelmstraße, stood the hulk of Spandau Prison, built to house 600 back in the 1870s, now home to seven Nazis who'd escaped the noose at Nuremberg, with their rotating shifts of Allied guards.

Back home, Americans seemed to expect a permanent division of the former European Theater. Lawrence Houston, head counsel for the defunct Strategic Services Unit and Central Intelligence Group, now for the CIA, had written the Central Intelligence Agency Act, passed by Congress in May and signed by Harry Truman on June 20, effective the same day as Public Law 110. Of course, it wasn't *really* public, since its terms allowed the Agency to use confidential fiscal and administrative procedures while exempting it from most limitations on federal spending. At the same time, it excused the CIA from disclosing its "organization, functions, officials, titles, salaries, or numbers of personnel employed," also creating program "PL-110" to handle defectors and other "essential aliens" who fell outside normal immigration rules.

In short, anything was permitted, as long as nobody knew.

Gantt had to smile at HQ's unofficial motto, lifted from the Gospel of John: "And you shall know the truth and the truth shall make you free." But free from what? Not fear, if people really knew the truth about their changing world.

Better to stick with the official motto, then: "The Work of a Nation. The Center of Intelligence." Which kept things nice and vague.

Speaking of fear, Americans were agitated by news of Russia's initial A-bomb test on August 29, codenamed "First Lightning." Washington's leaders were taken aback, withholding reports of the blast at Semipalatinsk, in the Kazakh SSR, for three weeks afterward.

In Hungary, meanwhile, Red leader Mátyás Rákosi staged a show trial for his leading rival, Foreign Secretary

László Rajk, convicting him of treason on September 24 and executing him three weeks later. Word out of Budapest said that Rákosi's second-ranking adversary János Kádár, had survived so far, but only after agents of the State Protection Authority beat him, smeared his skin with mercury to block pores from breathing, and pissed into Kádár's propped-open mouth. Rákosi called himself "Stalin's best pupil," while enemies labeled him the "bald murderer," wishing him dead but unable to pull it off.

Perhaps the CIA could help with that.

In Greece, the civil war ended one day after László Rajk's death in Hungary. A bitter rift between Stalin and Tito had demoralized Red insurgents, Moscow's leader warning that America and Britain would "never permit Greece to break off their lines of communication in the Mediterranean." Stalin advised the rebels to *svernut*—"fold up"—and so they had, as tension grew between the Greek Communist Party, pledged to follow Stalin and its failing Democratic Army. The result: peace was declared under a plan called *Peristera* ("dove"), while more than 100,000 suspected Reds were imprisoned, exiled or shot.

Another big win for the West.

Things hadn't gone so smoothly in the Far East though. Take Indochina, where all-out war had raged between French and Việt Minh forces since December 1946, with Hồ Chí Minh and his Red government retreating underground. France tried to stabilize the region in May 1949, creating a Federation of Associated States that merged Tonkin, Annam, and Cochinchina under former Emperor Bảo Đại, ruling a new State of Vietnam with "partial autonomy" from France, but that only provoked resistance from Laotian and Cambodian nationalists. Hồ, for his part, despised Bảo Đại as much as he hated the French and the war continued.

Incessantly rejected by America since 1945, Hô's rebels finally, reluctantly, accepted military aid from Moscow and the Red regime lately established in Peking by Mao Zedong.

That was the news that sent tremors through Washington, rivaling Russia's detonation of its first A-bomb. Congress was seething and demanding answers: how had the United States "lost China" after saving it in World War Two? Gantt could have told them, it was obvious. Millions of Chinese citizens loathed Chiang Kai-shek and his Kuomintang. Aside from being brutal and corrupt, supported in large part by dealing opium, the KMT proved it couldn't fight its way out of a paper bag. Suffering defeat after defeat, Chiang's troops retreated from Canton, Chungking, Chengtu and Sichang before finally leaving the mainland entirely and massing on the islands of Taiwan and Hainan, calling their shrunken regime the Republic of China. They'd already "pacified" Taiwan in February 1947, killing some 10,000 dissidents, imposing martial law—"White Terror," to the locals—that imprisoned tens of thousands more and still remained in force today. In Chiang's absence, Mao established the People's Republic of China on September 29, and no one in the States professed to understand it.

Gantt could've told them in a heartbeat. Deal with gangsters and you wound up getting burned unless you double-crossed them first. And that, he thought, might be the single greatest lesson of the Cold War shaping up ahead.

————

1678 Broadway, Manhattan: December 15, 1949

Birdland was jumping, Payton Sawyer immersed in its

music, laughter, crosstalk, and the incessant *clink* of glasses. It was opening night for the jazz club, situated below street level, just north of West 52nd Street on the northern edge of Hell's Kitchen.

Thursdays were also one of Payton's nights off from his job, the other being Tuesdays. Both were light days for the firm that had employed him since he'd graduated from Monroe College in June, with his associate's degree in criminal justice, and he'd wanted to take in Birdland's premiere.

Payton already knew its backstory; purchased from mobster "Joe the Wop" Catalano by a consortium of partners including Oscar Goodstein and the Levy brothers, Morris and Irving, named for headliner Charlie "Yardbird" Parker. Parker was onstage right now, milking his tenor saxophone for all that it was worth, heading a lineup billed as "A Journey Through Jazz." Other musicians standing by to rock the house included Lester Young, Stan Getz, Maxie Kaminsky, "Hot Lips" Page, and Lennie Tristano, with vocals from Harry Belafonte.

A night to remember and then some, but Payton was all by his lonesome, in spite of the jubilant mob underground. He eyed the girls but had none of his own—well, nothing steady, anyhow—busy around the clock working and studying up for NYPD's written entrance exam.

The physical tests he knew would be no great problem —except, perhaps, for his race. The department had hired its first black cop, Sam Battle, in 1911. There were more today, though still greatly outnumbered, mostly stuck in lower ranks. When Battle made lieutenant, finally, in 1935, the brass had sidelined him as a parole commissioner.

Onstage, Parker jumped straight from "Yardbird Suite" to "Ornithology," having already raised the roof with other hits including "Bird of Paradise" and "Bird Gets the Worm."

Oddly, he didn't have a piece of Birdland, but that hardly mattered to the hepcats dancing, clapping, and cavorting on the jam-packed floor.

Payton was still eleven months away from being legal when it came to buying liquor or enlisting as a cop. While waiting, he was picking up the best experience he could working for Ace Security in Harlem, run by one of his old man's pals in the neighborhood.

His father was another hurdle, dead set on his eldest living son going for some profession like the law or medicine, instead of wading through the same shit he'd been saddled with for over thirty years, fired from the Bureau of Investigation for his race, then hunting Chinamen and ghetto dope-fiends for the FBN. Payton had seen his old man struggle with the racism he faced, coupled with the everyday frustrations of a thankless job, but none of it changed his mind. He still hoped to do better, make the world at least a slightly cleaner place.

Naïve? Well, he was young enough to try, before he fell into the rut of apathy and cynicism, anyway.

And if that happened to him over time, at least with crime rates rising as they were, he'd always have a steady job —unless it killed him first.

CHAPTER 4

COLUMBIA UNIVERSITY LAW SCHOOL: MAY 17, 1950

THE SKY DRIZZLED rain that morning, but it mercifully stopped before commencement exercises started. After the dean's obligatory speech, Dave Jordan watched the graduates rise from their seats and file across the stage, receiving their degrees and automatically shifting the tassels on their mortarboards from left to right, as a symbol of passage. They all wore light blue caps and gowns, the hoods dangling behind them lined in purple, the chosen color for the law. Dave noted that Fiona's hood bore velvet trim, denoting her new status as a Juris Doctor.

When the ceremony was completed and the graduates began dispersing to their families, Fiona found him in the crowd, smiling as she approached. Dave forced his eyes away from the twin patches sewn onto her gown above each breast, bearing the crown adopted by Columbia nearly three centuries ago, when it was still King's College in the eighteenth century.

He knew already that her parents hadn't made it to commencement: her father Declan tied up with his FBI work down in Washington these hectic days, her brother also working for the Bureau in Miami, and her mother loath to travel on her own. They'd sent regrets and cash stuffed into greeting cards, and while Dave feigned disappointment at the news, in truth he'd been relieved.

Jordan knew bits and pieces of the complicated history between their families, although he'd never broached it with Fiona during any of their conversations: fathers law school classmates back in 1917, both bound for war when one—Fiona's dad—had been diverted to the Bureau and a draft exemption, while Dave's father had enlisted, gone to France, returning with assorted scars and medals to denote his service "Over There." Declan O'Hara had been with the FBI for over three decades, still hanging on in his mid-fifties, while Greg Jordan had returned planning a law career and wound up serving no one but the Giordano family.

That could've made for awkward holidays together, never mind the ancient camaraderie between *patres familias*. Fiona's father was a manhunter; Dave's was a mobster, more or less. It wouldn't help much that the FBI kept hands off anything related to the Syndicate unless their boss saw a potential headline in it, like the puppet show where Lepke Buchalter surrendered to him personally, back when Dave had been fifteen years old.

It still impressed and *de*pressed Jordan that Fiona, though one year his junior, was already clear of law school, starting on a whole new life, while he was only wrapping up his junior year and wouldn't graduate until next spring, with three more years of law school still lying ahead of him.

And then...what?

Jordan let it go and greeted her with his best smile. "Congratulations, Doctor! What's your next big move?"

"Still not a lawyer yet," she answered back. "I have to pass the bar somewhere."

Meaning New York, D.C., or in another state where she could find the kind of clients she was looking for: innocent "criminals," or at the very least, accused felons who never got an even break because of race, class, status, or whatever.

Jordan thought it sounded like a hunt for unicorns, but what in hell did he know? If he hadn't gone and got himself blown up in Italy...

Fiona looped an arm through his, saying, "Somebody promised me a feast."

"That would be me," Jordan confirmed. "And I've got reservations at Fraunces Tavern. If we grab a taxi—"

"What? That's too much money, Dave. You know—"

"I know I'm paying, Ma'am."

"But I was hoping we might hit Katz's again. Remember our first lunch together?"

"How could I forget?" They hadn't gotten far since then, in terms of intimacy—still no scar show that he knew would horrify Fiona—and her seeming sentiment surprised him now. "You want pastrami, it's pastrami you shall have."

She gave her gown a little shake. "But showing up like this..."

"It's great. You'll be the star."

"Well..."

"Trust me, eh?"

"I do."

They went to hail a cab, still arm-in-arm. Nearly a year spot-on since their first lunch together at the deli, and he hadn't been convinced that it was anything special to her, before today.

Was that a problem?

Could be, absolutely.

Now, despite his strong attraction to Fiona, he would have to find some way to spare her from his scars—and from his family.

————

EAST HARLEM, Manhattan: August 19, 1950

IKE SAWYER WAS WORKING on a Saturday, but no one back at his apartment seemed to mind. Payton was gone, of course, moved out when he'd started his full-ride scholarship at Monroe College, now renting a small place of his own— what realtors called a "studio apartment," meaning one L-shaped room around 500 square feet, with the bathroom tucked around a corner and a Murphy bed that folded up into one wall. The other kids would be off somewhere with their friends: Keisha hanging with Eulis Jordan, her alleged fiancé, though Ike hadn't seen a ring; Fred likely playing football, planning on a promotion to the varsity lineup next year.

As for Talitha, she'd be at her ladies' club most of the afternoon, sampling wine and sharing in the trash-talk about husbands who were either out of work or usually gone.

That's me, Ike thought. *Forever chasing something I can't reach.*

Payton had been the focus of his worry for a while now since he'd gone to college with a view toward joining the NYPD as soon as he was old enough, three months from now. Another worry had arisen on June 25, when North

Korean troops invaded South Korea and conscription came back with a vengeance, the call-up increasing more than twentyfold, from less than 10,000 draftees in 1949 to some 220,000 in the current year. If Payton nailed a job on the police force he would be exempt, but he would still be facing the disdain of white "brothers in blue" and risking death each time he hit the streets.

Nothing that I can do about it now, Ike told himself, for the umpteenth time.

Now, here he was in East Harlem, a little off his normal turf and looking for a bum he'd turned as an informant back in 1942. The neighborhood had been known as Italian Harlem then, more often tagged today as Spanish Harlem or *El Barrio*. The Puerto Rican population had topped 60,000, bringing in *bodegas* and *botánicas*, but tension between races hadn't gone away, far from it, and Sawyer drew comfort from his badge, more from his holstered .45.

Today, he sought Eugenio Giannini, a "made" man of the former Luciano—now Costello—family who'd started smuggling penicillin from the States to Italy after the war, at Lucky's invitation. Sadly for Eugenio, police in Naples recently had nabbed him with a suitcase full of counterfeit U.S. dollars and locked him up in Poggio Reale prison until FBN Agent Charles Siragusa pulled strings to get him released. Now Gene, as his *goombahs* called him, was back in New York, but rumor had it that Luciano was wise to his game as a double agent and had put a price tag on his head.

Ike knew the threat was real, especially considering the fate of California informer Abraham Davidian, gunned down in Fresno six months earlier. So far, he'd had no luck in finding Giannini, but he kept on trying, feeling he owed it to the punk for putting him at risk initially.

In other drug news, fierce commercial competition had

been boosting amphetamine sales and consumption, all the more this year since Smith, Kline & French had introduced Dexamyl, a blend of dextroamphetamine and the barbiturate sedative amobarbital. Ostensibly intended to reduce amphetamine's frequent, unpleasant agitation and quell anxiety without drowsiness, Dexamyl was now advertised as a cure for everyday "mental and emotional distress," doubling as a weight-loss drug to spare fatties the agony of dieting and exercise. Competitors were circling SKF, promoting Abbot's Desbutal and Robins's Ambar, blends of methamphetamine and pentobarbital or phenobarbital, respectively. All, needless to say, were addictive as hell.

Meanwhile, George Hunter White—a hero of the FBN since he'd busted the Hip Sing Tong in 1936 while posing as a Chinaman—had come back to the fold after his wartime service with the OSS as a lieutenant colonel, teaching classes in counterespionage. Since his return in '46, he'd busted Arthur Zweier's Mexican drug ring, cracked another in France led by Lucien Santoni, compiled evidence in Rome that sent heroin exporter Marcello Enzi to prison, and dropped by Istanbul as a counterfeit merchant seaman, taking down smuggler Severt Dalgakiran. Treasury had given White its highest award, the Medal for Exceptional Service, in 1949, and earlier this year Director Anslinger loaned White to the Kefauver Committee when Edgar Hoover refused to play ball, Anslinger hailing White as "one of the great experts on the Mafia."

That all looked great on paper, but Ike knew things hadn't been so rosy in White's life. His wife left him at war's end, calling White a "fat slob," and his last OSS psych report detailed how White compensated for that humiliation via alcohol and forays into sadomasochism.

All of which led White—and the whole FBN—into

some very murky waters. White wasn't alone on his wartime involvement with the OSS, as it turned out. Director Anslinger was right there in the middle of it too, advising Wild Bill Donovan on research into hypothetical "truth drugs" for use on captured Axis agents. Peyote and sodium amytal proved ineffective, so they'd switched to the "killer weed" marijuana and a derivative, tetrahydrocannabinol (THC) acetate, which reportedly produced a high "more spiritual and psychedelic than that of the ordinary product," thirty minutes after ingestion. On one occasion, White had volunteered to smoke a THC-laced cigarette, later griping that all he'd achieved was to "knock myself out."

Since those giddy days, another of White's many irons in the fire was his ongoing contact with fellow OSS veteran James Jesus Angleton, appointed in May 1949 as head of Staff A for the CIA's Office of Special Operations, making him responsible for collection of foreign intelligence and liaison with the Agency's counterpart organizations abroad.

Some Jesus, Ike thought. *More like Judas.*

Racial matters, as the FBI called them, had not improved to any great degree this year. Tuskegee University in Alabama had begun compiling stats on lynchings dating back to 1882, and professors there reported only two such crimes thus far for 1950, with one of those victims being white. Officially, lynching occurred when five or more persons teamed up to slay one or more victims "under the pretext of service to justice, their race or tradition," so Ike guessed the definition fit both crimes on file.

The first victim, in February, was Charles Hurst, white operator of a "rolling store" around Pell City, Alabama. He'd done something to upset the Klan led by "Grand Dragon" Alvin Horn, a so-called Christian minister who'd led four other Kluxers out to Hurst's place, packing guns. Hurst's son grabbed a rifle to defend his father and was wounded by the fusillade that killed his dad. Since the victim was Caucasian, a grand jury indicted all five raiders for murder, and one drew a five-year manslaughter sentence while another was acquitted and the other charges disappeared like ghosts the morning after Halloween.

The other lynching, filed just yesterday, involved a Negro, one Jack Walker, found riddled with bullets in a creek near Gay, in Georgia's Meriwether County. Nobody claimed to know exactly who or how many assailants murdered Walker, but the local wags said he had worked for white men and was snuffed for "knowing too much" about the details of their moonshine business.

Feeling anxious for his son, his *mafioso* squealer, and the world in general, Ike put his old sedan in motion, cruising down Third Avenue and watching for the only man on Earth he might have any chance to save.

———

THE LUBYANKA BUILDING: October 2, 1950

IT WAS good to be back in Moscow, even if the new Cold War had matters more unsettled than ever between East and West. The chance of never coming home at all had been a very real one, and it would've been a lie for Leonid Babin to deny he was relieved.

He knew exactly how the FBI had nabbed him—Sasha Yushkov, the old *sooka*, had betrayed him—and Babin had passed that on to the attorney whom the Russian UN delegation had provided for him in captivity. There'd been no bail, of course, because the damned U.S. attorney labeled him a spy and flight risk (both correct), so Babin sat in jail while prosecutors tried to frame a charge against him for his trial. They'd ultimately failed, thanks to a rare food allergy of Yushkov's that had killed him in protective custody, but not before the trial of Judith Coplon and her so-called lover, Gubischev.

Before that happened, Soviet Ambassador Panyushkin tried to get Gubischev off the hook, as an *amerikantsy* might say, dispatching an unprecedented letter to the U.S. State Department via Embassy First Secretary Lev Tolokonnikov. That missive reminded State that Gubischev had entered the United States in July 1946, bearing a diplomatic passport as the third secretary for the Soviet Ministry of Foreign Affairs. Therefore, Panyushkin said, his aide could not be held or tried on any charge. The state and the courts demurred, noting that Gubischev specifically waived diplomatic status on his application to serve the UN Secretariat, thereby becoming a private employee accountable for any felonies he might commit.

At trial in New York, both Gubischev and Coplon were convicted on March 9, sentenced to fifteen years apiece. Both appealed, then Gubischev gave up the fight eight days later when Justice agreed to deport him instead. On March 20, Gubischev, his wife and daughter left New York Harbor aboard the Polish liner M.S. *Bathory,* dubbed a "lucky ship" for surviving multiple military actions during the Second World War. She'd been lucky for Babin as well, another passenger who'd been ignored by shouting reporters and newsreel photographers as he boarded.

Arriving back in Moscow, Babin learned what he had missed during his sojourn in America. In January, while he sat in jail, Stalin had laid the groundwork for war in Korea, instructing Ambassador Terentii Shtykov in Pyongyang,

"Tell Kim Il-sung that I am ready to help in this matter." Two weeks later, hedging his bets, Stalin had signed a mutual defense pact with Mao Zedong's People's Republic of China.

Babin's debriefing had been arduous, but he was ultimately cleared of any wrongdoing and was thanked in fact, for his part in exposing Sasha Yushkov before he caused the Russian network any further damage. Babin, for his part, had reached out since his return, ensuring that no harm had come to Mark and Isabella Barnes before they could be graced with the arrival of his son, Stefan.

So far, so good. Babin retained his rank as a major general of state security, with full authority and all the privileges he'd earned before the unexpected side trip to New York. And he arrived home for the bloody climax of the "Leningrad affair," although it had begun in January 1949.

That was the month when Pyotr Popkov, Aleksei Kuznetsov and Nikolai Voznesensky organized a Leningrad Trade Fair to boost the city's postwar economy and aid survivors of the Nazi siege. Although their effort won approval from the State Planning Commission, *Izvestia* and other propaganda organs accused fair planners of tapping Moscow's federal budget in a bid to restore Leningrad—formerly Saint Petersburg—to its pre-revolutionary status as Russia's capital. Deputy Chairman Georgy Malenkov led the attack, charging more than 2,200 officials in Leningrad Oblast with treason masked by an "unauthorized business."

But what was to be done with them?

Moscow formally abolished capital punishment in May 1947, decreeing that henceforth the stiffest penalty for any crime in Russia should be twenty-five years in prison, but the death penalty was restored in January 1950. Tried behind closed doors, six defendants—Premier Mikhail Rodionov; P. G. Lazutin, chairman of Leningrad's municipal government;

Y. F. Kapustin, second secretary of Leningrad's Party Committee; plus trade fair planners Kuznetsov, and Popkov and Voznesensky—were convicted shortly after midnight on September 30, all sentenced to die. Granted, their "crimes" had been committed during the legal moratorium on executions, but the court waived that technicality to apply the new law retroactively. A firing squad mowed down the six condemned one day after their sentence was imposed.

As for the rest of those accused, more than 200 drew prison terms ranging from ten to twenty-five years, their families deported to Siberia. Another 2,000 public officials were driven from office, exiled from Leningrad, some to the Gulag. Politburo member Alexei Kosygin, a close friend of Voznesensky, escaped criminal charges but was sidetracked from career advancement while Stalin remained in charge.

All good, thought Babin, *while the weight falls onto someone else.*

He had his own agenda to pursue, a child at stake, and he refused to let the fate of others hold him back.

———

NEW YORK CITY POLICE ACADEMY: November 18, 1950

PAYTON SAWYER SCANNED the faces that surrounded him, judging them each on sight. Of forty-five new NYPD applicants, all male, only one other aside from him was black— or a "high yellow," as his old man might have said. Another was Latino, probably a Puerto Rican, and from what Sawyer could see he'd barely measured up to the department's minimum of five foot seven, lucky if he tipped the scales at

150 pounds soaking wet. The rest all looked like cops Payton was used to seeing around Harlem, pallid, half a dozen of them freckled redheads he marked on sight as Irish.

Well, I got this far, he thought. *I'm in the running, and I'm still alive.*

That last had been a toss-up, sweating out the new, accelerated draft since June, when North Korean troops crossed the 38th parallel, capturing Seoul in three days, running head-on into U.S. soldiers on July 1. The Yanks and South Korean soldiers had recaptured Seoul in late September, pushed back across the 38th parallel four days later, and rolled on from there until they'd met Red Chinese reinforcements two weeks ago, on Sawyer's twenty-first birthday.

By then, guys Payton knew were being plucked from Harlem into military service, but he'd stayed the course, passing NYPD's cursory physical and Civil Service written exam, presenting proof of age and residency with his transcripts from Monroe College and a letter of recommendation from Ace Security. The only obstacles remaining in his path were the physical agility test and a pre-hire interview conducted by a desk-riding lieutenant and two sergeants, all of them undoubtedly Caucasian.

All the tests so far had been conducted in the "new" police academy—in point of fact, a vacant former public school on Hubert Street, across from St. John's Park in Lower Manhattan—and the agility test was no exception. They'd gathered outside for this one, in a spacious, fenced-off parking lot where they could run around like draftees in boot camp and show what they were made of to a pair of white, gray-haired and paunchy officers in T-shirts and sweatpants.

Payton, dressed much like his judges but with gym

shorts in the place of sweats, didn't imagine that the final test would be much of a challenge. It included half a dozen elements, beginning from a kneeling, weapon-ready posture, whereupon each applicant would sprint fifty feet and scale a six-foot wooden barrier. Next up, he'd have to mount a six-stair pyramid arrangement, back and forth three times. A physical restraint simulation followed up, requiring each applicant to grapple and "subdue" an inanimate tactical training device. From there, he'd launch into a "pursuit run," covering 600 feet around preset concrete traffic cones, without clipping any. The "victim rescue" phase involved each applicant dragging a 176-pound mannequin for thirty-five feet, and the capper was a weapons exercise with an unloaded .38 revolver, held inside a metal ring nine inches in diameter, remaining there while the recruit executed sixteen trigger pulls with his dominant hand, fifteen with the other.

All that was for time, the stopwatch running until all phases of the exam had been completed or the applicant fouled up somehow and didn't make it through.

No sweat, thought Payton, and he hit the course as if his life depended on it—which it might, if he was cut out of the running and wound up in the wrong uniform, sent overseas.

He wouldn't let it beat him, *couldn't* let it beat him. He had plans, goddamn it, and no obstacles laid out on dusty blacktop were about to hold him back.

———

HOLLYWOOD: *November 27, 1950*

SOMETIMES, Devon Gantt drove past the movie studios—

Paramount and Universal with their arched gateways, MGM with its lion—imagining what life was like on a soundstage, where the problems vanished anytime directors shouted, "Cut!"

Nothing like life as Gantt knew it.

A week after Thanksgiving, all the news he heard was bad. Halfway around the world, Red Chinese troops had the U.S. Marines surrounded at someplace called Chosin Reservoir with no relief in sight. This very morning, at a press conference broadcast via radio, the president said he was prepared to launch an A-bomb strike on North Korea "to achieve peace," if need be.

Some fucked up time to try raising a son, now three years old, who might be orphaned or incinerated before he made it to kindergarten.

Nothing in the global news had quelled Hollywood's zeal for hunting Reds. The Supreme Court had denied review for the Hollywood Ten, and they'd started serving one-year terms in various federal lockups. One of the defendants, screenwriter Dalton Trumbo—best known for *Thirty Seconds Over Tokyo*—was philosophical about it, telling interviewers that he did, indeed, hold Congress in contempt.

Closer to home in June, a pamphlet titled *Red Channels* had hit the streets, branding 151 movie industry professionals "Red Fascists and their sympathizers." Those identified joined the ever-growing blacklist, while one of the original Ten, director Edward Dmytryk, won early release from prison by changing his tune, admitting he'd once joined the Communist Party, naming a list of "comrades" including RKO producer Adrian Scott, who's movie *Crossfire* won Dmytryk an Oscar in 1947.

In L.A. politics, Dick Nixon had set his sights on the U.S. Senate, encouraged when incumbent Sheridan Downey announced his retirement in March. Ex-actress Helen Gahagan Douglas, star of 1935's thriller *She* and a congresswoman since '45, wanted fellow Democrat Downey's seat, but Nixon had other ideas. Cross-filing in both party primaries, Nixon tagged Douglas as "the Pink Lady," claiming her liberal votes in the House made her "pink" if not red, from politics "right down to her underwear." Voters ate it up, giving Nixon a 59-percent victory on November 7, ratified by 100 percent of the state senate to cinch his appointment. Aside from the promotion, Nixon earned a nickname: "Tricky Dick."

Gantt spent as much time as he could these days watching the Mob, although it brought him no rewards and he had to hide his interest from SAC Stafford. Back in February, some of Jack Dragna's gorillas bombed Mickey Cohen's house on Moreno Avenue, near the Brentwood Country Club, blowing a ten-foot hole in the wall of a bedroom where Cohen normally slept. Alas, Mickey had been forewarned by a newly installed radar alarm system, saving both himself and wife Lavonne before the estimated thirty sticks of dynamite went off. Needless to say, that didn't keep his neighbors, with their shattered windows, from labeling the self-styled King of Los Angeles "an intolerable nuisance."

Meanwhile, across the state line in Nevada, Las Vegas was prospering. Encouraged by profits from the Flamingo, Cleveland's mob built the Desert Inn with 300 hotel rooms, frontman Wilbur Clark taking the blows while partners Moe Dalitz, Sam Tucker, Morris Kleinman and Sam Tucker raked in the skim. Hank Greenspun, Bugsy Siegel's former PR man now published the *Las Vegas Sun,* unfazed by his July conviction and $10,000 fine for smuggling weapons to Israel.

The big news Mob-wise was a national Senate probe into organized crime. The impetus for that had come last year, from the American Municipal Association, representing more than 10,000 cities nationwide, led by Mayor deLesseps Morrison of New Orleans, seeking a federal spotlight to shine on corruption. In early January, Tennessee's Estes Kefauver introduced Senate Resolution 202, permitting the Judiciary Committee to investigate organized crime's role in interstate commerce, but the rival Senate Committee on Interstate and Foreign Commerce claimed that privilege and its attendant headlines. The final compromise: the creation of a Special Committee to Investigate Crime in Interstate Commerce, with Vice President Barkley casting the tie-breaking vote May 3.

With that debate still in progress in mid-April, President Truman announced his own investigation of interstate racketeering, led by Attorney General McGrath. McGrath took all of four days to declare he'd found no evidence of any Syndicate, after allegedly reviewing the files of federal grand juries nationwide. Edgar Hoover quickly sided with his boss, while Indiana's Homer Capehart countered their opinions, telling fellow Senators that America's bookies were united in "a loose and unofficial working arrangement." Telephone and telegraph companies weighed in with unanimous opposition to any proposed legislation banning interstate transmission of gambling information.

Spawned from dissent and confusion, the new committee chaired by Kefauver, had four other members, including Wyoming's Lester Hunt, Maryland's Herbert O'Conor, New Hampshire's Charles Tobey, and Wisconsin's Alexander Wiley. The panel started with a budget of $150,000 and a deadline fixed at January 31 of 1951. Their road show hadn't reached L.A. until November, but Gantt found it worth the wait, including testimony from Nevada lieutenant governor and casino owner Cliff Jones, clueless Desert Inn "owner" Wilbur Clark, Flamingo vice president Moe Sedway, LAPD Chief William Parker, Mickey Cohen, L.A. County Sheriff Eugene Biscailuz, San Diego hitman and *caporegime* Frank Bompensiero, and San Francisco D.A. Edmund "Pat" Brown."

The results were decidedly mixed, as expected. Lawmen typically denied knowledge of Mob activities within their bailiwicks or claimed old problems had been solved by their administrations. Some proved stubborn, like the three Internal Revenue Bureau agents suspended for "improper transactions" with gangsters in California and Nevada. Identified mobsters either hid behind the Fifth Amendment or defective memories. Bompensiero *did* admit a May meeting in Tijuana, with *mafiosi* "Silver Dollar Sam" Carolla, Frank "Three Fingers" Coppola, and Ciro Gallo, but he insisted they met by chance and were "just drinking." David Kessel, a Frisco "businessman" born in Romania, stalled for two hours, drawing citations for perjury and contempt.

Sound and fury, signifying nothing yet. Gantt guessed he'd have to wait and see if anything resulted from the hearings, but he wouldn't hold his breath. Some things in L.A. and across the country never seemed to change—at least, not for the good.

———

FBI Headquarters: December 7, 1950

Nine years since Pearl Harbor and America was back at war again. The only consolation Aloysius Gantt derived from that was knowing his son Devon should be reasonably safe, drawing a paycheck from the Bureau in Los Angeles. As for Devon's twin brother, Colby, Gantt hadn't a clue where he might be, what risks he might be taking at that moment for the CIA.

Things had been bad enough in Washington, where two Puerto Rican nationalists had tried to kill the president at Blair House—Harry Truman's temporary home during a White House renovation—on November 1. The shooters, Oscar Collazo and Griselio Torresola, killed White House Police officer Leslie Coffelt but failed to spot Truman himself, peering from an upstairs window after gunfire roused him from a nap. Before he dropped, Coffelt killed Torresola, but not before he wounded two other policemen. Secret Service agents wounded and captured Collazo, rushing him to a hospital where doctors patched him up for his eventual trial.

Gantt wished the Alger Hiss case could've been resolved so easily. After his mistrial in July of '49, Hiss faced a new jury in November, this time convicted of both counts on January 21. New judge Henry Goddard sentenced him to five years on each count, the sentences to run concurrently at the federal pen in Lewisburg, Pennsylvania. At sentencing, Hiss told the court, "I want only to add that I am confident that in the future the full facts of how Whittaker Chambers was able to carry out forgery by typewriter will be disclosed."

That had Gantt sweating since he knew *exactly* how it was accomplished. Thankfully for him, no testimony at the second trial addressed that crucial matter, and the defense once more failed to cross-examine FBI typewriter "expert" Ramos Feehan. Hiss posted $10,000 bond pending appeal, denied by the U.S. Court of Appeals for the Second Circuit this very morning.

And would that be the end of it? Gantt didn't have a damned idea.

Judith Coplon's case was another source of agitation at Bureau headquarters. Despite dual convictions in Washington and New York, the latter including Soviet spy Valentin Gubischev, the case was falling apart. Gubischev waived his appeal in favor of deportation, thus escaping prison while Coplon—like Hiss—had taken her case to the Second Circuit, but with very different results. Two days before their Hiss decision on December 5, the same three judges reversed both of Coplon's convictions. While granting that her "guilt was plain," the panel couldn't stomach warrantless wiretaps that eavesdropped on her conversations with attorneys or the failure of G-men to swear out an arrest warrant. In short, she walked, although Justice still had the open charges pending, searching madly for some way to win another trial without the Bureau's tainted evidence.

And then, there were the A-bomb spies.

On January 31, five months after Russia tested its first atomic bomb in Kazakhstan, President Truman had ramped up the nuclear arms race by announcing the development of a hydrogen bomb, hundreds of times more powerful than the bombs dropped on Japan to end World War Two. That news was barely out of Truman's mouth when British authorities jailed German-born atomic scientist Klaus Fuchs on February 2, for violating the Official Secrets Act by leaking crucial data to the Soviets. Fuchs pled guilty on March 1 at the Old Bailey, after fingering his courier, Manhattan Project chemist Harry Gold.

Gold was born Heinrich Golodnitskiy, to Russian-Jewish

parents living in Switzerland, age four when his family immigrated to the States in 1914, Americanizing their surname. Jacob Golos—né Yakov Reizen, a Ukrainian-born founder of the CPUSA—recruited Gold as a spy in 1934, but Gold remained mostly inactive for the next decade, until Soviet case officer Semyon Semenov became his handler. By then, the Manhattan Project was well advanced, and Moscow yearned to know all about it.

Bureau agents arrested Gold on May 23, and he instantly followed Fuchs's example, rolling over to identify accomplice David Greenglass, employed during wartime at the Clinton Engineer Works uranium enrichment facility at Oak Ridge, Tennessee, then at the Los Alamos laboratory in New Mexico. Arrested by G-men on June 15, Greenglass claimed brother-in-law Julius Rosenberg recruited him and his wife Ruth as spies, passing data to Russian agent Anatoli Yatskov. Justice charged David and Ruth the next day, while Oetje Rogge took charge of their defense, urging both clients to testify against Rosenberg and wife Ethel.

Things had moved quickly from there. On the same day, charges were filed against David and Ruth, G-men questioned Julius Rosenberg for the first time. Born in Manhattan to immigrant parents, Rosenberg joined the Army Signal Corps Engineering Laboratories at Fort Monmouth, New Jersey, in 1940, spending the war as an engineer-inspector, then was canned when the army discovered his CPUSA membership. By then, he'd already shared data on radar and guided missile controls with Moscow.

Urged on by handler Alexander Feklisov, Julius recruited Greenglass through David's sister Ethel, who'd married Julius in 1939. Others on the traitor's list included Joel Barr and Alfred Sarant, friends of Rosenberg's from Fort Monmouth; Barr's fiancée, Vivian Glassman; General

Electric engineer Morton Sobell; engineer Russell McNutt, who'd helped design Tennessee's Oak Ridge National Laboratory; and William Perl, a jet propulsion physicist whose application to the U.S. Atomic Energy Commission was pending when the case broke.

Once the dominoes started falling in June, Vivian Glassman passed money to Barr, Perl and Sarrant, advising all of them to flee the country. Only Perl refused, perhaps deluded as to the extent of trouble he was in, taking his chances with ACLU attorney Raymond Wise, who recommended turning state's evidence. A federal grand jury in New Mexico indicted Dave Greenglass for espionage conspiracy on July 6, followed eleven days later by similar counts against the Rosenbergs in New York. G-men caught Julius shaving and slapped on the cuffs. Morton Sobell was charged on August 3, *in absentia*, hiding in Mexico with his wife and two kids. Ethel Rosenberg appeared before a federal grand jury four days later, indicted on August 11 and held in lieu of $100,000 bail. Six days later, the grand jury charged both Rosenbergs and Anatoli Yatskov with eleven overt acts of espionage.

Sobell thought he was safe in Mexico, but when he tried to run for Europe he lacked proper travel documents. On August 16, unidentified gunmen snatched the whole family, handing them over to FBI agents at Laredo, Texas, just across the Rio Grande. It took six days to formally arraign him and transport him to New York for trial.

Seldom fully satisfied, Justice had filed a superseding indictment on October 10, charging the Rosenbergs, Sobell, David Greenglass, and Yakovlev with fresh counts of conspiracy to commit espionage. Greenglass pled guilty eight days later, with sentencing deferred, while the other four denied everything.

This time Gantt thought, *convictions that should stick. No wiretaps and no one forgot arrest warrants.*

Of course, that didn't mean that you could trust the courts. These days, it seemed that anything could go awry.

───────

GW Delicatessen, Washington, D.C.: December 15, 1950

THERE WERE TIMES—AND more of them lately—when Declan O'Hara to get out of headquarters and go somewhere he could breathe. The GW Deli on G Street, in Foggy Bottom, was one of his favorite places to slip off and hide from the rat race, however briefly.

Declan was halfway through a meatloaf sandwich with a side of fries and slaw, counting his blessings. Abigail was well, Nolan was safe as any Bureau agent could expect to be in Florida, and maverick Fiona breezed through the New York bar exam in late July. That likely meant he wouldn't see her for a while, and Declan wasn't thrilled by her new job with the Legal Aid Society, but she was headstrong and he couldn't tie her down.

At least he wasn't sacrificing any children to the mayhem in Korea. Newspapers were calling it a "police action," which was ludicrous. That very morning Harry Truman declared a state of national emergency.

Bureau headquarters inaugurated two new programs during spring. The first, kicked off in March, precipitated by a question from International News Service editor-in-chief William Hutchinson, asking Edgar Hoover to identify the "toughest guys" at large on active federal complaints. Hoover deferred replying, passed it to Guy Hottel, SAC of the D.C.

field office. Thus was born the list of "Ten Most Wanted Fugitives," among the thousands sought by G-men nationwide, and so far the results had been encouraging.

Publicity from newspapers netted six of the Top Ten so far this year, including jewel thief and prison escapee William Nesbitt; murderer and burglar Omar Pinson; safecracker Lee Downs; Leavenworth escapee Orba Jackson; Barker-Karpis gang alumnus Glen Wright; kidnapper Henry Shelton; and Morris Guralnick, sought for attempted murder and maiming a cop whose finger he'd severed.

The other new project was Hoover's Sex Deviates Program, inaugurated in April when he sent the White House and assorted other agencies a list of 393 government employees busted for "sexual irregularities" in Washington since 1947. That program was part of a larger, more sinister "Lavender Scare" set off by Republican National Chairman Guy Gabrielson's claim that "sexual perverts who have infiltrated our Government in recent years" were "perhaps as dangerous as the actual Communists." Undersecretary of State John Peurifoy, an FDR appointee, replied that State "allowed"—that is, *forced*—ninety-one homosexuals to resign in recent months. The risk, allegedly, was fear of being fired that made "deviates" prone to blackmail by the Reds, transforming them into spies. Joe McCarthy was quick to join in the witch-hunt, telling newsmen, "If you want to be against McCarthy, boys, you've got to be either a Communist or a cocksucker."

Declan saw the irony in that, considering some of the rumors circulating around McCarthy himself, not to mention his new aide Roy Cohn, a closet queen if ever there was one. Senator Kenneth Wherry of Nebraska summed it up for most Republicans when he pontificated, "You can't hardly separate homosexuals from subversives." Granted, there *was* some overlap between the Reds and homosexuals, particularly in the Mattachine Society, founded on the West Coast in July by CPUSA defector Harry Hay. North Carolina Senator Clyde Hoey's Committee on Expenditures in Executive Departments reported that all federal agencies "are in complete agreement that sex perverts in Government constitute security risks."

But were they, really? Wasn't it, in fact, the fear ginned up by Bible-thumpers on the right that gave "perverts" the panicked urge to hide?

Another burden for the Bureau since September, was the Internal Security Act, authored by Nevada Senator Pat McCarran, passed on September 20, vetoed by Truman two days later, then passed again over his veto that same afternoon. Its subsections were labeled Subversive Activities Control and Emergency Detention, which pretty well told you McCarran's agenda for Reds. Aside from establishing a Subversive Activities Control Board to investigate suspected traitors, the law required communist organizations to register with the Attorney General. Said groups were defined as any promoting the establishment of a "totalitarian dictatorship," and while that theoretically included fascists, no one seemed to give a damn about them anymore. Even the act of picketing a federal courthouse become a felony if carried out "to obstruct the court system or influence jurors or other trial participants."

Farewell free speech, and you could scrap the First Amendment too.

One bright spot—hell, call it hilarious—had been the January fraud conviction of HUAC Chairman J. Parnell Thomas. Rumors of his corruption dated back to 1940, Thomas taking kickbacks from a clerk to keep her off the tax rolls, and newspapers started chasing the stories in '48.

When called before a grand jury, sweet irony, Thomas pled the Fifth Amendment just like all the so-called Reds he'd pilloried. Conviction earned him an eighteen-month sentence, and he'd resigned from Congress on January 2. Sweeter still, for anybody with a sense of humor, Thomas was serving his time at Connecticut's Danbury Prison, where "Hollywood Ten" members Lester Cole and Ring Lardner Jr. were locked up for contempt of HUAC.

O'Hara thought about the latest rash of Smith Act trials while he was finishing his lunch. Convictions of the CPUSA's leaders stripped the party of legitimacy in the eyes of most Americans, even though they'd only been sentenced for speaking and reading, not one of them caught at an actual crime that harmed anyone else. By now, he knew that roughly half the Party's members were informers for the Bureau or some local Red Squad, characters like Lou Budenz and Harvey Job Matusow, yet another in the growing stable of repentant Reds trying to cleanse his soul and make a killing as a stool pigeon. Recently, the Party expelled Matusow as a useless drag on resources and he'd been excised from the Bureau's payroll, but it looked like he was doing even better from the rash of government committees and private investigating firms.

One target of Chief Hoover's who had finally been nailed was Harry Bridges, convicted with two codefendants in June of fraud and perjury for denying CPUSA membership on his nationalization application back in 1940. A judge slapped him with five years in prison and revoked his hard-won citizenship.

In August, Bureau agents raided the CPUSA's Pittsburgh office, arresting Stjepan Mesaros (aka "Steve Nelson") and two other Reds on sedition charges. Still marking time until the first Smith Act defendants settled their appeals, Justice handed Nelson over to the Allegheny County D.A.'s office, which charged him with twelve counts of plotting to depose the U.S. and state governments under a Pennsylvania law dating from 1919—the same year that "Nelson," then sixteen, immigrated from Croatia with his mother and three sisters. He joined the Party's Young Workers League in 1923, later spent two years in Moscow with his wife, and served as a "political commissar" with the Abraham Lincoln Brigade during the Spanish Civil War. Illegal Bureau bugs and wire-taps indicated he'd been spying on a phase of the Manhattan Project during World War Two, but nothing stuck, so G-men let the Keystone State have him. He hadn't gone to trial yet, but Edgar Hoover counted on a win.

The big news recently, in Washington and elsewhere, had been Senator Joseph McCarthy from Wisconsin. Farm-born to strict Catholic parents, he left school at fourteen to raise chickens, then manage a grocery store. Back in high school at twenty, he completed a four-year course in one year, then talked his way into Milwaukee's Marquette University, earning a law degree in 1935 and passing Wiscon-sin's bar the same year. When his practice failed to prosper, he earned his living playing poker.

Politics beckoned, and McCarthy—an early FDR supporter—switched parties to win an election as a Repub-lican circuit judge, shocking locals with a gutter campaign wherein he lied about his rival's age while calling him both senile and corrupt. In 1942, though draft-exempt, he joined the Marine Corps to boost his prospects for higher office, commissioned as a lieutenant and posted as an intelligence briefing officer with a bomber squadron in the Solomons. He'd flown twelve training missions, later claiming it was thirty-two in combat, and left the Corps a major in April 1945, calling himself "Tail-Gunner Joe." While still on active duty, he'd campaigned for a Wisconsin Senate nomination, losing out to the incumbent with a miserable 27 percent of the popular vote.

Back in civilian life, McCarthy ran unopposed for his old judgeship, then geared up for the 1946 GOP senatorial primary race. His backers included Wisconsin's Republican boss, Thomas Coleman, and—ironically, as it turned out—the CPUSA-controlled United Electrical, Radio and Machine Workers union. Waging another dirty race, he'd accused the three-term incumbent Robert La Follette Jr. of dodging the draft (at age forty-six) and of war profiteering; false charges that hurt while McCarthy's posters showed him in full combat gear, with belts of machine-gun ammo strapped across his barrel chest. That time, McCarthy swept the field with 61 percent of ballots cast.

On his first day in the Senate, McCarthy staged a press conference to air his thoughts on a CIO coal strike in progress. His proposal: draft union leader John L. Lewis and his strikers, order them all back to work, and then if they refused, court-martial and shoot them all for insubordination.

Surprisingly, Tail-Gunner Joe pulled his head in after making that splash, spending the first half of his six-year term in relative obscurity. That changed when he'd addressed the Republican Women's Club of Wheeling, West Virginia, on Lincoln Day, brandishing a sheet of paper no one else was privileged to see, saying, "The State Department is infested with communists. I have here in my hand a list of 205—a list of names that were made known to the Secretary of State as being members of the Communist Party and who nevertheless are still working and shaping policy in the State Department."

That number waffled with McCarthy's mood, changing

erratically. Supporting his first claim, he'd referred in the Senate to a 1946 letter from then Secretary of State James Byrnes to Maryland congressman Adolph Sabath, claiming that security investigation of State employees had cleared out seventy-nine of 284 suspects. That left 205 alleged subversives on the payroll, but as Declan learned from Bureau files, only sixty-five still remained, all of whom were subsequently cleared.

And that left *zero* Reds, according to O'Hara's calculation.

Still, it didn't stop McCarthy's sounding off. While *Washington Post* cartoonist Herb Block coined the term "McCarthyism" to denote slanderous demagoguery, Wisconsin's bad boy made a five-hour Senate speech on February 20, referring this time to eighty-one identified "loyalty risks" serving the State. When asked for names, he'd given "case numbers" instead, compiled as Declan had discovered from the so-called "Lee List," a report compiled in 1947 by Robert E. Lee—not the dead Confederate general, but rather an ex-Bureau agent turned Director of Surveys and Investigations on the U.S. House Appropriations Committee. Reviewing that list at the time, said committee cited "incidents of inefficiencies" in the security reviews of 108 past and present federal employees.

So it went, round and round, with McCarthy inflating his nameless suspects into "card-carrying Communists." Trying to sort it out, February's Senate Resolution 231 authorized a special subcommittee to make "a full and complete study and investigation as to whether persons who are disloyal to the United States are, or have been, employed by the Department of State." Maryland Senator Millard Tydings had chaired those hearings, conducted between March and June.

Appearing as a witness, Joe McCarthy dumped his Lee List in favor of charges against nine specific "subversives." Some had never worked for the State at all, while others were long gone, but the tail-gunner forged ahead, naming Esther Brunauer, Gustavo Durán, Haldore Hanson, Philip Jessup, Dorothy Kenyon, Owen Lattimore, Frederick Schuman, John Service, and Harlow Shapley.

Declan, intrigued, checked them out himself. Brunauer, a longtime civil servant, ardently supported government loyalty screening and had written, in 1948, "There is certainly nothing vindictive or arbitrary in the attitudes of the people who are carrying out this program, and I have the feeling that, as unpleasant as this situation is, it does provide an opportunity for straightening up the record and being protected in the future." By the time she testified for the Tydings Committee, she'd been bombarded by telephone death threats.

Durán, conversely, looked suspicious: an ex-lieutenant in the Spanish army, he'd been named special assistant to the Assistant Secretary of State in 1946, then quit to join the UN's Refugee Division before future HUAC chairman Parnell Thomas branded him a Comintern member and an agent of the Soviet NKGB.

Hanson was a one-time foreign correspondent who covered China's civil war and Japanese invasion, later working for the State Department. McCarthy denounced his "pro-Communist proclivities" and accused Hanson of being on "a mission to communize the world." Although Hanson insisted that he was a loyal American, his Virginia neighbors signed a petition to drive him from their midst, one calling him a Russian spy.

Kenyon, an outspoken advocate of women's equality, called McCarthy "an unmitigated liar" and "a coward to take shelter in the cloak of Congressional immunity." Questioned by the *New York Times* next day, McCarthy claimed that he'd lost interest in her case.

Lattimore—a "top Russian spy" in McCarthy's opinion, *sans* proof—had worked for the Institute of Pacific Relations, turning its journal into a "forum of controversy," appointed by FDR in 1941 to serve as U.S. advisor to Chiang Kai-shek. Chiang and his defense secretary, Wang Ch'ung-hui, accused Lattimore of "understating Soviet involvement" in Xinjiang and Outer Mongolia, but Roosevelt had still named him to lead the Pacific Theater's Office of War Information in '44. Four years later, a defector from the Soviet embassy in Athens labeled Lattimore a spy, again with no proof, but that was enough for McCarthy.

Fred Schuman, a history professor at the University of Chicago and Williams College for over three decades, had already survived charges of Red affiliations in 1943 from the Dies Committee and kept his side job as an analyst of Nazi radio broadcasts, but any random smear was grist for Joe McCarthy's mill.

John Stewart, one of State's veteran "China Hands," had been embroiled in 1945's *Amerasia* affair, but a unanimous grand jury refused to indict him on any charges, despite a Bureau bug suggesting that he'd passed one State Department memo on to editor Phillip Jaffe. Now, it was convenient to blame Stewart and his former colleagues for the "loss" of China, as if Washington had ever owned it in the first place.

Last but not least, Harlow Shapley—head of the Harvard College Observatory since 1921—had been outspoken in support of FDR's New Deal and Truman's Fair Deal, which earned him a HUAC subpoena in 1946. Specifically, because he'd joined the Independent Committee of the Arts, Sciences and Professions, also opposing Republican Joseph Martin Jr.'s reelection bid to Congress. Shapley faced grilling over HUAC Chairman Ed Hart's designation of the ICASP as an unproven "major political arm of the Russophile left."

McCarthy had no evidence for any of the charges he laid out, nor did hired witness Lou Budenz, called to buttress McCarthy's accusations against Lattimore. It hurt that Budenz hadn't mentioned Lattimore's name once, during 3,000 hours of FBI debriefing, more specifically informing *Collier's* magazine in 1949 that Lattimore had never "acted as a Communist in any way." By 1950 though, with fresh payments in hand, he'd suddenly recalled that Lattimore was both a CPUSA member *and* an active Russian spy.

From day one of its hearings, the Tydings Committee was riven by partisan infighting split along strict party lines. Tydings himself labeled McCarthy's charges a "fraud and a hoax," serving only to "confuse and divide the American people to a degree far beyond the hopes of the Communists themselves." Indiana Republican William Jenner returned fire, accusing Tydings of "the most brazen whitewash of treasonable conspiracy in our history."

The Senate at large was likewise divided, although seven Republicans led by Maine's Margaret Chase Smith signed a "Declaration of Conscience" condemning McCarthy's witch-hunt. McCarthy replied by branding Chase and company "Snow White and the six dwarfs." In its final report, published in mid-July, the committee's majority cleared McCarthy's nine suspects of all allegations, but a subsequent review board found "reasonable doubt" of John Service's loyalty, prompting Secretary of State Dean Acheson to fire him.

One thing you could say about Tail-Gunner Joe, he never forgot or forgave. In November, he'd campaigned for

Republican hopeful John Butler against Millard Tydings, telling crowds that Tydings was "protecting Communists" and "shielding traitors." McCarthy's minions faked a composite photo of Tydings acting chummy with CPUSA boss Earl Browder. Tydings lost to Butler by some 43,000 votes, and McCarthy also helped elect Everett Dirksen, replacing Democratic Senate Majority Leader Scott Lucas, whose image had also been tarnished by the crime-fighting Kefauver Committee.

In fact, McCarthy seemed to live for rough-and-tumble tactics, often fueled by too much alcohol. In May, spotting critical columnist Drew Pearson at Washington's Gridiron Club, McCarthy had grabbed his detractor, snarling, "Someday I'm going to get a hold of you and really break your arm." Seven months later, on December 12, they'd met again at the Sulgrave Club on DuPont Circle. That time, after some verbal sparring over dinner, McCarthy trailed Pearson to the cloakroom, pinning his arms and kneeing him twice in the groin. Richard Nixon intervened, prompting McCarthy to complain, "You shouldn't have stopped me, Dick." Facing reporters afterward, McCarthy minimized the assault, although admitting that "I slapped him hard."

Is this what we've become, O'Hara wondered, while he paid his tab. *And if it is, how could the Commies be much worse?*

———

SEOUL, South Korea: December 15, 1950

COLBY GANTT STOOD AT A DISTANCE, watching as five South Korean army riflemen finished their execution of 800 political prisoners, the echo of their gunshots whipped away by icy winds.

The slaughter had gone on for forty minutes, five men armed with MI Garand rifles, reloading after each clip of eight rounds was expended, needing more than one shot each for some of the survivors. Victims had been herded into trenches that would be their graves, gouged from the frozen earth by bulldozers at dawn. The government labeled all of them as Reds and saboteurs or murderers, though Gantt himself spotted children who were barely grade-school age. Since 1948, free education had been deemed compulsory for South Korean kids, but Colby reckoned this lot would be missing class.

United Nations officers, including Yanks, Brits, and Australians, stood with Gantt to watch the slaughter going on, some of them taking notes, all grim-faced. Whether they'd file reports of what they saw would be hashed out some other time, but Colby knew President Syngman Rhee would shrug it off, deny the whole damned thing. Gantt would report his observations to the CIA, where he fully expected nothing to be done.

The massacre, repeated on a smaller, local scale at sites scattered around the countryside, was spawned by paranoia following the Red recapture of Pyongyang ten days earlier. Rhee's government was purging communists, including those merely suspected or imaginary, a pursuit that Foggy Bottom heartily endorsed. Meanwhile, morale among Rhee's soldiers plummeted while their president—officially earning a mere $37.50 per month, revelling in what one war correspondent called "the worst excesses of corruption." Common soldiers went unpaid for months on end, while officers embezzled their pitiful salaries and hundreds more "ghost soldiers" existed solely on paper, their pay siphoned into official pockets.

It didn't help that Rhee had been a tyrant since the day of his election, severely curtailing dissent and paying an army lieutenant to murder rival Kim Gu in July of 1949. Rhee's troops had executed more than 14,000 so-called rebels on Jeju Island that year, plus another eighty-eight— including thirty-two children—at Mungyeong. By the time war broke out in June, Rhee had some 30,000 alleged Reds in prison, with 300,000 more enrolled in a "re-education" program called the Bodo League. After the North Korean invasion, Rhee's firing squads liquidated most of those captives as well.

All of which paled beside Rhee's role in jump-starting the Korean War. Both Rhee and Kim Il-sung wanted to reunite the peninsula under their respective governments, but the U.S. stalled about providing Rhee with heavy weapons in advance of June's attack. Months before the said invasion, journalist John Merrill reported "a major insurgency in the South and serious clashes along the 38th parallel," with at least 100,000 people slain in "political disturbances, guerrilla warfare, and border clashes."

The cold, unspoken truth: both sides had fudged across the parallel repeatedly before June 25, and one day after North Korea's "unprovoked attack," the *New York Times* reminded readers that "on a number of occasions Dr. Rhee has indicated that his army would have taken the offensive if Washington had given consent."

Of course, Korea wasn't the CIA's only hot front in this Cold War. In February, East Germany created the *Staatssicherheitsdienst*—SSD, or Stasi—whose motto translated as "Shield and Sword of the Party." Led by Minister of State Security Wilhelm Zaisser and deputy Erich Mielke, the Stasi was fast shaping up as Eastern Europe's most effective and repressive secret police agency.

Mao's Red China was another worry since the People's Liberation Army had driven KMT troops from Hainan in May, forcing General Xue Yue, Chiang's "God of War" into exile on Taiwan. Five months later, the PLA had invaded Tibet, told months before by Britain's House of Commons that it would "recognize Chinese suzerainty over Tibet, on the understanding that Tibet is regarded as autonomous."

Fat chance of that, Gantt thought.

Since August, the CIA had been fanning the flames in China with Airdale, a Delaware-based corporation soon renamed Air America, purchasing 40 percent of Claire Chennault's old Civil Air Transport firm while KMT investors owned the rest. As Air America spread its wings, it ferried spies throughout Southeast Asia—and some claimed, though Colby hadn't tried to prove it, loads of opium outbound for Europe and the States. Its role as a "civilian" airline would be handy for evasion of treaties prevailing in the region, and of those as yet unsigned.

More trouble loomed in Indochina, where Peking and Moscow had recognized Hồ Chí Minh's Democratic Republic of Vietnam in January, equipping Việt Minh soldiers with military advisors and modern weapons, including American-made hardware abandoned by the KMT army in flight. By month's end, General Võ Nguyên Giáp had transformed his guerrillas into six conventional army divisions. In February, Washington and France recognized Bảo Đại's regime in South Vietnam, while Hồ attacked French outposts along the Chinese border. In July, President Truman authorized $15 million in military aid to the French, but they still couldn't hold, losing 6,000 men and large stores of supplies in September. Soon afterward,

Washington created a Military Assistance Advisory Group (MAAG) in Saigon to aid the French Army. CIA officers went along for the ride, but French discouragement had thus far restricted their actions. An Agency report warned Truman that "if these attacks develop into a coordinated, large-scale offensive, French maintenance of control over Indochina—by means of their own forces alone—will be seriously threatened."

Through it all, the CIA kept growing and expanding its scope and influence wherever it could. On September 30, Truman approved National Security Council policy paper No. 68, providing for the global militarization of the Cold War, rejecting the alternative policies of friendly détente and peaceful containment of the Russkies. That pleased Walter Bedell Smith, who'd taken over as Director in October and brought Allen Dulles along as Deputy Director for Plans, the Agency's covert operations arm abroad.

The home front was another proposition altogether. While the CIA was barred by law from operating there, it hadn't stopped wartime experiments in search of "truth" drugs, started by the OSS. Of course, it had expanded now, with Operation BLUEBIRD launched in April, constantly in search of newer, better chemicals.

One such turned out to be ergotamine, first isolated from the ergot fungus by Swiss biochemist Arthur Stoll at Sandoz Pharmaceuticals in 1918, marketed as Gynergen to fight migraines and stop postpartum hemorrhage in 1921. Today, its new derivative was lysergic acid diethylamide (LSD), first synthesized by Albert Hoffman at Sandoz in 1938. Its psychedelic properties weren't recognized till 1943, marketed four years later as Delysid for various psychiatric uses. Now Sandoz was looking for investors with deep pockets. Two CIA agents had flown to Basel and returned with free samples, anxious to see how it worked.

Colby would definitely keep his eye on BLUEBIRD's progress, watching out to see how it could help him rise within the Agency while taking care that no false steps outside the law could bring him down.

Winning the future, as his father] predicted back in 1941, and loving every minute of it—most particularly when it kept him out of Washington, away from working at a desk.

―――――

MANHATTAN: *December 30, 1950*

GREG JORDAN KNEW that he should count his blessings as another year ended, but whenever he tried, they slipped between his fingers and were lost like sand on Coney Island's beach. Not that he ever went there anymore, or any other place he once regarded as a rollicking good time.

Of course, he *was* thankful, albeit silently. His son was on the dean's list at Columbia, his third straight year, and set to graduate with honors in the spring. Gemma and husband Paulo had a settled life with three-year-old Lucia, and Greg would've said that things were back to normal between him and Abigail, after her fury over Dave's enlistment and her anguish at his grievous wounds.

As for the rest of Jordan's family—the Giordanos, that would be—Carlo was still in charge, though trusting Greg to keep him out of trouble, serving as the family's attorney, primary accountant, and all-around *consiglieri*. Nephews Dominic and Angelo were on a path that didn't seem to worry anyone but Uncle Greg, and that was something else he could be thankful for, in a left-handed way: son David hadn't followed them into the murky realm of crime.

On foreign fronts, newspapers told him that Charlie Luciano had been photographed in Palermo, talking to *Don* Calò Vizzini's bodyguards outside the Hotel Sole, widely known as Calò's second home. Vizzini's *soldatos* bloodied the photographer, but he decided not to tell police after *Don* Calò paid him off and bought him a new camera. Elsewhere in Sicily, anti-communist bandit Salvatore Giuliano had outlived his usefulness to both the government and Mafia, killed in July while "resisting arrest."

Meyer Lansky also had business abroad, with a new heroin pipeline running from Turkey, through Marseilles' processing labs to America's streets. His front men in the States included Paul Mondolini, Antoine D'Agostino, and Corsican Pierre Lafitte—a descendant of Jean Lafitte, the pirate captain who helped America win the War of 1812. Pierre, in fact, was multifaceted, fencing for big-time thieves and playing some role with the CIA that Jordan hadn't worked out yet.

Politics in New York remained nearly as cutthroat as those overseas, though actual bloodshed was rare. Mayor Bill O'Dwyer resigned in August, three months before the expiration of his term. Before boarding the 20th Century Limited to California, he'd made his chauffeur a police commissioner and secured his own lifetime pension "in the best interests of the city." When reporters questioned his abrupt departure, O'Dwyer replied, "That question will have to be answered by the President." As to D.A. Miles McDonald's rackets probe, he simply said, "I have no further comment." Harry Truman's answer came in late November, when he named O'Dwyer the U.S. ambassador to Mexico.

Bill's resignation doomed his hopes of ever being governor, and two-term incumbent Tom Dewey was facing stiff opposition from Democratic congressman Walter Lynch, out of Queens. Lynch hammered on the theme of Dewey freeing Luciano as a favor to Frank Costello, a claim branded "gross misinformation" by the State Parole Board's chairman. On Election Day, Dewey reaped 57 percent of the popular vote, shading Lynch by 572,668 ballots, while three other contenders shared 242,494.

Long before that, all anyone could talk about in Gotham was the Kefauver Committee's hunt for mobsters nationwide. One of the first surprise results had come from Kansas City on April 5, when gunmen killed *capo crimine* Charles Binaggio and bodyguard Charles Gargotta at the Jackson County Democratic Club, leaving Binaggio sprawled beneath a huge portrait of Harry Truman. A federal grand jury grilled Gargotta in February, while tension had been crackling between Binaggio and *Cosa Nostra*'s ruling Commission. While Anthony Gizzo stepped up to lead the local family, the murders turned a spotlight on Binaggio's support for sitting governor Forrest Smith, likely dooming his hopes for reelection or advancement in 1954.

At first, the Kefauver Committee seemed chiefly focused on gambling—ironic, Greg thought, since Kefauver himself loved to put a bet down when he could—but by May its interest had expanded to narcotics trafficking, counterfeiting, and all manner of political corruption. Chief counsel Rudolph Halley did the groundwork, aided by chief investigator Harold Robinson and a staff eager to please. In the committee's early days, the Continental Press Service of Cleveland admitted earning $2.4 million from its "flash" racing news last year, whereupon FCC chairman Wayne Coy suggested prosecuting Continental as an illicit monopoly. He also ordered Western Union to preserve all relevant telegrams as potential evidence, while President Truman told the Internal Revenue Bureau to give the committee gamblers' tax returns. After top layoff banker Frank Erickson testified behind closed doors, he faced a sixty-count indictment for bookmaking and conspiracy.

That hit close to home, but no subpoenas had arrived so far, for any members or employees of the Giordano family.

In Washington, committee members heard Under Secretary of the Treasury Edward Foley Jr. described his increasing difficulty nailing racketeers for tax evasion, also reporting that the Reconstruction Finance Corporation had loaned money to known gamblers, thus tying the government indirectly to their crimes. Kefauver also received a list of eighty "legitimate" firms with mobsters as silent partners —a figure, Greg knew, which barely scratched the surface.

In St. Louis, the panel questioned Vincent Chiapetta, recent successor to *capo crimine* Pasquale Miceli, but missed underboss John Vitale. Other reluctant witnesses included Anthony Lopiparo and bookmaking "overlord" William Molasky, who was ordered to deliver the books for his Pioneer News Service. Well-connected lawyer Morris Shenker, recently appointed to the Democratic National Finance Committee, ably represented Molasky and five other witnesses, ensuring that none were slapped with contempt citations.

The committee hit Kansas City in July, buoyed by support from the city's new Board of Police Commissioners, reviving a 1947 stolen-ballots scandal, probing the Binaggio-Gargotta hit, and hearing Governor Smith claim he'd barely known Binaggio. Asked under oath if he belonged to the Mafia, Anthony Gizzo replied, "What's the Mafia? I don't even know what that is." Opposition came from Missouri Democrats, including Harry Truman, who called K.C. home when he wasn't in Washington. Congressman Thomas Hennings Jr., seeking to replace Senate incumbent Forrest Donnell, asked Kefauver to postpone local hearings til after Election Day, but Estes demurred, pleading inability to control his fellow committee members' choice of where to go next. Hennings wound up winning anyway, but Truman held a grudge.

After reporting that mobsters had siphoned $34 million from Kansas City's political coffers, Kefauver tried to soften the blow, calling K.C. "a place that is struggling out from under the rule of the law of the jungle." He also spoke ill of the dead, telling his audience, "If ever a human being deserved the title of 'Mad Dog' it was Gargotta."

On its first pass through Gotham in August, the committee researched 1940s gambling in war plants, along with black market dealings in wartime, expressing concern that Korea might spawn more of the same. Spokesmen for the Port Authority of New York and New Jersey complained of the Peoples Express Company's "ridiculously low" rental bid on an unoccupied terminal in Newark—promoted, they claimed, by bribes in high places.

September's target was Chicago, and the panel struck a mother lode. Police corruption was so notorious—typified by Daniel "Tubbo" Gilbert, chief investigator for the U. S. Attorney's office and "world's richest cop" with $360,000 in the bank—that a reporter claimed one-fifth of the city's police captains were "slated for the skids." Those revelations scotched Gilbert's bid to become Cook County's sheriff, and U.S. Senate Majority Leader Scott Lucas went down in flames, taking dual hits from Kefauver and the Tydings Committee.

One Chicago boy anxious to serve Kefauver's panel was Jack Ruby, né Jacob Rubenstein, who'd returned from a

Dallas sojourn to contact key committee lawyer Luis Kutner, an associate of gangsters since his teens who was himself accused of taking $60,000 in exchange for empty promises that top Windy City mobsters wouldn't have to testify "on specific issues." Kutner handed Ruby off to Rudolph Halley and "Mafia expert" George White, on loan from the Federal Bureau of Narcotics, who reported that "Ruby is a syndicate lieutenant who had been sent to Dallas to serve as a liaison for the Chicago mobsters," serving there as "the payoff man for the Dallas Police Department." Halley told Ruby thanks, but no thanks, and Jack went back to Dallas.

Another would-be witness huddling with Kutner was ex-Chicago PD Captain William Drury, fired in 1947, who possessed substantial information. Drury warned Kutner, "I'm awfully hot," and Kutner offered protection, but it didn't help. On September 25, in separate attacks gunmen nailed Drury and Marvin Bas, lawyers for Republican Cook County Sheriff nominee John Babb. Drury was clearly slain to silence him, while a peek into Bas's safety deposit box revealed $21,000 in unexplained cash. The State's Attorney John Boyle questioned Kefauver subpoena dodgers, Paul Ricca and Lou Campagna—as if they'd have pulled the hits themselves—then freed them without charges.

October featured hearings in New York and environs. Lansky ducked questions about open gambling in Saratoga, while Kefauver claimed "large sums" from betting went to Luciano overseas. In Philly, the panel cited Nig Rosen for contempt and "threw the Philadelphia Police Department into a turmoil from top to bottom." Kefauver's approach made New Jersey State Attorney General Theodore Parsons suddenly investigate gambling in Hackensack, where subpoenas finally caught up with Joe Adonis and Willie Moretti.

Both testified in Washington, in mid-December. Adonis was tight-lipped, but Moretti stole the show, evoking frequent laughter in his role as the class clown. Loopy from tertiary syphilis, he played to TV cameras, waffling between claims of defective memory and wisecracks. Asked if he "operated politically," Willie denied it, adding, "If I did, I'd be a congressman." How had he missed newspaper reports of his pending subpoena? "I'm not a reader; my eyes are bad." Had he financed road trips for potential committee witnesses? "That sounds so ridiculous, sir, I have to answer that by saying it's impossible." Had legal heat forced his tardy appearance? "What heat? It's cold weather outside." As to his finances, "I've lost my records and I can't answer anything truthfully." And the capper, when asked if he was a *mafioso*: "What do you mean by a member, carry a card with 'Mafia' on it?"

Hearings in Wisconsin were an anticlimax, even when a bookie from Kenosha claimed two city councilmen had put the arm on him for $15,000, finally accepting half of that to keep the town wide open. It was hard to follow Willie's act, but Jordan wondered if his duck-and-weave performance might not turn around and bite him in the ass.

Oh, well, Greg thought. Willie could take care of himself, and if he couldn't, that was his tough luck. Each day that passed without subpoenas calling in the Giordanos was another blessing—although thinking of it that way made it sound like sacrilege.

Another day til New Year's and Greg reckoned he could make it that far, anyway. Beyond that, whether safe at home or on the witness stand, he'd have to keep his fingers crossed.

———

MIAMI FBI FIELD OFFICE: December 30, 1950

NOLAN O'HARA sometimes found it difficult to keep track of the Bureau's irons, glowing at white heat in the coals of different fires. Each one demanded his attention—even those he had been cautioned against watching by Austin Hunnicutt, his SAC.

Cuba's proximity to Florida kept it on every special agent's mind, particularly on occasions like the visit from Cuban Bureau of Investigation Lieutenant Sigfredo Diaz, ostensibly to watch FBI firearms training. Nolan guessed that was a pretext since the Cubans had no problem shooting one another—or their politicians in a pinch. Carlos Prío was still hanging on as president, but mayhem in the countryside suggested a revolution in the making.

Back at home, in what the Bureau labeled "racial matters," Florida's Supreme Court had affirmed the Groveland rape convictions and death sentences. Two Klans competed for attention and recruits, the older of them founded back in 1944 by three Orange County residents, now claiming 30,000 members. Upstart Bill Hendrix, a Tallahassee plumber, led the newer Southern Knights—briefly Southern and Northern Knights, with Hendrix as its "national adjutant," scaled back again when no one from the North signed up. Both factions were well armed and building up to trouble, if O'Hara read them right.

But of late, his focus was the Mob, despite SAC Hunnicutt's insistence that there couldn't be one because Edgar Hoover said so. And the root of syndicated crime in Florida, as Nolan knew by now, was gambling. The first casino—Colonel Edward Bradley's Beach Club in Palm Beach—opened its doors in 1898, two years after Miami was incorporated as a city. It ran til 1946 with only one police raid, by a rookie cop of low IQ who didn't understand he was supposed to let the rich folk have their fun in peace.

Meanwhile, in 1923, a Miami grand jury found that "in much of the city, residents and tourists alike could find numerous slot machines, punchboards and other gambling devices that even little children may play without being molested." Meyer Lansky arrived six years later, renting a Spanish-style home on Biscayne Bay while his bookies infested hotels. Al Capone soon followed, leasing the Hollywood Country Club as a casino, and Broward County offered competition from the It Club, among others. Broward's sheriffs tended to be "liberal" where gambling was concerned, assuming they had been elected to preserve the status quo.

In 1931 state legislators legalized pari-mutuel betting on horse and dog racing as a form of Depression relief, overriding Governor Doyle Carlton's veto. Betting on jai-alai was added to the list in '35, along with legal slot machines, until a change of heart in Tallahassee banned the slots again in '37. Broward County Sheriff Walter Clark won the first of nine biennial elections in 1930, endorsed by outgoing incumbent A.W. Turner in a newspaper ad that declared, "I have every reason to believe that he is a man of unquestionable character." Eddie Lee got one crack at reforming the county in 1939-40 before voters returned Clark to his roost in '41, and there he stayed until the Kefauver Committee rolled around.

Under Clark's protection, carpet joints sprang up like mushrooms, catering primarily to wealthy tourists, welcoming crowds of 2,000 per night. The It Club soon faced competition from La Boheme, the Colonial Club, the Greenacres, and the Plantation Resort—grown up from its beginning as a bookie joint in a tomato packing shed. On any given night, players might see the likes of Longy Zwill-man, Jimmy "Blue Eyes" Alo, or Chicago's Julian "Potatoes" Kaufman. Cops directed traffic at the big clubs and escorted owners to their banks, which proliferated until Hallandale was dubbed the "Wall Street of South Florida."

Miami, not to be ignored, boasted the Beach and Deluxe Clubs, Sunny Isles Casino, the Island and Palm Island Clubs, the Turf and Teepee Clubs (a huge faux tent), the 86 Club (on 86th Street), the Tennis Club, plus two joints owned by Miami Beach councilman Art Childers: the Royal Palm Club and Little Palm (a favorite hangout of Walter Winchell). A private group, the Law Enforcement League of Dade County, filed injunctions against some casinos, but sporadic raids for show only resulted in small fines and more business as usual.

By the mid-1930s, Luciano family *caporegime* Anthony Carfano, aka "Little Augie Pisano," had casinos in both counties, while Lansky backed Tropical Park, Gulf Stream Race-track and the Hollywood Kennel Club, handling off-track bets through "The Farm" in Hallandale.

And then, along came Melvin Richard, transplanted from Brooklyn in 1930, graduating from the University of Florida law school three years later. He'd started making waves with a column in the student-run *Florida Alligator,* skewering the *Tampa Tribune* for its coverage of crime so often that *Tribune* editor Edwin Lambright recommended he be boiled in oil. Lambright also attacked the university, vowing to dry up operating funds til Richard was expelled, but Mel stood fast, the rival *Gainesville Sun* saving his bacon when it printed up the *Alligator* free of charge. A graduate in private practice, Richard earned a princely $120 his first year in Miami Beach, then somehow got elected as a municipal judge. The first bookie who stood before him drew a thirty-day suspended sentence and a warning: next time, prison. Richard never had another gambling case assigned to him, but he had found a new crusade that would consume his life.

Troubles began for Miami's gamblers in January 1940. Police Chief Leslie Quigg was "liberal," but Vice Squad Lieutenant C. O. Huttoe disagreed, spilling his guts to a federal grand jury. Public Safety Director Daniel Reynolds demanded a cleanup, and Quigg gave the job to Huttoe, while City Manager L. L. Lee warned Quigg to "clip the wings" of overzealous vice detectives. In April, the DOJ issued a 653-page report detailing pervasive brutality and corruption within Miami PD. By October, Quigg declared Miami "closed to gamblers," whereupon Huttoe embarrassed him with sweeping raids. In November, the City Commission fired Lee and put Quigg on a paid leave of absence for sixteen months, until he retired. Pearl Harbor doomed the Palm Club, requisitioned as a Coast Guard barracks, and a postwar fire demolished it.

In Broward, the Colonial Inn closed in 1941, reopened under Lou Walters for five days in June 1945, then sold to Lansky for a record $80,000. Frank Costello, Carlos Marcello, and Santo Trafficante Sr. bought into the club as partners. Colonel Bradley died in 1946, willing the demolition of his Beach Club to create a public park, but its competitors kept thriving. Sheriff Clark barely noticed, preoccupied with running a numbers racket from his office.

Before war's end, in 1944 a brand-new operation organized. Founders Sam Cohen, Charlie Friedman, Jules Levitt, Eddie Rosenbaum and Harold Salvey called their outfit the S&G Syndicate, with the "S&G" defined either as "syndicated gambling" or "stop-and-go," depending on who told the tale. Dade County Sheriff "Smiling Jimmy" Sullivan, elected that same year, welcomed S&G as it corralled more than 200 of his county's bookmakers, splitting their daily take fifty-fifty with syndicate headquarters in the Mercantile Building on Brickell Avenue. Holdouts were raided by Miami Beach's one-man bookie detail, Pat Perdue, until they fell in line or left for parts unknown. To keep things cool, the syndicate paid yearly "fines" of $70,000 and contributed a like amount to local charities.

Not much overall, when S&G's gross ranged from $26 million to $40 million per year. Even Edgar Hoover, visiting Miami Beach in '46, had to admit, "If you put a dragnet around 23rd and Collins and slapped every mobster you caught into jail for life, you'd end organized crime in America."

What organized crime? SAC Hunnicutt dared not venture a guess.

There'd be no dragnet, naturally, but there *was* an outfit called "The Secret Six," comprised of *Miami Herald* publisher James Knight, *Daily News* publisher Dan Mahoney, radio WKAT owner Frank Kazentine, Florida Power and Light president McGregor Smith, Hialeah Race Track owner John Clark, and Burdine's department store owner George Whitten. Merged with the Dade County Bar Association, they formed the Crime Commission of Greater Miami, led by ex-FBI agent Dan Sullivan, running articles that profiled local mobsters with their home addresses, airing a radio series titled "The Sinister Blot" with the same information. Embarrassment could only go so far, however, when Miami Police Chief Walter Headley declared, "If there is no charge pending against a man with a criminal record, he can live here as long he likes."

Mel Richard had resigned his judgeship to spend World War Two in the navy, then returned in '46 to find the S&G

Syndicate going strong. His first encounter with the Mob involved construction of a four-wall handball court, bankrolled by Jules Levitt, whose patronage drove Richard to boycott his favorite sport. Running for City Council in 1947, he promised to rid Miami Beach of bookies, declaring, "If the chief of police won't arrest them, then I'll do it myself till we get a new chief."

Richard lost that campaign, and rebuffed Levitt's offer to make him mayor if he turned "liberal." No bluenose himself, Richard told anyone who'd listen, "I don't gamble because I don't think there's any chance of winning. I think people are stupid to invest in something where your chances of winning are one in five million."

One big winner was Sheriff Sullivan, who'd increased his net worth from $2,500 to $96,000 on a salary capped at $12,000 yearly. In Broward Sheriff Clark and his brother-assistant "Handsome Bob" gladly accepted campaign donations from the Lansky brothers, while grossing $1.1 million from their own slots and bolita games between 1945 and '47. In the latter year, Frank Erickson came down from Jersey, paying innkeeper Meyer Schine $45,000 for bookmaking rights at his Roney Plaza Hotel.

That deal meant trouble, since S&G had operated from the Roney since 1944. They hated losing money, and Miami Beach Police Chief Phil Short personally led the raid that sent Erickson's bookies packing. That briefly solved one problem, but the outsiders kept coming: Detroit's Zerilli family to the Grand Hotel, Cleveland's Al Polizzi to the Sands. By 1948, the *Miami Herald* counted fifty operations owned by Lansky. When local lawyer Fuller Warren ran for governor that year, William Johnston—heir to murdered Chicago racetrack mogul Ed O'Hare—put up $154,000 of Warren's $400,000 campaign fund.

Some locals resisted. When Hollywood reformer Lee Wentworth led an anti-gambling crusade, three Lansky aides showed up to offer him $25,000 or a bullet, but he saw them off with a shotgun. When Chicagoan Harry "The Muscle" Russell met S&G opposition in 1949, he got help from Governor Warren and Sheriff Sullivan, launching selective raids against S&G bookies, doubling down by cutting off their access to the Continental wire service. Overnight, Russell became S&G's sixth partner.

Jealous New Yorkers stepped up, leading with creation of a new tabloid, the *Morning Mail,* which welcomed Frank Costello as "a gentlemanly person" who "lives quietly, and apparently, a life of rectitude." When *Daily News* published *Morning Mail* editor Harry Voiler's own criminal record, he sued for libel, then the *Mail* shut down in its fifth week of publication.

Mel Richard bounced back in 1949, running for City Council again on a promise to put S&G out of business. Evicted from his law office, he moved campaign rallies to S&G's Lincoln Road doorstep, blaring his message over loudspeakers. He won that time, but Council votes usually outnumbered Richard's lone voice, and he started getting threats instead of bribe offers.

Another guy with problems was Lieutenant C. O. Huttoe, fired in '44 by Director of Public Safety Dan Rosenfelder for "taking part in political campaigns" by criticizing his crooked superiors. Florida's Supreme Court reversed his dismissal, but violence awaited cops who tried to do an honest job. After Patrolman Dallas Carroll raided a protected bookie joint in January 1949, his boss put him on a midnight shift where he was ambushed and beaten. Six months later, a departmental "investigating committee" called the beating a hoax. Meanwhile, Detective Chief J. O.

Barker and ex-cop W. W. Davenport beat up Lieutenant Huttoe at his girlfriend's house. The brass suspended both Huttoe and Barker. Ex-chief Quigg chimed in from the sidelines, telling reporters Huttoe "has been at odds with his superiors for years."

By trying to enforce the law, that is.

As 1949's winter season approached, civic leaders were worried. Mayor Harold Turk and the Miami Beach Hotel Owners' Association denounced crusading newspapers, aided by Mickey McBride's WMIE radio station. The *Miami Beach Times* blamed Mel Richard for persecuting S&G, thereby inviting outside mobsters to move in. Ben Cohen called on Richard at his office, threatening to toss him out the window, then a cooler head offered him $200,000 to leave Florida. Richard rejected that bribe, and asked Florida Senator Spessard Holland for help, just as the Kefauver Committee was forming. Richard promised testimony if the panel made it to Miami.

Nolan O'Hara was excited by that prospect, culling files for anything that Kefauver might need, but SAC Hunnicutt shut him down in no uncertain terms. The FBI officially denied existence of a Mafia or Syndicate, and it would not be helping the committee, period. Case closed. Governor Warren tried the states' rights angle in a letter to Kefauver panelist Herbert O'Conor, saying, "I think state sovereignty as conceived by the founders of our Government is something more than a fading memory to rest in the nation's archives."

Hearings began in Miami on May 26, with Kefauver reading a list of gangsters who'd dodged his subpoenas— including all six of S&G's bosses. Mel Richard gladly testified, along with ex-G-man Dan Sullivan, chairing the Crime Commission of Greater Miami. Along with S&G, Sullivan's chart of local gambling dens and their owners included the Lansky brothers, Joe Adonis, Frank Costello, Vincent Alo, Frank Erickson, and Gotham numbers racketeer "Trigger Mike" Coppola.

Before it left town, the committee documented $1 million in annual payoffs to local lawmen. One of those, Sheriff Clark from Broward, squirmed on the hot seat and feigned amnesia. When Kefauver read off a list of casinos in his bailiwick, Clark claimed they were "not gambling places to my knowledge."

Miami Beach Police Chief Philip Short admitting telling alleged vice cop Pat Perdue, "I don't want to know anything about the books," adding, "I know what hot potatoes are." S&G's missing owners claimed they were out of business, an assertion refuted by Mel Richard.

To the press, Richard said, "And if they have, I think they should go to jail anyway."

Dream on, thought Nolan. So far, the only ones facing indictment were Harry Russell and Frank Erickson, both out-of-state gamblers, plus Sheriff Sullivan, who got his charges quashed by Florida's Supreme Court in November. As far as Nolan knew, the committee's main contribution to South Florida was the flight of Santo Trafficante Sr. and his son to Cuba, holing up while aged Charlie Wall described his battles with the Tampa Mafia. In Santo's absence, place-holder James Lumia had started criticizing him, a dumb mistake resolved in June when shooters killed him on a Tampa street corner.

Kefauver's heart was in the right place Nolan guessed, but as far as any lasting changes were concerned, he'd have to do a whole lot more. And with a January deadline facing him, good luck with that.

CHAPTER 5

DAVE JORDAN'S family hadn't turned out in force to watch him graduate, but that was as he'd planned it, more or less.

His parents were on hand, of course, dressed to the nines and smiling in a way he hadn't seen them look at one another since he'd come back from the war a broken man. *My fault?* Dave asked himself, then put it out of mind. His sister couldn't make it, stuck at home with nearly-four-year-old Lucia running wild around the home she shared with husband Paulo. Paulo, for his part, was generally tied up managing his two print shops and seeking a location for the third he had in mind.

As for the other Giordanos, whose surname Dave's father had abandoned prior to college nearly half a century ago, Dave received a card and five C-notes from Uncle Carlo, who was swamped with work around his *ristorante* and with other things he only spoke about to Dave's father and maybe to his sons.

Dave hadn't bothered to invite his cousins Dominic and Angelo. They likely would've laughed it off, or if they'd come, wouldn't have fit in with the college crowd. Dave seldom saw them anymore, and they made no attempts to reach him, settling for holiday encounters or the rare family get-togethers, reminiscing over those who'd died.

It was enough to have his parents present, watching David graduate *summa cum laude,* in the top 5 percent of his class. Four years of study, and three more still waiting for him when he entered law school in the fall.

That part was covered, thankfully. His 3.96 GPA helped, together with a score of 179 on the Law School Admission Test in April. Thinking of Fiona, as he often did, Dave realized the LSAT was one thing she hadn't been encumbered by when she started her legal studies at Columbia. The test had been established one year after she began, in 1948, dreamed up by leaders of the year-old nonprofit Law School Admission Council.

Speaking of Fiona, she was also MIA from David's graduation, and he missed her more than any absent members of his dodgy family. He understood, of course: it was a Wednesday morning, and she couldn't take time off from working for the Legal Aid Society, handling both criminal and civil cases for Manhattan's indigents. From their brief and sporadic contacts, Dave knew she was swamped, often in court, habitually bringing files home to the small apartment he had never seen. On the occasions when their paths crossed nowadays, Dave sensed that she was torn between the reams of paperwork and pity for her clients on one hand and love of her chosen profession on the other.

Would *he* feel the same three years from now, after he'd passed the bar and entered private practice? Who, besides his parents—in their fifties now—would even care how Dave was getting by?

Fiona, for her part, was moving on, and good for her. She'd meet somebody sometime, if she hadn't yet, an up-and-coming lawyer who could make her happy, blessed with two good legs, his body not a pale patchwork of scars.

More power to her, Dave thought, as his row of graduates rose from their chairs and marched off toward the stage where their diplomas waited for them. Why in hell would someone with Fiona's looks and charm want to be saddled with a gimp?

Of course, she *had* sent him a card, and while it had no money tucked inside, she'd signed it "Love" and "XOX," for hugs and kisses. He'd called up to thank her for it, and they had agreed to meet up soon, as time allowed, maybe on neutral ground at Katz's Deli.

Call it mustard, mayo and pastrami, without any burden of commitment. Chalk it up as one more in their series of non-dates. Time would take care of separating them for good, Dave knew, but he wasn't inclined to jump the gun on that.

At least they weren't likely to meet in court—or meet at all, if Dave decided he should try his hand somewhere out west.

For now, he plastered on a smile and heard his name called, striding toward a future that was still obscure to him.

———

FBI HEADQUARTERS: June 2, 1951

ALOYSIUS GANTT SUSPECTED that the fucking Reds were out

to kill him. Not by undermining the United States, mind you, or toppling its government, but by afflicting him with headaches, heartburn, and no end to sour moods.

He'd been pursuing them for thirty-four years now, since he was twenty-one, and nothing ever seemed to change. The course of history and shifting times kept spitting out new radicals, while Gantt was slowing down. He wasn't the same youngster, relatively speaking, who had it out with public enemies and toasted victory in bars with sawdust on the floor. His sons were grown men now, involved in government careers at his suggestion, and Gantt wondered now if that had been his worst mistake.

Screw it. More Reds waited for him to find them, everywhere he looked.

And some, like Judith Coplon, were about to wriggle off the hook. Convicted twice, facing an aggregate of twenty years in prison, she'd appealed both verdicts, and in June, D.C.'s Court of Appeals had overturned them. While declaring that her "guilt was plain," the three-judge panel found that wiretaps violated Coplon's right to private consultation with her lawyer, and the Bureau's failure to obtain a warrant prior to arresting her was yet another fatal flaw.

Would Justice bring her up for trial again? What was the point, when all their evidence had been thrown out?

The Alger Hiss problem was something else again. In January, his request for a new hearing on his failed appeal had been denied, and the Supreme Court refused to hear his case in March. Ten days after that loss, he entered the federal pen at Lewisberg, Pennsylvania, a medium-security lockup 100 miles west of Manhattan.

Case closed? Not so fast.

Hiss's lawyers were crafting a retrial motion that had

Bureau headquarters in a dither. They hadn't filed it yet, but Alan Belmont, newly appointed head of the Domestic Intelligence Division, penned a memo reminding all and sundry that the case rested primarily on matching questioned documents to a typewriter Hiss once owned but never personally used, leaving his wife to punch its keys.

And that I.D., as Gantt well knew, was total crap. He'd personally been in charge of faking up the Woodstock typewriter—Exhibit UUU at trial—that had convicted Hiss. He hadn't done the soldering himself, of course, but if shit hit the fan eventually, most of it would land on him, while Edgar Hoover, Tolson, and the rest pled injured innocence.

Deniability was everything.

At least the A-bomb spying case had gone without a hitch. On January 31, a federal grand jury returned a superseding indictment, charging the Rosenbergs, David and Ruth Greenglass, Morton Sobell, and Anatoli Yatskov with espionage, a capital crime. Eight days later, the Joint Committee on Atomic Energy met secretly with AEC Chairman Gordon Dean and prosecutor Myles Lane, also form the Hiss trial. Dean declared, "It looks as though Julius Rosenberg is the kingpin of a very large ring, and if there is any way of breaking him by having the shadow of a death penalty over him, we want to do it."

Ohio Senator John Bricker asked, "You mean before the trial?"

To which Dean had replied, "*After* the trial."

U.S. Attorney Lane agreed that Julius was a "keystone to a lot of other potential espionage agents," but admitted that his case against Ethel was "not too strong," in that Dave Greenglass still denied his sister's guilt. Lane hoped facing the chair would crack Julius, but failing that, he said, "If we can convict his wife too, and give her a stiff sentence of twenty-five to thirty years, that combination may serve to make this fellow disgorge and give us information on these other people." Their primary hope, Lane allowed, was drawing "the strongest judge possible" at trial.

That was Irving Kaufman, ex-aide to Tom Clark and a jurist who idolized Edgar Hoover. He was also an old family friend of backup prosecutor Roy Cohn, who hadn't yet met Joe McCarthy. On February 7, Chairman Dean advised Justice that he'd spoken privately to Kaufman—a clear violation of the ABA's ban on *ex parte* communications—and that Kaufman "is prepared to impose death if the evidence warrants."

But death for whom?

David and Ruth Greenglass strengthened the prosecution's case on February 24, when they revised their former testimony, telling G-men Ethel *was* involved in spying after all. It must've slipped their minds before. As a result of that "re-interview," Ruth saw her charges dropped, proof positive that squealing can pay off.

Trial convened on March 6, Judge Kaufman granting a motion to sever Yatskov's case, along with that of David Greenglass, who had already confessed. Agents caught up with fugitive William Perl nine days later, jailing him on an espionage charge. The prosecution's case included Elizabeth Bentley. She'd never met the defendants, but somehow identified Ethel's husband as the same "Julius" who'd phoned her several times in the early Forties, passing info to her then-lover and handler, Russian agent Jacob Golos.

The defense called no one but the Rosenbergs as witnesses, and neither helped their case. Both denied any guilt but pled the Fifth Amendment when asked about their politics and CPUSA membership. They came across as cold, contemptuous, despite their situation and long separation from the children they presumably adored. Jurors convicted all three remaining defendants on March 29. Sentencing Julius and Ethel to death a week later, Judge Kaufman blamed them both for spying *and* for the ongoing slaughter in Korea. "I consider your crime worse than murder," he said, then relented a bit, handing Morton Sobell a thirty-sentence, Dave Greenglass fifteen. Harry Gold, who pled guilty in July of 1950, was already doing thirty years.

Reactions to the verdicts were immediate. A National Committee to Secure Justice in the Rosenberg Case organized, its members ranging from outspoken Reds to playwright Jean Cocteau, Albert Einstein, and Nobel Prize-winning chemist Harold Urey. Critics blamed anti-Semitism for the death sentences, and Nobel Prize-winning philosopher Jean-Paul Sartre called the trial "a legal lynching which smears with blood a whole nation."

At Justice, the response was somewhat different. No one admitted any doubts about the jury's verdict, but Chief Hoover and Attorney General McGrath still craved confessions from the Rosenbergs. To that end, they prepared a schedule whereby each defendant would be questioned by a rabbi on the eve of execution. If they told all, Ethel at least might win a presidential commutation. As appeals began, expected to drag on for months or years, all they could do was wait.

Like me, Gantt thought. *And going nowhere fast.*

He'd thought about retiring at age sixty, five years down the road, but that made him wonder what he would do without the Bureau in his life.

If he could only answer that...

———

HARLEM: August 4, 1951

THE FIRST SHOT sounded like a car backfiring, but no vehicles were passing and you shouldn't hear a muffled scream after a backfire. When the second round went off, there could be no mistaking it, or how the scream was suddenly cut off.

His second day walking the beat as a probationary cop, and Payton Sawyer was already in the shit.

"Get to the callbox on the corner, Rookie. Phone it in right now."

The order came from Ace Dupree his training officer, a Negro sergeant who'd been on the Harlem beat for fifteen years. His parents hadn't named him Ace, but that was what the other cops called him, a few white assholes smirking that it meant he was the "ace of spades."

It was Dupree's job to teach Payton what he called "the shit they never say at the academy," lessons on how to get along with people in the ghetto, as if Sawyer hadn't done exactly that his whole damned life.

He began absorbing Dupree's pearls of wisdom yesterday, a Friday, fresh from twenty weeks of formal training, and he still had eighteen months to go before he finished his probationary period.

That is, if he survived his second day.

The corner callbox was exactly that: a metal box, once red, now weathered to a kind of pink, bolted to a utility pole at the corner of West 136th and Lenox, just south of the block called "Strivers Row." A sticker on the dented door, open to anyone in an emergency, had once read "CALL POLICE FROM HERE," but some vandal had painted "FUCK YALL" over that.

At least the phone was still inside, not stolen like so many others, and when Sawyer hoisted the receiver he could hear a dial tone hum. Before an operator answered from the 28th Precinct, however, more gunfire rang out, and Payton dropped the phone, spinning to face that sound.

Dupree was down, unmoving on the sidewalk, peaked cap lying to his left, blood soaking through his short-sleeved navy shirt. He'd drawn his gun but hadn't had a chance to use it when two stickup men—a salt-and-pepper team, one white, one black—burst out of the drugstore they'd just robbed and cut him down.

Payton's mind went into autopilot, right hand dropping to his new department-issue Smith & Wesson Model 10. It cleared his holster as one of the shooters—Whitey—turned and spotted him, raising a sawed-off twelve-gauge pump. The shooter was about to grin, it looked like, but he lost it when the Smith & Wesson bucked in Payton's firm two-handed grip and drilled his forehead with a .38 Special from twenty-odd feet out.

Whitey dropped, stone dead before he hit the cracked pavement, then Blackie was turning, calling someone a motherfucker, leveling an automatic that looked like an army Colt. Payton fired two more rounds, center of mass, and knocked the second bandit over backwards, sprawling so that his head kept the drugstore's door from closing.

Sawyer's mind was slowing down now, asking, *What the fuck was that?*

He reached back with his left hand for the dangling telephone receiver, lifted it and heard a female operator asking him, "Is anybody there? Do you have an emergency?"

Somewhere, he found his voice and answered back, "Probationary Officer Sawyer, badge number thirteen thirty-one." Somehow, the codes he'd learned at the academy were clear in mind. "I've got a ten-thirteen, shots fired, officer down. Repeat, officer down. I need an ambulance, a supervisor, and a shooting team at West 136th and Lenox Avenue. Repeat!"

She gave it back to him, breathless, and told him to stand by; too late for that, he was already racing toward Dupree, crouching beside him, trying to avoid a spreading lake of blood as he checked for a pulse below one ear and got nothing. He didn't bother with the punks he'd shot, except to kick their guns beyond the reach of lifeless hands.

A crowd had started gathering as Payton stuck his head inside the drugstore's entrance, still propped open by the black guy he'd gunned down. He spotted two more bodies crumpled on blood-stained linoleum. One of them, a man, had nearly lost his face to buckshot, but Sawyer knew Leon Tate, the pharmacist who'd run the place since Payton was a kid. The girl lying beside Tate in a ventilated smock still wore a nametag—"MARCY"—that would make her the cashier.

There seemed no point in checking them for pulses. Neither Tate no Marcy seemed to be breathing, and anyway, the wail of sirens told him help was on the way.

First on the scene was a lieutenant Payton hadn't met, red-faced and paunchy in his too-tight uniform, one gold bar on each collar tab, his badge a starburst pattern, unlike a patrolman's shield. He stared at Ace Dupree a moment, scowling, then pinned Sawyer with his gimlet eyes and moved to face him with the dead thugs' guns lying between their polished shoes.

"So, tell me, Rookie."

Sawyer told him what had happened, finishing each sentence with a "Sir." Before he finished, two more squad cars arrived, disgorging Irish types in blue, one of them with a sergeant's chevrons on his sleeve. The ambulance came next, from Harlem Hospital on Lenox, then an NYPD shooting team, two white detectives, who instructed Sawyer to go through it all again.

While he repeated what there was to say—not much— another car pulled up, this one unmarked but plainly a police vehicle. Its lone occupant got out and cut in line before the two-man shooting team could start to question Sawyer. They deferred to him immediately, and no wonder: his white shirt, gold eagles on his collar tabs, pegged him as an inspector, five steps down the ladder of command from Chief of the Department.

"You took care of this?" he asked Payton.

"Yes, Sir."

"Your second day on the beat, from what I hear?"

"Yes, Sir." But how in hell had he learned that so fast?

"Sorry about your partner, Rookie. But you made it right."

It didn't feel that way, but Payton bobbed his head once. "Yes, Sir."

"We've been after these two fuckers for a month of Sundays," the inspector said, still not giving his name. "You've closed the book on fifteen stickups, maybe some we still don't know about, and three more homicides."

"Six now," Payton corrected him, and nearly choked on it. "Two more inside the drugstore."

"Shit. You've had a busy day, Rookie. You know the drill on shootings, right? They tell you that at the Academy?"

"Yes, Sir."

"You'll be on desk work for a day or two, but don't get used to it. A deal like this, there won't be any trouble from the shooting team."

"I hope not, Sir."

"I *know* not. When they clear you, come and see me at the 28th. I want to talk to you about a fork in your career path."

"Fork, Sir?" Payton hoped he wasn't getting forked himself.

"You ever heard of Boss?"

"Yes, Sir."

Sawyer knew it was an acronym for NYPD's Bureau of Special Service Investigations—technically abbreviated BOSSI, though most cops dropped the "I," only a few smart alecks calling it "Bossy." That name had been imposed in 1946, but the detachment had been formed as the Italian Squad in 1905, renamed the Neutrality Squad ten years later, changed again to the Radical Squad in 1923, then to the Alien Squad in 1931. Some cops and reporters called it the "Red Squad," for its emphasis on shadowing subversives.

"Something tells me you might have a flair for what we do," said the inspector. "Not the gun work, necessarily, although we need men who can drop the hammer when they have to. So, come see me when you're off the desk, unless you love walking a beat."

"No, Sir. I mean, yes, Sir! I'll absolutely be there."

"Good."

Not a promotion—not yet, anyway—but getting posted to Intelligence would be a huge reward for someone only two days on the street.

As the inspector turned back toward his car, Payton said, "Um, excuse me, Sir. I didn't get your name."

"Well, shit. I oughta have a card here, somewhere."

He produced one from a pocket, handing it to Sawyer. Payton read "Inspector Patrick Flannery, NYPD" above a phone number.

"You'll definitely hear from me, Inspector Flannery," said Payton to the Irish cop's retreating back.

Before the unmarked car had time to pull away, the two-man shooting team was back in Sawyer's face, both of them frowning at him as one of them said, "Okay, Rookie. Let's hear your version of what happened here."

————

Serpukhov, Moscow Oblast: August 10, 1951

Leonid Babin drank his vodka straight, and he was working on his third glass at the moment, still not feeling it. He left Moscow for a long weekend at his dacha, deserted now except for him, a brief but welcome getaway from turmoil in the capital.

His mind turned toward young Stefan as it did approximately twice an hour these days. The boy was nearly four years old and presently en route to Canada via Albania, and on from Canada to the United States, his journey ending in New Jersey, where adoptive parents Mark and Isabella Barnes were waiting to receive him. It was out of Babin's hands now, but he wouldn't rest until he got the coded bulletin announcing Stefan's safe arrival in Trenton.

Meanwhile, more changes at the MGB preoccupied Babin during his waking hours, and it must be said he didn't get much sleep of late.

First thing, there had been "Operation North," involving deportation of Jehovah's Witnesses to exile in Siberia. There had been few, if any, in the USSR prior to annexation of the Baltic States, but now they numbered 3,048 families—9,389 persons in all—every one of them believing Armageddon might come any day, relieving them of fealty to any earthly government that wielded power on behalf of "Babylon the Great." Stalin approved their deportation in November 1950, and rubber-stamped the plan detailed by Viktor Abakumov in February. When all was said and done, each family in transit was allowed to keep 330 pounds of private property to get them settled in the East. Remarkably, the exodus had been accomplished without incident, conducted overnight between March 31 and April 1.

Next up came a continuation of the so-called Doctor's Plot, and that had set foxes amidst the MGB henhouse. First, in March, Deputy Minister of State Security Mikhail Ryumin told Minister Abakumov that an alleged Zionist, Dr. Yakov Etinger, had committed deliberate malpractice to murder prominent Party members Alexander Shcherbakov in 1945 and Andrei Zhdanov in '48. Abakumov attended Etinger's fatal interrogation but came away unconvinced of the plot. Worse yet—for Abakumov—he fired Ryumin for embezzling MGB funds and killing Etinger. Ryumin huddled with Georgy Malenkov, then sent a note to Stalin saying that Abakumov had murdered Etinger to hide a Jewish plot against Mother Russia. On July 4, a commission led by Malenkov dismissed Abakumov for concealing the mythical plot and creating "a bad situation in the MGB." Arrested ten days later, Abakumov was tortured and accused of concealing the "criminal Jewish underground." Surprisingly, while most of his Jewish subordinates were purged from the MGB's ranks, Abakumov himself still survived in prison.

His successor, Deputy Director Sergei Ogoltsov, had a brief and undistinguished tenure as acting head of the MGB from July 14 to August 9, when Stalin named Semyon Ignatyev to lead the reeling agency. The son of Ukrainian peasants and an engineer by training, Ignatyev continued investigation of the nonexistent Doctor's Plot, fueling another wave of Russian anti-Semitism under Lavrentiy Beria's watchful eye. Babin did his best to stay out of the limelight while suspicion spread.

Still hanging fire was the Mingrelian affair, another fabricated case concocted to purge Communist Party members whose roots were traceable to Samegrelo Province in western Georgia. Stalin himself initiated that lethal farce, claiming those targeted were members of a "Mingrelian nationalist ring" seeking independence from the USSR, collaborating with Georgian émigrés in Paris. That spelled bad news for Beria himself, whose "Georgian Mafia" still troubled Stalin. There had been no executions yet, but accusations of conspiracy had driven most Mingrelians from government positions, some into the Gulag, while more vanished into exile.

Babin watched that chaos from the sidelines, kept his nose out of it when he could, and concentrated on his son's transit to the United States. With luck, his vengeance against Edgar Hoover's FBI would bear grim fruit in time—but would he live to see it realized?

————

MANHATTAN: *November 20, 1951*

GREG JORDAN SAT at home and watched his TV set, like countless others citywide, caught up in Senator Kefauver's live road show. The panel had been slated to dissolve on January 31, but an entranced public swamped Congress with letters clamoring for more, so the deadline had been extended to September 1, with fresh appropriations added to the pot.

In New Orleans, the committee heard how criminals tried to silence one reformer with the offer of a new church building, while Sheriff Frank Clancy's ex-wife said he'd banked $50,000 in six years, while legally earning $300 monthly. Clancy and his gambler buddies wouldn't talk, earning contempt citations, although "Diamond Jim" Moran got in a plug for his casino-restaurant, which dished up "food for kings." Carlos Marcello pled the Fifth Amendment fifteen times, prompting Kefauver to label him "one of the worst criminals in the country."

February took the panel to Detroit, learning that mobsters under Harry Bennett doubled as "security" for Henry Ford. Otherwise, the men in charge of Motown— Peter Licavoli, "Black Bill" Tocco, the Perrone brothers and company, either blew town or else relied on the advice of their attorneys to keep silent. St. Louis hit a snag when gambler James Carroll angrily refused to let himself be tele-vised. Kefauver, preening in the spotlight, smiled and answered, "Television is a recognized medium of public information. I refuse to permit the arrangements for this hearing to be dictated by a witness." Still, that case was on its way to court, with warnings issued to Kefauver by the ABA.

Then it was back in March to Gotham for a grand finale of the circus. Bill O'Dwyer, safe in Mexico and shielded by diplomatic immunity, volunteered to testify, then suddenly took ill and had to put it off. When Frank Costello took the ex-mayor's place, he balked at having TV cameras in his face, so they were focused on his nervous hands while Frank sat fidgeting, mopping his sweaty forehead with a handkerchief, and finally stormed out, pursued by a contempt citation.

Witness Virginia Hill proved far from camera-shy, arriving in a mink cape, silk gloves, and a hat to die for, spilling tidbits about Bugsy Siegel, Charley Luciano, and a list of others, always stopping just in time to claim she'd never meddled in their business. She was vague on where her money came from—some of it from "friends in Mexico"—but under pressure, she turned waspish. "Do you really want to know?" she challenged Senator Tobey. Assured that he was serious, Virginia sneered, "Because I'm the best cocksucker in town." Greg couldn't vouch for that, himself, but he admired her style. Stalking out of the hearing room on Foley Square, she'd decked one female journalist and told the rest, "I hope an A-bomb falls on all of you!"

The day after Kefauver turned up as a guest on "What's My Line?," O'Dwyer finally felt well enough to testify, but that was a mistake. He grudgingly admitted errors in the handling of Albert Anastasia's case, accused Senator Tobey of accepting cash from "mysterious forces" during his last campaign, then winged off back to Mexico for a siesta in the sun. The panel's third interim report, published in April, sketched a grim picture of crime in Gotham, unfettered by interference from the mayor or governor. No great surprise: they pulled that off without a word concerning Operation Underworld.

Kefauver's visit coincided with dramatic changes in New York's Five Families. Gatano Gagliano died from natural causes in February, succeeded by underboss Tommy Lucchese, and Vincent Mangano disappeared in April. Two days later, brother Phil turned up dead in a swamp near Jamaica Bay, Queens, putting Al Anastasia in charge with support from Frank Costello, while Vito Genovese gnashed his teeth in envy.

It wasn't just the *Cosa Nostra* changing though. By May Day, Kefauver fired the FBN's George White as unreliable, then lost all but two members of his legal and investigative staff as they resigned *en masse*. Hiring a dozen new lawyers took time, as did selecting twenty new investigators from sources including NYPD, Maryland's State Police, and Treasury's Alcohol Tax Unit. Justice grudgingly pitched in a file clerk, while Hoover's FBI remained aloof. Harry Anslinger shrugged off White's dismissal and replaced him with another famous narc, Charles Siragusa.

And it couldn't be denied that leaders of the Syndicate were taking heat. In May, jurors convicted Joe Adonis of gambling and he pulled two years in New Jersey State Prison. Four months later, New York prosecutors charged Meyer Lansky with the same offense in Saratoga Springs. Still, poor Willie Moretti got the worst of it, dubbed unreliable and loopy after his comic performance for Kefauver. Persons unknown slew Willie on October 4, while he was waiting to meet Jerry Lewis and Dean Martin at a restaurant in Cliffside Park—a mercy killing, in the words of *la Commissione*, to spare him further suffering from tertiary syphilis.

Before that bloodletting, on August 31, the Kefauver Committee published its final report, 11,000 pages packed with testimony from 600 witnesses in fourteen major cities. The report included twenty-nine recommendations for federal, state, and local authorities: "constant vigilance" and further investigation; creation of a National Crime Coordinating Council and a racket squad at Justice (both opposed by Edgar Hoover and Attorney General McGrath); plus a list of suggestions for battling drug addiction that included a hopeless global ban on growing opium.

When the smoke cleared, Kefauver's results were modest. The Revenue Act of 1951, effective on November 1, levied wagering excise and occupational tax on illegal gamblers, while Tom Dewey finally ordered New York's State Crime Commission to investigate the Mob-owned waterfront. Beyond that, television was the big winner, claiming 30 million viewers—one in every five Americans— watched Kefauver's broadcasts. A Gallup poll listed Kefauver among the year's most admired individuals, along with General MacArthur, Albert Einstein, and Pope Pius XII.

And which fool was it who'd proclaimed crime didn't pay?

———

SAIGON: December 10, 1951

COLBY GANTT HAD NEVER BEEN to Vietnam before, but after spending months in Burma during World War Two, it almost felt like coming home. Saigon's name was derived from native designation of the kapok trees that were abundant in the area. Western travel books sometimes referred to Saigon as "the Paris of the East," but having seen both cities now, Gantt found no rational comparison.

Simply another Asian capital immersed in vice, surrounded by a war that never seemed to end.

Korea's seesaw battle for supremacy continued. "Operation Killer" gained some ground for the UN in February, and "Operation Ripper" seized more in March, before President Truman relieved General MacArthur of command in April, replacing him with General Matthew Ridgway. Reds took advantage of the switch and launched their spring offensive two weeks later, stopping just north of Seoul. Moscow surprised everyone in June, calling for armistice talks. August witnessed the Rhee regime's worst scandal yet, with National Defense Corps General Kim Yungun and five aides shot for corruption after they stole their soldiers' pay, leaving an estimated 70,000 conscripts to starve or freeze on a three-week death march through the blighted countryside. Rhee tried to cover that by asking soldiers from the British Commonwealth to leave Korea, claiming that London was "sabotaging the brave American effort to liberate fully and unify my unhappy nation." As for America, come November General Ridgway announced an end to offensive operations in favor of "active defense."

Laos, meanwhile, was on the brink of its own civil war. French troops returned to claim their former colony in January 1946, resisted by Prince Souphanouvong with Việt Minh support. A native Red movement, the Pathet Lao ("Lao Nation") soon joined the fight, backed by the Indochinese Communist Party. By October 1951, the French-backed Royal Laotian Army had 5,000 soldiers in the field, while members of the French Foreign Legion—including some former SS men—trained paratroopers and waged guerrilla warfare independently.

Still, Vietnam was where the action lay right now, hence Colby's presence in Saigon. In January, 20,000 Việt Minh soldiers under General Võ Nguyên Giáp stormed French positions in the Red River Delta, stretching from Hanoi to the Gulf of Tonkin. Two months later, only naval gunfire and air strikes kept Giáp from seizing Mạo Khê near Haiphong. Giáp lost 10,000 soldiers in June, attacking the De Lattre Line southeast of Hanoi while France obtained another handout from the White House in September, yet

Giáp battled on. By yesterday morning, French casualties in Vietnam officially topped 90,000.

Things were just as hectic for the CIA at home, where OSS veteran Frank Wisner had become the Agency's second Deputy Director of Plans in August. Ostensibly created to resolve conflicts between the Office of Special Operations (OSO) and the Office of Policy Coordination (OPC), the Directorate of Plans was also dabbling in covert actions that included recruiting foreign agents and continuing experiments in chemical and biological warfare.

In the latter realm, between September 1950 and February 1951, some genius released the bacterium *Serratia marascens* into San Francisco's general population. Typically seen in hospitals a result of catheter-related problems, the rare bacterium infected eleven patients at one Frisco hospital, prompting publication of an article in the *Journal of the American Medical Association*.

More secretive, but no less risky, was Operation BLUE-BIRD, renamed Operation ARTICHOKE in August 1951, forging ahead with studies on the creation of amnesia, hypnotic couriers, and unwitting assassins. Club-footed chemist and poison expert Sydney Gottlieb had joined the Agency in April, heading the Office of Technical Service, soon earning nicknames as the "Black Sorcerer" and "Dirty Trickster." In typical OTS experiments, subjects were driven to a remote safe house, subjected to interrogation followed by whiskey and two grams of Phenobarbital, which induced sleep. Subsequent interrogations were conducted under intravenous chemicals, with the goal of inducing false memories and implanting "trigger words" for future action.

Gantt read one OTS document from September, titled "SI and H experimentation" for *sleep induction* and *hypnosis*. It described the case of two women put through the

ARTICHOKE mill, ordered to build bombs in a hypnotic state and awake with no memory of their actions, until an unknown person dubbed "Jim" telephoned the safe house, engaging each subject in mundane conversation and dropping a code word, whereupon each subject passed into an SI trance with eyes wide-open, seeming normal to any observer. Each then went to meet Jim at a separate location, carrying her bomb inside a briefcase. When Jim met her and pronounced the trigger phrase "New York," each subject readily displayed her bomb, instructing Jim on how to set its timer and conceal it in a standard office desk.

Another ARTICHOKE document, dated December 3, described the Agency enlistment of a psychiatrist "reported to be an authority on electric shock." His specialty, it said, was using electroconvulsive therapy, not to relieve mental illness such as schizophrenia, but rather to induce amnesia.

Meanwhile, George White, on loan from Harry Anslinger's FBN, found a new wife for himself in Gotham. She seemed to adore him, ignoring his numerous quirks, and all was bliss in their spacious apartment on West 12th Street in Greenwich Village, visited by a parade of politicians, diplomats, lawmen, artists and writers. Presumably, the second Mrs. White knew nothing of her hubby's secret life, including LSD experiments conducted on the CIA's behalf.

Where would it lead? Gantt didn't know and wasn't terribly concerned, as long as it contributed to national security and to his own advancement in the Agency. The key, as always, would be plausible deniability in case some piece of covert shit should hit the fan.

Above all else, he couldn't have it blowing back on him.

———

FEDERAL BUREAU of Narcotics Manhattan Field Office: December 13, 1951

THESE WERE DAMNED tough days to be a narc; worse yet to be a Negro in the service of a white man's government. Ike Sawyer knew that very well and had for thirty-five years now, but it was hammered home anew each day when he reported for his job or opened up a newspaper.

George White served as a perfect case in point. The Kefauver Committee dismissed him on two counts—for pissing off the president by linking him to Kansas City mobsters, then writing a memo that suggested Tom Dewey was paid for letting Lucky Luciano out of prison. In retaliation, Dewey briefly banished White from Gotham, but while that ended White's hope of a promotion to serve Harry Anslinger as district supervisor of New York, George came out smelling like a rose, regardless. Anslinger appointed him as Boston's district supervisor, although White was rarely in Beantown, preferring to assist the CIA with its *sub rosa* drug experiments. Before leaving Manhattan, he hooked up with Corsican Pierre Lafitte to bust a drug ring run by Joe Orsini, alias "Dornay."

It was hilarious how things always worked out for White simply because he was...well, *white.*

One white man who'd run out of luck was Waxey Gordon—but, of course, he was Jew and three-time loser when FBN agents arrested him up for selling heroin in August 1951. Gordon had been paroled from Leavenworth in 1940, stripped of cash and property, still owing Uncle Sam $2.5 million in overdue taxes. He'd gone to San Francisco, peddling a "revolutionary type of cleaning fluid" until cops jailed him for vagrancy, but he raised $10 bail and run back to New York. Reporters pestered him, but he insisted, "Waxey Gordon is dead. From now on, it's Irving Wexler, salesman."

Of course, he didn't specify *what* he was selling.

Gordon was sixty-three years old when Agent John Cottone nabbed him for delivering $6,300 worth of smack to an informer. Bursting into tears, Waxey begged, "Please Johnny, don't arrest me. Don't take me in for junk. Let me run, then shoot me." Instead, he was tried as a four-time loser, drawing a sentence of twenty-five years to life at Sing Sing.

At sentencing, Judge Francis Valente told Waxey, "You have demonstrated repeatedly that there is no crime or racket to which you would not resort in order to make a dollar. Your latest and most dastardly offense is typical of your hostility, and it should bring down the curtain on your parasitical and lawless life."

Thanks to Gordon's arrest and the Kefauver Committee's suggestions, Harry Truman signed the Boggs Act in November, amending the Narcotic Drugs Import and Export Act of 1922 with minimum sentencing standards. Henceforth, dope peddlers would be fined $2,000 for a first offense, imprisoned for two to five years, with five to ten years for a second conviction, and ten to fifteen for each subsequent charge. Perspective skewed, as usual, Congress imposed a $20,000 fine plus two to ten years for a *first* conviction on marijuana possession.

Ike could live with that, although the gross discrepancy rankled. Conversely, when he thought about the state of Negroes halfway through the present century, he wasn't sure how anyone could live with that in silence.

According to Tuskegee University, there'd only been one lynching during 1951—a Negro citrus worker whom Florida

Klansmen murdered "by mistake"—but headlines proved the plague of racism was far more deadly. In May, Reverend Joseph Mann was doused with gasoline and torched in Norfolk, Virginia, during a reunion of Confederate soldiers. He'd lived two days in agony, while cops dismissed his immolation as "a male lovers' spat gone bad."

In July, 4,000 white residents of Cicero, Illinois, rioted to bar a black family from their newly rented apartment while police did squat. In Dixie, the Southern Regional Council reported bombings of at least a dozen Negro homes this year, and a Louisiana sheriff's deputy had slain one of three black men who'd filed a lawsuit to obtain their voting rights in St. Landry Parish. The cop claimed victim John Mitchell was "acting rowdy" at a juke joint, forcing him to kill Mitchell in self-defense. Needless to say, the case pending in federal court was merely a coincidence.

One theoretical bright spot on the horizon was the UN's Convention on the Prevention and Punishment of the Crime of Genocide, ratified in December 1948, finally taking force in January 1951. One of the first cases presented came from the Detroit-based Civil Rights Congress, a 237-page petition titled *We Charge Genocide: The Crime of Government Against the Negro People*. It recited chapter and verse of the Jim Crow legislation, disenfranchisement, lynching, police brutality and murder, but Ike knew the odds of getting anywhere with that were on a par with the proverbial snowball in Hell.

Nor did he see much hope in the Kefauver panel's wish list for the eradication of narcotics. It was easy to sit down in Washington, advising other agencies to share information and promote narcotics education, but getting them to move was like pushing a glacier uphill, wearing handcuffs and shackles. Every move involved a pissing contest, and the players wound up getting nowhere.

Four more years until retirement, Ike thought. *Jesus, let me last that long.*

———

FBI HEADQUARTERS: December 22, 1951

THREE DAYS LEFT TIL CHRISTMAS, and for once Declan O'Hara had his shopping done on time. He'd bought a pair of ruby earrings and a matching necklace he could ill afford for Abigail, but what the hell. At fifty-six and still in harness, it was time to live a little, right? Before it was too late.

For Fiona, he'd acquired the brand-new fourth edition of *Black's Law Dictionary,* after asking what she'd like and figuring her basic casebooks would be readily available from Legal Aid. Still not exactly thrilled to have her living in New York, Declan was proud of her achievements so far and expected many more.

For Nolan, being practical, he'd packed and shipped a Colt Commander, shortened by a half-inch from the M1911 Declan carried til it got too heavy for him, but with all the older weapon's knockdown power plus spare magazines. He hoped that Nolan wouldn't need it, but the way things had been heating up in Florida, you never knew.

In Washington, things were about the same. Chief Hoover expanded the Bureau's Sex Deviates Program in June, with a new uniform policy for handling complaints of "perversion" among federal employees. All the sound and fury made sure no one looked too closely at himself and Clyde Tolson, while Hoover did his best to purge the government of "lavender" from lowly clerks to White House aides.

Where witch-hunts were concerned, there was a new sideshow in town: Pat McCarran's Senate Internal Security Subcommittee, created in December 1950 so Nevada's blotchy-faced yahoo could steal his share of HUAC's limelight. It had started by investigating shopworn claims against the Institute of Pacific Relations, smearing Owen Lattimore and company again, while trotting out the usual hired "experts." Liz Bentley, looking older than her forty-three years thanks to booze, recalled that Red ex-lover Jacob Golos warned her to avoid the IPR, saying it was "as red as a rose, and you shouldn't touch it with a ten-foot pole." Lou Budenz, nice and comfy with the $70,000 he'd banked as a professional witness, agreed that the CPUSA had cautioned him against involvement with the IPR, saying that its "galaxy of communists" made it too ripe a target. McCarran wound up calling the IPR "a specialized political flypaper in its attractive power for Communists," apparently so tempting that subversives must be turned away for lack of openings.

The same hysteria continued hounding William Remington. Once again, when Remington faced trial in late December 1950, Liz Bentley and William's ex-wife Ann were first in line to label him not only a Red, but also an accomplished Russian spy. Granted, neither of them could recall specific cases but coached by prosecutor Roy Cohn, Bentley could provide details of Remington's half-baked invention to produce synthetic rubber out of garbage. Defense attorneys pointed out that John Brunni—foreman of the grand jury that had indicted Remington—had a side deal to co-author Bentley's memoirs, but jurors let that pass, convicting Remington of perjury in March. Judge Gregory Noonan slapped him with the maximum: five years.

For all of that, the big noise in D.C. was Joe McCarthy, still chasing targets who had been exonerated last year by the Tydings Committee, branching out from there to chastise Democrats for "twenty years of treason," focused now on Harry Truman, but the president fired back as was his want, calling Tail-Gunner Joe "the best asset the Kremlin has" for sowing chaos on the home front. Secretary of Defense George Marshall was McCarthy's latest target, blasted from the Senate floor and in the pages of a book ghostwritten for McCarthy, titled *America's Retreat From Victory*, that blamed Marshall for "a conspiracy so immense and an infamy so black as to dwarf any previous venture in the history of man." When Truman fired Douglas MacArthur for insubordination, Joe claimed the dismissal was planned during late-night sessions when Reds "had time to get the President cheerful" on bourbon and Bénédictine, opining that "the son of a bitch should be impeached."

Aside from cursing Joe at any given opportunity, Truman had gone one better, naming former target Philip Jessup as a delegate to the UN, and when the Senate failed to approve him, Truman circumvented them by making it an open-ended "interim appointment" as ambassador-at-large.

Meanwhile, from coast to coast grand juries handed down Smith Act indictments against dozens of "second-tier" CPUSA leaders. They wisely waited until June 4, when the Supreme Court affirmed the first eleven 1949 convictions by a vote of seven-to-two, in *Dennis v. the United States*. Dissenter Hugo Black expressed his hope that "in calmer times, when present pressures, passions and fears subside, this or some later Court will restore First Amendment liberties to the high preferred place where they belong in a free society," but that was just a daydream here and now. Two weeks after the *Dennis* ruling, seventeen defendants were indicted in Manhattan. August saw six charged in Pittsburgh, six in Maryland, and seven more in far-off Honolulu.

Only yesterday, another twelve were slapped with charges in L.A.

As the fresh deluge of indictments spread, there was old business to resolve from the original convictions. The defense attorneys all served jail time, while New Jersey and New York disbarred Abe Isserman and Harry Sacher. Four of their clients skipped bail, posted by the Civil Rights Congress, whose leaders faced their own grand jury in July. Grilled by U.S. Attorney Irving Saypol—hailed in *Time* as "the nation's number one legal hunter of top Communists"—CRC President and mystery novelist Dashiell Hammett pled the Fifth Amendment, repeating that performance later before HUAC, which earned him a contempt citation, packed off for six months' toilet scrubbing at a federal lockup in West Virginia.

As a result, the CRC refused to post bail for the second-tier defendants, who were also running short of lawyers as defense attorneys felt the heat and shied away from representing Reds.

With or without counsel, defendants faced the stable of hired "experts" that now seemed obligatory, chief among them Bentley, Budenz, and Harvey Matusow. Harvey's latest triumph, prior to going on the courtroom circuit, was defaming folksinger Pete Seeger, whose "Goodnight, Irene" topped the charts for thirteen weeks last year. Seeger's offense, according to Matusow, had been leading People's Songs, a group supporting Henry Wallace back in '48. According to Matusow, People's Songs employed 126 Reds—a neat trick, since it only had 100 employees.

A second trial at Gotham's Foley Square led off the latest inquisition, its defendants including CPUSA National Committee members Elizabeth Gurley Flynn and Trinidadian immigrant Claudia Jones, already jailed and facing deportation on a 1950 Smith Act conviction. Aside from being Reds, both women were renowned as feminists and advocates for birth control, a double no-no for conservatives. All were branded as conspirators with the eleven Party leaders formerly convicted. Polish-born defendant Victor Jerome also faced trial for the "overt act" or writing a pamphlet titled *Grasp the Weapon of Culture.*

Pittsburgh's Red half-dozen included CPUSA National Committee member and district organizer Steve Nelson, born Stjepan Mesaros in his native Croatia. Others included state organizer Irving Weissman, district board members William Albertson and James Dolsen, Party treasurer Benjamin Carethers, plus county chairman and "steel organizer" Andrew Onda, facing trial sometime next year.

With Baltimore, L.A. and Honolulu in the mix, it added up to five big trials and doubtless more to come, all followed by a string of long-winded appeals, while taxpayers picked up the tab.

What were they getting for their money?

Declan realized he didn't have a damned idea.

———

FBI Field Office, Los Angeles: December 26, 1951

Devon Gantt glanced at the Timex watch he received for Christmas from his wife Camille and saw he'd only spent an hour at his desk so far.

Time flies, my ass, he thought.

A fun fact no one gave a shit about: when Thomas Olsen bought the Waterbury Clock Company ten years ago, he changed the name to Timex, not because it manufactured watches, but to merge the title of *Time* magazine with Kleenex, first invented by the Japanese around the end of World War One.

And what was Olsen thinking when he tumbled out of bed that morning? Was he three sheets to the wind?

Around one-quarter of the G-men in L.A. had booked vacation time today, stretching the celebration with their families, but Devon took advantage of it, seized the opportunity to leave Camille with fourteen-month-old Wyman and stake out some breathing room.

Crime never sleeps.

The local "werewolf killer" had apparently gone on hiatus, maybe locked up on some other charge—hell, maybe even flattened by a bus—but other goons kept making headlines. Back in June, a jury had convicted Mickey Cohen of evading $156,000 in taxes between 1946 and '48, plus lying to Treasury agents. Similar charges against his wife had been dropped when a critical witness dropped dead, but they lost their house and Mickey's property went up for auction while he caught the boat to Alcatraz.

Before all that, in February, Estes Kefauver's committee returned, quizzing a cast of characters including Mayor Fletcher Bowron; police chiefs William Parker of L.A. and Clinton Anderson of Beverly Hills; Dallas police lieutenant George Butler, alleged rejecter of Chicago bribes; master lobbyist and "Boss of California" Art Samish; and two partners in the Desert Inn, Moe Dalitz and Sam Tucker. Ex-convict Tom McGinty, once a bootlegger, also held points in the DI, along with Morris Kleinman, one-time "Al Capone of Cleveland." Needless to say, when Kefauver proposed a 10-percent federal tax on all gambling Nevada's Pat McCarran never let it reach the Senate floor.

In August, a pair of Kansas City thugs dubbed the "Two Tonys"—Anthony Brancato and his buddy, Anthony Trombino—caught a fatal dose of lead in Hollywood. No geniuses by any means, they'd robbed the sports book at the Fabulous Flamingo back in June, Brancato recognized by bookie Hy Goldbaum, whom he had robbed before, two years ago, in Beverly Hills. Escaping with $3,500 and dropping Brancato's hat in the process, they fled to Frisco, where they were arrested, posted bail, then skipped to hide out in L.A. Jack Dragna got the word and farmed a contract out to Nick Licata, who in turn recruited hitman Aladena Fratianno, aka "Jimmy the Weasel." Fratianno invited the Tonys to join him in robbing a high-stakes card game, then set a final meet where he and "Charley Bats" Battaglia put them to sleep. When cops arrested Fratianno and Battaglia as suspects, Licata and a list of other witnesses swore up and down the shooters were at Nick's club in Burbank all night. Case closed, and no one mourned.

Devon's excuse for working one day after Christmas was the latest LAPD scandal, breaking just last night, when drunken cops spent ninety minutes beating seven teenage prisoners at Central City Jail, breaking some bones and damaging internal organs. Five of those subjected to the clubbing had been Mexican Americans and all were underage, which made the case a civil rights nightmare. At least 100 cops had been involved in what the press was calling "Bloody Christmas," and for once, Gantt thought a few of them might actually land in prison, even though the *Times* headlined its précis on the case "Officers Beaten in Bar Brawl; Seven Men Jailed."

It all depended on your point of view, and who was slugging whom.

Many Angelenos, mostly white and middle class, were

less concerned by blue-on-brown brutality than with the second coming of HUAC to Hollywood. Actor Larry Parks, who'd played Al Jolson twice on screen, met the committee as a "friendly witness," but earned a swift contempt citation when he asked the panel of inquisitors to be more "sportsmanlike." Others avoided jail with Fifth Amendment pleas but found themselves blacklisted anyway. Some patriotic witnesses—directors Elia Kazan, Edward Dmytryk and Frank Tuttle, screenwriter Budd Schulberg—named dozens of colleagues and torpedoed their careers. Actor Lionel Stander, conversely, faced the committee and labeled its members "a group of fanatics who are desperately trying to undermine the Constitution of the United States by depriving artists and others of Life, Liberty, and the Pursuit of Happiness without due process of law."

Despite that hubbub, as on HUAC's first pass through L.A., no evidence of any Red conspiracy surfaced. One witness recalled Stander whistling the leftist anthem *"L'Internationale"* on film while his character waited for an elevator. Another complained that screenwriter Lester Cole had a football coach tell his fictional team it was "better to die on your feet than to live on your knees," words uttered by Republican heroine Dolores Ibárruri during Spain's civil war.

Slim pickings all around.

Of course, that didn't stop the current rage of Smith Act fever from infecting La-La Land. In October, a federal grand jury indicted twelve CPUSA members including California leader Albert Lima; State Chairman William Schneiderman; organizational secretary Loretta Stack; *Daily People's World* founder and editor Al Richmond; L.A. Party chairperson Dorothy Healey; Rose Chernin, executive secretary of the Committee for the Protection of the Foreign Born, founded last year; plus lesser members Philip Connelly, Ernest Fox, Carl Lambert, Henry Steinberg, Oleta Yates, and Mary Doyle.

Prosecutors held the twelve in lieu of $50,000 bond, apiece, prompting the case of *Stack v. Boyle*, argued before the U.S. Supreme Court on October 18. The Boyle in question was U.S. Marshal James Boyle, custodian of the defendants pending trial. Chief Justice Fred Vinson ruled on November 5, finding that the Constitution's Eighth Amendment banned the current bond on charges with a maximum fine of $10,000, and that bail jumping by four New York Reds in a separate case was no justification. Another month elapsed before the Ninth Circuit Court of Appeals set bond at $10,000 for defendants Doyle, Lambert, Lima, Schneiderman, Stack, Steinberg and Yates, while Connelly, Fox, Healey, Kusnitz and Richmond owed only $5,000 apiece.

District Judge William Mathes reviewed the case, retitled *United States v. Schneiderman*, on December 11, citing problems with the October indictments and voicing his "assumption that all defects in the existing indictments will be promptly cured." They were, in fact adding defendant Frank Carlson when new charges were filed on December 14. Bail wasn't an issue for Carlson, a Polish immigrant already doing time for a 1950 Smith Act conviction, marked for deportation when he made parole.

Good riddance, Devon thought. For all he cared, the whole damned gang of Red termites could go to Russia, since they loved the fucking place so much. What were they even doing here, except spreading dissension and mayhem?

One thing his old man had been right about from the beginning, anyway.

MIMS, Florida: December 26, 1951

THE FRAME HOUSE looked as if a giant had come by some-time last night and stopped to rest, parking his ass atop the southeast corner so that it collapsed, but that wouldn't explain the blackened boards flung out across the yard.

No, this had been a bomb. Nolan O'Hara had no doubt of that. The smoke had long since dissipated, but O'Hara smelled the sickly-sweet lingering odor left by dynamite, known to induce what some folks called a nitroglycerin headache.

And given who the occupants of this wrecked home had been, explosives couldn't be in doubt. Yesterday, crusader Harry Moore and his wife Harriette had welcomed their grown children, celebrating Christmas and the Moores' twenty-fifth wedding anniversary. After the guests left, they'd gone to bed, and then a blast from the crawlspace shattered their bedroom. Harry died before his ambulance could reach the nearest Negro hospital. His wife was barely hanging on, prognosis grim.

"The Klan, you think?" asked Agent Rupert Downes.

"Likely, but maybe with some help," Nolan replied.

Mims lay in Brevard County, 220 miles north of Miami and forty miles east of Orlando. Since 1949 it was best known for Cape Canaveral, home of the Joint Long Range Proving Ground, completed in time for its first V-2 rocket to launch in July of last year. Downes and O'Hara had flown up at the crack of dawn, from Miami International to McCoy Air Force Base, then drove to the crime scene from there.

Nobody had to tell them that Orange County, Brevard's neighbor to the east, ranked sixth in lynchings for the South at large since Reconstruction in the 1870s, or that Sheriff

Dave Starr and all his deputies were rabid members of the KKK. The latest Orange County lynching occurred in March, when Klansmen kidnapped Melvin Womack, flogging him, then shooting him "by accident," as local white folks claimed. The Klan's intended prey was Womack's brother, whom the rumor mill accused of child molesting. Two years earlier, young Willie Vincent had been tossed out of a moving car onto a Negro preacher's lawn, his skull fractured.

Police were crawling all over the shattered house, ostensibly collecting evidence. After the two G-men watched them for a while, standing apart, Downes asked O'Hara, "What do we do now?"

O'Hara fought an urge to shrug, replying, "Question Mrs. Moore, I guess, if she's in any shape to talk."

In fact, Nolan had no doubt that the bombing—one of many recent blasts in what some newspapers now called "the Florida Terror"—was linked to the Groveland rape case. Harry Moore, already loathed by bigots in the Sunshine State, had done his best with lawyers from the NAACP to get those verdicts overturned. In April, just a few days after Melvin Womack's death, the Supreme Court ordered a new trial for death row defendants Sam Shepherd and Walter Irvin, base on Florida's exclusion of nonvoting Negroes from state jury pools. Justice Robert Jackson opined that Groveland's case "presents one of the best examples of one of the worst menaces to American justice."

White Florida groaned, ground its teeth, and prepared for the retrial. On November 6, a rainy night, Sheriff McCall retrieved the prisoners from Raiford, headed southward toward Tavares and Lake County's jail. Along the way, he claimed his captives starting whining that they had to pee, so he'd pulled over on the road near Umatilla and removed them from his car, still handcuffed, to relieve themselves.

What happened next depended on who told the tale.

McCall claimed that his prisoners attacked him, forcing him to shoot them both in self-defense at point-blank range. Soon Deputy James Yates arrived upon the scene, finding McCall battered, the handcuffed prisoners both seeming dead.

But there had been a miracle of sorts. Irvin was still alive.

From his hospital bed, he told a very different story from McCall's to Bureau agents. Irvin said the sheriff stopped his car without warning, ordered his prisoners to step out on the shoulder of the road, then shot them both in an attempted murder. Irvin clung to life when Yates arrived and heard McCall boast to his underling, "I got rid of them, killed the sons of bitches."

Yates checked Irvin, told McCall, "This nigger's still alive," then pulled his own pistol and fired what be supposed would be the *coup de grâce* through Irvin's throat. McCall and Yates then tore the sheriff's clothes and mussed his hair, making it look as if he'd been attacked.

Incredibly, Irvin survived the final shot as well, his story validated when G-men dug up a .38 slug buried ten inches below the spot where he had fallen, proving he'd been shot while lying supine on the ground.

Not that it mattered to Lake County's coroner, who'd cited evidence that McCall looked "pretty bumped up, so something happened to him."

He cleared McCall of any wrongdoing, while one typical local told the press, "We're proud as all get-out." Judge Futch, in turn, rejected the Bureau's forensic evidence, refusing to call a grand jury, while the *Mount Dora Topic* warned Florida's critics that they "should certainly not take chances of starting the Civil War over again."

Justice also refused to move against McCall, despite persuasive evidence that he was guilty of cold-blooded murder and attempted murder, so the case was closed—except for Harry Moore, who'd circulated a petition for the sheriff's recall til a bomb had snuffed him out.

Of course, Moore's murder hadn't been the only recent bombing, but the twelfth so far for 1951. Miami's Carver Village housing project opened up to Negroes in August and suffered three blasts from September to early December. October alone had seen three other bombs planted at synagogues and Jewish schools. Miami's police chief, Walter Headley, claimed to see no link between those incidents, attributing the Carver Village bombings to "professionals," the rest to "amateurs."

Klan spokesmen naturally disavowed any involvement in the terrorism, while boss Klucker Bill Hendrix announced his run for governor in 1952.

From what Nolan observed, most white Floridians cared little about violence toward Negroes, but they were excited by the Kefauver Committee, and not always in a good way. In January, the National Association of State Racing Commissioners convened in Miami Beach, voicing fears that Uncle Sam might ban interstate transmission of racing news. Tampa's Bar Association and the Chamber of Commerce Board of Governors denounced Kefauver's hearings as both "unfair" and "un-American." Up in D.C., Federal judge Fred Letts absolved gambler Harry Russell of all contempt charges filed by the committee. Broward County's D.A. dismissed Sheriff Clark's gambling charge, and while a new indictment followed, leukemia beat Justice to the punch, killing Clark before his trial.

When all was said and done, fears that Miami would become a ghost town without gambling were not realized. In fact, Mel Richard started getting calls and letters from hoteliers, thanking him for getting S&G bookies out of their hair. Tourists kept flocking to the Gold Coast, and in spite of dire predictions, no grass sprouted from the streets.

Now, Nolan mused, *if only they could welcome citizens regardless of their race, we might be getting somewhere after all.*

CHAPTER 6

SARDI'S, WEST 44TH STREET, MANHATTAN: MAY 16, 1952

"THIS SCAMPI'S GREAT," Fiona said. "I'm glad you thought of coming here."

Dave Jordan smiled and swallowed back his ravioli to avoid the embarrassment from talking with his mouth full. "Glad you like it."

"Quite a waiting list, I understand," she said.

"I took a shot. Besides, my uncle knows a guy."

"Aha! The family you never want to talk about?"

"Nothing to say, I guess."

"Nothing to be ashamed of, either, I suppose?"

He changed directions in a hurry, not about to spill about his bloodline with the daughter of a longtime FBI agent. "So, are you still happy at Legal Aid?"

Fiona rolled her eyes. "Happy's a stretch," she said, "but it's fulfilling work. A *lot* of work for someone starting on the bottom."

"Helping the masses," he picked up where she'd left off. "Uplifting the downtrodden."

"Do I hear sarcasm?" she asked him, frowning.

"Not a bit of it. I honestly admire you, Fee. Truth is, I still don't know what I should shoot for when—or *if*—I pass the bar two years from now."

"Oh, Mr. Modest, is it? Graduating *summa*, and your GPA right now is...what, again?"

He almost blushed and ducked his head to hide it, skewering another ravioli with his fork. "First year, 3.93," he said.

"Keep that up, any firm in town would love to nab you."

Jordan snorted. "Sure, for eighty-hour weeks and all the scut work they can shovel at me."

"On the partner track."

"Well..."

His first year at Columbia Law had ended on Wednesday. Now here it was, an early Friday evening, and Fiona O'Hara had surprised him by accepting his dinner invitation. The first time in several months, now that Dave thought about it, between her long hours and his load of class work—and still, he supposed that he couldn't count it as a "date."

Just as well.

Columbia Law's first-year curriculum was labeled foundational, laying the groundwork for all that would follow with basic courses on contracts and civil procedure, criminal and constitutional law, torts and property, plus Legal Methods I and II—intense as hell, though fairly brief—two Legal Practice workshops, and foundation year moot court, as close to the real thing as hoary veterans could make it. Some of it he understood already, just from conversations with his dad, but there were times when Dave felt that his head was so jam-packed it might explode.

"So, what was your first-year elective?" asked Fiona.

"Evidence."

CL first-years got their first crack at an elective in the spring semester. Later on, they'd hit him in a swarm.

"You want to be a litigator," she said, smiling. Not a question.

"Otherwise," he answered, "what's the point?"

"I know, right? All the paperwork and filings, well, you have to wade through that regardless. But it's *court* where all the action happens."

The course on evidence explored how facts were proven in court, whether the case was criminal or civil, starting off with interplay between the hearsay rule and Constitution, moving on to means of introduction and impeachment of opposing witnesses. New York still hadn't drafted a Code of Civil Procedure, so they studied California's groundbreaking model enacted in 1872, then followed up with the federal Rules Enabling Act of 1934, repealing the archaic "conformity principle" used by American courts going back to their earliest days.

He didn't have to tell Fiona that, of course. She'd been through all of it in class and now was using it in real life, hoping she could change the world.

One of the many things that he admired about her, but he didn't dare think *loved*.

Her voice cut through his reverie. "So, no thoughts whatsoever on your graduation plans? Didn't you say your father heads a firm?"

"A one-man show, semi-retired," Dave said. "Besides, he only handles matters for the family."

Shut up! the little voice inside his head commanded. *Let it go!*

"Very mysterious," she teased him.

"Very boring," Dave replied. And changed the subject once again. "You really like the scampi?"

"It's divine."

"Religious shrimp?"

She laughed and nearly choked. "Smart guy," she chided him, when she could speak again.

Humor was better than discussing families, which led David into the same old swamp. Besides, he knew already how tonight would end: maybe a light peck on the cheek if he was lucky, then Fiona would be whisked away in one of Gotham's famous taxi cabs, painted canary yellow so you couldn't miss them on the street. Medallions only for a lawyer on the rise, none of those shady "gypsy" cabs.

Just keep your chin up and get through it, part of David's mind was saying. *And since nothing's bound to come of it, think twice before you ask her out again.*

A sad thought, and no matter how David munched on his next ravioli, it had trouble slipping past the tight lump in his throat.

————

180 West 135th Street, Harlem: August 23, 1952

Payton Sawyer spent his fair share of time as a kid at the Harlem YMCA, but it was different now, being an undercover cop for BOSS. He didn't stop in at the Y to shoot hoops but to play a part that had been scripted for him, posing as a Muslim in his black suit, white shirt, and bowtie.

The Harlem Y had been established in 1901, then moved across the street in 1932, into a redbrick building that took up most of the block between Lenox and Seventh Avenue.

Back then, it had housed the Harlem History Club, a ghetto study group nicknamed the "living room of the Harlem Renaissance." Since 1946, one of its tenants had been the Nation of Islam's Temple No. 7, Payton's target as an infiltrator for NYPD.

Joining the NOI hadn't been difficult, since it was avidly recruiting in the neighborhood. He'd had to study up on the *Qur'ān*, observe the dietary rules on "lawful" and "unlawful" food—no pork, no carrion or blood products, no meat from proscribed animals or those slaughtered by five forbidden means—and shun intoxicants. Beyond that, he memorized the Nation's twelve-point roster of beliefs and ten-point list of "What the Muslims Want," broadly stated as equal justice under law, full and complete freedom, plus separation from the white race in a state or territory of their own.

Simple, if you could just go back to day one of creation and start fresh.

Sometimes, Payton thought back to conversations with his father, as to how Ike started with the Bureau of Investigation, spying on Marcus Garvey's Universal Negro Improvement Association and affiliated groups, doing his part to land "Black Moses" in prison, followed by deportation back to his native Jamaica. Payton didn't miss the irony in his present career path, but he knew what he was doing, understood the risk NYPD saw in the Nation and didn't believe he was a traitor to his race—at least, not yet.

No one with half a brain could doubt the Nation's history was shady. Founding father Wallace Fard Muhammad—aka "Fred Dodd," according to his FBI file—born sometime between 1877 and 1893, maybe in New Zealand or Afghanistan. Nobody knew for sure. In 1914 he'd married and fathered a son in Oregon, then turned up claiming to be single in Los Angeles, signing his draft card

"Wallie Dodd Ford." The 1920 census listed him as white, though others later knew him as a "white Arab" or "light-skinned Negro." By that time, he'd acquired another wife, but there was nothing on the record to identify his parents or his date of immigration to the States.

Sometime later, he'd landed in Chicago as a member of the Moorish Science Temple of America run by Timothy Drew, aka "Prophet Noble Drew Ali." In March of 1929, Drew was arrested on suspicion of killing a rival, "Sheik" Claude Greene, and while police released him, he died mysteriously four months later, possibly from injuries sustained in custody or else murdered by friends of Greene. Whichever, Fard assumed command, tagging himself a "master" and a "prophet" in his own right, then absconding to Detroit in 1930 where he started up the NOI. One of his first recruits, Elijah Poole, the last known person to see Fard alive, when Fard boarded a plane at Wayne County Airport, flying off to parts unknown in May of 1933.

Elijah Poole thus became "Elijah Muhammad," assuming command of the Nation to "teach the down-trodden and defenseless Black people a thorough Knowl-edge of God and of themselves, and to put them on the road to Self-Independence with a superior culture and higher civilization than they had previously experienced." He'd proclaimed his missing mentor the "Almighty God incar-nate" and began enlisting more recruits. In 1942, Elijah and a number of his followers were jailed for violating the Selec-tive Service Act, refusing to defend the nation that enslaved their ancestors. Released in 1946, he got straight back to organizing and opened the Nation's seventh temple in Harlem, the heart of Black America.

And in the process, he recruited Malcolm X, born Malcolm Little in Nebraska to proud activists for Marcus

Garvey's movement. Threats from the Klan prompted his family to pull up stakes and settle in Milwaukee, but it didn't help. A Ku Klux spin-off, the Black Legion, killed his dad when Malcolm was a six-year-old, and he would later claim four of his uncles died at white men's hands. His mother wound up in a lunatic asylum shortly after Malcolm turned thirteen, and he'd gone off the rails, locked up for burglary in Massachusetts at twenty. His first acquaintance in prison turned out to be a member of the Nation, and he started studying its precepts, signing letters "Malcolm X" after the Nation's practice of discarding his "slave name." In 1950, he sent one of those letters to Harry Truman, claiming that he was a communist and hated the Korean War. Truman passed it to the FBI, which opened up a brand-new dossier.

Already signed up with the Nation, having sworn off pork, liquor, tobacco and a life of crime, Malcolm hit the streets in 1952 and hastened to Chicago, where the Nation's headquarters had transferred from Detroit two years after its founder caught his flight to who knew where. Malcolm, who'd cultivated and refined an innate gift for oratory, was the Nation's minister to watch, a young man on the rise.

Payton could understand why BOSS and white society, in general, were wary of the Nation. Sure, its spokesmen hated interracial marriage just as much as any cracker in the South and they were all for racial separation, but instead of Jim Crow, they were shooting for a state or nation of their own, and not just going "back to Africa" where none of them had ever been to start with. As for white folks, they were "blue-eyed" devils spawned from weird experiments by Yakub, a black scientist described in Wallace Fard's writings, who'd lived "6,600 years ago" and created the first whites by "grafting" them from Negroes on the Greek island of Patmos.

Ridiculous? Hell, yes—but no more so than the white-supremacist two-seedline creed of British Israelism preached by some Klansmen, wherein Eve had sex with snaky Satan in the Garden of Eden while Adam wasn't looking, thus producing Cain, the first murder and patriarch of all Jews, defined by founder William Branham as "a big religious bunch of illegitimate bastard children." Jews, in turn, had also dabbled in mad science, racists claimed, thereby creating all nonwhite "mud people."

Flipsides of the same coin when you thought about it, both crazy as hell. More to the point, the Nation sought "an immediate end to the police brutality and mob attacks against the so-called Negro throughout the United States," enforced by federal law, coupled with "justice applied equally to all, regardless of creed or class or color." And then, the kicker: for their separate all-black domain, Nation ministers proclaimed, "Our former slave masters are obligated to provide such land and that the area must be fertile and minerally rich." Not only that, but "We believe that our former slave masters are obligated to maintain and supply our needs in this separate territory for the next twenty to twenty-five years, until we are able to produce and supply our own needs."

Try getting *that* through Congress, much less past a white cop on the ghetto beat.

Aside from riding herd on obvious fanatics, Payton saw his time with BOSS as a ticket to advancement within the NYPD. Ideally, he could make detective, starting out at third-grade, working up from there to first, then trying his luck at the tests for supervisory rank as a sergeant, lieutenant, and captain.

All pie in the sky for the moment, while he earned his spurs with BOSS and tried to please Inspector Patrick Flannery. And that, of course, depended on his managing to stay alive while playing Judas to the Nation, without winding up like his late training officer.

Payton was taking it one hour at a time, thankful he didn't have a wife and kids at home to mourn for him if something should go wrong.

———

FEDERAL BUREAU of Narcotics Manhattan Field Office: September 22, 1952

IKE SAWYER CLOSED the file in front of him, stamped with the name of Mafia informer Eugenio Giannini, and pushed it aside. The stool pigeon he'd turned originally ten years earlier. As Ike had feared in 1950, after Giannini had been jailed in Rome, then liberated by the FBN, his double agent's role had been seen through by Lucky Luciano, and the die was cast—with emphasis on *die*. Two days ago, three men pumped him full of bullets in East Harlem, left him in a gutter with the other trash and made their getaway.

Word on the street named Giannini's slayers as one "Joe Cago" Valachi and the two Pagano brothers, Joseph and Pasquale, taking orders from Anthony Strollo—"Tony Bender" to his friends in *Cosa Nostra*—presently a *capo* working under Vito Genovese. Not that anyone would sing that song in court, risking a death sentence themselves. Then again, another rumor blamed the hit on Tommy Lucchese's 107th Street Gang, but what difference did it make? The rats were all in it together, come what may.

One rat, at least, was dead and gone. Waxey Gordon had been moved from Sing Sing to Attica Prison in March, then shipped out to San Francisco in April, one of two dozen defendants facing a federal narcotics charge to match his New York state conviction. He'd pled not guilty in May, then suffered a massive heart attack and croaked on June 24. The prosecutor who announced his death claimed Waxey had rolled over and was ready to rat out his various accomplices.

Meanwhile, more than 500 suspects had been indicted so far under the Boggs Act, while the Food and Drug Administration estimated that amphetamine and meth-amphetamine production had quadrupled over the amount turned out in 1949. The FBN didn't subscribe to any of the new preventive programs aimed at steering teenagers away from dope, although it grudgingly produced a pamphlet titled "Living Death—The Truth about Drug Addiction." That screed toed the headquarters line, stating that "Teen-age drug addiction in its inception and in its continuance is generally due to vice, vicious environment, and criminal associations, but it cannot be too strongly emphasized that the smoking of the marijuana cigarette is a dangerous first step on the road which usually leads to enslavement by heroin."

Of course, that hadn't stopped George White from peddling poison on the CIA's behalf.

On February 1, Attorney General McGrath hired ex-Gotham City Council member Newbold Morris as special assistant to investigate rumored corruption in the DOJ. Morris hired White, who wrote a questionnaire for top Justice officials, sniffing out malfeasance, and Morris passed it around while demanding unlimited access to McGrath's personal records. That got him fired after barely two months on the job, and *that* got McGrath fired by Harry Truman later the same day. A Manhattan grand jury subpoenaed White, and he spent a night in jail for refusing to name his informants, also claiming that a member of the U.S. prosecutor's staff was tied in with Tommy Lucchese's family. At least he had the CIA to fall back on and seemed prepared to make the most of it.

As for the racial front, Ike wasn't pleased to hear son Payton was working undercover for BOSS, inside the Nation of Islam. Ike had traveled down that path himself before Chief Hoover dumped him from the Bureau of Investigation for the crime of being black, but he supposed Payton would have to learn that lesson for himself.

In Dixie, while the year passed without a lynching listed by Tuskegee University—the first time within living memory—Atlanta's Southern Regional Council logged forty Negro homes bombed by racists. "Bombingham," in Alabama, was the epicenter of that terror, but there had been thirteen blasts in Dallas, others scattered across Florida, Georgia, and North Carolina. Fighting back in Mississippi, Dr. Theodore Roosevelt Howard founded the Regional Council of Negro Leadership, leading a boycott of gas stations that barred Negroes from restrooms, campaigning to expose police brutality, and encouraging deposits to the black-owned Tri-State Bank of Nashville that made life a little easier for Negroes mired in debt.

At least it was a start, and if Rome wasn't built within a single day, he figured neither would Jim Crow be laid to rest.

———

FBI HEADQUARTERS: October 14, 1952

JUST WHEN ALOYSIUS GANTT thought he was free and clear, somebody stirred the shit again to make him sweat. The way he'd tried to calm himself of late, he guessed that sweat must smell of Jameson Black Barrel, prompting him to pop a couple more Altoids into his mouth.

In January, someone who had worked with Horace Schmahl—the former OSS man and the Bureau's double agent on the Hiss defense team—tipped attorney Chester Lane that Alger probably was framed via the art of "forgery by typewriter." Lane called on a civilian expert, one Martin Tyrell, to build a Woodstock indistinguishable from the one the Hisses might have owned back in the 1930s, and he'd managed it with some finagling. Filing his motion for a new trial, Lane informed the court of his belief that state Exhibit UUU—the Woodstock manufactured *after* Hiss acquired his one and only typewriter—was "a deliberately fabricated job, a new typeface on an old body."

Which, if proved in court, would place the fraud directly in Gantt's lap, end his career, and maybe even land his ass in prison.

Judge Goddard denied the motion in July, saying he didn't think Whittaker Chambers had the knowledge or resources to produce a fake machine. No one suggested that it might've come from somewhere else—such as the FBI's own workshop—but that still wasn't the end of Gantt's headaches.

In May, Chambers published his memoirs titled *Witness*, which shot straight to the top of the *New York Times* best-seller list and stayed there for three months. So what? The trouble was that every time Chambers described his tenure in the CPUSA he moved the dates around and made himself appear as what he was, in fact: a clumsy liar.

In his early HUAC testimony, under oath, Chambers stated that he had "entered into the Washington picture" as a Red in summer 1935, then left both D.C. and the Party at the tag end of December '37. Later, prodded by Dick Nixon for accommodating details to hang Alger Hiss, he fudged his exit back to "early 1938." At Alger's second trial, he pinned it down to April 15, 1938—explaining how the documents he claimed Priscilla Hiss had typed for him bore dates ranging from January 1 to April 1 that year. Chambers freely admitted that his other statements had been "incorrect," but naturally, no one ever thought of charging *him* with perjury.

Even though the new trial motion failed, it agitated Edgar Hoover, who in May ordered his agents to re-interview three former Woodstock engineers "at some length," to determine if Exhibit UUU could have been manufactured as late as July of 1929, thus contradicting records from the manufacturer and testimony from ex-salesman Tom Grady, who'd retired in 1927. Nothing came of that, but when the negative replies reached Hoover's desk, Judge Goddard had already solved the problem for him. Gantt was spared again but still kept waiting for the other shoe to drop, another revelation to destroy him.

There'd be no eleventh-hour save for either of the Rosenbergs, at least. The U.S. Second Circuit rejected their appeals in January and again in February, followed by the clincher yesterday when the Supreme Court denied both defendants a writ of certiorari. Nothing stood between them and Old Sparky now but presidential clemency, and that was clearly off the table. They could still confess, of course, in hope of leniency, but so far they were standing mute.

Jesus, Gantt thought, crunching the breath mints into fragments with his teeth, *I need a fucking drink.*

FBI Headquarters: November 25, 1952

DECLAN O'HARA CHECKED his small desk calendar, confirming what he knew already, that Thanksgiving was the day after tomorrow. Abigail already had a turkey prepped for roasting, plus ingredients for stuffing and one of her famous pumpkin pies, a drawn-out day of slaving in the kitchen that she claimed to love, but all Declan could think of was the people who had no reason for giving thanks this year.

A case in point: defendants in the Smith Act trials would find no cause to celebrate, assuming members of the CPUSA even saw fit to recognize the holiday. Six Reds in Baltimore had been indicted in mid-January and convicted of conspiracy in June. The Fourth Circuit Court of Appeals affirmed their convictions on July 31 and denied a rehearing in early September, leaving only the Supreme Court to review their case if it saw fit to, probably sometime next year.

January ended with the conviction of Steve Nelson and four other CPUSA members in Pittsburgh after Andrew Onda's case was severed from the rest. Nelson, as the alleged ringleader of the "plot" to read and speak, was handed twenty years in prison, a $10,000 fine, a $13,000 debt to reimburse his prosecutors for their time, and was locked away pending his motion to appeal. Pennsylvania's Superior Court affirmed those convictions on November 12.

The second Party trial at Foley Square in Gotham, convened on April 24, with an emotive speech by Helen Gurley Flynn, serving as counsel for her own defense. She told the jury, "Our ideas may be new and strange to you. Probably you have never seen or met a Communist before. We don't ask you to agree with us but to listen with an open mind and not to accept as gospel truth the sensational tales of stool-pigeons and planted agents who will be the government's chief, if not sole, witnesses." As to the CPUSA's conspiracy, she said, "I came to the conclusion that socialism could be achieved, not by one splurge of violence, but by the persistent political activities of the workers and the people. And so in order to participate in political activities in the effort to achieve socialism, I joined the Communist Party. We are asking you to decide this case on the evidence—or, more correctly, may I say, on the lack of evidence— which we are confident will be glaringly revealed long before this trial is over." That trial was still ongoin, and would be, O'Hara guessed, for many months to come.

As a footnote to that trial, on March 10, the Supreme Court affirmed contempt convictions of all five defense attorneys from the first trial held at Foley Square, affirming their jail terms for disrupting proceedings in that case.

On September 12 in rainy Seattle, G-men arrested seven Party members tagged in newspaper reports as "dangerous criminals" over their thoughts and statements. Attorney John Caughlan led the defense team for CPUSA members Paul Bowen, John Daschbach, Barbara Hartle (named by Justice as "Washington's top woman Communist"), Henry Huff, Karley Larsen, Terry Pettis, and William Pennock (an eight-year state legislator). Harley Mores, a farmer and Bureau informer, was the state's "surprise witness." Held in lieu of $40,000 bail for Huff, $25,000 apiece for the other six, the defendants filed an Eighth Amendment appeal in September, winning the reduction of their bonds to $25,000 for Huff and $10,000 for the rest. Caughlan filed a motion for dismissal of all charges in November, instantly denied, and that trial, too, would not convene until next year.

Twelve days after the Seattle roundup, Bureau agents

arrested CPUSA members James and Dorothy Forest, Marcus Murphy, Robert Mankowitz, and William Sentner in St. Louis. All their charges were identical to those in other Smith Act cases, but objections and appeals stalled their trial so far and might for months to come.

Meanwhile, in early January, seven Honolulu Reds challenged their August 1951 indictment with ten separate complaints. In February, Chief District Judge James Mclaughlin denied four of their motions and deferred the rest as being premature. October brought them back to court, protesting Judge McLaughlin's ruling before Judge Jon Wiig, but he denied the motions save for granting each defendant one additional strike for prospective jurors at trial. That trial opened on November 5, Judge Wiig presiding, with no rapid end in sight.

One Red charged on his own, without a mob of codefendants, was Alexander Trachtenberg, born in Ukraine, a longtime activist for the Socialist Party of America and later for the CPUSA, founder and manager of International Publishers of New York. At issue were two of his own works he'd published since the Smith Act craze got rolling: *Books on Trial* and *Publisher on Trial*, relating his view of the charges filed against him. That was all it took these days, apparently, although his trial had not commenced as yet.

With hired "experts" in high demand across the nation, these were salad days for characters like Liz Bentley and Harvey Matusow. They'd met up this year, at her publisher's office, whereupon Harvey opined, "She used alcoholism to ease her pain and she had a lot of pain," prompting him to take her home each night and "pour her into bed. She didn't understand the hostility. She never got to the point where she could handle it. She felt that she'd been used and abused."

Another witness who cashed in on his fame was Herbert Philbrick, publishing a bestseller called *I Led Three Lives: Citizen, 'Communist', Counterspy*. That had already spawned a radio drama, "I Was a Communist for the FBI, " and there was talk of making it a TV series soon.

Defendant William Remington was also back in headlines, Judge Learned Hand of the Second Circuit reversing his perjury conviction, ruling that jury instructions as to "membership" in the CPUSA were too vague, further criticizing Assistant Attorney General Thomas Donegan for "judicial improprieties" in his abusive questioning of Remington and wife Anne, and also scolding grand jury foreman John Brunini for conflict of interest based on his business ties to Liz Bentley. Hand ordered a new trial, with no date determined as yet.

In the Senate, so far no one seemingly dared to oppose Joe McCarthy. Marine Corps headquarters had lately given the faux tail-gunner thirty-two combat missions he'd claimed but never flown, thereby making McCarthy eligible for an unearned Distinguished Flying Cross and multiple awards of the Air Medal. Gloating over that stolen glory, Joe had also cultivated servants in the press, particularly columnist Jack Anderson, whom he allowed to eavesdrop on McCarthy's phone calls to fellow Senate Republicans Robert Taft and William Knowland, feeding them Anderson's questions for use in his columns.

At the same time, Joe received numerous Bureau files on people Edgar Hoover hoped to target with a timely smear. Dean Acheson, for instance, had the bad judgment to serve as Harry Truman's Secretary of State, catching hell both for the "loss" of China and for being "a pompous diplomat in striped pants." On the other hand, Catholics seemed to love Joe, and he'd forged a tight bond with the Massachusetts

Kennedy clan, cuddling up to patriarch Joseph, welcoming second son John to Congress, dating sisters Patricia and Eunice, even serving as godfather to brother Bobby's first child, Kathleen.

What do they see in him? Declan asked himself. The only answers he could think of had been power and influence, fleeting as those were in Washington.

McCarthy picked Harvard lawyer Bobby Kennedy as counsel for his committee, but that only lasted six months, until Kennedy found out he couldn't stomach Roy Cohn. In February, McCarthy pulled strings to land nemesis Owen Lattimore on the hot seat with McCarran's Senate Internal Security Subcommittee, grilled once again over the Institute of Pacific Relations, faced with more bullshit from Lou Budenz. In the end, McCarran branded Lattimore "a conscious articulate instrument of the Soviet conspiracy" and slapped him with seven counts of perjury. Those charges were still hanging fire, while defense attorney Abe Fortas blamed McCarran for nitpicking trivial crap from the 1930s. McCarthy was dead right for once, when he praised Budenz In 1952, for testifying "in practically every case in which Communists were either convicted or deported over the past three years."

Of course, there *were* some real bad guys around. In February, NYPD nabbed "Top Ten" fugitive Willie Sutton—a bank robber dubbed "The Actor" for his love of quirky disguises. A Gotham salesman, Arnold Schuster, spotted Sutton on a Brooklyn subway and reported him, then died by gunfire after sitting for a TV interview. The leads on that crime all led back to hitman Frederick "Angel of Death" Tenuto, who took his own spot on the Most Wanted list in May but was still on the loose.

Two months later, another "Top Ten" fugitive, Gerhard

Puff, had slain Bureau agent Joe Brock at the Hotel Congress, on Manhattan's Upper West Side. Other G-men on the scene shot Puff and took him into custody, awaiting trial for first-degree murder.

Puerto Rican militant Oscar Collazo hadn't personally killed anyone in his 1950 attempt to murder Harry Truman, but it didn't matter. He was sentenced to fry anyhow, until Truman showed mercy, commuting his sentence to life in prison.

Speaking of Truman, he was eligible for another term despite 1951's Twenty-second Amendment, but he'd grown tired of Washington, battered by scandals involving his aides and an embarrassing loss to Estes Kefauver in New Hampshire's March Democratic primary. From there, Estes rolled on to win eleven more primaries, losing only three to hopeless "favorite son" candidates. He was supremely confident of nomination by July when his party convened at Chicago's International Amphitheatre, but a rude surprise awaited him. Instead of rewarding his 3.1 million primary votes, party bosses had tagged Illinois Governor Adlai Stevenson II, who'd scored a mere 78,000 primary ballots.

Why Stevenson? Incumbent Truman hated Kefauver, and while he hoped diplomat Averell Harriman would land the nomination, Harriman had never held elective office. Vice President Alben Barkley was too old at seventy-four, while Truman's third choice, Georgia Senator Richard Russell Jr. was a diehard segregationist referred to as "brother" by Dixie Klansmen. On the convention's second ballot, Truman threw his weight behind Adlai, and so the deal was done. Alabama Senator John Sparkman, every bit as racist as Russell, was chosen as Stevenson's running mate, neatly dividing the ticket.

Not that it mattered, finally. The GOP, also convening in

Chicago at the same venue, virtually guaranteed success by nominating war hero Dwight "Ike" Eisenhower and Red-hunter Dick Nixon. The party's platform promised America more nuclear weapons, plus dismissal of the State Department's "loafers, incompetents and unnecessary employees." For those who missed the point, Everett Dirksen vowed that Republican victory would purge D.C. of its simpering "lavender boys."

Despite unbalanced tickets, it was still a hard-fought race. Republicans campaigned against Truman *in absentia*, blaming him for China's "loss," Korea's war, and firing Doug MacArthur. When they got around to Stevenson, they branded him an "egghead" because he was bald and worse yet, intellectual, a graduate of Princeton. (Ike had been too old for the U.S. Naval Academy, but made it through West Point, a true "man's man.") Democrats flogged "Tricky Dick" Nixon for his dirty political record and chastised Ike for failing to repudiate McCarthy's witch-hunting.

Edgar Hoover, cringing at the notion of another Democrat calling his shots, did all he could to help the GOP, mining Bureau files for innuendo on Stevenson's personal life, putting G-men on the trail of Adlai's ex-wife, once diagnosed as suffering from "persecution paranoia." When Joe McCarthy went on television, nine days prior to the election, claiming Stevenson "endorses and would continue the suicidal, Kremlin-directed policies of this nation," concluding that "there is no such thing as being a little bit disloyal or being partly a traitor," every word out of his mouth came straight from Bureau files.

Columnist Maurice Childs called the campaign America's dirtiest on record to date, but voters ate it up. On Election Day, Ike and Dick swept the field, claiming 55 percent of the popular vote and carrying thirty-nine states. In Dixie,

Florida, Texas and Virginia voted Republican for the first time since Reconstruction.

Eisenhower recognized Chief Hoover's contribution to that landslide and rewarded him with a personal sit-down shortly after the election. Following their chat, Ike told the press, "There has come to my ears a story to the effect that J. Edgar Hoover, head of the FBI, has been out of favor in Washington. Such was my respect for him that I invited him to a meeting, my only purpose being to assure him that I wanted him in government as long as I might be there and that in the performance of his duties he would have the complete support of my office." In return, the Chief graced Ike with Bureau dossiers on countless enemies, including the NAACP and Wild Bill Donovan, who'd campaigned for Ike in a bid to replace "Beetle" Smith as Director of Central Intelligence.

Joe McCarthy was up for reelection in '52, turning public criticism to his own advantage with the slogan "McCarthyism is Americanism with its sleeves rolled," releasing another ghostwritten book titled *McCarthyism: The Fight For America*. Hank Greenspun tried stopping him, printing rumors of Joe's homosexuality in the *Las Vegas Sun,* but it was like pelting a runaway bull with peanuts. When pal John Kennedy ran for a Senate seat, McCarthy shied away from GOP incumbent Henry Cabot Lodge Jr., and JFK repaid the favor by denouncing some of McCarthy's Democratic opponents. On November 4, McCarthy won with 54 percent of Wisconsin's ballots, while Eisenhower got 60 percent.

Business as usual, in short—at least until the country reached those "calmer times" that Justice Black had mentioned while dissenting in the *Dennis* case last June. But would O'Hara be around to see that day?

If anyone had asked him, with his life dependant on the answer, he couldn't have said.

———

THE LUBYANKA BUILDING: December 3, 1952

STEFAN—NOW "STEPHEN BARNES"—WAS safe and sound in Trenton with adoptive parents Mark and Isabella, all the necessary papers signed and notarized, a great relief to Leonid Babin after his years of anxious planning for revenge. The hardest part was done. Now all the boy needed to do was grow up strong and smart, matriculate through five successive tiers of public education with outstanding grades, consider military service or at least fulfill the statute that required draft registration, then apply and be accepted to the FBI.

Oh, yes, and he must also manage to survive to manhood in America, rife with disease, crime, and the ever-present threat of crippling or fatal accidents. So far this year, the worst polio epidemic in U.S. history had struck 58,000 victims, killing 3,145 and leaving 21,269 paralyzed. An average 7,250 Americans fell prey to murder yearly, while more than 36,000 died in car wrecks. Other lethal diseases, accidents and natural disasters claimed their share, including seventy-seven lost in three airplane crashes. The world was perilous indeed, and no less so the gleaming Capitalist Paradise.

At home, the MGB continued its time-honored machinations against fascists. Fifteen such—all of them Jews, ironically—had gone to trial in May, accused of treason. Those so charged included Solomon Lozovsky, Director of the Soviet Information Bureau and Deputy Commissar of Foreign Affairs; Boris Shimeliovich, Medical Director of Moscow's Botkin Clinical Hospital; and Lina Stern, a biochemist and first female professor at the Russian Academy of Sciences. The other twelve were Yiddish poets, novelists and editors of varying renown. Their trial before three military judges, *sans* prosecutors and defense attorneys, climaxed in July with most defendants condemned. Firing squads shot thirteen in the Lubyanka's basement on August 12, while Solomon Bregman, a leading member of the wartime Jewish Anti-Fascist Committee, lapsed under torture into a coma from which he would never awake. Only Stern survived, sentenced to forty-two months in prison and five years' exile. Today, sentimental Jews still mourned what they referred to as "The Night of Murdered Poets."

That was old news by September when arrests of suspects in the Doctor's Plot began at last. From the first roundup of thirty-seven suspects, hundreds more soon followed them to prison, Stalin demanding "accelerated" interrogation to finally unearth some evidence of Zionist conspiracy. TASS and *Pravda* churned out reams of anti-Semitic propaganda to that end but proof, so far, remained elusive.

The fever spread to Prague in November, with a series of show trials purging the Czech Communist Party (KSČ) of Jews and half-hearted Stalinists. Russian "advisors" led the charge, aided by Czechoslovak State Security officers, compiling a list of defendants that included Rudolf Slánský, General Secretary of the KSČ; Deputy General Secretary Josef Frank; Bedřich Geminder, International Section Chief of the Party Secretariat; Otto Šling, Regional Party Secretary in Brno; Minister of Foreign Affairs Vladimír Clementis and his deputy, Vavro Hajdů; Ludvík Frejka, Chief of the

Economic Committee in the Chancellery; Deputy Ministers of Foreign Trade Evžen Löbl and Rudolf Margolius; Deputy Minister of Finance Otto Fischl; Deputy Minister of National Security Karel Šváb; Deputy Minister of National Defense Bedřich Reicin; Deputy Minister of Foreign Affairs Artur London; and Otto Katz, aka "André Simone," editor of the KSČ newspaper *Rudé právo* (*Red Justice*). In the end, all were shot except Hajdů, Löbl and London, sentenced to life in prison.

No skin off me, thought Babin, falling back on an old American idiom. His future and his legacy now lay primarily in the United States, where Stefan—make that *Steven*—had been planted like a slowly ticking time bomb in the homeland of his mortal enemies.

———

MANHATTAN: December 7, 1952

KEFAUVER HEAT WAS STARTING to subside, at last, replaced by good old Red hysteria and fear of homosexuals at large, which pleased Greg Jordan to no end. Above all, Kefauver had failed at his bid for the presidency, after pissing off so many topflight Democrats they wouldn't nominate him even though he as a TV star who'd carried more than three-fourths of the primaries.

Dumb move, Davy, Greg thought, remembering Kefauver's campaign photos in a coonskin cap, some of them posed aboard a dogsled.

But the Tennessean's failure hadn't helped William O'Dwyer, ruined by his testimony on TV. After that grueling bout, O'Dwyer returned to service as U.S. ambassador to

Mexico, then quit his post just yesterday but stayed south of the border, as if frightened to return.

Speaking of Latin matters, Cuban *presidente* Carlos Prío hadn't made it to his scheduled reelection race in June, deposed on March 10 by Fulgencio Batista and his military pals. Batista declared himself "provisional president," backed by U.S. corporations that owned 40 percent of Cuban sugar plantations, 90 percent of its mines and mineral concessions, 80 percent of its utilities, plus nearly all its cattle ranches and oilfields. President Truman recognized Batista's regime on March 27, three days after White House speechwriter Arthur Schlesinger Jr. complied with Truman's order to assess the new regime. That report read, in part: "The corruption of the government, the brutality of the police, the government's indifference to the needs of the people for education, medical care, housing, for social justice and economic justice is an open invitation to revolution."

Of course, that didn't worry the casino managers from Stateside or the estimated 11,500 hookers working in Havana alone, where Batista's underlings welcomed bribes and passed that loot up the chain of command.

At home, Syndicate business proceeded more or less as usual, with just a few hiccups. Milwaukee's *Don* Joseph Vallone died from natural causes in March, briefly replaced by Salvatore Ferrara until Chicago's Outfit ousted him in favor of John Alioto. Greg and brother Carlo had attended an April meeting of eighty-odd *Cosa Nostra* bosses at Raymond Patriarca's home in New England, rubber-stamping Ray's succession to *Capo Crimine* Philip Buccola, hiding in Italy from tax-evasion charges. Missouri Governor Forrest Smith survived his embarrassment by the Kefauver Committee to serve as the lead delegate to the

Democratic National Convention in July, but voters in the Show-Me State had seen enough to dump him in November. Anna Genovese had broken precedent by suing ex-husband Vito for spousal support, but she was still alive, against all odds. In August, a contempt citation finally caught up with Frank Costello, and he'd drawn a prison term of eighteen months.

And yet, for all that, the year's weirdest news involved a couple of civilians, unconnected to the Syndicate in any way. Nobody Arthur Schuster had the bad luck to spot fugitive bank robber Willie Sutton on a subway train and pointed cops in his direction, ending up with Sutton back in Pennsylvania's Holmesburg Prison, which he had escaped from five years earlier. So far, so good, but Schuster gave a TV interview and Albert Anastasia caught it, raging, "I hate squealers. Hit that guy." Freelancer Fred Tenuto did the job, then Anastasia had *him* whacked, while Edgar Hoover put Tenuto on the FBI's "Most Wanted" list, almost a comedy of errors.

But the long arms of the law and Death had passed Greg's family by this year, so far. With Christmas coming up, he kept his fingers crossed and hoped their luck would hold.

———

FBI Field Office, Los Angeles: December 16, 1952

Devon Gantt was still amazed by the hypocrisy of Hollywood. The major studios shelled out something like a million bucks to Mob extortionists, averting costly strikes, then welcomed John Rosselli back as an uncredited producer. Now, with all of America entranced by Estes

Kefauver, those selfsame studios were filming law-and-order movies as if they'd been on the right side all along.

First up in March, was United Artists' *Captive City,* inspired by Kefauver's hearings and screened for him privately in D.C. before director Robert Wise spliced him into the film's prologue and epilogue. One month later, Republic's *Hoodlum Empire* hit screens nationwide, followed in November by Paramount's *The Turning Point.* All of which confirmed Devon's assessment that crime paid off very well, for those on both sides of the law.

Except, maybe for drunken members of LAPD. Charges from "Bloody Christmas" made it into court by March, leading with six of the seven beating victims—all Latinos— convicted of battery and disturbing the peace. Unfortunately for his officers, Chief Parker couldn't keep his mouth shut, talking up his "war on crime," claiming that criminals were trying to unseat him with false charges of brutality, signing off on a 204-page internal report claiming "none of the prisoners was physically abused in the manner alleged." A new grand jury disagreed, indicting eight cops for assault, while others suddenly were stricken with amnesia. By November, five of the eight stood convicted, drawing short jail terms, while fifty-four others were transferred and thirty-nine were temporarily suspended without pay.

On L.A.'s Mob scene, Mickey Cohen's tax conviction ended his long war with Jack Dragna, leaving Dragna in control of vice and bribery that carried on as usual. In Vegas, the Strip sprouted two more mobbed-up joints: the Sahara, backed by Chicago money, and the Sands, run by Meyer Lansky's hand-picked front man, Jack Entratter.

Meanwhile, HUAC returned for yet another round of witch-hunting, adding director Jules Dassin to the ever-growing blacklist. He left America for France, then resettled in Greece. The Screen Writers Guild kowtowed, pledging to "remove from the screen" any individuals who'd had failed to placate the committee by naming names. Vying for headlines, the American Legion "disapproved" of United Artists' *Moulin Rouge,* suspicious of Puerto Rican star José Ferrer, who'd won the year's Distinguished Dramatic Actor Award and Outstanding Director Award. Ferrer, no fool, immediately wired Legion headquarters and offered to join their "fight against communism."

United Artists fought back in July, abstractly, with *High Noon*, the story of a lone marshal—ironically portrayed by HUAC "friendly witness" Gary Cooper—who defends his frontier town from outlaws while fair-weather friends desert him. Screenwriter Carl Foreman had earlier refused to meet with HUAC. Now, his allegory of the Red Scare won Oscars for Best Actor, Best Editing, Best Score and Best Song. Foreman also got a nomination, with the film's director and producer, but they went home empty-handed.

Finally, in August, L.A.'s Smith Act trial saw fourteen local CPUSA members convicted of conspiracy, sentenced by Judge William Mathes to one year in prison for each of eleven criminal counts, their terms to run concurrently. Appeals were underway and might take years to settle, by which time Devon suspected the Red Scare would be a fading memory. Caryl Chessman, likewise, was continuing his series of appeals, but unlike the Smith Act defendants, failure in his case meant execution in San Quentin's gas chamber.

Good riddance, Devon thought and wished that he could get his teeth into a meaty case like that, catch some publicity, and start making a reputation for himself.

———

THE "FLORIDA TERROR" was slowly fading, but Nolan O'Hara saw no prospect for cessation in Klan-ridden counties. Bill Hendrix followed through on his threat to run for governor, but his campaign took a hit with his conviction of mailing libelous postcards, accompanied by a three-year suspended sentence. Briefly quitting the Klan, he formed an Orlando-based American Confederate Army, half-jokingly, but found enough takers to start commissioning "colonels." In May's Democratic primary, he'd run fourth in a field of five candidates, his 11,208 votes buried by winner Dan McCarty's 624,463.

The year-old bombing murders of Harry and Harriette Moore remained officially unsolved, though Nolan had identified four Klansmen as prime suspects: Tillman Belvin, Earl Brooklyn, Joseph Cox, and Edward Spivey. All had histories of violence, and Brooklyn had been exiled from his Georgia Klavern as "a renegade." He'd also shown floor plans of the Moore home at Klan meetings, requesting volunteers for a "special assignment." Cox killed himself after an interview by Nolan and his partner, Rupert Downes. Belvin, a friend of Brooklyn, died from natural causes in August, and only this morning, Brooklyn joined his old buddy in death, one year to the day since the Moores were murdered. That left Spivey, and he wasn't talking—not yet, anyhow.

In Groveland's phony rape case, Walter Irvin received his second trial in February, the proceedings shifted to Ocala, although Judge Futch still presided. Prosecutor Jesse Hunter, lately diagnosed with a terminal illness, offered Irvin life imprisonment if he'd confess to rape, but Irvin doggedly refused. Jurors deliberated only ninety minutes on

Saint Valentine's Day, convicting Irvin once more, and Futch promptly returned him to death row.

Nolan had nearly given up on finding justice for the Moores or any other victims of Jim Crow, and he faced more frustration on another front. Despite the Kefauver "cleanup" in southern Florida, the Syndicate was still alive and well. In May, G-men logged a gathering of *mafiosi* somewhere in the Keys. Details remained elusive, but O'Hara was determined to keep digging, even though Chief Hoover deemed the Mob a nonexistent menace to society. If he could hold on long enough, something was bound to change the Old Man's mind and force him to face facts.

———

MANHATTAN: December 29, 1952

"HERE SHE COMES," George White said, peering over Colby Gantt's left shoulder while he raised one hand as if to scratch his eyebrow. "Check her out, but don't be obvious about it."

Gantt turned, feigned a sudden interest in the fashions on display behind him through a boutique's display window. Shooting glances to his left, he saw a young brunette approaching, longhaired and full-figured, with blue eyes and just a smattering of freckles. To his right, White was hunched over, fumbling at a newspaper dispenser. When the woman moved past them without noticing, White swung around once more and beamed, "What do you think? She's hot, right?

Gantt responded with a noncommittal grunt. "Who is she?"

"Barbara Crowley Smithe," White said. "Crowley, like the magician, and Smithe with an 'e'."

"British?"

"Hell if I know. Only met her yesterday, but I can tell you she's nineteen, married, and has a twenty-month-old daughter. Friendly, and likes to talk about her family. Maybe too much for her own good, you get my drift."

"So, what's the plan?"

"Soon as I get this place lined up in Greenwich Village, I'll invite her to a party, drop some acid on her, and see where it goes from there."

"What makes you think she'll take it?"

"She won't *know* she's taking it, okay? And hell, I'll put her husband on the invite too. All open and aboveboard."

White was chuckling now, reminding Colby of why he didn't like the guy. He was so hyped up on his job with Operation ARTICHOKE, feeding his own mental and sexual quirks, that Colby feared he might go rogue at any time and jeopardize the Agency.

A document from ARTICHOKE that Gantt had seen in January posed the question, "Can we get control of an individual to the point where he will do our bidding against his will and even against fundamental laws of nature, such as self-preservation?" One answer, posited by a collaborating army general, Paul Gaynor, argued that experiments should target "weaker" and "less intelligent" subjects collected from Europe, Southeast Asia and the Philippines.

One test had blown up in their faces already, involving subject Dimitre Dimitrov, codenamed "Kelly." His dossier described Dimitrov as "young, ambitious, bright, a sort of a 'man-on-a-horse' type but a typical Balkan politician." That was before the Agency spun him a yarn about his imminent assassination, clapped him into Greek "protective custody," where he was tortured for six months, then handed back to the CIA for confinement at Forts Amador and Gulick in the Panama Canal Zone. There, they fed him LSD and heroin, along with more torture, until he wound up as a "psychopathic patient" at Fort Clayton, yet another base in Panama. His jailers, judging accurately that Dmitrov was by now "extremely hostile" to the Agency, prescribed "an 'ARTICHOKE' approach to see if it would be possible to re-orient him favorably toward us." The last notation in Dmitrov's file claimed that by March he'd been "successfully given the ARTICHOKE treatment in Panama for a period of about five weeks."

George White, for his part, liked working close to home.

His duties for the FBN were running out of steam by April 1952, when he'd first met Dr. Sidney Gottlieb and embraced him as a kindred spirit. Harry Anslinger had given White a strong nudge toward the Agency, and White dosed his first unwitting subject—a Gotham thug known only as "Tony" on paper—with LSD in September. One of his sidekicks was a fellow OSS alumnus, Albert Hubbard, once jailed for eighteen months on a Volstead Act violation, lately nicknamed "Captain Trips" for his belief in handing LSD to anyone and everyone available, whether or not they knew they'd be receiving it. Encouraged by that method, White dosed neighbors Gil and Patricia Fox with acid, likely to scramble their memories of sadomasochistic episodes they'd glimpsed involving White and sundry hookers.

Talk about a shitstorm in the making, but it wasn't Colby's job to reason why.

October saw a new Agency program, "Project MKDELTA," spun off from its parent, ARTICHOKE, but it was a cosmetic change, still working ardently with drugs and plans for mind control. In Washington last month, President Truman created the National Security Agency, led by Lieutenant General Ralph Canine. His name spawned countless jokes at Agency headquarters, but Director "Beetle" Smith wasn't amused to have more competition in the intelligence field.

And how could he be, with a world on the edge?

In Laos, the Royal Lao Army bulked up in its war on Reds, including eighteen companies by year's end, all suckling at Washington's teat. In Vietnam, Việt Minh fighters drove the French out of Hòa Bình and the De Lattre Line, then foiled Operation Lorraine, inflicting another 1,200 casualties, and ambushed the stragglers at Chan Muong. Even Korea had been heating up again, with "human wave" attacks against UN defenders at godforsaken sites like Old Baldy, Pork Chop Hill, and the Iron Triangle.

Things were also tense in Europe, where Greece and Turkey—though uneasy neighbors— signed on with NATO's original dozen nations, putting the blocks to Soviet expansion on the Aegean. London's *Daily Express* exposed the Gehlen Org in March, telling the world that it was top-heavy with "former" Nazis such as Alois Brunner, ex-*Schutzstaffel* commander at Drancy internment camp outside Paris, who'd shipped 140,000 Jews to their deaths in Poland as part of the "Final Solution." CIA headquarters took that hit on the chin and defended its choice, noting that only survivors of Hitler's *Abwehr* had a handle on fighting the Reds in Europe.

One Agency success story, kept tightly under wraps, was the Congress for Cultural Freedom, an advocacy group formed in West Berlin two years earlier, recruiting artists of all kinds—musicians, dancers, authors and philosophers, you name it—to counter Moscow's claim that that liberal democracy was less compatible with culture than communism. CCF founding members included psychologist John Dewey, historian Benedetto Croce, playwright Tennessee Williams, and so on through the arts and sciences. Breakaway Red journalist Arthur Koestler penned the CCF's manifesto, with thoughtful amendments from British historian Hugh Trevor-Roper. Even the Boston Philharmonic Orchestra was part of the scheme, codenamed OKOPERA.

If anyone knew where the money came from, they were wise enough to keep it under wraps. They absolutely knew where it was going though: to frequent conferences spreading the capitalist gospel from Western Europe to Rangoon, Tokyo, and back around the world to Mexico. The good news also spread in print, through a variety of publications: *Cuadernos del Congreso por la Libertad de la Cultura,* printed in Paris for Latin American distribution; *Encounter* in the United Kingdom; Denmark's *Perspektiv*; and *Preuves* (*Evidence*) in France.

Colby had to smile when he considered it.

Who knew he would grow up to be a missionary?

CHAPTER 7

HARLEM: APRIL 20, 1953

IKE SAWYER INKED ANOTHER "X" over this Monday on his kitchen calendar. He'd never been one who could sit and wish his time away til recently, but now he had begun to count the days, weeks, months until retirement. It was still more than two years away, and while he felt a bit like he was tempting fate, Ike couldn't help himself.

The job he used to love—well, *like,* at least—had turned into a grind, and these days, catching up on the daily news was even worse.

Another United Nations Opium Conference had just wrapped up its latest meeting, producing another treaty that was long on verbiage, while it promised few real-world results. Under this year's Protocol for Limiting and Regulating the Cultivation of the Poppy Plant, the Production of, International and Wholesale Trade in, and Use of Opium, the UN's sixty member states recognized that global opium growing still quadrupled Earth's medical requirements, agreeing that henceforth stock inventories and estimates of licit opium needs would be submitted to that bulwark of temperance, the Permanent Central Opium Board, created in 1909 at Shanghai and morphing through various names for the past four decades.

Under the latest Protocol, seven specific nations were authorized to produce opium for export, the lucky winners being Bulgaria, Greece, India, Iran, Turkey, the USSR and Yugoslavia. Forget about where most of it, in fact, came from the so-called "Golden Triangle" where Burma, Laos and Thailand met at the confluence of the Mekong and Ruak Rivers; and its recent competitor, the "Golden Crescent," nestled in the mountainous peripheries of Afghanistan, Iran and Pakistan. To those regions, for backup, add Colombia and Mexico—not one of them allowed to export opium or heroin under prevailing law.

But did that stop them? Hell no, not a bit.

Meaning Ike would go to work each day for the remainder of his tenure with the FBN, working the same old cases, shadowing the same old syndicates, seizing some drugs from time to time, but seeing little or no progress for his effort.

Progress for his people in pursuit of basic civil rights was just as slow and tedious. So far, it was another lynch-free year according to Tuskegee University, but colored folks still died on both sides of the Mason-Dixon Line, gunned down or bludgeoned by police, picked off in random homicides on ghetto streets and rural Dixie highways. "Grand Dragon" Thomas Hamilton's Association of Carolina Klans had run amok until the FBI belatedly stepped in last year, making arrests for interstate kidnapping, and a pair of Tarheel newspapers—the *Tabor City Tribune* and the *Whiteville News*

Reporter—shared a Pulitzer this month for standing up to sheeted terrorists.

Something more interesting, to Ike's mind, occurred in Baton Rouge two months ago. Louisiana's capital raised its bus fares, while formally abolishing race-based reserved seating, the only bus line in the Old Confederacy that allowed Negroes to sit up front. Drivers—all white, of course —went out on strike to protest the new ordinance, idling most buses for a week until Frederick LeBlanc, ex-mayor of Baton Rouge now state attorney general, declared the law a violation of Louisiana's constitution. Now, Negroes led by Reverend Theo Jemison were boycotting the buses, in what some pundits believed might be a growing trend.

Not much of one in Ike's opinion. After eight short days, the buses rolled again, but now with only two front rows and two in back reserved for whites and blacks. Call that progress, if you were so inclined, but it still felt like Sisyphus from Greek mythology, pushing that boulder up a hill all day only to have it roll back down when he got near the top.

And what could one man with a badge in Gotham do about it? Squat.

Just keep on keepin' on until you die, Ike thought. *Or maybe just til you retire.*

———

INTERVALE STREET, Dorchester, Boston: June 19, 1953

PAYTON SAWYER WAS a long train ride outside his comfort zone, 210 miles northeast of the Harlem neighborhood where he'd grown up and transformed into a cop. For all that, standing opposite Nation of Islam Temple No. 11, watching people of his own hue come and go, it felt vaguely like home.

Dorchester had what some white folks would call "a history": claiming Boston's first integrated neighborhood on Jones Hill, harboring a founder of the old Niagara Movement that later became the NAACP. Suffragettes had also based their Massachusetts operations there before the 19th Amendment gave women the vote and rendered their cause obsolete. It thus seemed only natural, therefore, that the NOI would have quarters here, although their choice of an ex-synagogue might strike some people as ironic.

Payton hadn't come simply to see the building, though. He'd traveled all this way with the permission of and a *per diem* from Inspector Patrick Flannery, to get a look at Malcolm X. Temple No. 11 was his baby for the moment, founded at the order of Elijah Muhammad after Malcolm served an apprenticeship as assistant minister of Temple No. 1 in Detroit—both a promotion and a step toward independence now, the Prophet recognized talent when he saw it.

And Malcolm was recognized by Edgar Hoover's FBI as well, which wasn't any black man's notion of an honor.

Hoover's Bureau began padding its dossier on Malcolm back in February, sharing some results—but only some—with BOSS at NYPD's headquarters on Centre Street, Manhattan. The file noted that Malcolm had his own Communist Index card, a holdover from his rash note to Harry Truman from prison, and listed four arrests in Massachusetts between 1944 and '46, when he'd been sent to prison, freed at last in May of 1952. It called the NOI a "cult" that branded the Korean War "a futile effort by the United States to prevent the coming Asiatic conquest of the world."

Imagine that, thought Payton as he checked his bowtie, making sure that it was straight, and crossed the street to get his first glimpse of the man who seemed to relish scaring white America.

———

A PHONE CALL overnight put a smile on Aloysius Gantt's normally somber face. His son, Devon, was being transferred back from California to the Seat of Government in Washington, together with his wife and Gantt's grandson. No reason had been given for the transfer, but there never was. All orders from the Chief were arbitrary til explained in his good time—if ever.

Still, it would be good to see Devon again, along with wife Camille and son Wyman. Gantt saw a fair amount of daughter-in-law Eileen and son Hardy, still residents of Washington, though Colby spent most of his time elsewhere, engaged in covert business for the CIA.

My plan, Gantt thought back to their talk after Pearl Harbor. *Now I get to live with it.*

At least one of his problems had been shelved, if only for the moment. The same three-judge appellate panel that spurned Alger Hiss's perjury appeal in January rebounded yesterday, dismissing his motion for a new trial. If anyone on the defense team was pursuing Gantt's finagling of Woodstock No. 230099, they'd kept their snooping under wraps so far.

And then there were the Rosenbergs. Make that *had been.*

The Supreme Court denied both spies a stay of execution on June 13, then Justice William Douglas, acting on his own, granted a brief stay four days later, vacated by the court meeting in special session on June 19. Between those two pronouncements, on the eighteenth six G-men from Gotham's field office, led by Alan Belmont, drove thirty-three miles to Sing Sing with a thirteen-page list of questions for Julius and Ethel. Honest answers, Belmont told the prisoners, might save their lives, but still, the Rosenbergs refused to blab.

At 8:00 p.m. on June 19, Julius sat in the electric chair. Bureau observer Anthony Villano on an open line to Hoover, estimated that it took two minutes to snuff out his life. Ethel came next, but something went awry: multiple jolts of electricity took five full minutes to silence her heart, smoke rising from her head all the while.

At Bureau headquarters, one agent thought the news deserved a dose of gallows humor. Others had to save him from a beating by Bob Lamphere, supervisor of the Soviet Espionage Unit, raging at the rookie, "We wanted them to *talk*, asshole. We didn't want them to *die*."

Too late.

David and Ruth Greenglass were recanting their sworn testimony that they'd watched Ethel type up the stolen A-bomb data before passing it along to Alexander Feklisov. David admitted lying under oath to save himself and Ruth. "I frankly think my wife did the typing," he now confessed, "but I don't remember. My wife is more important to me than my sister, or my mother or my father, okay?"

Another story Edgar Hoover would be keeping under wraps until the end of time, buried in what he called his "Secret and Confidential" files, for dusting off at need if he should ever come under attack. In that case, all the Bureau's fuck-ups would be everybody's fault except his own.

And where did that leave Gantt, on some day yet to be revealed?

———

Katz's Delicatessen, Manhattan: July 4, 1953

Another lunch break with Fiona O'Hara, off work from her job at Legal Aid for Independence Day, but subject to recall if any of their clients landed in a cell and needed help. Dave Jordan didn't mind. He was on summer break and had the afternoon free until clocking in at Glassman's restaurant that night.

Fiona took a short break from her lunch—half a corned beef sandwich with matzo ball soup—to meet his eyes across their small table and say, "So, look at you. Nearly a lawyer."

"Nearly? Fee, I've still got a whole year to go, before I even take my first run at the bar exam."

"One run is all you'll need," she answered back, sounding supremely confident. "I've kept up on your grades, if you recall."

"Well..."

"Well, *nothing*, David. Straight A's all the way, so far, unless you've been pulling my leg."

The way she smiled at him made Jordan wish he had been pulling on her leg—or easing both of them apart—but then he thought about his own leg and the other scars he carried from the war, halting that train of thought before his damned imagination got away from him.

His courses at Columbia this year had run the gamut from administrative law to complex litigation, state and local government law, American jurisprudence, pretrial commercial litigation, trial practice and tax policy. He chose classes seeking a balance between criminal and civil law, still not entirely sure which field would be his specialty, assuming that he had one.

When Fiona spoke again, she caught him with a mouthful of brisket, her question seeming as if she'd read his mind. "So, any thoughts yet on what you'll be doing, once you're free and clear?"

"Thoughts?" he answered when he'd had a chance to swallow. "I've got thoughts up the wazoo, but no conclusions."

"We could always use a mind like yours at Legal Aid."

"What would I do with all that dough?" he teased.

She suddenly went serious. "I didn't study law just to cash in, you know. I love the work I'm doing, even when it gets me down."

"Sorry. I know you do. It's what I—"—*don't say, "love," you idiot*—"what I admire about you most of all."

"Oh, most of all?" Now she was teasing him. "What else do you admire?"

"Your courage, confidence, and character, the way you try to make the world a better place."

"Jesus, the Girl Scouts' creed? No wonder you've got women lining up around the block."

"Not so you'd notice," Dave replied, and bent back to his sandwich with a will, suddenly wishing he were anyplace but there.

———

FBI Headquarters: August 24, 1953

MONDAY WAS Devon's first day back after returning from Los Angeles, and here he was, waiting beside his father after being summoned first thing in the morning to Director Hoover's office.

What the hell?

He'd asked his dad, but Aloysius didn't seem to have a clue. "Just wait and see," he cautioned. "You can bet he's got something in mind for both of us."

"Like what?" Devon asked, and got only a bland shrug in reply.

The intercom on Helen Gandy's desk gave out a chirp, and she glanced up at the two of them, deadpan as usual. "He'll see you now."

They passed into the Chief's office, Devon surprised to find Clyde Tolson wasn't joining them. Maybe he had a facial lined up for this morning, trying to stay young against all odds. Hoover remained seated at his desk as they entered and Devon closed the door behind them. Every bit as taciturn as Miss Gandy, he greeted them.

"Agents Gantt and Gantt. I have a special task for you today."

Devon waited beside his father, knowing better than to speak, til Aloysius said, "Yes, Sir?"

"I trust you followed the Kefauver circus while it was in progress?"

"Yes, Sir." This time, both of them answered in unison.

"I found it...disconcerting," Hoover said. "And an advantage to one Harry Anslinger, espousing fables of the so-called Mafia."

Devon could think of no response. His father didn't even try.

"Your new assignment," Hoover said, "is to prepare a

monograph documenting the nonexistence of organized crime in America."

Devon thought he just might choke on that, but he managed to suppress a cough.

"In furtherance of that pursuit, I offer this," Hoover declared, still seated as he passed a sheet of paper to the senior Gantt. Devon accepted it in turn and saw it was a memo written by Assistant Director Alan Belmont to Assistant Director Mickey Ladd. It read: "The Maffia is an alleged organization active in Sicily. The organization's existence in the U.S. is doubtful."

Christ, thought Devon, *he can't even spell it right.*

"You have the Bureau's files at your disposal," Hoover said, concluding his directive. "Use them well and in a timely fashion. I expect the finished monograph within two weeks from now. Agreed?"

"Yes, Sir," Gantt's father answered for them both, then they were out and moving through the bustle of another morning at HQ.

"What in the hell—" Devon began before his father hushed him with a glare.

"Not here, all right? You feel like lunch?"

Devon glanced at his watch. "It's only half-past nine."

"So what? We need some peace and quiet."

"Sure. Okay."

His father drove to Mangialardo's Deli, in the 1300 block of Pennsylvania Avenue. They ordered at the counter, took a number, then retired to a small table by the window. Aloysius checked under the table, finding only wads of dried-out gum, then put a quarter in their table's Seeburg Wall-O-Matic diner jukebox, punching up three tunes from the fifty 45-rpm single records on tap. Before he started talking, even with that cover, Devon's dad waited to hear their number called out and retrieved their food: a pair of "G-Man" sandwiches heaping with ham, salami, mortadella, pepperoni, and two kinds of cheese.

Suddenly hungry, Devon took a bite, then said, "Okay, we're here. No bugs under the table. Now, can you believe this shit?"

"I don't have to," his dad replied. "Neither do you. We just have to produce as Speed requires."

"To prove crime isn't organized? Has he ever heard of Vegas? Just this year, so far, Meyer Lansky's cronies opened up a new hotel they're calling the Algiers, to handle overflow guests from the Thunderbird. They've spent a million dollars renovating the Flamingo, which they murdered Bugsy Siegel for. And then there's Hollywood. Does *From Here to Eternity* ring any bells?"

"I saw it with your mother on opening weekend," his father answered.

"Nine Oscar nominations," Devon said, "and it won eight of them, including Frank Sinatra for Best Supporting Actor."

"So?"

"So, Harry Cohn at Columbia only cast Sinatra because John Rosselli *told* him to. They had an argument about it, Cohn despising Frank the way he does, and Cohn says, 'John, if we have a problem here, I'm going to have to make some phone calls.' Hinting around at his ties to the Mob. Rosselli comes back with, 'If we have any problem, you're a fucking dead man'."

"And your point is?"

"My point is that the Mob *exists,* okay? Hell, they've been watching over Frankie from the time he was a kid in Hoboken, back when his mama did backroom abortions. When he wanted to ditch Jimmy Dorsey and go solo with Columbia Records in '43, who smoothed it over with his old contract? The late Willie Moretti, at gunpoint. Three years later, Frank's crooning to the whole damned 'nonexistent' Mafia down in Havana, making headlines when those nuns caught him passed out with hookers in his hotel suite."

"Old news," his father said. "We've got a file on him, and you're missing the point."

"Which is?"

"You ought to know by now. We serve one master, and his name's John Edgar Hoover. He gives orders and we follow them, or we find someplace else to work. And if you think he'll recommend you for another decent job, you need to pull your head out of your ass, and do it quickly."

"So we just lie about the Syndicate, the Mafia, whatever? Even though New York started a list of thirty 'top hoodlums' this year, compiling dossiers?"

"Headquarters has millions of files, Devon. Few of them go to court, as you already know. Justice will prosecute a mobster here and there, for flagrant federal violations. Meanwhile, Edgar likes his tips on races and investments, his rooms comped for those inspection tours with Clyde, and so forth. Ours is not to reason why."

"Okay. But lying's one thing. 'Documenting nonexistence' of a fact is something else."

"You think so? Finish up your lunch and let me show you how it's done."

———

Serpukhov, Moscow Oblast: September 8, 1953

Leonid Babin sipped his second vodka, lounging in an easy chair before his dacha's fireplace as he read once more the letter from Trenton, New Jersey. That was not reflected in the envelope's return address, of course. It had been mailed from Montreal to Paris, on from there to Neuchâtel in Switzerland, next to Podgorica, Yugoslavia, and only then to Serpukhov.

His name appeared nowhere, either outside the envelope or on the short letter. In both cases, he was addressed as Misha Egorov, the name he'd used when purchasing the dacha, and its signature—"Your Comrades"—gave nothing away. The text was brief without, he hoped, being so cryptic that it might excite a nosy censor: "*U nas vse khorosho. Byt' bezopasnym.*"

Translation: *All is well with us. Be safe.*

From that, he knew Stefan was doing well at nine years old. If there'd been any problems—with his health, in school, with the authorities—the message would reflect it, while remaining just as bland.

No doubt, the couple to whom Babin entrusted his sole child must be aware of sudden and dramatic changes in the USSR, and across the Eastern Bloc at large. In January, Beria pressured the Politburo to publicize the "Doctor's Plot," hoping those headlines would divert attention from the more embarrassing Mingrelian Affair. To ensure it, *Pravda* trumpeted the charges filed against some of Russia's preeminent doctors, reviled in print as "Vicious Spies and Killers under the Mask of Academic Physicians." MGB "investigation" soon established the accused were covert terrorists, killing off their patients with false diagnoses, concealment of actual ailments, and murder cast as therapy.

Among the victims named were Aleksandr Shcherbakov, First Secretary of Moscow's Communist Party from 1938 to 1945; Andrei Zhdanov, Chairman of the Soviet of the Union for eleven months in 1946-47; Red Army

Marshals Leonid Govorov (slain in March), Ivan Konev and Aleksandr Vasilevsky (both of whom had somehow managed to survive); plus two more fortunate survivors, General Sergei Shtemenko and Admiral Gordey Levchenko. The nine accused—six of them Jews—included Stalin's personal physician, Dr. Miron Vovsi.

Ironically, with Dr. Vovsi locked away, a stroke felled Stalin on March 1, leaving him paralyzed and incoherent until he died after four days. An autopsy revealed the cause of death, but rumors of assassination—possibly by Lavrentiy Beria—ran wild. Georgy Malenkov replaced Stalin as Premier, while Nikita Khrushchev became First Secretary of the Party, impatiently waiting his turn at command. The "Doctor's Plot" evaporated overnight, all charges dropped and branded fabrications.

Also lost to illness, only nine days after Stalin, was Czech Communist Party leader Klement Gottwald, whose repressive actions mirrored Stalin's on a smaller scale. By April 3, Sergei Ogoltsov was out as First Deputy Minister of State Security, accused by Beria of murdering Jewish actor and producer Solomon Mikhoels in 1948. At the same time, Beria merged the MGB with his MVD, deposing Semyon Ignatyev as Minister of State Security and packing him off to Bashkir ASSR as a minor Party secretary.

Ogoltsov was still in prison, awaiting trial and presumed execution, when the wheel turned on Beria in June, with his arrest at a special meeting of the Presidium. Confined under heavy guard, while Ogoltsov was freed and "rehabilitated," Beria himself now faced trial and certain death on charges of treason, terrorism, counter-revolutionary activity during the Russian Civil War, and—almost incidentally—a long series of rapes involving young women, some of whose imprisoned relatives were used as leverage to ensure submission. Beria's replacement, Sergei Kruglov, received the Order of Suvorov, First Class, for his role in deporting thousands of Chechens during World War Two.

As if upheavals in the Russian capital were not enough, East German workers oppressed by ever-rising production quotas staged a wildcat strike on June 16, expanding into a full-scale rebellion the following day, with demonstrations staged in more than 500 towns and villages. Red Army troops and *Volkspolizei* brutally suppressed the uprising, prompting charges that GDR Minister of State Security Wilhelm Zaisser had failed to promptly mobilize the Stasi in response. Stripped of authority and branded an enemy of the people, Zaisser was allowed to live, but only as a lowly translator at East Berlin's Institute of Marxism and Leninism.

How hath the mighty fallen, Babin thought and smiled before he fed his letter from America into the fire.

As if to celebrate, the USSR detonated its first hydrogen bomb on August 12, at Semipalatinsk Test Site, using data furnished by now-imprisoned spy Klaus Fuchs. Although it lagged nine months behind the first American H-bomb exploded at Eniwetok Atoll, it delivered a yield equivalent to 400 kilotons of TNT—twenty-two times that of the "Fat Boy" Nagasaki bomb.

That guaranteed a new arms race, and ample work ahead for agents of the MGB. All Babin had to do now, was to keep his wits about him while the aftershocks of cutthroat politics rocked Moscow and the world at large.

———

FBI Miami Field Office: October 18, 1953

WHILE RACIAL VIOLENCE appeared to be slowly subsiding in the Sunshine State, the Ku Klux Klan maintained most of its post-war strength, albeit under altered leadership. Newspapers told Nolan O'Hara that Bill Hendrix had resigned his post as leader of the Southern Knights, replaced by River Junction furniture salesman C. L. Parker. Once installed, Parker renamed his faction the United Klan, claiming 100,000 members and inviting Negroes to participate in segregated chapters, but none took him up on it.

In March, frustrated by its inability to pin a federal crime on any known Klansmen, Justice convened a grand jury probing the order's reign of terror between 1949 and '51, grilling more than 100 witnesses. When the hearings concluded in June, seven Kluxers—six men and one woman —faced perjury charges for lying to G-man or the grand jury, some accused of falsely denying Klan membership on federal job applications. The twelve-page list of charges called the Klan "a cancerous growth," responsible for "a catalog of terror that seems incredible," but O'Hara wasn't counting on convictions. As further proof of that, the Bureau had already closed its inquiry into the Moore bombing at Christmas 1951.

In politics, Governor Dan McCarty was inaugurated on January 6, then stricken with a crippling heart attack on February 25 and died before September's end. Successor Charley Johns, a segregationist and leader of the legislature's far-right "Pork Chop Gang," promoter of the state's first portable electric chair, stepped in as acting governor to finish the remainder of McCarty's term. Closer to home, Mel Richard ran for reelection to Miami's city council, but some wily adversary sank him on election eve, plastering "Vote for Mel Richard" stickers on car windshields citywide, obscuring their drivers' view, infuriating voters as they were headed for the polls.

In Tampa, drive-by gunmen missed their shot at Santo Trafficante Jr. in January, leaving their target to feign confusion, claiming "I don't have an enemy in the world. I think it was a case of mistaken identity." In fact, he blamed longtime rival Charlie Wall, now in his seventies, but Wall was hiding out, for now, so Santo Sr. sent his only son off to Havana, learning how to manage posh casinos for the Syndicate.

Cuba was drawing mobsters like a magnet these days, since Fulgencio Batista deposed "cordial president" Carlos Prío last year. His new law on gambling, with tax breaks for foreign investors, welcomed any Stateside thug, although their mentor Meyer Lansky, had to finish off a New York prison term before he could take full advantage of the altered rules.

Meanwhile, there was a revolution brewing in Cuba, led by young lawyer and frustrated would-be Big League Baseball pitcher Fidel Ruz and his brother, Raul. After he blew a tryout for the New York Yankees, Castro played briefly for a home team called the Barbudos ("Bearded Ones"), then circulated a petition to depose Batista following his military coup in March of 1952. The courts rejected that initiative, so Castro stockpiled guns, recruiting some 1,200 rebels from Havana's angry working class, training them in the guise of skeet shooters.

Only 135 fighters turned out for Castro's first raid, staged on July 26 at the Moncada army barracks in Santiago de Cuba. Fifty-two rebels died in the attack or were summarily executed before fifty-one others faced trial in September. While two dozen lawyers defended most of the defendants, Fidel represented himself, treating the court to a four-hour speech on October 16, declaring, "Condemn me, it does not matter. History will absolve me." Instead of execution, he was spared, handed a fifteen-year term at Presidio Modelo prison, on the Isle of Pines. Brother Raul received a thirteen-year sentence. Twenty other rebels got ten years apiece, while three who fled before the shooting started drew three years.

But would that be the end of it? O'Hara doubted it, since malcontents who idolized Fidel christened their association the 26th of July Movement—M 26-7 for short—in honor of the Moncada skirmish. Arms were trickling into Cuba, and unless O'Hara missed his guess, that trickle would become a flood before the Castro brothers breathed free air again.

Corruption and the *Cosa Nostra* versus revolutionary zeal: which one would win out in the end?

Given Cuba's dramatic history, O'Hara wasn't placing any bets.

———

FBI Headquarters: October 30, 1953

Declan O'Hara finished skimming over an internal Bureau document titled "The Mafia: A Myth," then tucked it out of sight in one of his desk drawers. At first, he'd been inclined to drop it in the trash can, but that would be tantamount to heresy, and who knew where it might wind up from there? The cover bore a stamp proclaiming CONFIDENTIAL: DO NOT CIRCULATE, and there'd be hell to pay if some custodian got hold of it and leaked it to the press.

No author's name was given on the monograph, but Declan recognized his former law school classmate's handi-work and understood why Aloysius Gantt spent the past few weeks huddled with son Devon, conversing in hushed tones while they poured over Bureau paperwork. As con jobs went, the document was adequate, discussing machinations of "the so-called Mafia" in Sicily and immigration of purported members to the States between the 1880s and the First World War, but that was where the authors parted company with evidence to tout the Chief's view of a National Crime Syndicate as unsupported by hard facts.

Whatever. The report would please Attorney General Herbert Brownell Jr., put his mind at ease about the state of crime in the United States, and it ignored established ties between Vice President Dick Nixon and the likes of Mickey Cohen, not to mention Nixon's gambling junkets to Havana. President Eisenhower, for his part, had proved to be an ideological ally of Edgar Hoover, averting his eyes from illegal bugging and wiretaps as long as he received prime dirt on political rivals including Eleanor Roosevelt, Democratic political advisor Bernard Baruch, and Supreme Court Justice William Douglas, a target of abortive impeachment proceedings after he briefly delayed the Rosenberg executions in June.

And speaking of wiretaps, two months of new hearings in Congress climaxed in July with the introduction of a bill by New York's Kenneth Keating, permitting the Bureau to tap phones at will in pursuit of traitors, saboteurs, spies, and others suspected of "similar offenses." Ex-Attorney General McGrath bitched to Congress about the inconvenience caused by lawyers who insisted on revealing covert sources. Larry Fly turned up, of course, debating House Majority Leader Charles Halleck's support for wiretapping on Edward R. Murrow's "See It Now" TV show. Milton Jones, chief researcher for the Bureau's Crime Records Section, reviewed that program in a memo to Hoover, claiming that

"Fly was extremely vindictive in his attitude towards the Bureau, and Halleck had trouble interrupting to rebut his statements." As before, the new bill crashed and burned in Congress.

A new member of the Bureau HQ hierarchy was Cartha DeLoach, nicknamed "Deke," who'd joined in 1942 and been promoted to Inspector nine years later. Just this month, Hoover made him Clyde Tolson's assistant, with a side order to "straighten out" the quarrelsome American Legion. Starting from the FBI's own Legion post, he'd so far lectured the outfit's "Americanism Committee" and seemed bent on rising through the ranks to a command position.

In April, Chicago G-men captured three suspects—including a lawyer and a court bailiff—alleged to have stolen nine framed paintings from St Joseph's Cathedral in Bardstown, Kentucky. At trial, third defendant "Gus Manoletti" revealed himself as one Pierre Lafitte, claiming the Bureau engaged him to retrieve the paintings at a cost of $35,000. Searching the records on Lafitte, Declan had been surprised to learn he was a Corsican drug smuggler with Syndicate connections on both sides of the Atlantic, who was also sometimes on the CIA's payroll.

Strange days.

Meanwhile, another special agent had been slain on duty. John Murphy was part of the team that cornered fugitive killer John Elgin Johnson in a Baltimore theater, dying when Johnson chose to shoot it out. Return fire killed him on the spot, too late to help Murphy.

Nationwide, the "Lavender Scare" was ongoing, a January memo noting that the State Department had discharged 425 suspected homosexuals so far. President Eisenhower fueled that fire in April, with Executive Order 10450. Ironically, while it dismantled Harry Truman's

Loyalty Review Board program from 1947, the new edict banned homosexuals from federal jobs across the board, regardless of their politics. Word was that it would axe 5,000 more employees when the FBI and Office of Personnel Management sorted them out. Edgar Hoover got things rolling in July, sending names from his Sex Deviates Program to the Civil Service Commission.

Not that the Red Scare had been sidetracked; far from it. A recent target of HUAC now chaired by Illinois Republican Harold Velde, was Lucille Ball, star of TV's "I Love Lucy" since 1951 with her husband, Cuban bandleader Desi Arnaz. Millions tuned in to the sitcom each week, but Lucy's joust with HUAC told the world she'd registered to vote for the Communist Party in 1936. Ten years later, Desi appeared in a show sponsored by the Hollywood Independent Citizens Committee of the Arts, Sciences and Professions, tagged by the Bureau as a Red front group. Neither revelation hurt ratings, but Hoover opened dossiers on the couple, keeping a close eye on both.

Another longtime subject from the Chief's watch list, unionist Harry Bridges, who won reversal of his 1950 deportation order from the Supreme Court in mid-June. The court, split four-to-three, with two judges abstaining, as to whether Bridges lied about his CPUSA membership, but a majority agreed the three-year statute of limitations had long since expired. Larry Fly, who represented Bridges in a single court appearance, got another memo in his Bureau file, branding him "a concealed communist."

Things hadn't worked out quite so well for William Remington. At his second trial in January, drunken Liz Bentley repeated her turn as the State's star witness, still whining to friend and fellow informer Harvey Matusow about her abuse by the press, confiding to a girlfriend that she might "step out in front of a car and settle everything." Booze and bellyaching aside, she scored a win for Justice, when jurors convicted Remington of perjury and Judge Vincent Leibell imposed a three-year term at Lewisburg Penitentiary. Chief Hoover praised Bentley for having "conducted herself in a credible fashion" and extended her Bureau payments for another three months.

As for the Smith Act trials, there'd been no letup and O'Hara saw no signs of one to come. Original Gotham defendant Robert Thompson—winner of the Distinguished Service Cross in World War Two, after he'd split from the Abraham Lincoln Brigade— jumped bail in 1949, but G-men recaptured him this year, the court adding four more years to his original sentence.

The National Lawyer's Guild, founded in 1937, stepped up to defend some "second-tier" Smith Act defendants, but its members soon backed off—and half of them resigned outright—after Attorney General Brownell threatened to list the NLG as a subversive group if it continued representing Reds.

There goes the Sixth Amendment, Declan thought but kept it to himself.

Across the landscape now, he noted new convictions in a host of federal courts. In May, Manhattan jurors returned guilty verdicts on Elizabeth Gurley Flynn and her twelve codefendants, sending them off for an average two years in prison. Honolulu's case saw all seven defendants convicted in June, immediately followed by one juror's raving mental breakdown. Judge Jon Wiig imposed prison terms of three to five years each, with fines ranging from $2,000 to $5,000.

In Seattle, seven more reds bit the dust in October, betrayed at the eleventh hour by an FBI informer who'd banked $10,000 for infiltrating the International Woodworkers of America while doubling as an active CPUSA recruiter. Judge William Lindbergh imposed five-year prison terms and $10,000 fines across the board, while defendant Barbara Hartle—an avid Red since 1933—renounced the Party to start working for the FBI and HUAC.

Detroit's trial of the "Michigan Six" ran true to form, all defendants convicted and sentenced to prison, though ripples were already spreading from that case. Star prosecution witness Milton Stanwire was hinting that he'd lied under oath on the stand, and a judge who'd observed the proceedings opined that the accused were "victims of Russianitis."

In Philadelphia, where Bureau agents arrested seven Reds during July and August, the Pennsylvania Civil Rights Congress was outraged enough to launch a newsletter titled *Let Freedom Ring,* emblazoned with a Liberty Bell, condemning a society that confused dissent with Communist conspiracy. It did no good, of course, as all of those accused were convicted of plotting to destroy the U.S. government, sentenced to five-year prison terms with their $10,000 fines.

Cleveland, in turn, had seemingly forgotten its motto of "Progress & Prosperity," holding seven Reds for trial on Smith Act charges that was set to drag on through next year. In Baltimore, six accused were spared Elizabeth Bentley's routine, but all were convicted on testimony from witness Mary Markward, who'd spent nine years reporting to the Bureau from inside D.C.'s Communist Party before she went public, also testifying in Manhattan. Immigrant Marxist Alexander Bittelman was vacationing in Florida when he was charged, tried, and convicted of conspiracy. Ditto Alexander Trachtenberg, founding publisher of Gotham's Marxist International Publishers, who served three months

MICHAEL NEWTON

before witness Harvey Matusow began recanting his lies under oath.

In Washington, Joe McCarthy began his second Senate term with an appointment as chairman of the Committee on Government Operations where, Majority Leader Robert Taft opined, "He can't do any harm." As it turned out, that may have been Taft's worst mistake so far in fourteen years of politics.

Unnoticed by Taft, McCarthy's committee included the Senate Permanent Subcommittee on Investigations, with a mandate flexible enough to let Tail-Gunner Joe scrutinize anyone, anywhere, for damned near anything. Appointing Roy Cohn as chief counsel and young Robert Kennedy as his assistant, McCarthy went right back to hunting Reds in government.

His wedge this time was Gerald David Schine, heir to his Latvian immigrant father's New York hotel-and-theater fortune, also a bosom pal of Cohn's. Cohn brought Schine aboard as a "chief consultant," based on a pamphlet he'd written in 1952, *Definition of Communism*, which wound up in every room of his family's hotel chain. The friends—some said lovers—embarked on a tour of Europe, allegedly investigating Red influence on the State Department's U.S. Information Agency, its overseas libraries and its radio program, "Voice of America." In Hamburg, *Die Welt* dubbed Roy and Gerald *Schnüffler,* German for "snoops." Theodore Kaghan, Deputy Director of the Public Affairs Division in the Office of the U.S. High Commissioner for Germany, mocked them as "junketeering gumshoes."

When the draft caught up with Schine, inducted as a private, Cohn immediately launched a near-hysterical campaign to win him special privileges, including phone calls to Secretary of the Army Robert Stevens and Schine's company commander. When that got him nowhere, Cohn threatened to "wreck the army" for holding his buddy "hostage" to muzzle McCarthy's committee.

While Joe and Roy geared up for full-scale hearings on the army brass, McCarthy named professional ex-Red Joseph "Doc" Matthews Sr. as his committee's staff director —the same post Matthews had earlier filled at HUAC. Lately, he'd sparked a heated controversy with his pamphlet *Reds in Our Churches*, opening with an observation that "The largest single group supporting the Communist apparatus in the United States is composed of Protestant Clergymen." While pastors nationwide denounced his strident lies, McCarthy welcomed Matthews as a kindred spirit in pursuit of covert enemies.

For his opening shot at the army, McCarthy—newly married to wife Jean, with an adopted daughter on the way —chose Irving Peress, a New York dentist drafted as a captain in October 1952 and promoted to major one year later. The rub: an anonymous complaint that Peress was promoted while "under surveillance for communist activities." McCarthy called the army "soft on communism," promoting the battle cry "Who promoted Peress?" while forgetting that the dentist's promotion was mandatory under the "Doctor Draft Law," which McCarthy himself voted to pass in 1948.

Even as McCarthy braced himself to take on the army, he didn't forget older enemies. Owen Lattimore, facing multiple counts of alleged perjury before Pat McCarran's Senate Internal Security Subcommittee, found a surprise supporter in George Boas, professor of philosophy at Johns Hopkins University, who founded a Lattimore Defense Fund to defray legal costs. In May, Judge Luther Youngdahl dismissed four counts of Lattimore's indictment outright, while requiring Justice to present specific evidence supporting three more charges. No proof was forthcoming, and despite the government's appeal of Youngdahl's ruling, the case, at last, died quietly.

Too bad they all can't, Declan thought, but knew America's hysteria had yet to run its course.

———

MANHATTAN: October 31, 1953

THE STREETS WERE full of ghosts, goblins and witches, wandering from door to door and shouting, "Trick or treat!" Watching them from the backseat of his Chrysler Custom Imperial, Greg Jordan saw a mummy trailing bandages along the sidewalk, trying to keep pace with Frankenstein's monster and a werewolf who looked slightly moth-eaten. Emerging from a corner shop, a stubby Satan trailed two little witches in his wake.

Halloween tableaux always reminded him of Dave and Gemma when they'd been that small and vulnerable, bent on seeking candy in the midst of Gotham's Castellammarese War and its parallel War of the Jews. He sent men out to cover them in those days, always fearful, but they'd managed to survive, though it was close in Dave's case. Both of them were vastly altered now: Greg's son nearly recovered from his battle wounds in Europe, Gemma a wife and mother who had given up her teenage visions of a university degree to keep house for a husband who was rarely found at home.

As for Greg, today he was a fifty-seven-year-old orphan, the younger of his parents' two surviving sons, a reasonably wealthy lawyer with a wife who mostly loved him and had more or less forgiven him for Dave's enlistment in the army, plus a practice limited to his own family's network of businesses, both legal and illicit. He no longer feared someone would pop out of the woodwork to accuse him of his role in killing Salvatore Maranzano two decades earlier, but he still walked a path fraught with danger on both sides of the law.

Take Meyer Lansky for example, one of the "untouchables," convicted of gambling in May, sentenced to three months in jail and three years' probation. *Capo crimine* Anthony Lima took a harder fall in San Francisco, locked up for grand theft and replaced by Michael Abati. Joe Adonis faced the double threat of a perjury rap and deportation to Naples, just as Frank Costello left prison after his stint for contempt of Congress. Time itself could also be an enemy, as in the case of Kansas City's *Don* Anthony Gizzo, stricken by a heart attack on April Fool's Day, leaving his empire to underboss Nick Civella.

In New York, Vito Genovese was still making waves, ordering a hit on soldier Steven Franse, whom he'd tasked to keep an eye on Vito's wife while Genovese hid in Italy during the war. Franse had dropped the ball big-time, as Anna Genovese enjoyed a series of adulterous affairs, then aired her husband's dirty laundry in divorce court. On June 18, Joe Valachi lured Franse to a Bronx restaurant, where Pasquale Pagano and nephew Fiore Siano took turns beating Steve, then strangled him slowly as per Vito's orders.

And so what? Jordan asked himself. This was the life he'd chosen, when he could've signed on with some major firm, worked grueling hours on the partner track, and likely been involved in deals as shady as the ones he'd managed for the Giordano clan. He would've made some money, maybe had himself some ulcers and a heart attack or two by now, but he knew one thing beyond doubt.

In the "legit" world, he'd have never been his own man as he was working for family, meeting the risks head-on and sharing equally in the rewards. On balance, not the worst life Jordan could imagine, but he rarely passed a day without wondering how and when it all would end.

———

Tehran, Iran: December 22, 1953

THE MILITARY TRIAL, all things considered, hadn't taken long. Prosecutor Hossein Azemodeh sought execution for ex-Prime Minister Mohammed Mossadegh, charged with treason, but the court had shown its version of leniency, sentencing him to three years' solitary confinement, followed by house arrest for life. Showing a flair for irony, Mossadegh told his judge, "The verdict of this court has increased my historical glories. I am extremely grateful you convicted me. Truly tonight the Iranian nation understood the meaning of constitutionalism."

How would Americans regard the recent *coup d'état,* Colby Gantt wondered, if they knew the whole thing had been planned and pulled off by the CIA?

The plot was codenamed "Operation Ajax," hatched by Director Dulles and Deputy Director of Plans Frank Wisner. London, as an equal partner in the scheme, preferred to call it "Operation Boot." Long story short, the ruckus dated back to 1951, when Iran's Parliament voted to nationalize the greedy Anglo-Iranian Oil Company. Prime minister Mossadegh, duly elected, bucked the will of monarch Shah

Mohammad Reza Pahlavi and supported keeping Iran's oil for Iranians. Britain imposed a crippling embargo on Iranian oil, and AIOC shoveled bribes to grasping local politicians while successive British prime ministers Clement Attlee and Winston Churchill nagged Washington to orchestrate a coup. President Eisenhower first refused, then caved into London's demands and gave the Agency free rein.

On August 19, Tehrani mobsters in the CIA's employ staged pro-Shah riots in the capital, aided by busloads of thugs from the hinterlands. To make matters worse, the pro-Soviet Tudeh Party, having failed to kill the Shah in 1949, now rallied in support of Mossadegh, whom they'd denounced until the riots started. Street fighting and reprisals from the Royal Iranian Army killed at least 300 persons, but the truth was the first casualty, derailed when one pro-Shah newspaper publisher accepted a CIA "personal loan" for $45,000 and a Mossadegh supporter saw his printing presses wrecked by vandals in the Agency's employ. Paid *agents provocateur* posing as members of the Tudeh Party faked a "communist revolution," while U.S. Major General Norman Schwarzkopf Sr.—former superintendent of New Jersey's State Police during the Lindbergh kidnapping fiasco—escorted Shah Pahlavi home from brief exile in Italy and stayed to train his new Organization of National Intelligence and Security (alias "SAVAK") to crush future dissent against the monarchy.

Colby had been an interested observer, handed out some bribes himself along the way, but now, sunburned and weary, he was ready to go home.

Stateside, where Allen Dulles succeeded Bedell Smith as CIA Director in February, freeing Smith to become Under Secretary of State, the Agency was falling into line with Ike's "New Look," anxious to flex its muscles further on the broad world stage. In March, when Joe McCarthy started to impugn the CIA's patriotism, agents first burglarized his office, then set about feeding him misinformation, diverting the tail-gunner's short attention span toward other branches of government.

At the same time, Dulles promoted the cause of a new and more secure Agency headquarters, handpicking 258 acres near Langley, Virginia, surrounded by federal parkland on three sides and private homes on the fourth. It was a start, but Colby knew it might take years to win approval from Congress, then complete construction of an adequate facility.

And in the meantime, Asia smoldered, portions of it bursting into flames.

Korea, for the moment, was at peace, although a fragile one. The warring sides signed an armistice—but no final peace treaty—at 10:00 a.m. on July 27, with combat suspended twelve hours later. Over Syngman Rhee's fierce objections and threats to fight on alone, the peninsula lay divided along the 38th parallel in perpetuity, a solution that some diplomats were now proposing for war-torn Vietnam.

The Agency was busy there as well, pulling strings behind the scenes, occasionally hampered by the State Department while Director Dulles sold Ike on the "domino theory" of Red expansion in Southeast Asia. In early April, the action shifted into Laos, where Việt Minh soldiers joined the Pathet Lao to raze French outposts. With General Giáp in command, the Reds conquered the border provinces of Phongsali and Xâm Neua, adjoining Vietnam and lying northeast from the Plain of Jars. By November, French General Henri Navarre was battling to preserve a small airbase in the isolated jungle valley of Điện Biên Phủ, in northwest Vietnam.

Worldwide, the CIA was pressing "Project HTLIN-GUAL," a massive campaign to intercept and read all U.S. mail addressed to the USSR or the People's Republic of China, collaborating on the sly—and in clear violation of federal law—with Postmaster General Arthur Summerfield. It was a herculean task, but clerks like Colby's wife thought they could handle it.

None of its foreign operations interfered with Agency experiments at home, into the mysteries of mind manipulation and control. Could LSD prompt Russian agents to defect, or could the MGB use it against the CIA's assets? By 1953, Sandoz opted to deal strictly with the FDA in Washington, but first, it held a kind of fire sale, offering the Agency ten kilos of acid—100 million individual doses—for the bargain price of $240,000. It was an offer too sweet to resist, and Allen Dulles snapped it up without a second thought.

How was it being put to use? A January document from Project ARTICHOKE described experiments conducted on two nineteen-year-old girls, reporting that "These subjects have clearly demonstrated that they can pass from a fully awake state to a deep hypnotic controlled state via the telephone, via some very subtle signal that cannot be detected by other persons in the room, and without the other individuals being able to note the change. It has also been shown by experimentation with these girls that they can act as unwilling couriers for information purposes, and that they can be conditioned to a point where they believe a change in identity on their part even on the polygraph."

Another ARTICHOKE file, labeled "Analogous Case #3," noted that a CIA Security Office employee "was hypnotized and given a false identity. She defended it hotly, denying her true name and rationalizing with conviction the possession of identity cards made out to her real self. Later, having had the false identity erased by suggestion, she was asked if she had ever heard of the name she had been defending as her own five minutes before. Apparently, she had true amnesia for the entire episode." Other methods under study included drugs, magnetic fields, sound waves, sleep deprivation, solitary confinement, and even surgical lobotomies.

For a time, the Office of Security and the Technical Services Staff shared responsibility for ARTICHOKE, but TSS pulled ahead under the leadership of Dr. Gottlieb. From ARTICHOKE, he changed the operation's name to Project MKDELTA, then again to MKNAOMI, and finally, in April, to Project MKULTRA, sanctioned and bankrolled by Director Dulles with a startup budget of $300,000. Indiana's Eli Lilly and Company pharmaceutical firm got $400,000 to rush production of more LSD.

As a brief change of pace, the Agency also released another blast of *Serratia marcescens* in San Francisco, producing more mysterious infections, but that was a sideshow to the main event. LSD was the new toy of choice, unwitting victims dosed in "normal" settings whenever feasible, while agents watched and noted observations. CIA agents also served as guinea pigs, one raving and sprinting into heavy D.C. traffic after a "friend" spiked his morning coffee with acid. He survived and later claimed hideous monsters drove the cars surrounding him. Other subjects included mental patients, prisoners, junkies and hookers—all "people who couldn't fight back" in Agency parlance. One Kentucky psych ward inmate was dosed for 174 consecutive days.

Aside from Dr. Gottlieb, others on the MKULTRA team included allergist and pediatrician Harold Abramson; Donald Cameron, president of the American Psychiatric Association; Harry Isbell, director of addiction research at the Public Health Service Hospital in Lexington, Kentucky; and Louis "Jolly" West, in charge of UCLA's Neuropsychiatric Institute—all honorable men, as Shakespeare might've said, with sterling reputations in their fields.

Needless to say, the Agency didn't confine its wild experiments to drugs alone. MKULTRA Subproject 54 sought to produce concussions from a distance using mechanical blast waves, noting that success "is always followed by amnesia for the actual moment of the accident." Subproject 62 declared that "certain kinds of radio frequency energy have been found to effect reversible neurological changes in chimpanzees." Subproject 119 reviewed existing literature on "techniques of activation of the human organism by remote electronic means." Subproject 35 built Georgetown University Hospital's Gorman Annex at a cost of $1.25 million, one-sixth of its floor space reserved for CIA dabbling. A collaborative project with the Defense Intelligence Agency, tagged "SLEEPING BEAUTY," studied "remote microwave mind-influencing techniques."

George Hunter White paddled at will through the entire polluted pool. His first "patient" in Manhattan was the same Barbara Smithe he'd pointed out to Colby late last year, dosed with a January hit of LSD unknowingly, sending her previously normal life into a tailspin that was still continuing. White acquired the Greenwich Village flat he'd told Colby about, on Bedford Street, rented in the name of "Morgan Hall," with Dr. Gottlieb picking up the tab. White dubbed his project "MIDNIGHT CLIMAX," hiring streetwalkers to lure men upstairs, where they engaged in kinky sex and soared on unexpected acid trips, each detail of the orgies lovingly preserved by hidden movie cameras and tape recorders.

Rather surprisingly, the only acknowledged MKULTRA

MICHAEL NEWTON

fatality thus far involved Dr. Frank Olson, employed by the U.S. Army Medical Command at Fort Detrick, Maryland. While visiting New York, ostensibly for consultation with CIA psychiatrist Harold Abramson, Olson received a dose of LSD in liqueur furnished by Dr. Gottlieb and subsequently leapt or fell from a window of his tenth-floor hotel room on November 28. Present when he took the plunge was Agency chemist Robert Lashbrook, who trailed Olson's corpse to the morgue for official identification. Detectives found a note in Olson's pocket bearing the address of George White's Bedford Street playpen, plus the initials "G.W." and "M.H."—the latter for White's "Morgan Hall" codename. Lashbrook feigned ignorance and a pathologist ruled Olson's death to be a suicide, but Colby wasn't altogether sure.

It didn't take much snooping to find out that while White attended his mother's funeral in California at the time Olson tried and failed to fly, two of his longtime cronies —Corsican drug runners Pierre Lafitte and François Spirito —were lurking around the victim's hotel, Lafitte in the guise of lowly repairman, Spirito lately freed from Atlanta's federal lockup after a course of drug experiments conducted by prison physician Dr. Carl Pfeiffer, yet another MKULTRA accomplice.

Through all of it, White drew one paycheck from the FBN as a "supervisor at large," another from the CIA. Any doubt of his overt agency's participation in MKULTRA was erased by a July entry from his not-so-secret diary: "Arrive Wash.—confer Anslinger and Gottlieb re CIA reimbursement for 3 men's services."

All one big happy family, Gantt thought, as he began the trek to his Tehran hotel, and on to Mehrabad International Airport. *All except for the hundreds of victims, that is.*

CHAPTER 8

A SIGN TAPED to the *ristorante*'s front door read: "CLOSED FOR A PRIVATE PARTY, WITH APOLOGIES."

Dominic Giordano nudged his brother with an elbow, grinning. "Private party. That's us, *fratellino*."

"About fuckin' time," replied Angelo.

"Hey, now. Remember to be humble, will ya? Show a little class for the old man."

It was their father's place. Where better for his two sons to become made men at last?

The *Cosa Nostra*'s rolls closed in 1932, after the big war of the families when Dominic was eight years old, his brother barely five. They'd only just reopened when New York's Five Families started running short of street soldiers, the roster whittled down by death, old age, and jail. Dom knew that Bill Bonanno—birth name Salvatore—had been inducted by his father recently, into the former Maranzano family, once run by *Cosa Nostra*'s last acknowledged "Boss of All Bosses."

Now it was finally his turn, and Angelo's, joining their father's small but still important family rooted in Little Italy.

Dom gave a coded knock, hoping he remembered it correctly, and his uncle Greg opened it for them, smiling at his two nephews. "*Buonasera signori*," he greeted them, formally.

Dom thinking, *That's the first time anybody's ever called us gentlemen.*

He answered back for both himself and Angelo. "*Buona sera, zio.*"

Dom always had some reservations about Uncle Greg, the way he'd swapped the family's surname for "Jordan" when he'd gone away to college in D.C., but normally they got along all right, despite that insult to the clan at large. He knew Greg wasn't keen on him and Angelo becoming *soldatos,* but Greg wouldn't buck his elder brother, Dom's old man. Jordan might be the *consigliere,* mouthpiece and bookkeeper for the family, but Carlo Giordano called the shots.

And here he came, all smiles, arms spread in welcome while their uncle closed and locked the *ristorante*'s street entrance behind them. After the obligatory hugs and back-slapping, *Don* Carlo led them all through the main seating area and past the kitchen, to a private banquet room in back.

The table there was set for four, no need for place cards. Their old man would take the head, his brother at the other end, with Dom and Angelo facing each other from opposite sides. Dead center on the tabletop, Dom saw a .38 revolver and a wicked-looking dagger, plus a single ashtray, box of matches, and what he took for two playing cards lying face down.

At Papa Carlo's order, all of them sat down, Dom on his father's right, Ange to his left. Dom caught a whiff of something from the kitchen, smelled delicious, but he didn't turn in that direction, keeping full attention on his dad.

"Tonight," his father said, all solemn-voiced, eyes shifting back and forth between his sons, "marks your rebirth as Men of Honor. We already share a bond of blood, but now you pass on to a higher level of the family. Before that happens, do you both acknowledge and submit to all the rules of *omertà*?"

"I do," each brother answered individually, in his turn.

"And do you understand the need for absolute respect toward any other member of the family and *Cosa Nostra*, which extends to every member of their families and to the females in particular?"

"I do," echoed from each side of the table.

"That no insult, whether physical or verbal, may be made toward any member of your new extended family? That any disrespect shown toward their loved ones is a serious offense? And that the worst offense of all is to become a *traditore* who informs to *la polizia*?"

"I do."

"Before you lay a gun and knife, the symbols of your promise to defend this family and tokens of the way your lives will end if you betray that trust. Gregorio?"

When his birth name was called, their uncle rose and circled to his left, reaching past Dom to lift the dagger. Next, his free hand gripped Dom's wrist before the blade came down and pricked his trigger finger, instantly rewarded with a drop of blood. That done, their uncle moved around the table to repeat the ritual with Angelo.

"This blood—shared blood—doubles our bond as family," their father said. "Pick up your cards."

When Dominic had his in hand, stained with his blood, he saw that it wasn't a playing card at all. Its face, rather, depicted a saint whom he didn't recognize from church, haloed and scowling up at him.

Now uncle Greg was back, taking a match out of the box in front of Dom and striking it, a smoky stench of sulfur spreading rapidly. He touched the flame to Dom's card, then circled back around the table, where he did the same for Angelo.

"Cup these saints in your hands," their father ordered, "and repeat this oath: If I betray my family, so shall I burn as does this saint."

Translated automatically in Dom's mind as he answered in Italian: "*Se tradisco la mia famiglia, anch'io brucerò come fa questo santo.*"

Dom's card was curling, shriveling, scorching his palms. He passed the dwindling ashes back and forth to minimize the pain, and at a signal from his father, brushed its scorched remnants into the clean ashtray. Across from him, wincing a little, Angelo did likewise.

When the last bit of each card had burned away their father, smiling once again, said, "So your lives begin anew. Who's ready for a feast of celebration?"

Dominic was smiling too, dabbing his bloody index finger with a handkerchief, as he replied, "*Grazie, padre e zio.* Right now, I could eat a horse."

Thinking, *A Man of Honor. Fuckin' ay.*

———

COLUMBIA UNIVERSITY LAW SCHOOL: *May 19, 1954*

THERE HAD BEEN times when David Jordan wondered if this day would ever come. Not for the classwork, mind you. Truth be told, although his courses and professors were exacting, he'd enjoyed most of them, finishing his last year off with criminal investigations and adjudication, comparative criminal procedure, real estate transactions and corporate taxation, international business transactions and property law. He'd cleared it all *summa cum laude,* with a 3.92 GPA in fact, but still, there'd been a toll to pay: in weariness from his work schedule outside of class, and in simple loneliness.

And if he had to pick, the loneliness was worse.

He had his family, of course: parents and sister Gemma, who surprised them all by showing for commencement this time, leading daughter Lucia, now seven years old, by the hand. Fiona hadn't made it, naturally being deskbound or tied up in court by Legal Aid, working for indigents and felons who reached out for help they couldn't reimburse.

Sometimes it seemed to Dave that she was caught up in an endless futile exercise, but he was also proud of her—not that he had a right to be, since everything she'd done was managed on her own, and they were simply friends, never romantically "involved."

After the ceremony, David huddled with his family, declining dinner at The Palm on Second Avenue—"The place to see and be seen"—yet again, his third time now.

His father wore a knowing smile. "No problem," he replied to Dave's polite refusal. "I imagine you've got plans with that O'Hara girl?"

"No plans. And she's a *woman,* Pop, besides being a full-fledged lawyer."

"Just like *you,*" Gemma chimed in. "I mean a lawyer, not a woman."

"I'm no lawyer yet, Sis," Dave reminded her. "There's still a two-day bar exam ahead of me, in late July, and if I pass that—"

"If?" his mother interrupted. "There's no *if* about it, Davey."

"When did you start telling fortunes, Mom?"

"I know my son, that's all."

"And I appreciate your confidence. But *if* I pass, there's still the little matter of a job."

His father frowned. Began to say, "You know—"

"I know, Pop. Thanks, but no thanks."

"Right." Changing his tack. "What did you say your lady's last name was, again?"

"First thing, she's *not* my lady. We are absolutely *not* an item, or whatever Hedda Hopper's calling it these days. And her last name's still O'Hara."

"Funny, that," his father said. "You know, I had a class-mate named O'Hara at GW. Declan O'Hara. When I signed up for the war, he joined the Bureau of Investigation. If he's still in harness, I suppose he must be heading toward retirement age by now."

"Like you?" Dave countered, steering clear of an admission that Fiona's father was a G-man.

"Ah, well. Practicing the law goes on forever."

"Or at least, it feels like it," Dave's mother said, drawing a nervous laugh from Gemma and a sidelong glance from Dad.

"I mean to say, we don't have rules about retirement, like they do with Civil Service."

"Funny thing about that," Dave replied. "J. Edgar keeps his agents out of Civil Service so that he can fire them anytime he likes without a legal brouhaha. Keeps them under his thumb."

His father frowned. "And how do you know that?"

Fiona told me, David thought. And answered, "It must've come up in class sometime."

"Well, Dave," said Gemma, "if you're *free* tonight—"

"Glassman's," he cut her off. "I'm putting in for longer hours, now that they won't need me at the law library."

"All right," his father said. "We have a reservation, and the *maitre d'* will want a bigger tip if we don't show on time."

Dave shook hands with his dad, accepted kisses on the cheek from Mom and Gemma, ending with a sly wink for Lucia. As they parted, Dave hoped that he'd covered for Fiona well enough, or rather, for her dad. He wasn't sure how Pop would take it if he thought his only kid was tied up with a G-man's daughter.

Not to worry, Dad, he thought. *We're friends and nothing more, damn it to hell.*

———

West 116th Street, *Harlem: May 25, 1954*

Payton Sawyer took his time approaching Temple No. 7, walking south on Lenox Avenue below Mount Morris Park, with Central Park still seven blocks ahead of him. The temple, Payton knew, had lately left its quarters at the Harlem YMCA for a storefront at 102 West 116th, the southwest corner. It was crowded during services and getting more so all the time, now that Malcolm X had been assigned to it after his last post in Philly.

So far, Payton hadn't found much dirt for BOSS. The NOI demanded fealty to the *Qur'ān* and Five Pillars of Islam from its members, and while many of its male recruits had been locked up at one time or another, their religion had them flying right today, for the most part, eschewing liquor and narcotics, steering clear of crime and "counseling" drug pushers to evacuate the ghetto if they wanted to stay healthy. None of that bothered NYPD, particularly, although Sawyer knew a fair share of detectives earned their bribes by keeping dope dealers, gamblers and whores in business. There would always be vice on the streets and in the tenements of Harlem, with its payoffs greasing wheels at City Hall.

No, Payton knew it was the Nation's view of black people as Earth's original inhabitants, not only predecessors to the white man but as his creator through deranged experiments, that marked Black Muslims as a breed apart, and dangerous to so-called "civilized" society.

And they were not the only group on Payton's radar at the moment, prompting Inspector Flannery's interest.

Another group, the Committee on Civil Rights for East Manhattan launched in 1950, had been making waves over housing discrimination, using that as a wedge to bare other forms of *de facto* segregation in Gotham. Lately, it was fielding 153 of its members in teams citywide, reporting back which restaurants refused Negroes outright or shunted them to "undesirable" tables near kitchens, swinging doors, bathrooms, in back corners, or on restricted balconies. As evidence, the teams were broken into pairs—some white, some black, some mixed—to see how treatment at their various targets adhered to color lines.

That "sneak" approach angered white proprietors and diners, not to mention politicians who depended on their votes and contributions at election time. Still, the CCREM couldn't hold a candle to Black Hebrew Israelites, as far as riling white folks was concerned.

The BHIs believed that colored people were the biblical twelve tribes of Israel, just as the all-white Anglo-Israelites believed said "lost tribes" were their own kind, Anglo Saxons and Teutonic folks, both black and white sects stolidly denying that the ancient Israelites were Jews. Since the early 1920s, Anglo-Israelites in the United States called their cult "Christian Identity," shunning contact with Jews and "mud people."

You had to give Black Hebrews credit for imagination though, Payton supposed. They'd parsed the twelve tribes out to designate the tribe of Judah as American Negroes, the tribe of Benjamin, West Indians; the tribe of Levi, Haitians, and so on through the Western Hemisphere until you hit the red-skinned tribe of Gad, the tribe of Reuben (Seminoles standing apart), and Asher (Mexicans). Somehow, oddly, they'd left out Africa itself entirely.

Crazy, Payton thought, as he approached the door to Temple No. 7 with its well-dressed guards outside. But crazy had already put him in plainclothes and off the walking beat. Who could predict where it would land him next?

———

LITTLE ITALY, *Manhattan: July 11, 1954*

"IT MAKES ME PROUD, YA KNOW?" said Carlo Giardano.

"What's that?" Greg Jordan asked dutifully, as if he didn't know.

"Bringin' my boys into the family as Men of Honor," Carlo answered.

"It's something, all right," Greg said, as if he hadn't heard

287

the same damned thing a hundred times or more, over the past four months.

He understood the urge, the need to keep their outlaw family growing in line with Gotham's other *Cosa Nostra* clans, but these were still perilous times to be a *mafioso*, anywhere you looked.

In April, five years after Charley Luciano and *Don* Calogero Vizzini opened their Palermo "candy factory," shipping heroin throughout Europe and North America, the Roman daily *Avanti!* published a front-page photo of the setup with a headline reading "Textiles and Sweets on the Drug Route." The plant closed that night, its chemists reportedly fleeing to other countries, while a heart attack killed Vizzini two months later. Stateside, that exposé raised new questions over Luciano's prison commutation back in 1946, aimed at embarrassing Governor Dewey and his would-be Republican successor, Irving Ives. Dewey ordered a special investigation, the panel decreeing that Lucky and friends had provided "many valuable services" to Naval Intelligence, but a separate congressional probe led by Virginia Democrat Patrick Drewry proved the SS *Normandie* was lost to human negligence, no saboteurs involved, and now contender William Harriman seemed poised to crack the GOP's hold on New York.

Nor was there any peace on Earth for *mafiosi*, near or far away. Warfare sputtered in Chicago, where racketeers bombed a new Howard Johnson's restaurant in May. When Cherry Nose Gioe intervened to end that ruckus, drive-by gunmen killed him in mid-August, as he left a meeting with associates. Two days later, a shotgun blast killed Frank Maritote, one-time bodyguard to Al Capone and a codefendant in the IATSE extortion case that sent both men to prison while leaving Frank Nitti dead. Police claimed they were looking for "three small fry" gangsters—Felix Alderisio, Marshall Caifano, and Albert Frabotta—but no one could decide if rival mobster Joey Glimco gave the orders, or they came straight from Tony Accardo.

In Gotham, the news was less bloody but equally glum. Federal jurors convicted Joe Adonis of perjury in March, resulting in a two-year prison term, and barely two days after that verdict, another panel found Johnny Dioguardi, from the Lucchese family, guilty of evading New York's income tax. He pulled sixty days, and seven weeks after *that,* Frank Costello stood convicted on three counts of federal tax evasion, facing five years inside and a $30,000 fine.

Greg's family, at least, kept dancing between the raindrops, but now instead of just himself and Carlo, he was forced to worry about nephews Dominic and Angelo, both clearly eager to wade in and prove themselves as fledgling *mafiosi*

He only hoped it wouldn't get them killed or locked up while they watched their lives pass by through prison bars.

———

FEDERAL BUREAU *of Narcotics Manhattan Field Office: July 29, 1954*

AT LAST, some progress on the Mafia. Ike Sawyer felt like gloating, but he'd knocked around the job too long to think that any victory was permanent. Besides, he had more in his life to fret over than logging drug arrests.

Payton was working undercover on the ghetto beat,

pulling some of the same shit Ike once carried out for Edgar
Hoover, risking life and limb each time he went out on the
street. On top of that, Ike's wife, Talitha, had been ailing
lately from some malady the doctors couldn't seem to diag-
nose, coughing a fair bit, otherwise just listless in a way Ike
hadn't seen from her since diphtheria carried off their first
son, Tillman, at the tender age of three.

Depressed now, Ike turned back to the file lying open on
his desk, intent on making sure no one had dropped a stitch
on the most recent busts. Five members of the present-day
Lucchese family were on the hook for smuggling an average
twenty pounds of heroin per month into the States and
Canada from their *amici* back in Italy. In order of impor-
tance to the family, those charged included Giacomo Reina,
son of the clan's original founder, who'd died in the Castellammarese War twenty-odd years earlier; Larry Quartiero,
the family's top fence for stolen furs and jewelry, aside from
running smack; and three street soldiers from Tony Strollo's
Greenwich Village crew, Pasquale Moccio, Pasquale Pagano
and Joseph Valachi.

Thanks to the Boggs Act, all five goons were facing
sentences doubled from what they would've been three
years ago, on top of which Pagano was a prime suspect in
the murders of federal informers Steve Franse and Gene
Giannini. Conviction on either of those counts would send
him to the chair at Sing Sing. Otherwise, the five *goombahs*
were looking at an average ten years in the Atlanta lockup.

Ike wished he could've said the same for the rednecks
who kept killing Negroes in the South. Tuskegee University
claimed 1954 was shaping up to be another lynch-free year,
but Sawyer couldn't figure out how they were keeping score.
Ike knew of three murders that qualified, at least to his

mind, both within the past three months alone, with no suspects in custody, no charges filed.

The first victim, in May, was Russell Charley, found hanging from a tree outside Vrendenburgh, Alabama. Police were calling it a suicide, failing to mention that Charley had been accused of dallying with a white woman in the neighborhood.

The next slaying, in June, claimed Arkansas farmer Isadore Banks, found chained to a tree, mutilated and burnt alive near Marion, four days after he'd left home for the last time, to pay off some employees. Crittenden County's coroner found no sign of robbery or struggle at the scene, although it must've taken several men to handle Banks—a strapping 300-pounder—while he was being bound, then slashed with knives and set afire. By some "coincidence," one of the local crackers who'd been hounding Banks to sell his farm now owned it, purchased for a song from grieving relatives after Banks died.

And then just yesterday, someone found the battered corpse of Izell Henry in a roadside ditch a mile from home, outside Greensburg, Louisiana. He was still alive when found, but died en route to Lallie Kemp Hospital, twenty-three miles south. His fatal beating came one day after Henry dared to vote in the state's Democratic primary. A complaint filed with the FBI was going nowhere fast.

The year's best news for Negroes—possibly the best news coming out of Washington since the Emancipation Proclamation— arrived in May, when a unanimous Supreme Court overturned the "separate but equal" rule of *Plessy v. Ferguson,* dating from 1896. The Warren Court's judgment deemed Jim Crow schools "inherently unequal," even if a given state spent the exact same money on a school for blacks as any white school—which, of course, they never did. The shockwaves from that ruling, labeled *Brown v. Board of Education of Topeka*, lumped five lawsuits into one, covering Jim Crow schools in Kansas, Delaware, Virginia, South Carolina, and the District of Columbia. It was a true red-letter day, but set no deadline prior to which desegregation must occur.

On June 10, agitated governors from twelve states met in Richmond to discuss a plan for circumventing *Brown* without a second Civil War. Of them all, only Kentucky, Maryland and West Virginia voiced their willingness to go along with *Brown,* and Ike expected trouble even in those states with relatively small black populations.

It began in Mississippi predictably, on July 11, when Robert "Tut" Patterson founded the first White Citizens' Council in Sunflower County, home of diehard racist Senator James Eastland. While the Councils disavowed any connection to the Klan, those groups shared overlapping membership and got their "news" from the same racist publications, some of them with roots in the Depression, cranked out by defendants who'd escaped conviction for sedition back in 1944. And while the Councils outwardly shunned violence Ike didn't trust them, most particularly since they'd started publishing the names of Negro activists in local papers, with their addresses and phone numbers, while cutting off their credit at assorted banks and stores, foreclosing mortgages, and urging any whites who had Negro employees to dismiss them. From all-black Mound Bayou, Dr. Theodore Howard's Regional Council of Negro Leadership fought back as best it could, promoting institutions like the Tri-State Bank of Memphis, owned by Negroes, to relieve financial pressure from white economic terrorism.

But could *real* terror in Dixie's classic style be far behind?

Not likely, Ike surmised, with four Klans active in the South that he could name right now, off-hand, and more likely to organize as a response to *Brown.*

As for the federal government, Attorney General Brownell seemed more concerned with deporting Mexicans, joining Immigration and Naturalization Service Commissioner Joseph Swing on July 15, to launch "Operation Wetback." Brownell himself named the project, telling journalists "the Mexican wetback problem was becoming increasingly serious," with illegal aliens "displacing domestic workers, affecting work conditions, spreading disease, and contributing to crime rates." The operation's goal: repatriating some 200,000 Mexicans from California, Arizona and Texas as soon as they could be packed aboard trains and buses. Brownell proposed an operation he deemed "swift and skillful, yet humane and fair." From the White House, President Eisenhower offered no objection to the scheme.

Another year, Ike thought, *and then I'm out. The government can take care of itself.*

And looking at it now, he didn't think that year could pass by fast enough.

————

FBI HEADQUARTERS: December 8, 1954

WATCHING the daily headlines in the *Post,* Declan O'Hara sometimes wondered if the world had slowed down to a halt or had begun an awkward journey back through time.

In spring, for instance, the Senate Judiciary Committee rehashed its 1953 debate over legalized federal wiretaps, repeating all the same old arguments for eavesdropping in the name of "national security." This time around, the House passed its version of the bill by an overwhelming margin of 378 to 10, but the Senate committee deadlocked and killed it after Larry Fly turned up again, defending privacy. His argument, in essence, was that while the bill forbade wiretap material being "divulged" outside the FBI, that amounted to "wishful thinking" and worse, "a dangerous pastime for attorney generals."

William Remington was also back in headlines, this time as a murder victim rather than a criminal defendant. In November, he'd been beaten while he slept, attacked by fellow inmates George McCoy and Lewis Cagle Jr., McCoy wielding a brick inside a sock and shouting, "Traitor!" when he struck. Remington survived for two days in a coma, then died on Thanksgiving Eve.

Lewisburgh's warden told reporters, "This wasn't a personal attack against Bill, just the actions of a couple of hoodlums who got all worked up by the publicity about Communists." The FBI preferred to call it "robbery," as if the victim had been hoarding valuable property inside his cell.

More of the same, likewise, as Smith Act trials proceeded near and far. Both attorneys, who had been disbarred after the first trial in New York, fought their cases all the way to the Supreme Court, where disbarment had been overturned for Harry Sacher in April and in October for Abe Isserman.

Things hadn't gone so well for Red defendants elsewhere. In St. Louis, after eighteen weeks in court, seven defendants were convicted of conspiracy in May, sentenced in early June to serve the maximum allowed. Cleveland's trial was two weeks shorter, but it ended with the same result: all six of the accused found guilty and sentenced to prison. Six more stood convicted in Denver, their cases now pending appeal. In Honolulu likewise, all defendants were found guilty with a twist: one juror had come home from court and suffered what appeared to be a nervous breakdown, dropping to his knees in front of relatives and "begging God for mercy, saying he had sinned, that he had lied in the eyes of God and the case was a frame-up."

Dramatic stuff, but it had zero influence over Judge Jon Wiig's final sentencing.

In Philadelphia meanwhile, jurors sat through ten weeks of testimony before they convicted Steve Nelson and his codefendants in mid-August. Suspects who stood alone included John Noto of Buffalo, chairman of the CPUSA for upstate New York, who'd gone "underground" in 1951, faced indictment in November 1954, but still remained at large. Another one, Eugene Cuebas Arbona, was a Puerto Rican realtor in Manhattan, charged with Smith Act violations on his native island in October, pending extradition if he couldn't beat the case in court. Judge Edward Weinfeld had refused to quash the October indictment but ordered settlement, which Declan knew could still go either way.

In Congress, Joe McCarthy pursued his chosen role as lightning rod for right-wing mash notes and leftist abuse. In January, he subpoenaed army dentist Irving Peress to appear before his Senate Permanent Subcommittee on Investigations, where Peress repeatedly declined to answer. McCarthy labeled him a "Fifth Amendment Communist" and "the key to the deliberate communist infiltration of our armed forces," while Peress fired back that Senators who equated invoking of the Fifth with guilt were themselves subversives.

McCarthy next fired off a letter to Secretary of the Army Robert Stevens, demanding that Peress be court-martialed, but the dentist received an honorable discharge instead. Tail-Gunner Joe recalled Brigadier General Ralph Zwicker from Japan in February, questioning his role in the promotion as commander at Camp Kilmer, but Zwicker declined to say who'd authorized it—also failing to note McCarthy's 1948 vote for the "Doctor Draft Law" that made it mandatory. Enraged, McCarthy told Zwicker he was "not fit to wear that uniform." Witness Ruth Eagle, an undercover agent for the Bureau and NYPD, appeared to claim Peress had been an active CPUSA member for twenty years, as well as joining the small American Labor Party. Secretary Stevens testified in March, confessing "some very bad mistakes" on Peress, which McCarthy took to mean that the promotion had been ordered by a "silent master who decreed special treatment for communists."

What horseshit, Declan thought. *But the rubes still love it.*

In the midst of that confusion, somebody on Joe's committee produced a doctored photograph of Roy Cohn's playmate, David Schine, posing with Secretary of the Army Stevens. Army lawyer Joseph Welch, blew the whistle on that fraud, accusing Cohn of trickery to polish up Schine's tarnished image. Shortly after that, Welch also proved a "confidential letter" that McCarthy said had passed from Edgar Hoover to Major General Alexander Bolling, warning of traitors within the Army Signal Corps, was another bogus document, found nowhere in the Bureau's files nor those of Army Intelligence.

In short, McCarthy was—no great surprise—a flagrant liar.

Even so, the Senate hearings lasted for thirty-six days, recording some two million words of testimony from thirty-two witnesses, while 20 million TV viewers watched, entranced and horrified. The committee's final report claimed that Secretary Stevens and Army Counsel John Adams "made efforts to terminate or influence the investigation and hearings at Fort Monmouth," and that Adams "made vigorous and diligent efforts" to block subpoenas for members of the Army Loyalty and Screening Board "by means of personal appeal to certain members of the committee."

McCarthy loved the TV ratings, but he wasn't smart or sober enough to make out writing on the wall. In successive Gallup polls from January and June, public support for McCarthy dropped from 50 percent to a mere 34, while negative opinions grew from 29 percent to 45. Late in the hearings, when McCarthy told committee critic Stuart Symington, "You're not fooling anyone," Symington replied, "Senator, the American people have had a look at you now for six weeks. You're not fooling anyone, either."

The hearings' most dramatic moment occurred between McCarthy and Joe Welch, when McCarthy branded a member of Welch's Boston law firm as a Red. Welch pinned the sweating Senator with gimlet eyes and told the world, "Until this moment, Senator, I think I never really gauged your cruelty or your recklessness. Let us not assassinate this lad further, Senator. You've done enough. Have you no sense of decency, sir, at long last? Have you left no sense of decency?"

TV commentator Edward R. Murrow devoted his March 9 broadcast to McCarthy, concluding that "the line between investigating and persecuting is a very fine one, and the junior Senator from Wisconsin stepped over it repeatedly. Cassius was right: 'The fault, dear Brutus, is not in our stars, but in ourselves'." McCarthy demanded equal time and fouled his own nest further, charging that Murrow served as an agent of Moscow's All-Union Society for Cultural Relations with Foreign Countries, created in 1925 as "the Russian espionage and propaganda organization."

Back home in Wisconsin, the *Sauk-Prairie Star* launched a "Joe Must Go" recall petition, collecting 404,000 signatures within two months. The issue never reached voters, but the clock was ticking on McCarthy, whether he knew it or not. Despite his marriage, rumors of McCarthy's homosexuality still flourished, now including claims that he shared young men with Edgar Hoover on occasion. Army lawyer Welch helped those claims along while challenging the tricked-up Schine photo, asking a committee staffer, "Did you think this came from a pixie?"

McCarthy butted in, sneering, "Will counsel for my benefit define—I think he might be an expert on that—what a pixie is?"

Welch kept his cool, answering back, "Yes. I should say, Mr. Senator, that a pixie is a close relative of a fairy. Shall I proceed, Sir? Have I enlightened you?"

The Senate audience roared. McCarthy seemed fit to piss himself.

On December 2 by a three-fourths vote, the Senate censured McCarthy on two charges: that he "failed to cooperate with the Subcommittee on Rules and Administration" and "repeatedly abused the members who were trying to carry out assigned duties." Specifically, when a Senate committee chaired by Utah's Arthur Watkins met to consider potential charges, McCarthy accused three members of "deliberate deception" and "fraud," branding the entire committee "a lynch party," further calling the panel the "unwitting handmaiden, involuntary agent and attorneys in fact of the Communist Party."

With that tirade alone, Watkins found, McCarthy had "acted contrary to senatorial ethics and tended to bring the Senate into dishonor and disrepute, to obstruct the constitutional processes of the Senate, and to impair its dignity."

December's judgment was only the sixth Senate censure vote since 1789, and while it imposed no specific penalties upon McCarthy, it effectively doomed his career. Worse, perhaps, were the jokes: Indiana Senator William Jenner, once a fan of Joe's, now likened him to "the kid who came to the party and peed in the lemonade."

Even President Eisenhower quipped that McCarthyism was now "McCarthy*was*m."

A nearly broken man, McCarthy drank more heavily than ever, and he'd also become addicted to heroin—an open secret within federal law enforcement, though concealed so far from voters. FBN Director Harry Anslinger served as McCarthy's pusher, cowed into submission after he confronted Joe and the tail-gunner told him, "I wouldn't try to do anything about it, Commissioner. It will be the worse for you, and if it winds up in a public scandal I wouldn't care. The choice is yours."

Anslinger's choice was to supply McCarthy from a pharmacy in Washington, his Bureau picking up the tab and giving Edgar Hoover one more reason to despise his rival in D.C.

O'Hara wished the Red Scare could be ended simply by dragging McCarthy offstage, but he knew that wasn't a realistic hope. It might take years yet to subside, with untold damage done in the meantime.

Once again, as happened frequently these days, Declan considered that it might be his time to retire. And once again, a part of his mind answered in the negative. *As long as*

Edgar and Clyde Tolson stay, as long as Ally Gantt hangs on, I'd better stick around.

———

FBI MIAMI FIELD OFFICE: November 3, 1954

FLORIDA HAD A BRAND-NEW GOVERNOR-ELECT, if that made any difference to life around the Sunshine State. Nolan O'Hara hoped it would, but as the old joke said, wish in one hand, shit in the other, and find out which fills up first.

Voters turned out Charley Johns in favor of Tom Collins, who preferred to use his middle name: LeRoy. He'd beaten five other contenders in the Democratic primary, mostly by damning the Supreme Court's *Brown* ruling, but whispers claimed he wasn't quite the die-hard segregationist as Johns and others of his ilk. O'Hara reckoned he would have to wait and see.

In January, Miami's U.S. attorney dismissed perjury charges filed last year against seven Klan members, claiming that his office had no jurisdiction over crimes they'd lied about to G-men and a federal grand jury. That decision smelled fishy to Nolan, since the lies themselves were federal crimes, but no one consulted him, as usual.

Evaporation of those charges encouraged Bill Hendrix, who'd founded a White Brotherhood, believed to be an underground unit of his American Confederate Army. No one was bombing Negroes at the moment, but a late September blast at Miami Beach's Fontainebleau Hotel felt like a message to the hotel's Jewish owners.

Then again, it might have been related to the Syndicate somehow. Meyer Lansky, out of prison in New York, had no desire to serve another stretch for gambling Stateside so he'd moved to Cuba, managing casinos there. Santo Traffi-cante Jr. served as his apprentice for a while, til stomach cancer claimed his father's life in August and he returned to lead the Tampa Mafia, with aging adversary Charlie Wall still on the lam.

In May, Fulgencio Batista revoked the orders handed down in 1952, amounting to a state of martial law. At the same time, leading a newly born Progressive Action Party, he'd nominated himself as a presidential candidate, with "free and honest" balloting scheduled for November 1. Two days prior to that election, rival Ramón Grau dropped out, leaving Batista unopposed. As soon as he could see above the landslide, Batista suspended the Cuban constitution, replaced Parliament with a handpicked Council of State, and dissolved all political parties aside from his own. Even so, the number of registered voters dropped from 80 percent in 1948 to 53 percent this year.

Mobsters welcomed the new regime, but it wasn't unani-mous. A federal grand jury recently charged three defen-dants—two Cubans, one American—with acquiring thirty surplus M-1 rifles, meant for followers of deposed president Carlos Prío, no longer as "cordial" as when he'd held office. The weapons never reached Cuba, but Nolan knew there were plenty more where those came from.

In Washington, meanwhile, the Supreme Court declined to review Walter Irvin's Groveland rape conviction. Thur-good Marshall fought on, having promised Walter's mother that he wouldn't let her son be put to death, but Nolan didn't like his chances now that Irvin had exhausted all appeals. His only hope was gubernatorial clemency, but LeRoy Collins had his hands full, reassuring rednecks that he wasn't liberal.

Still, Nolan thought, *it could be worse.* He could be marking time in Mississippi, Alabama, or some other Deep South state where violent resistance to the *Brown* decision might break out at any time.

And when it did, he knew there would be bloody hell to pay.

––––––––

FBI MANHATTAN FIELD OFFICE: December 14, 1954

ANOTHER TRANSFER, and this time Devon Gantt would get to see more of the Mob up close, although the monograph he'd written with his father, "proving" there was no such thing, had barely earned a shrug from Edgar Hoover.

Gantt's wife and son were fairly settled for the moment in an Ainsworth Street apartment, out on Staten Island, a short walk from Great Kills Park. It was the best a lowly G-man could afford without crossing the line to Pennsylvania or New Jersey, and the park—created on the shore of Lower New York Bay only five years ago—should offer some diversion for Wyman, assuming that Camille found time to take him there and keep a wary eye on him.

Manhattan, for its part, was every bit as crazy as Devon imagined. Street crime and the Syndicate aside, the cops were still trying to find Con Ed's worst enemy, dubbed the "Mad Bomber" in headlines, who started planting charges back in 1940 and was still at it, after a ten-year lull from '41 to early '51. During his downtime, the psycho had sent numerous ranting letters and postcards to police, the press, Con Ed itself, and even private citizens. His bombing count was up to twenty-five, most recently a blast that wounded four persons in an audience of 6,200 while they watched Bing Crosby's *White Christmas* at Radio City Music Hall. So far, the bomber's crude homemade devices left eight persons injured, but he hadn't killed a soul.

Not yet.

Gotham's field office had been cheered by news of Gerhard Puff's electrocution at Sing Sing in August, for the death of Agent Joe Brock two years earlier. Some of the G-men present at the shooting scene still wished they'd killed him, but to Devon, dead was dead. Puff made the fifth federal execution since President Eisenhower was inaugurated, counting the Rosenbergs and a pair of sadistic kidnappers who'd killed a six-year-old in a botched Kansas City ransom kidnapping.

Gantt had his share of work to do in his new posting to America's largest field office, but he still found time to keep up with his former interests from when he'd worked Los Angeles. Chief Hoover might regard the Mafia as nonexistent, but its leaders still kept meeting to discuss their business, observed from time to time by G-men who refrained from interfering. The most recent sit-down occurred in Mountainside, New Jersey, only yesterday, twenty-two miles east of where Devon sat at his desk. Two other get-togethers had been witnessed and reported since July, one in L.A., the other in a posh Chicago suburb. Those reports were filed in triplicate and then, presumably forgotten, since Chief Hoover didn't care.

Out west, the Red Scare's aftershocks were still reverberating like tremors along the famous San Andreas Fault. One casualty was screenwriter Louis Pollock, blacklisted when the American Legion confused him with Louis Pollack, a clothier who'd defied HUAC. Gossip columnists were dishing up "communist" names like *hors d'oeuvres* at a Hollywood party, filling columns from snoops such as Walter Winchell, Hedda Hopper, Victor Riesel, Jack O'Bryan and George Sokolsky. One victim who fought back, actor John Ireland, secured an out-of-court settlement from the Young & Rubicam advertising agency after they'd cost him the lead role in a TV series.

And bizarrely, some of those who'd sold their friends to HUAC were now trying to cash in on betrayal, with a thinly veiled message that tattling to Big Brother was good for you. In July, when *On the Waterfront* hit theaters and started reaping Oscars, it bore the names of "friendly" HUAC witnesses Elia Kazan and Budd Schulburg. While ostensibly a gangster movie, *Waterfront* couldn't fool everyone, one critic noting its "embarrassing special pleading on behalf of informers." Hollywood didn't care, awarding two of the film's eight Academy Awards to Kazan as Best Director and to Schulberg for Best Screenplay.

The industry and viewing public were not so forgiving when the shoe was on the other cinematic foot. Upon parole from prison, "Hollywood Ten" director Herbert Biberman went independent, scraping up enough cash to film *Salt of the Earth,* a tale of striking Mexican-American miners in the New Mexico desert. Along for the ride came some of his fellow black-listers: producer Paul Jarrico, writer Michael Wilson, actors Will Geer and Rosaura Revueltas. Distributors boycotted *Salt,* the projectionist's union refused to run it, while radio stations and newspapers shunned its advertisements. *The Hollywood Reporter* claimed that *Salt* was filmed "under direct orders of the Kremlin." Nationwide, barely a dozen theaters had screened it since it was released in March.

Gantt shrugged it off and went back to his paperwork, watching the clock and counting down to lunch, when he could try a new kosher deli on Second Avenue some other guys around the office had been going crazy for.

If only nothing came along to interrupt...

———

THE LUBYANKA BUILDING, *Moscow: December 19, 1954*

LEONID BABIN'S unacknowledged bastard son passed his eighth birthday in March, presumably receiving gifts and cake from his adoptive parents in New Jersey. He was enrolled in what Americans would call third grade—*nachal-noye* or "beginning" level in Moscow—and making decent grades according to the quarterly reports Babin received, noting with special pleasure Stefan/Steven's aptitude for math and schoolyard sports.

He was a balanced young man in the making, nothing yet to bar him from a future application to the FBI.

At home, more changes put Babin's world at risk, but he weathered all of them so far. With Beria cremated and his ashes scattered in a forest outside Moscow, the MGB and MVD merged again, then split apart once more on March 13. The MVD survived, handed responsibility for criminal investigations and correctional facilities. A new unit, the *Komitet Gosudarstvennoy Bezopasnosti*—Committee of State Security, abbreviated KGB—was tasked with handling polit- ical police duties, intelligence, counterintelligence, and personal security for Party leaders.

The KGB's first chairman was General Ivan Serov, pres- ently fifty-four years old, who'd earned his nickname of "Ivan the Terrible" as Beria's Deputy Commissar of the NKVD, protecting No. 1 after Stalin's demise when he helped put Beria's head on the chopping block. Today, he reigned over a maze of eighteen separate directorates. The Ninth, assigned to safeguard Party bosses, had some 40,000 soldiers of its own; 200,000 more worked for the Border Guards Directorate; while Operations and Technology ran Laboratory 12, concocting drugs and poisons for the state.

In short, the KGB was now an army of its own.

Within that pyramid, Babin now held the rank of Colonel General, First Chief Directorate, with three stars on his golden epaulettes. Duties assigned to his directorate all dealt with "foreign operations"—meaning espionage conducted abroad. That suited Babin to a tee, permitting him to keep an eye on the United States legitimately, without sneaking it and drawing unwelcome attention to himself.

Less fortunate was former Minister of State Security Viktor Abakumov. Imprisoned without trial since July 1951, he'd lately been dragged into court with five former interrogators from the MGB's Section for Investigating Specially Important Cases. Following a hopeless six-day trial, Abakumov and three others were shot immediately after hearing their death sentences pronounced. The other two were treated to vacations in the Gulag, one for twenty-five years and the other for fifteen.

Babin cared nothing for the outcome of that trial, since it didn't affect him, but he'd watched with interest a month-long inmate uprising at Kengir, one of many Gulag camps located in the Kazakh SSR. Inmates seized the prison's service yard on May 16 and held it til June 25, when troops backed up by tanks arrived to crush their vain rebellion.

Some fools never learned from their mistakes, but Leonid Babin was not among their number. When death came for him, as it did for every man, he planned to be prepared and make his final moments count.

———

NO DOUBT ABOUT IT, these were great days for a spy. Who else was free to roam the world at government expense, meet interesting strangers, and conspire to have them killed at virtually no risk to himself?

I definitely made the right decision, Colby Gantt assured himself. Brother Devon, tied down with Edgar Hoover's FBI, could never hold a candle to his twin's globe-hopping exploits—nor could he escape from home and family, a kid now seven years of age and stuck in second grade when not entrusted to a nanny, while his mom filed paperwork at CIA headquarters.

It was pretty much like being single, just with family to visit on the odd weekends and holidays.

Saigon was steaming, which was normal—and a lot like Guatemala, now that Colby thought about it. He'd been there, promoting "Operation PBSUCCESS," helping replace duly elected President Jacobo Árbenz Guzmán with a military junta under Lieutenant Colonel Carlos Castillo Armas. Sure, the Guatemalan people liked Árbenz, casting 60 percent of their votes for him in 1950, but they weren't the ones who mattered. Those would be the United Fruit Company's honchos, ably represented by New York lawyer John Foster Dulles. When Árbenz passed an Agrarian Reform Law in '52, splitting up 1,700 mostly foreign-owned estates among 500,000 peasants, John Dulles had a word with brother Allen, Director of the CIA, and Allen took their case to Ike at the White House.

Voila! Árbenz became a commie overnight, earmarked for removal by the Agency, first with abortive "Operation PBFORTUNE," in 1952, replaced by PBSUCCESS two years later, when the first effort misfired. The so-called uprising began on June 28, when Castillo invaded Guatemala from Honduras, leading 480 soldiers armed, trained, and cheered on via radio by CIA handlers. It lasted for nine days, until Castillo supplanted Árbenz after gunpoint "negotiations" and the Agency at once began to justify its actions with "Operation PBHISTORY," fabricating evidence of Soviet incursions prior to the coup. Now, Guatemala was embroiled in a civil war that might drag on for decades, but that wasn't Colby's problem—nor was it United Fruit's, while they remained on top and gave the nod to death squads in the hinterlands.

Back in the States, counseled by Allen Dulles, Eisenhower was on board for broader, better spying all around the world. Gantt thought he likely missed his days as Supreme Allied Commander in Europe, when things were simpler—go here, kill Axis soldiers, then rinse and repeat—instead of being deskbound and confined by flimsy guidelines from the Constitution. Ike eagerly approved plans for the Lockheed U-2 spy plane, nicknamed "Dragon Lady," that would fly at altitudes of fifteen miles, beyond the reach of Russian fighters, missiles, or radar, snapping off photos of Earth that covered a 1,700-mile radius. Granted, Lockheed would pocket some $23 million, not counting unpredictable cost overruns, but who could really put a price on national security these days?

Maybe the Dulles brothers, for a start?

If the Dragon Lady ever flew, she'd have a wide, wild

world to cover, starting in unsettled Europe, where Moscow ruled its Eastern Bloc with an iron hand. The Agency's "tame" Nazis were among the latest casualties, chief among them Alois Brunner from the Gehlen Org. French and West German prosecutors belatedly indicted him for slaughtering more than 140,000 Jews, but they were forced to do it *in absentia,* as Brunner fled to Syria. Paris and Bonn both sentenced him to die, but what of it? The ruling Ba'ath Party met him with open arms, trading a lifelong sanctuary and a fat paycheck for Brunner's expertise at torture. In retrospect, even U.S. Army Intelligence grumbled that Gehlen had duped his CIA masters by loading his staff with "some pretty bad people."

If Europe was dicey, Asia was worse. Indochina in flames was both a threat and opportunity for Agency "spooks," as some pundits were now calling spies. Unknown to most of its people, America had already embarked on a course of undeclared hostility toward Indochinese Reds, described in Top Secret memos as "acts of sabotage and terror warfare." Deeply entrenched throughout the region, Agency saboteurs drew their dubious mandate from the Geneva Accords, signed in July by diplomats from Britain, France, Russia, Red China, and three Associated States of Indochina: Laos, Cambodia, and Vietnam. Hô Chí Minh signed for his Việt Minh, as did Bảo Đại for his southern domain. America agreed to "respect" the Accords but wouldn't sign. Displeased by the division of Vietnam along the 17th parallel, Washington hoped to see the country reunited—and non-communist—after a general election scheduled for July of 1956.

In the meantime, anything could happen and frequently did.

U.S. Air Force Colonel Edward Lansdale assumed

command of the CIA's Saigon Military Mission in June, operating undercover as "Assistant Air Attaché." While not an Agency employee in his own right, Lansdale had served with the OSS and knew precisely what was meant by his orders to wage paramilitary operations against the Việt Minh and train the South Vietnamese in tactics of psychological warfare, collaborating with the U.S. Information Agency.

By then, America had already spent $1 billion supporting French troops, bearing 80 percent of the cost for their hopeless resistance to Hô. Defeat at Dien Bien Phu spelled the end of French dominance in Indochina, elevating misinformation to an art form. As French troops abandoned Saigon, Agency plants called for a weeklong victory celebration—or, in effect, a seven-day work stoppage in Hô's new capital. It nearly worked, but Hô caught on and ordered workers back to their appointed jobs after a mere three days.

South of the 17th parallel, meanwhile, U.S. spooks had trouble understanding Vietnamese politics and social divisions. How could a Roman Catholic minority hope to rule a nation wherein some 80 percent of the people were Buddhists? Could Bảo ĐạI keep control when avaricious younger men hoped to depose him? As a stopgap measure, Washington donated $93 million and its Seventh Fleet for "Operation Passage to Freedom," evacuating 310,000 mostly Catholic refugees from North to South Vietnam. At the same time, with no U.S. aid, some 130,000 "revolutionary regroupees" moved north, expecting to see Vietnam united under Hô Chí Minh in 1956. Another 60,000 Việt Minh troops stayed behind, to serve as what Hô called a "politico-military substructure within the object of its irredentism."

So battle lines were drawn, even if they were never clear

and shifted constantly. America would guarantee "freedom" for Vietnam below the new dividing line, though even Eisenhower knew that effort might be futile. Earlier this year, he'd written, "I have never talked or corresponded with a person knowledgeable in Indochinese affairs who did not agree that had elections been held as of the time of the fighting, possibly eighty percent of the population would have voted for the Communist Hồ Chí Minh as their leader rather than Chief of State Bảo Đại. Indeed, the lack of leadership and drive on the part of Bảo Đại was a factor in the feeling prevalent among Vietnamese that they had nothing to fight for."

Clearly, that would have to change, via adoption or creation of leader who was strong enough to fight, agreeable enough to recognize his orders came from Washington. For now, at least, that man appeared to be Ngô Đình Diệm, a former mandarin of the Nguyễn dynasty, lately appointed Prime Minister by malleable Bảo Đại while Diệm and his CIA backers plotted Bảo Đạl's removal.

While Vietnam simmered, the People's Army of Vietnam launched two invasions of Laos, each crushed within a month. That didn't matter to the CIA, convinced that it must buttress toppling dominoes wherever they appeared. Laos declared independence in August as French troops withdrew, but Americans and wily Corsicans remained. Air America flew anything, anytime, anywhere, and only lost one plane in May, a Fairchild C-119 Flying Boxcar brought down by ground fire with two crewmen killed. The *Unione Corse* had better luck, flying drugs from Laos to South Vietnam aboard cargo planes collectively nicknamed "Air Opium."

Offshore, the First Taiwan Strait Crisis erupted in August, when Chinese Premier Zhou Enlai demanded "liberation" of Taiwan, shelling the KMT-occupied islands of Kinmen and Matsu. On September 12, the U.S. Joint Chiefs of Staff recommended nuking China, but Eisenhower demurred, settling instead for a Sino-American Mutual Defense Treaty with Chiang Kai-shek. On a broader scale, the Southeast Asian Treaty Organization was born, including America and Britain with Australia, France, New Zealand, Pakistan, Thailand, and the Philippines.

Asian opium aside, drugs remained the Agency's dirty little secret Stateside, where Henry Luce's *Life* and *Time* magazines published laudatory articles on LSD. Both Henry and wife Clare dropped acid regularly, Clare later claiming "it saved our marriage," but the weekly glossies never mentioned Agency involvement, much less George White's role in drugging human guinea pigs. One such, ex-actress and hooker Liz Evans, received multiple doses from White in New York, saying she "hated every minute of it" and once contemplated suicide while on an acid trip.

But for the Agency, LSD was a means to an end. A February MKULTRA document titled "Hypnotic Experimentation and Research," described one young woman who, entranced, overcame a lifelong fear of guns and readily agreed to shoot another woman for infuriating her by failing to awaken on demand. She'd gone through with it, but the pistol was unloaded that time.

Colby had to wonder whether it would always be.

On the side, George White continued to play narc from time to time. Sent to ferret out corruption among Houston's cops, his efforts led to one honest detective being murdered before White exposed the chief as a drug addict, touching off a scandal that sent the police commissioner packing and ended with restructuring of the entire department—all, again, without a whisper of White's CIA connections.

Some bastards have all the luck, Gantt thought. *But it won't last forever. You can count on that.*

————

FBI H*EADQUARTERS*: *December 22, 1954*

S*OMETIMES*, Aloysius Gantt felt that he was surrounded by his enemies, just as the First Marines had been at Chosin Reservoir, three years ago this month. Of course, he wasn't *literally* cornered, but he was convinced that he would rise no further in the Bureau's hierarchy, even though he'd been around for almost forty years and Mickey Ladd vacated the number-three position back in February.

And who got the nod, instead of Gantt? That goddamned Deke DeLoach, with barely twelve years on the job. Ridiculous!

At fifty-eight, Gantt knew he was too old for an assignment in the field, where G-men had been making news all year. The "Top Ten Fugitives" program was going strong, eleven bad guys picked off within days of being listed just this year. A California veterinarian spotted cattle rustler Chester Davenport one day after his January listing, ironically while Chester milked a cow. Armed robber James Lofton tied that one-day record for his Louisiana capture. Burglars Basil Beck and Ray Menard each lasted two days on the list, with Beck facing a murder charge as well. Double killer Apee Chapman remained at large for one week in February. Two weeks was the limit for burglar and car thief Nelson Duncan, while strangler Sterling Groom, armed robber John Hopkins, and car thief Everett Krueger lasted three weeks, Krueger telling G-men, "I'm glad it's over.

I was tired of running." Another robber, John Allen, spent three months on the list before cops in Fort Smith, Arkansas, recognized him from a WANTED poster. Four months was the limit for Alex Whitmore, who'd axed and robbed a Virginia hitchhiker.

Of course, the big news in D.C. this year had been the Puerto Rican nationalist raid on Congress, four zealots including one woman smuggling pistols and a Puerto Rican flag into the House Ladies' Gallery—in fact, a balcony for visitors of both sexes—on March 1. After unfurling their banner, the quartet sprayed bullets around the House chamber, wounding congressmen from five states but killing no one. Pedro Albizu Campos, leader of the Puerto Rican Nationalist Party, played no role in the attack, but J. Edger Hoover used it as a prime excuse for tightening surveillance on Albizu and his followers, collaborating with the CIA and Puerto Rico's Insular Police.

At trial in June, before Judge Alexander Holtzoff, the shooters faced charges of assault with intent to kill. Thirty-three witnesses described the attack, while the defendants spoke alone in self-defense, Lolita Lebrón insisting she'd fired only at the ceiling, though she'd planned "to die for the liberty of my homeland." Attorneys furnished by the American League for Puerto Rico's Independence did their best under the circumstances, but jurors convicted the accused, reducing Lebrón's charge to assault with a deadly weapon. Although the prosecution sought capital punishment, Judge Holtzoff settled for prison terms, ranging from sixteen to seventy-five years. A second trial in New York, on charges of conspiracy to overthrow the U.S. government, ended with four more convictions in October, Judge Lawrence Walsh adding six years to each prisoner's time.

As the shooters trooped off to prison, Alger Hiss

emerged in November, two weeks after his fiftieth birthday. Rumors among New York publishers suggested he was working on a memoir, guaranteed to resurrect the charge of forgery by typewriter that still gave Gantt his share of sleepless nights.

Last thing I fucking need, he thought, but couldn't see a way out of his jam.

CHAPTER 9

Lower East Side, Manhattan: April 4, 1955

THE CAR and license plates were both stolen, a double-blind in case somebody spotted it and felt like ratting to the fuzz. The driver and his sidekick hadn't bothered with disguises, being made men now and on a mission for their family, feeling damned near invincible.

Besides, they both had guns.

"Somebody oughta clean this up," Angelo grumbled from the shotgun seat, eyeing the bars, pool halls and thrift shops lining both sides of Delancey Street.

"Somebody might," Dominic answered, "but it won't be us. Grunt work. We got one more collection, then we're off the clock."

"Nucci," Angelo said.

"Fat bastard is behind on principal *and* vig. Tonight we catch 'im up or leave a fuckin' message."

"Pop said—"

" 'Pop said'," Dom cut in, with a sneering tone. "He told us not ta rub the welcher out. Didn't say nothin' about givin' 'im a little tune-up. The prick can take a lot before he croaks."

They were coming up on Clinton Street, the east end of Delancey where it met the Williamsburg Bridge and crossed the East River to Brooklyn. Opened in 1903, the bridge had carried trolley lines and railways until the city paved two lanes for cars in 1932, adding three more in '41. Newspapers called the bridge unsafe, in need of renovation or whatever, but that didn't interest Dominic. He didn't plan on crossing it tonight, just do his job and then skedaddle back to Little Italy, dumping their ride somewhere along the way.

"Whatcha think about Badami?" Angelo inquired.

"Hey, people die," Dom answered, trying to sound casual.

"We all die," Angelo agreed. "But *Cristo,* stabbed like that in front a ever'body in a friggin' restaurant? That's cold, man."

"Cold is how ya gotta be sometimes, *fratelli.*"

Stefano Badami, first boss of the *Cosa Nostra* in Trenton, had been branching out since Newark *capo* Gaspare D'Amico ran back home to Sicily under the gun, in 1937. Ever since, Badami had been taking over one racket after another in Elizabeth and Newark, until someone literally cut him short, clearing the throne for underboss Filippo Amari.

"Here we go," said Angelo.

They'd reached Matteo Nucci's pawnshop, which you would've taken for a goldmine in that neighborhood, but somehow Nucci was the only pawnbroker in New York City who kept *losing* money. Gambling had a lot to do with that, and Nuccio borrowed three grand from Dom's family—one of their lenders, nothing that was traceable to Papa Carlo—

spinning a line of shit about how that could get him back into the black.

Stupido stronzo.

Dom double-parked their car and led the way inside, Angelo on his heels. Nucci was all alone behind the register when they entered, his fat face going pale.

"Hey, *miei amici*. What brings you around?"

"As if ya didn't know," Dom said.

"The money, right?" Nucci was sweating now. "I know it's late, but—"

"If you know it's late," Dom snarled, "then where in fuck *is* it?"

"Good news! I got some of the vig right here." As Nucci spoke, he keyed open the register.

"*Some* a the vig. You hear that, Ange?"

"I heard," said Angelo.

"Some a the vig ain't good enough, is it?"

"Don't think so," Ange replied.

"I fuckin' *know* it ain't. So, Fat Man, do you cough up *all* the vig plus two, three hunnerd of the principal, or do you want us to redecorate this shithole for ya?"

"Fellas, please..."

"Awright," Dom said. "Redecorate it is. Startin' with you."

———

East 161st Street, The Bronx: May 20, 1955

THE LEGAL AID SOCIETY's office stood on the same block as the Bronx Hall of Justice and Criminal Court, five blocks south of Civil Housing Court. It made good sense to David Jordan, lawyers congregating where their clients were.

Inside the lobby, clean but nothing to compare with any of the major private firms in town, he passed tables bearing pamphlets that detailed the basic legal rights of every Gotham citizen, dumbed down a bit to suit the standard supplicants who would be long on need and short on formal education. Posters artfully arranged on walls of painted cinderblocks advised all passers-by to KNOW YOUR RIGHTS and DON'T BE SATISFIED WITH SECOND CLASS.

An overweight receptionist in her mid-thirties smiled at Jordan, not quite meaning it but putting up a show. From his attire—a three-piece suit, light gray, accented by a navy tie—she knew he wasn't one of Legal Aid's usual suspects.

"May I help you, Sir?"

"Yes, please," he said. "I have a ten o'clock with Mr. Cronkite."

"And your name is...?"

"David Jordan."

She was checking on a clipboard when a bright, familiar voice hailed him. "David? My Lord, that *is* you!"

Taken by surprise, he turned to find Fiona O'Hara approaching, all smiles, looking both conservative and sexy in a suit of Kelly green, jacket and pencil skirt, that played well with her auburn hair. Spare makeup, nothing overdone that might be too provocative among male lawyers or their low-rent clientele. Instead of hugging Dave, she shook his hand and let it go.

"What brings you here?" she asked.

"I might ask you the same," he said. "Weren't you in Queens?"

"Until last month. With Legal Aid, we move around."

Last month? Had it been that long since they'd talked?

"Keeping you busy," he allowed.

"They are. Congratulations on that bar exam score, by the way."

He'd scored 952, which placed him in the ninety-fifth percentile, but it wasn't common knowledge.

"I got by," he said. "But how did you—?"

"Your mom called me."

"She *what*?"

"We chat from time to time."

That was the first he'd heard of it. Was his mother trying to fix him up? Dave covered with a smile but came up short for words. "Well..."

"Put that together with your GPA, firms must be beating down your door."

"I've had some interviews."

"So modest." Teasing him. "So, what's your business here today?" she asked again.

"I'm seeing Mr. Cronkite."

"Sam? You'll like him, unless— Hey, you don't have someone suing us, do you?"

"Another interview," Dave said.

Her eyes went wide. "You've made an application *here*?"

Dave hoped his shrug seemed casual. "The firms I've talked to all seemed kind of...stuffy. I was thinking, why not try to do some good before I jump into a rut and spend the rest of my life money-grubbing."

"Well, that's...I mean...I thought you and your dad- -"

He helped her out. "We get along okay, but he only works with relatives. I wanted something...more diverse."

"I hear you. That's the main reason I stayed in town, instead of going home to Washington. The politics, back-rooms, all that."

Behind Dave, the receptionist chimed in, "Excuse me, Mr. Jordan? You can go on through to Mr. Cronkite now."

He thanked her, smiled at Fee, and told her, "Here goes nothing."

"I look forward to you working here," she said, and David watched her walk away, hips swaying without any seeming artifice.

Asking himself, *What have I gotten into now?*

———

FBI MANHATTAN FIELD OFFICE: May 24, 1955

DEVON GANTT WONDERED if he was getting somewhere with the Bureau, finally. A chance arrest, with one agent for backup, and he earned a commendation from D.C., as well as a mention in the *Times* and the *New York Post,* which managed not to botch spelling his name. Of course, it was a "team effort," like everything else with the FBI, reflecting more on Edgar Hoover than the agents who put in their hours and "voluntary" unpaid overtime each day, but getting noticed was a start.

And his catch was a murderer, to boot: Patrick McDermott, a small-time mobster who dabbled in medicine before he shot a crusading newsman in Canton, Ohio, for exposing his ties to dirty cops. Okay, an NYPD beat patrolman had spotted McDermott first, working as a Gotham ambulance attendant, but Gantt and rookie agent Tom Hardesty reeled him in.

When Devon wasn't busting fugitives or looking into thefts of government property, he turned his eyes westward, keeping track of events in his old stamping grounds. The Vegas Strip had sprouted three more carpet joints—the Riviera, Royal Nevada, and the Dunes, all well mobbed-up behind the scenes—and now boasted its first desegregated joint, the Moulin Rouge, in West Las Vegas, which you'd have to call Sin City's ghetto. In March, with a nod to appearances, the Nevada Tax Commission created a Gaming Control Board, rumored to be working on a slim "Black Book" of gangsters whose mere presence in a hotel or casino would be ample grounds for license revocation.

Devon reckoned he'd believe *that* when he saw it, and he wasn't counting on a roster that excluded anyone who mattered. Relative old-timers like Moe Dalitz and his Desert Inn crowd or convicted two-time murderer from Texas Benny Binion, proud owner of Binion's Horseshoe down on Glitter Gulch, would be grandfathered in, their sins washed clean by sleight-of-hand.

HUAC hadn't been back to Los Angeles lately, but its public reputation took another hit in January when Pennsylvania's Francis Walter succeeded Harold Velde as chairman. Velde had been a G-man before drifting into politics, which graced him with a certain credibility. Walter, meanwhile, was best known for giving Harry Truman a letter opener carved from a Japanese soldier's humerus carved in 1944—though not by Walter, who had never served a day in uniform—and for coauthoring the McCarran-Walter Act, passed over Truman's veto eight years later. Generally viewed as a reactionary white supremacist, Walter had also served as a director of the Pioneer Fund, a foundation organized in 1937 "to advance the scientific study of heredity and human differences."

Devon guessed he'd have fun hassling certain groups from the Attorney General's subversive list—the Civil Rights Congress and Committee for the Negro in the Arts, at least —while steering well clear of the Klan; whatever kept his name in print and got him reelected by his fans in eastern Pennsylvania.

No skin off me, Gantt thought, and hoped someone would spot another Top Ten fugitive somewhere within his reach. Or maybe he could get an angle on the Mad Bomber, who'd touched off three more blasts so far this year. That wouldn't land the psycho in a federal court, but Gantt imagined the publicity and had to smile.

Something to think about, while he was doing paperwork and wishing he was back out west.

Benjamin Franklin High School, Harlem: June 3, 1955

Payton Sawyer clapped and fought the urge to whistle as his younger brother's name was called and Frederick crossed the stage, collecting his diploma from the principal. Beside Payton, his parents wore their Sunday best, although his mother's finest go-to-meeting dress hung loosely on her now, reminding him how gaunt she had become.

Damned worthless doctors. None of them so far could pin down what was wrong with her, why she kept losing weight, although they claimed to have ruled out TB and cancer with their endless tests. Did anyone just waste away in these days, leaving no clue to what ailed them?

Payton's father, on the other hand, was slim and fit as ever, though he had a worried look around his eyes that likely came from watching his wife fade. Keisha, his parents' youngest, cheered for brother Fred, but if he had to guess, Payton would've bet most of her mind was on her husband, Eulis Jordan, who'd been called in to replace a sickly driver at the trucking company he worked for and missed out on the graduation ceremony.

Payton didn't care for Jordan—sometimes thought of him as "Useless," rather than Eulis—but he never voiced that view aloud. Some things a person had to find out for herself, even when that person was your beloved younger sister.

Brother Fred, by contrast, seemed to have it all nailed down. At seventeen, he was their high school's football quarterback, a star who had been scouted by at least three colleges that Payton knew of, settling on the University of California at Los Angeles. Payton had done his homework on UCLA, learning its athletic scholarships were funded by sports ticket sales, alumni, and corporate contracts, with no state money spent. Based on his sport and academic records from Ben Franklin, Fred qualified for a full ride: paying tuition, fees, plus room and board. He was already looking forward to playing for Head Coach Henry Sanders, up from Vanderbilt, who'd led the UCLA Bruins to Rose Bowl victories in 1953 and '55. They likely would've taken 1954 as well, but Rose Bowl rules required a winning team to sit out every other year and give somebody else a chance. Even so, in '54 the Bruins compiled a 9-0 record and climbed to the top of the Coaches' Poll.

It was amusing, Payton thought, that the first Sawyer boys who'd gone to college owed it to athletics. Fred hadn't picked out a major yet, but he was leaning toward political science, wherever that might take him.

At work, "BOSSI" had dropped a letter, officially becoming "BOSS," known to most cops as the "Red Squad." It focused on the CPUSA and so-called "fellow travelers," but still had ample men, money and time to keep an eye on Negroes and rambunctious Puerto Ricans with occasional assistance from the FBI. Its files had rapidly expanded to include raw dirt and baseless innuendo on a quarter-million citizens.

And one of those, as Payton knew from personal experience, was Malcolm X. Before landing in Harlem, he'd established Nation Temples No. 13 in Springfield, Massachusetts, 14 in Hartfort, Connecticut, and 15 in Atlanta. Hundreds of new members were joining monthly, drawn by Malcolm's personal charisma and dramatic style of preaching, nearly mesmerizing to the crowds that followed him. He was engaged to marry a young convert, Betty Sanders—"Betty X," now—who was nine years younger and willing to let the Nation's rules guide their romance: no one-on-one dating, replaced instead by Temple gatherings or group visits to various museums and libraries.

A part of Payton wished them both a happy life but didn't see it happening in Harlem, dwelling under scrutiny from BOSS, the Bureau, and whoever else might listen in. Was he ashamed to play a part in that? Sometimes. But going in to work each day meant that he had to trust Inspector Flannery and all the brass above him to know what in hell was *really* going on, and how potential danger could be curbed.

If all of them were wrong...well, he would have to live with that, the way his father had.

———

Serpukhov, Moscow Oblast: July 18, 1955

Another letter had arrived from the United States, moving halfway around the world in fits and starts to place itself in Leonid Babin's hands. His son Stefan—now perfectly inhabiting the skin and fabricated life of Stephen Barnes—was nine years old and in the fourth grade, doing well in class and on the playing field, no aberrations noted on the home front by the sleeper agents who'd adopted him.

Call it another twelve years before he could earn a bachelor's degree, three more if FBI standards required him to go on and study law or the dry numbers of accountancy. Unless there was a change on that side, Stefan/Stephen couldn't join the Bureau until 1970, at which time Babin would be eighty-one years old. The odds of him surviving that long, much less clinging to his influence within the Russian government, struck him as verging on the realm of fantasy.

No matter. It would be enough for him to die knowing he'd sown the seeds of ruin for his enemies. If he and Edgar Hoover died before that crop was harvested, it made no difference. Babin's impact on history, although anonymous, would be ensured.

Meanwhile, it was more critical than ever for Babin to watch his back. The world was bristling with tools of mass destruction, daily edging closer to the brink of an apocalypse. West Germany claimed its independence from the former Allies on May 5 and then joined NATO four days later. Ten days after *that*, Moscow announced the creation of the rival Warsaw Pact, including Mother Russia and her Eastern European satellites: Albania, Bulgaria, Czechoslovakia, East Germany and Hungary, Romania and Poland. Echoes of alliances before the First World War were obvious, but now more threatening than ever.

Even so, with Yugoslavia outside the fold, Khrushchev and Tito sat down long enough to sign June's Belgrade Declaration, Moscow making its first admission that "different forms of Socialist development are solely the concern of the individual countries." With that in mind, Khrushchev nurtured the five-year-old Sino-Soviet Treaty of Friendship, Alliance and Mutual Assistance; did his best to pacify Pyongyang's Kim Il-Sung; and welcomed Hô Chí Minh to Moscow in July, with promises of military aid where the U.S. had failed Hô time and time again.

The world might well explode at any moment, nothing Babin could do to prevent it, even as a Colonel General within the KGB. *But if it blows*, he thought, *perhaps that would be victory enough.*

———

MIAMI FBI FIELD OFFICE: August 25, 1955

FLORIDA WAS CALMING DOWN, at last, Nolan O'Hara thought, although it might take years for any southern state to fall in line with Washington's stopgap approach to Negro civil rights. The Bureau had already closed its file on the Moore bombing, with three suspects dead and one vanished, but Governor Collins reviewed the Groveland case of Walter Irvin and commuted Irvin's death sentence to life imprisonment.

Why not just set him free? Collins told the media, "My conscience told me it was a bad case, badly handled, badly tried. I was asked to take a man's life. My conscience would not let me do it." But a blameless man might still die behind prison walls.

Mob leaders in the Sunshine State were suffering no pangs of conscience. Hitmen finally caught up with Charlie Wall in April, slitting the septuagenarian's throat and bludgeoning him with a baseball bat for his presumed attack on

Santo Trafficante Jr. two years back. Of all the gamblers once embarrassed by the Kefauver Committee, only Jules Levitt was brought to book, at last, slapped with a two-year suspended sentence and $5,000 fine for his role in the S&G Syndicate. Melvin Richard reclaimed his city council seat, then faced a recall, claiming malfeasance in office, but Florida's Supreme Court found that petition hopelessly vague and Richard hung on.

Offshore, Meyer Lansky's Casino Internacional changed hands, sold to Cleveland partners Moe Dalitz and Sam Tucker, who kept the skim flowing Stateside. Lansky was busy setting up the Riviera, financed in equal parts by the Mob and government-run Cuban banks. President Batista signed a new gambling law, permitting casinos in any night-club or hotel worth a million dollars or more—the Riv came in at $17 million—while Minister of Labor Suarez Rivas issued two-year visas to American dealers, stickmen and pit bosses.

Havana ran like clockwork, but Batista made one mistake—in Nolan's view, perhaps a fatal one. In May, he granted amnesty to all political detainees, and by June the Castro brothers were in Mexico, huddled with Argentine radical Ernesto "Che" Guevara and Alberto Bayo, a Republican leader in Spain's civil war, to plot Batista's downfall.

Nolan would've liked to stick around and see what happened next, but he received new orders, shipping him to Birmingham, where things were heating up between the white establishment and restless Negroes. He didn't like taking his wife and kids to Ground Zero, but it was either move or quit the Bureau.

And what else was Nolan fit to do by now?

———

SAIGON: October 26, 1955

COLBY GANTT WAS BACK in Vietnam, observing what the CIA had wrought. He'd been promoted recently, within the Agency's Directorate of Operations, more specifically to third in charge of a division labeled "Ideas to Solutions"—I2S, for short.

It was a tag that might conceal a multitude of sins.

In Europe for example, "Operation GOLD" finished tunneling beneath Berlin in May, permitting taps on cable lines used by the KGB and Stasi. The Baghdad Pact, although excluding the United States, for now, united "free-dom-loving" nations like Iraq, Iran, Turkey and Pakistan with Britain to prevent more dominoes from falling in the Middle East. At the same time, America *had* joined Australia, France, New Zealand, Pakistan, the Philippines, and Thailand in the Southeast Asia Treaty Organization (SEATO), with the same goal of Red containment in mind.

While ex-French Indochina stood apart, North Vietnam settled in Moscow's orbit now, the region dominated covert talk in Washington. In January, French and Thai advisors had begun training Laotian troops and pilots, while a U.S. Operations Mission in Vientiane spent 80 percent of its budget arming the Royal Laotian Army.

That same month witnessed the first overt shipment of U.S. arms to South Vietnam, as Washington backed Prime Minister Diệm's maneuvers to unseat alleged "Head of State" Bảo Đại. In May, Diệm fielded troops to crush Saigon's powerful Bình Xuyên crime syndicate, while suppressing the Cao Đài and Hòa Hảo religious warlords in the country-side. Guillotines mounted on caissons toured the hinter-lands, beheading opposition leaders. In October, Diệm staged a plebiscite, claiming victory with 5,784,752 ballots in a nation with only 5,335,668 registered voters. Bảo Đại sought refuge in Paris, while Diệm filled public offices with relatives and other fellow Catholics, proclaiming a new Republic of Vietnam, buoyed by President Eisenhower's pledge of military aid.

The stage was set for chaos, Diệm's "Civil Action" teams invading regions sympathetic to the Việt Minh, while north of the 17th parallel, "people's tribunals" tried and executed hundreds of wealthy landowners, sending thousands more to Red "reeducation" camps. How long until the whole damned place exploded? At the moment, Colby didn't know and didn't care.

At home, Congress approved the purchase of land preselected by Alan Dulles for construction of the CIA's new headquarters at Langley. President Eisenhower authorized a construction budget of $46 million, but no one had yet found a suitable architect.

Strictly undercover, CIA researchers dumped another load of *Serratia marascens* in January, this time in Pennsylvania. MKULTRA files detailed the operation's quest for a myriad of different types of mind-altering substances: some promoting "illogical thinking and impulsiveness" to discredit subjects in public; others to increase perception and mental acuity; another to retard or accelerate aging; others amplifying alcohol's intoxicating impact; more to produce short-lived symptoms of known diseases, whose sudden disappearance would mark subjects as malingerers; materials inflicting short- or long-term brain damage and loss of memory; drugs to help captives resist interrogation and "brainwashing"; drugs to produce amnesia, anemia, paralysis or blisters; surreptitious physical methods inducing shock and confusion; drugs enhancing a subject's dependence on others; undetectable methods of lowering ambition and work performance; drugs temporarily impairing vision or hearing; plus "safe" and surreptitious knockout drugs administered through food, drink, cigarettes, or via aerosol propellants, suitable for use by agents "on an ad hoc basis."

George White, already double-dipping on the CIA's payroll with Harry Anslinger's approval, proved that he was game for anything. This year, while serving as the FBN's regional chief in San Francisco, he'd set up another MIDNIGHT CLIMAX pad on Chestnut Street, signing the lease once more as "Morgan Hall." The duplex served both of his masters, acting as a lure for drug dealers whom White arrested—one of them State Narcotics Agent Fred Braumoeller, who padded his income selling drugs he'd seized on raids—while kinky dope-fueled orgies were filmed and recorded for the Agency. In the safe house, poised overlooking San Francisco Bay, White kept photo albums filled with snaps of prostitutes in bondage, being whipped and tortured.

White paid hookers a C-note nightly for their services, together with a promise that he'd intercede on their behalf if they were jailed for peddling sex. His research into "sexual proclivities" followed the same strain of occultism he'd hinted at with Colby in New York, two years ago, specifically rituals once employed by Aleister Crowley, the late British showman who'd dubbed himself "The Beat 666," while reporters called him "the wickedest man in the world." Satanic imagery merged with "sex magick" in the stranger practices.

But then, how did you even judge "strange" when consorting with the likes of Crowley or George White?

An operation far removed from White's weird sex-and-drugs freak show was "Operation SRPOINTER," lately changed by Agency taxonomists to "Operation HTLIN-GUAL." Under any name, while putatively tracking Soviet illegals, HTLINGUAL agents read and copied mail sent to or from alleged leftists including civil rights attorney "Battling Bella" Abzug, novelist John Steinbeck, chemist and peace activist Linus Pauling, adolescent chess master Bobby Fischer, homosexual playwright Edward Albee, and former racket-busting mayor of Minneapolis Hubert Humphrey, who'd learned the hard way to collaborate with establishment Democrats. Anyone, in fact, might be included on the suspect list, including politicians, media celebrities, and Negroes challenging Jim Crow on both sides of the Mason-Dixon Line.

That was the price you paid, thought Gantt, *for national security.*

———

FBI HEADQUARTERS: November 1, 1955

DECLAN O'HARA HATED WATCHING Edgar Hoover preen, but what could he expect when the president graced him with the National Security Medal in May? Harry Truman established the award in 1953 and galled Hoover by giving Wild Bill Donovan the first one, but the Chief was still strutting around, proud as a peacock with his shiny bauble.

Five months later, he cut a deal with journalist Don Whitehead, winner of two Pulitzers, to write the Bureau's history direct from files selected by the Chief to put the best spin possible on everything G-men had done since Hoover was appointed as Director back in 1924. Whitehead was calling it *The FBI Story,* due out sometime next year from Random House, but only after Hoover personally edited the manuscript.

Under old business, Larry Fly was still collecting hostile memos in his dossier, unknown to him, but it pleased Hoover to keep stalking him. Old Roger Touhy, former gangster framed by G-men for a kidnapping that never happened in the heady days of 1933, won successive orders for release in 1954 and '55, based on judicial notice that the case had been a frame-up, but appeals by Justice were still keeping him inside.

Hoover never forgot, never forgave.

At least Harry Bridges was in the clear, final attempts to strip him of his citizenship quashed in court, from which the government didn't appeal. Further embarrassment had come from paid informer Harvey Matusow when he published *False Witness,* a memoir of how McCarthy, Cohn, and every other Red-hunter in Washington had paid him off to lie while under oath. Some critics recognized Matusow's jab at fellow former Communist Whittaker Chambers and his book *Witness* but they had downplayed the "coincidence."

The "Lavender Scare" gained new momentum in October, with the revelation of a predatory "homosexual underground" in Boise, Idaho, of all places. Bureau agents weren't involved, but it made news from coast to coast, more than 100 teenagers claiming they'd been victimized, cops grilling 1,500 suspects before charging and convicting just sixteen of them, their sentences ranging from life to simple probation. The local *Idaho Statesman* chased a still-unknown, probably mythical ringleader known as "The Queen," blaming the YMCA for criminal negligence, and rallying scared citizens to "Crush the Monster!" Another editorial demanded "This

Mess Must Be Removed," warning that boys "victimized by these perverts" would "grow into manhood with the same inclinations." One teacher, never charged, had been so terrified he'd fled to San Francisco and vanished.

Meanwhile, the Smith Act frenzy wasn't running out of steam. Among New York's original defendants, two had won early release from prison—John Williamson, deported to his native England, while John Gates went back to working for the CPUSA, editing its newspaper the *Daily Worker*. John Noto, upstate New York leader of the Party, finally emerged from hiding and was nabbed by G-men in August.

The Honolulu case kept lurching along, lately with lawyer Harriet Sawyer facing disciplinary action from the state bar's Legal Ethics Committee, for making an out-of-court speech regarding the case in July 1954. It took a year for the committee to consider the matter, but it agreed that her speech was "improper," issuing a reprimand and recommending Sawyer's suspension "for such period of time as the Court may deem just and proper."

Solo cases on the docket involved the convictions of Junius Scales, a CPUSA member from North Carolina who'd gone on the dodge in 1951, staying at large until Bureau agents traced him to Memphis in '54; and Claude Lightfoot, a black Red from Chicago, charged simply for joining the Party, without any overt attempt to spread its message any further. Both were out on bail pending appeals, but Declan didn't like their chances of success.

Despite his censure by the Senate, Joe McCarthy was still hanging on and making noise, warning President Eisenhower against meeting with Nikita Khrushchev, since "you cannot offer friendship to tyrants and murderers without advancing the cause of tyranny and murder." That was rich, O'Hara thought, coming from someone who'd opposed the trial in 1949 of Waffen-SS soldiers who'd slaughtered more than 750 Allied prisoners in World War Two. Still, he was fading lately, largely thanks to booze and drugs, described by one reporter as "a pale ghost of his former self."

Even so, he kept flailing away with help from the Bureau. Perennial target Owen Lattimore faced new perjury charges after Judge Youngdahl dismissed the last round in 1952. They hit the same snag this time, and when the U.S. Court of Appeals upheld Youngdahl's latest dismissal on First Amendment grounds, Justice finally dropped the pointless crusade.

O'Hara wished that it could always be that easy, but he knew it never would. And so what? He was looking forward to a special party in December, touching base with an old friend, and had to book his days off now, before the Christmas rush.

———

DENVER, Colorado: November 14, 1955

IT WAS a rare road trip for Aloysius Gantt, but he enjoyed the break from headquarters, despite the nature of his mission. He'd been ordered to assist the FBI's Disaster Squad in picking over the wreckage and identifying victims from United Airlines Flight 629—known as "Mainliner Denver"— when the DC-6 exploded in midair, en route to Portland on November 1. All forty-four persons aboard were lost, scattered over six square miles of Weld County, ground fires raging for three days despite the best efforts of firemen.

Flight 629 was America's third-worst airline disaster to date. The topper, Eastern Air Lines Flight 605, had claimed fifty-two lives in May 1947 when it crashed in Maryland while traveling from Newark to Miami. The dubious runner-up in second place—another United DC 6—had gone down in Utah, while en route from L.A. to Chicago, in October '47, killing fifty-one.

Of course, those two crashes were accidents, while Colorado's case turned out to be mass murder. G-men couldn't prove it yet, but they were looking closely at Jack Gilbert Graham, whose mother was among those killed aboard Mainliner Denver. The Bureau's file on Graham listed charges of embezzlement, check fraud and bootlegging. Acquaintances spoke of a grudge he'd held against his mother, for a miserable childhood in an orphanage where she had left him, and he'd taken out a life insurance policy on Mama just before she caught her flight. (Oddly, his mother hadn't signed the policy, which made it worthless.) If all that wasn't enough, a restaurant his mother owned suffered a mysterious explosion earlier in 1955, and searchers recovered more bomb-making parts from Jack's garage. Gantt reckoned they could build a case against him, but since there was no federal law against destroying airliners in flight, it would come down to state charges of homicide.

At least Gantt thought he knew where Graham got his bright idea: from a Canadian named Joseph-Albert Guay. In September 1949, Guay sought to free himself up for a teenage mistress by killing his wife, putting a bomb in her suitcase before she boarded Canadian Pacific Flight 108, en route from Montreal to Baie-Comeau, Québec. The blast killed Mrs. Guay and twenty-two others, nearly identical to Colorado's bombing, down to the insurance policy that would have netted Guay $15,000 for his trouble. In his own defense, at trial, Guay noted that Québec's strict Roman

Catholic regime forbade divorce, but jurors showed no sympathy. Guay also named his lover and bomb-maker Généreux Ruest as his accomplice, resulting in death sentences for all concerned. Transported to the gallows in a wheelchair, stricken with tuberculosis, Guay told witnesses, "*Au moins, je meurs célèbre*"—"At least I die famous."

That's something, anyway, Gantt thought. How many others in this crazy world could say the same? *Not me, and that's for goddamned sure.*

———

Manhattan: December 9, 1955

Another day, another killing in Chicago. Greg Jordan had long since ceased being surprised by anything the Windy City's Outfit did, simply relieved that it was far removed from Gotham and the city's *Cosa Nostra* families.

The latest mark was Alex Greenberg, known in Chi-Town as the "financial wiz" who'd shown Al Capone how to launder his money through real estate, service industries, and entertainment venues. He'd been slain last night, outside a South Side restaurant while leaving with his wife —who, naturally, hadn't seen a thing to help police.

Louis Campagna of Chicago was another recent goner, but at least his death was natural: a heart attack while fishing from his lawyer's boat on Biscayne Bay, in Florida. He'd caught a thirty-pound grouper but never got to pose for pictures with his final victim. When the Roman Church denied "Little New York" a funeral, relatives planted him at Mount Carmel Cemetery with the Capone and Genna brothers, Dean O'Bannion, Hymie Weiss, Frank Nitti, and a host of other gangland notables, balanced by a stellar cast of Catholic bishops and cardinals.

Among the living, Tom Clark still believed in paying off old debts, appointing John Crown—son of Henry, named by columnist Drew Pearson as a one-time mobster, now the Empire State Building's owner—to serve as Clark's law clerk at the Supreme Court in D.C.

Friends in need were friends for life.

Thirteen hundred miles by air from Gotham, lavish new hotel-casinos were still springing up in the Vedado district of Havana, pouring cash into Fulgencio Batista's pockets and the Syndicate's coffers at home. Meyer Lansky was in charge, but greasing all the local squeaky wheels to keep things running smoothly. Greg's brother Carlo, considered investing in a club down there, but gave up on the notion when he read an article about the Castro brothers and their revolution in the making.

Smart or dumb?

Greg couldn't say, as of yet, but he was just as happy keeping family investments close to home in times like these, when anything could happen without warning. Taking risks was dicey for the younger guys, and now, at nearly sixty, Jordan didn't feel the urge.

———

Federal Bureau of Narcotics Manhattan Field Office: December 26, 1955

Another year closing, and this would be Ike Sawyer's last one as a lawman. People liked to say that all good things must end, but how would Ike rate his career at sixty-two, after he'd spent the better part of four decades in federal service? He supposed he'd done some good along the way, though most of it boiled down to boredom and frustration.

And nobody ever talked about the *bad* things ending, being swept away, whether that meant narcotics or the way Negroes were still treated across America.

He knew the government was pleased with what the FBN had managed to achieve so far. A new report from the Hoover Commission, chaired by the country's thirty-first president, praised Harry Anslinger, saying, "Fortunately for us, the head of this bureau has stood for twenty-five years as the greatest single bulwark against the spread of drug addiction throughout the world." No mention, naturally, of his feeding heroin to Joe McCarthy or collaborating in the CIA's illegal mind-control experiments.

The less said about any of that shit, the better, Ike supposed.

You knew frustration was a fact of life when the Supreme Court had to repeat its decision in the *Brown* case, this time ordering desegregation of the country's public schools "with all deliberate speed." Still no specific deadline, but the South's foot-dragging wasn't sitting well with Earl Warren and his colleagues, projected by one pundit, based on Dixie's present pace, to fully integrate classrooms sometime in A.D. 2026.

Would they comply now, with the ruling dubbed "*Brown II*"? Ike had his doubts, as recent laws in Alabama and North Carolina openly defied the Warren Court, requiring pupil placement based upon "ability, availability of transportation, and academic background." Neither was he encouraged by the Warren Court's November ban on racial segregation in public recreational facilities. Three weeks later, the Interstate Commerce Commission barred Jim Crow from all modes of public transportation crossing state lines, but southern cops still hadn't got the message, based upon reports of ongoing arrests.

And if the cops weren't bad enough, there was the KKK, its latest incarnation dubbed the U.S. Klans, chartered by Georgia in October. Auto paint-sprayer Eldon Edwards was the group's "Imperial Wizard," already putting out feelers to half a dozen nearby states.

Most of the year's mayhem, so far, had been confined to Mississippi. In Belzoni, Reverend George Lee and store-keeper Gus Courts founded Humphreys County's first NAACP chapter in 1953, using Lee's pulpit and his commercial printing press to recruit ninety-two Negro voters. Undaunted by obstructive registrars and boycotts by the White Citizens' Council, they'd persevered until May 7, when drive-by killers shot Lee as he drove home after dark. Medgar Evers, Mississippi's NAACP field secretary, investigated the slaying, which Sheriff Ike Shelton called a "traffic accident." In Shelton's view, buckshot pellets extracted from Lee's face during his autopsy were "fillings from his teeth. When G-men offered him that evidence of murder, he'd snarled, "Keep 'em." Bureau agents couldn't make a federal case, but they'd identified two of Lee's likely killers, both members of the "nonviolent" Belzoni Citizens' Council. Sheriff Shelton wouldn't charge them nor would the grand jury.

Fourteen weeks later in Brookhaven, a white man shot and killed another Negro suffrage activist, sixty-three-year-old Lamar Smith, in front of witnesses on the Lincoln County courthouse lawn. Sheriff Robert Case first sent the gunman home, then grudgingly arrested him and two accomplices a few days afterward. A white grand jury failed to indict the trio, while the white D.A. blamed terrified black witnesses for failure to cooperate with his so-called investigation.

Barely two weeks after that assassination, Mississippi slayers struck again, this time at Money, in Leflore County. Fourteen-year-old Emmett Till was on vacation from Chicago, visiting his mother's family when he supposedly made a suggestive comment to a white storekeeper's wife. The outraged husband and his half-brother snatched Till from his great-uncle's home, tortured and beat him, shot him with a .45, then dumped his body in the Tallahatchie River, chained to an old fan extracted from a cotton gin. Searchers retrieved the bloated corpse on August 31, and since the killers had been boasting of their crime, they *were* indicted on a murder charge with two eyewitnesses identifying them. After a three-day trial, a jury stacked with Citizens' Council members found the pair not guilty. The two witnesses who'd fingered them in open court fled Mississippi to preserve their lives.

Gus Courts, meanwhile, was still trying to register black voters in Belzoni. Threats and boycotts didn't faze him, but he finally packed up and left after persons unknown fired through a window of his grocery and hit him in the arm.

December's victim was a Negro schoolteacher from Drew, in Sunflower County, the birthplace of Senator Eastland and the White Citizens' Council. James Evanston was fifty-two years old when he vanished from home on December 21, his corpse found by a farmer on Christmas Eve, floating below a bridge at nearby Long Lake. Before spotting his body, that same witness found the dead man's car. Inside it, cops reportedly discovered a crude note reading: "Can't stand sickness and worries any longer." An autopsy called his death a suicide, no evidence of foul play noted, although Evanston's kin were unaware of any illness or associated "worries" in his life. Three months before his death, he'd attended the sham trial of Emmett Till's slayers.

The only other death Ike new about off hand, occurred in Mayflower, Texas, during the third week of October. Several Negro teenagers had gathered in a small café, discussing the Supreme Court's *Brown* II ruling, when bullets smashed the windows, killing John Reese, leaving two other victims wounded. As so often happened in Dixie, two shooters bragged until they wound up facing charges, but it hardly mattered. Even though they'd boasted of their plan to scare "uppity niggers" out of pushing for school integration, D.A. Ralph Prince called the drive-by "a case of two irresponsible boys attempting to have some fun by scaring niggers."

The defense urged acquittal, telling jurors to "call it a bad day and let the boy go on in life." Amazingly, jurors convicted the shooter of "with malice aforethought," then recommended mercy in the form of a five-year suspended sentence. His sidekick never went to trial at all, and both of them were back at home that afternoon.

The only bright spot of the year so far came from Montgomery, Alabama, where NAACP member Rosa Parks went to jail and paid a $14 fine for refusing her seat to a white man. Mindful of Baton Rouge in '53, Negroes were boycotting the city's buses, costing the Montgomery Bus Line and its parent company, National City Lines, hundreds of dollars daily since December 6. They'd organized taxis and private cars to pull it off, while thousands joined the new Montgomery Improvement Association, led by local NAACP leader Edgar Daniel Nixon and a new young preacher from Atlanta, Martin Luther King Jr. White cops and politicians raged, the Citizens' Council's membership doubled, but when black cabbies suddenly lost their insurance, Lloyds of London gladly signed them up. Lately, the city's white fathers dusted off an anti-boycott law from 1921, charging the MIA's leaders with criminal conspiracy, but the accuses seemed pleased to pray and sing old hymns in jail.

How long before the terrorism started in Montgomery? Ike didn't know, but if he'd had to guess—

"Would that be Agent Sawyer? As I live and breathe."

Ike pivoted, still reaching for the whiskey flask he carried in an inside coat pocket, and gaped, amazed, to see Declan O'Hara standing there.

"How does retirement feel," the G-man asked, before Ike had a chance to speak.

"I haven't tried it yet." As they shook hands, Sawyer inquired, "What brings you up from Washington?"

"You kidding me? I wouldn't miss this party for the world. I even brought a present."

From behind his back, O'Hara drew a floppy parcel wrapped in butcher's paper, handing it across to Ike. When Sawyer eased the package open, he beheld what seemed to be a folded pillowcase, then saw an empty eyehole staring back at him.

"For old time's sake," said Declan. "Just in case you're thinking I forgot I owe you one."

Sawyer replaced the tape, smiling. "You ever catch up with that sheriff?"

"Funny you should ask. He showed up in D.C. in '25, when his folks had their big parade down Pennsylvania Avenue."

Ike nodded. "Yeah. I read about that at the time."

"We had a little chat at his hotel, after the party got rained out. From what I hear, he hasn't been the same since then. Had to give up his job, still walking with a limp, they say."

"Well, that's a goddamn shame."

"Ain't it the truth?"

"You want something to drink? Stronger than Kool-Aid, maybe?"

"How could I say no?"

"You must be close to handing in the badge, yourself."

Declan frowned. Said, "I considered it, but then, what would I do? Where would I go? We're not with Civil Service, as I'm sure you know."

"Old Edgar Hoover."

"Hanging in there. I'm a few months younger than he is, so I've been thinking, if he doesn't quit and no one boots him out...well, what's my hurry?"

"Jesus, now *I* need a drink," said Ike. "You want to get away from here before some damned fool starts in singing 'Auld Lang Syne'?"

O'Hara's smile came back as he replied, "I thought you'd never ask."

EPILOGUE

DIRECTOR HOOVER SAT ERECT, almost rigid, behind his desk, facing two former college classmates, longtime Bureau agents Aloysius Gantt and Declan O'Hara. As usual, he didn't smile, speaking in the clipped tones they'd learned to recognize over the decades, first in university debating classes, then as his employees at the FBI.

"It's been some time, I think, since you two worked together on a case."

"Yes, Sir," O'Hara said. Thinking, *You know exactly how long, why the game?*

"I thought it might be useful if you put your heads together this time, for the Bureau's benefit. We have a problem brewing in Montgomery."

O'Hara had a mind for trivia. He knew eight towns and fifteen counties nationwide were named for General Robert Montgomery of the Continental Army, killed invading

347

Canada before there was a USA. He also guessed that only one of those applied but kept it to himself.

"The bus thing," Aloysius said.

"Succinct, if oversimplified," Hoover replied. "But yes, 'the bus thing.' More particularly, who's in charge of it."

O'Hara thought he knew the answer. "Edgar Nixon, Chief. His Negro friends call him 'E. D.' A former Pullman porter, union man, mixed up for years in civil rights, but he's an old man now."

Hoover stiffened. Replied, "He's seven months younger than *I* am."

"Sorry, Sir. I didn't mean—"

"In any case," the Chief pressed on, while Nixon did the groundwork for this 'bus thing,' he is no longer the man in charge."

"Reverend King," Gantt said.

"The so-called *reverend,* in fact, a second-generation Baptist preacher from Atlanta, where his father heads the biggest Negro church in town. That would be Martin Luther King *Senior*, born Michael King, then changed his name, presumably to sound more pious. Spent two years at Dillard University, New Orleans, followed by Atlanta's Morehouse School of Religion. He took over Ebenezer Baptist when its preacher died—coincidentally or otherwise, King Senior's father-in-law."

"Now the son's in Montgomery," Declan supplied.

"And that apple fell close to the tree," Hoover said. "According to his birth certificate, he also was born 'Michael,' but his father claims that was an error by the hospital. He grew up in the church, wanting to be a preacher on his own. Skipped high school and went straight to Morehouse College, graduated at eighteen with a B.A. in sociology, then managed to ignore his father's blandishment for

Morehouse Divinity, opting for Pennsylvania's Crozier Theological Seminary instead. Graduated there in 1951, emerging with a fascination for Mahatma Gandhi and a 'calling,' as he puts it, to relieve 'the burden of the Negro race'."

"Sounds like you know a lot about him, Sir," Declan allowed.

"Indeed *we* do, Mr. O'Hara, but it still isn't enough. Now, Martin Junior has his own church in Montgomery, and he's earned a Ph.D. from Boston University at the same time."

"A busy bee," Gantt said.

"Too busy for his own good or Montgomery's," Hoover replied. "He also studied briefly—or, perhaps I should say, was *indoctrinated*—at the Highlander Folk School in Tennessee, listed since 1932 for teaching revolutionary principles to unionists and Negroes. Not so long before the bus boycott, both King Jr and Rosa Parks, the seamstress *heroine* who paid a fine for sitting in a seat reserved for whites, were both at Highlander, together with known members of the CPUSA. Now, magically, they both turn up as icons of the ballyhooed Montgomery Improvement Association."

"Wouldn't this be handled out of Birmingham, Sir?" Declan interjected.

"So it would. And that office will oversee events as they unfold. You gentlemen shall cast a wider net, collecting any information you can turn up on the Kings, father *and* son, which might be useful in exposing their proclivities for meddling with the status quo."

Dig up the dirt, in other words, O'Hara thought. But simply said, in unison with Gantt, "Yes, Sir!"

TO BE CONTINUED....

Book VI of *The Bureau—In Honor's Name*—spans events
from January 1956 through publication of the Warren
Report on President John Kennedy's assassination, encom-
passing: the Black civil rights movement and southern resistance by organized terror, plus the Hungarian rebellion and
escalating warfare in Southeast Asia, the election of America's first Roman Catholic president and his Attorney
General brother's campaign against organized crime, the
Bay of Pigs invasion and the Cuban missile crisis, JFK's
assassination in Dallas and suppression of its conspiratorial
details. Robert Kennedy's resignation as Attorney General
ends the "Camelot" era, while the Gulf of Tonkin incident
propels America toward full-scale military involvement in
Vietnam. Series protagonists confront unexpected chal-
lenges, none of them emerging unscathed, costing some of
them their lives. Their children grow, pursuing various
careers in law enforcement or the realm of crime, some
undergoing transformations that divert the courses of their
lives forever.

ABOUT THE AUTHOR

A California native, Michael Newton has published 215 books under his own name and various pseudonyms since 1977. He began writing professionally as a "ghost" for author Don Pendleton on the best-selling Executioner series and continues his work on that series today. With 104 episodes published to date, Newton has nearly tripled the number of Mack Bolan novels completed by creator Pendleton himself.

Newton's first book under his own name was *Monsters, Mysteries and Man* (1979), a survey of unexplained phenomena for younger readers. While 156 of Newton's published books have been novels—including westerns, political thrillers and psychological suspense—he is best known for nonfiction, primarily true crime and reference books.

www.ingramcontent.com/pod-product-compliance
Lightning Source LLC
Chambersburg PA
CBHW020838020726
47497CB00005B/1155